Ophelia's Revenge

Rebecca Reisert is the author of *The Third Witch*

'A fascinating alternative storyline to the play . . . powerful, evocative. One of the most original first novels you're likely to find in this or any other year.' *Birmingham Post*

'What a book! Rebecca Reisert's mediaeval story is priceless.' *Bangor Chronicle*

'This clever slant on Macbeth is excellent . . . the central characters give it a warmth that will stay in the memory.' *Coventry Evening Telegraph*

'Original, atmospheric . . . Reisert balancing the intrigue and bloodlust of the royal court with the human drama unfolding below the stairs.' *The List, Glasgow*

'Whether Macbeth interests you as an historical person or as a Shakespeare play, *The Third Witch* is a book you will enjoy.' *Writing Scotland*

'A powerful retelling of *Macbeth*.' *Good Book Guide*

By the same author

The Third Witch

About the author

Rebecca Reisert has taught creative writing, drama and literature in both high school and college for 26 years. The author of more than thirty plays, she has twice been the recipient of a National Endowment for the Humanities fellowship to study literature. She teaches at a boys' high school in Louisville, Kentucky and directs a travelling improvisational theatre company.

REBECCA REISERT

Ophelia's Revenge

To Dick and Patty—
   What fun it was to
visit with you both this
summer! I'm so glad to have
cousins like you.
   May your deepest dreams
lead you closer to your
truest selves.
                    Love,
                    Rebecca Reisert
                    August 2003

flame

FLAME
Hodder & Stoughton

Copyright © 2003 by Rebecca Reisert

First published in Great Britain in 2003 by Hodder and Stoughton
A division of Hodder Headline
A Flame paperback

The right of Rebecca Reisert to be identified as the Author
of the Work has been asserted by her in accordance with the
Copyright, Designs and Patents Act 1988.

1 3 5 7 9 10 8 6 4 2

A CIP catalogue record for this title is
available from the British Library

ISBN 0 340 77119 4

Typeset in Plantin Light by
Palimpsest Book Production Limited,
Polmont, Stirlingshire

Printed and bound in Great Britain by
Mackays of Chatham plc, Chatham, Kent

Hodder and Stoughton
A division of Hodder Headline
338 Euston Road
London NW1 3BH

For Gabriel

No book is the product of one person, and this is certainly the case with *Ophelia's Revenge*. Nothing valuable in my life would have been possible without the love and devotion of my parents, John and Carolyn Reisert, or the emotional support of those other important Reiserts: John Mark, Jane, Courtney, Ian, Glenn, and Gabriel. Thanks also to my friends who believed in me as a writer even during those times I doubted myself: Judy Payne, Maria Jones, Dale Durham, Bob and Barbara Larkin, Mary Ann Bowman, Anita Tucker, Doris Harris, LeAnn Benevento and Susan Popp. My wonderful theatre colleagues provided inspiration and sanctuary for my creativity: Ray and Eileen Day, Bette Weber Flock, Paula Spugnardi, Jerry Ernstberger, Kerry Jones, Rick Knoop, Victoria Young, Jack and Susie Walker, Jennifer Day, Mark Saurer, Bob and Judy Silva, Linda Perez, and Mike Reynolds. It's impossible to list all the writing teachers who have helped me hone my craft, but I am particularly grateful to Richard Brengle, Howard Ashman, Michael Erwin, Carolyn Gorman, Trudi Krisher, Arlene Morse, Mary Quattlebaum, and the faculty of the Antioch Writers Workshop. My agent, Fred Morris, and my editor, Carolyn Caughey, were the wise and incredibly competent midwives for this book. I owe my life to my miracle worker of an oncologist, Dr David Doering, as well as to Cheri and the rest of his talented, skilled medical staff.

In addition, I owe a huge debt of gratitude to my witty,

sagacious, and fiercely intelligent colleagues at St Xavier and Providence High Schools. I especially want to thank my fellow English department members for doing so much to help me develop both as a writer and a person. I don't have space to list them all, but I am especially grateful to Sarah Watson, Bro. James Kelly, Mindy Ernstberger, Karen Benham, Irene Rapier, Martha Newcomb, Linda Winkler, Mike Johnson (Providence), Mike Johnson (St X), Glennda Tingle, Erin Burke, and Kathryn Jacobi. Finally, thanks are due to my St Xavier and Providence students for being my greatest teachers and to the actors and tekkies from my plays for being my ultimate heroes, wizards, and muses.

ACT ONE

My First Murder

I

By my sixteenth birthday, I'd murdered two kings, my father, my brother, a queen, a prince and my husband.

Nothing in my early life gave any indication of the villainy into which my later years would descend. Certainly not my early childhood spent in a village perched like a crumb above the upper lip of an island outlined by a grey northern sea. I lived in the house of Myg the Starcher. Starching is a nasty business. Back then, even though we didn't wear the great cartwheel ruffs that are all the current rage, prosperous folk nevertheless wore broad flat collars that had to be properly starched. Myg – a small, knobby woman with flesh pulled as tight across her sharp bones as a collar across a pair of starching irons – didn't like me overmuch, but I was useful to her since she had no daughter to follow her in her trade.

I spent mornings assisting Myg at her work. I hated it. I hated everything that went into making the starch – the daily draining and refilling of water from the gluey mess of wheat, the hours of beating it to a smooth paste without a single lump, more hours of boiling it with Myg's particular mixture of water and sweet milk, the sticky business of straining it through a succession of cloths, and the tedium of spreading it out on linen panels in the sun and having to rush out every few minutes to turn it so it dried evenly. Some of our starch was then scraped into packets to sell to the kitchens, but most of it we used in starching clothes. Worse even than making the starch was laundering the collars and other clothes, for these pieces were often greasy and smelly from contact with their owners' bodies, and collars in particular often bore stains from food and drink that we had to scrub away. At a pinch, we could bleach out some stains with asses' urine, boiled and poured through the discoloured cloth.

My only point of gratitude was that Myg didn't trust me to do the actual ironing. Her tiny fingers were nimble, and her sense of how long to hold the hot irons to the cloth was as finely tuned as a minstrel's harp. Every few months, Myg would say, 'Give another try to the pressing, for surely now you've skill enough.'

She always gave me the headpieces from the nearby convent of Saint Anna for this practice, reasoning that the nuns were women of God and should eschew vanity if their headpieces were a little singed. Nevertheless, no matter how much I swore to focus on the task, my mind would drift from the miles of bland white linen in front of me, and a smell of burning cloth would prompt Myg once again to clout me on my ear and snatch the ironing tongs out of my hands.

Often I tried to hint that I didn't wish to follow in her path. 'Someday I'll sail all the known seas,' I used to say. 'I'll see at least one undiscovered kingdom.' Or: 'I'll dance at a grand ball at a castle.' Or: 'I'll travel with a band of players all the way to Italy.'

Foolish, she called me, and at least once a week she'd say, 'You have dreams too big for your head and a heart too big for your chest.'

I hated the way our cottage reeked of the sharp, clean starch whose smell sliced through the nose like a knife. It was true, our cottage didn't stink like the house of Bi who lived directly downwind of her father's slaughter house or like that of Hvalp, son of the tanner. His house was filled with the vats of urine that his father used to soften leather. Whenever I felt sorry for my lot, I tried to remind myself that at least I didn't have to do the morning work of Hvalp who not only had to spend hours rubbing the urine into the smelly hides, but who also had to run around the village collecting it from various animals. Often he couldn't join us in the afternoons until he'd filled the jars with urine enough for the next day's work. Sometimes his friends would take turns pissing into the jar in order to make up the difference, but even a whole band of children can't produce the same quantity of urine as one healthy heifer.

In those days of childhood, I had no name of my own. I was simply called The Girl or Myg's Girl although my foster brother and twin was known as Piet. He was a small, big-eyed, solemn, silent boy. Unlike me, Piet didn't like to burrow into the deeper possibilities of things. Piet was a lover of surfaces. He loved the curve of a line, the spread of a shape, the blur of a shadow. Form, not meaning, was his grail. In our cottage, he spent hours on end next to the hearth, spreading out the ashes flat as the top of a spice chest. With a stick he'd draw a shape in the ashes, trying to use as few lines as possible to capture its essence. Out in the countryside, he'd do the same in any patch of dirt he could find. One of our games was for him to begin to draw some object or other and me to see how fast I could guess what he was drawing. 'Bowl,' I'd call out, or 'Eagle.'

Perhaps what I admired most about him was that after he'd achieved a perfect representation of a thing, a line drawing that looked so real you half-fancied you could reach down and pick it up and set it, plop, down next to the original like a long-lost brother, Piet would rub it out so he could draw something new. He loved the process, but he grew bored once the results were achieved, caring only about beginning the next challenge.

Me, I don't like to let go of anything once it's mine.

Myg was one of the wealthiest villagers, prosperous enough

to buy bread from the baker. Only the poorest folk in the village fashioned their loaves at home. I didn't quite understand how Myg's starching brought in as much money as we spent, but it's not in a child's nature to delve into the source of her family's income. I assumed her dead husband must have been a warm man who could squeeze a coin until it bled, and so she supplemented her earnings from the starch trade with money he'd left her. When Piet and I were about six, though, the baker and most of his family were carried off by a bout of sickness that swept through the village, and until the new baker arrived, Myg set me and Piet to making our daily bread.

In truth, breadmaking was near as tedious as starching. We had to bake daily since cottage fireplaces weren't large enough to bake more than a single loaf at a time. To beguile my boredom, Piet began fashioning the loaves into different shapes. One he shaped like a hare, another like a boar. Then he made a whale, a cottage, a Viking ship, a castle. To my surprise, Myg was pleased by his talent, clapping her raw hands together in delight. 'What a fine future you will have, my son,' she crowed. 'You will make a master subtler and have your pick of place at any nobleman's court.'

Piet looked bewildered, so she told us about castle folk from her youth when she'd toiled in the castle's laundry shed, how nobles were never content eating plain fare but must have their victuals disguised by spices or fancied up by pastes and crusts and such so that a herring pie might be made to look like a fairy ship sailing across gruel dyed blue to look like the sea. The subtler was king of the kitchen, the man in charge of creating marvels out of common foodstuffs, the wizard transforming ordinary fare into magic. 'My son will find his trade in a castle kitchen!'

She shot a meaningful glance at me.

I had no idea how to interpret this look, but I didn't

inquire because her temper was as uncertain as a November sky.

Once Myg disappeared for an entire afternoon. When she returned at dusk, she pulled a large, heavy parcel out from under her cloak and set it on the table.

'This is your future, Piet,' she told him. She then ordered me to fetch her a mug of beer.

Piet carefully unwrapped the parcel. Inside were three books. Piet and I looked at each other blankly. Neither of us could read, so this gift made no sense.

Myg laughed at our puzzled faces until she choked. 'The pictures,' she gasped. 'Study the pictures, Piet. With your doughs and such, learn how to make the things in the pictures and then your future will be assured.'

A single book could cost more than most folk made in a year, so Piet and I couldn't fathom how Myg afforded three of them or even where she got them, but we dared not ask for fear of her wrath. Instead, we each in our own way fell in love with the wondrous drawings inside the leather covers.

One volume contained all manner of beasts. There were cats and dogs and rats and seagulls like the ones seen round the village, but there were many more beasts as well. Piet's favourite was a creature shaped something like an ox with a curving single horn on its nose, while I favoured one that had the head and breasts of a maiden, huge wings like an eagle, and the haunches of a giant cat. How I yearned to be that flying cat-girl. I began to make up stories for Piet and the other children of the village about the adventures of the Flying Catgirl and how she travelled to distant lands. In truth I didn't know where my tales came from. I'd open my mouth and whole sentences would tumble out like peas from a sifter. The other children huddled together, wide-eyed and mouths gaping like those of landed cod as I spun the terrifying adventures of the Flying Catgirl who was as bold and dread as a Northman. The other children took my tales as history, and, in truth, as I spoke them they felt even more real than history.

Because it was a peaceful, prosperous time, we children had most afternoons to play. One day I had the idea of turning my playfellows into a band of actors to perform my Flying Catgirl stories. We all loved watching the players that came once or twice a year to our village. Every Yule, we adored seeing the men of the village and their comical play about the adventures of Dumpling, the youngest of three sons, who would trick the Devil. Each year the story was a little different according to whether Dumpling was played by the miller or the net mender or someone else entirely. We'd shriek with laughter at the silly things Dumpling did, wearing a chamber pot on his head for a helmet or riding a broom into battle. We cheered him on in his final battle with the Devil, a vigorous scene that usually upset a pot or two in the alehouse before it was finished.

Now every few weeks, we children performed a new adventure of the Flying Catgirl for the folk in the village. In each play, the Flying Catgirl faced a terrible enemy and overcame him through her courage and wit. At different times she defeated the Man under the Mountain, the Wizard of Rain and Thunder, the Witch of the Moors, the Flood God, Loki the Trickster, and even the Devil himself. The other children were willing but not particularly skilled, so I took on me the hardest two roles, playing both the Flying Catgirl and the Storyteller. Piet refused to speak any lines, but he was always willing to play a silent beast and to help fashion the costumes and swords and such. Finn, the third son of the fishmonger, usually played the villain of the piece and made a passable piece of work of it, but I secretly longed for a stronger opponent. Not only was Finn smaller than me, but if the stories got too real, he was prone to run away. None of the other children, though, would attempt the villain. They said I frightened them when I was caught up in the righteous passion of the Flying Catgirl who fought to save both herself and the kingdom of the Catpeople. I tried to soften my performance to appease Finn and the others, but as soon as I plunged into my part, I forgot to be meek and mild.

Our plays were popular with the village folk, although many of them asked if we could give them instead a good comedy.

'I hate comedy,' I'd say, my eyes flashing with indignation. Life was meant to be a heroic endeavour. As far as I was concerned, life itself made them look foolish. I wanted my plays to show folk how to be champions, not clowns.

The pictures in Piet's books inspired my plays. From the second book that apparently told stories from the Bible, I got ideas for destroying the Flying Catgirl's enemies. At different times they were dragged behind horses, crushed in a collapsing temple, drowned in a sea divided in two, trampled under the hooves of beasts struggling up a mountain to escape a flood, torn apart in a pit by a hungry lion, ripped by bears, and eaten alive by a cloud of insects. I loved the high drama of these deaths although I regretted I hadn't the means to show them directly on the stage but had to rely on a messenger to rush in with a speech describing the disaster.

The third book was my favourite. It was filled with pictures of distant lands where neither the clothing nor the buildings looked the same as ours. Sometimes I thought I'd die of impatience to witness these marvels for myself.

'When we are older, we'll travel to all these places,' I told Piet.

'No,' he said calmly, patting dough into the shape of one of the half-timbered cottages of our village. 'Unless they're sailors, people shouldn't leave their homeland.'

I stamped my foot with vexation. 'Doesn't that anger

you? Doesn't that drive you mad with frustration and long-ing?'

'No.' He carefully pressed down the nutmeat door. 'It's good to be rooted.'

'Vegetables are rooted. People are made to seek adventure.'

'No,' he said again, and began to draw a twig back and forth to make the dough roof look like it was made of thatch.

I looked over at the starch pots and blew out my breath in a tempest of despair.

Even though I was known as Myg's Girl, I always knew that she wasn't my mother. I don't know how I stumbled upon this understanding. Perhaps it came because Piet called her Mam, but I addressed her as Myg like the others in the village. I assumed my parents were dead and Myg had taken me in to raise. This wasn't unusual. The village was littered with orphans. Women died with regularity in childbirth, and the sea swallowed lots of our men. Children who were strays were taken in by some family or another. From time to time I considered asking Myg what had happened to my parents, but I didn't want to feel the blow of her hard hand against my face so I kept my peace. Partly, I must confess, my hesitation to ask the question was from fear of what I'd find. As long as I didn't know who my true parents had been, I was free to make up stories about my origins – how I'd been found as a babe, swept overboard from a foreign ship and how one day someone from an exotic country with domed churches and single-horned oxen would escort me to my real home.

At the age of thirteen or fourteen, most children in our village became apprenticed to a trade. From my tenth year onward, I dreaded the approach of my thirteenth birthday. I had no doubt but that Myg would formally apprentice me as a starcher. Apprentices no longer had the afternoons free to play, so I'd be forced to stay inside, starching from dawn to dusk, six days a week. Worse than that, Piet would then be apprenticed to the master-subtler at Elsinore Castle, and I'd see him but once a year.

Many afternoons, Piet and I took the long walk westward to gaze at Elsinore. I made up stories about the people passing to and fro across its moat and dreamed of being a princess within its thick walls. Deep within my soul I was sure I was superior to the village folk, better even than my beloved Piet. I knew for certain that I was the stuff from which princesses were made. I hugged that secret knowledge deep within me, unwilling to call forth the scorn of the village while I bided my time until I was summoned to my real life. Our second best walk took us to a ruined monastery and its wealth of grounds. Nestled next to its collapsed church and the cloister that had housed an order of monks before the plague came calling, there was a huge graveyard with stone monuments as large as sheds. Piet loved to study their intricate carvings for their artistry while I liked to study the effigies on top and speculate about who they'd been in life. Myg told us that even though the church was no longer used, this was still the traditional burying place of kings and nobles. I kept hoping someone in the castle would die so I could witness a grand state funeral and see all the royal folk close up, but this didn't happen. I knew our king was named Hamlet, but I didn't know what other royals lived with him at Elsinore, and I could find no way to persuade Myg to tell me more about them. 'Mix curs with greyhounds, and mongrels abound,' she always said when I pressed her to talk of the noble folk.

If I had to be apprenticed, then I wished I could have been apprenticed to the woman who lived in the cottage next to ours. One reason I felt a kinship with our neighbour was because, like me, she wasn't known by a proper name. Everyone called her the Herbwife because her trade was making potions out of herbs. Her husband had been a sailor who'd glimpsed her in an English port. He'd fallen sick with love, haunting her shop and gulping down every nasty mixture she could concoct until finally she'd agreed to sail with him to Denmark. They'd produced four lusty sons, each with her thundercloud of dark hair and stormy black eyes and his rosy cheeks and love of the untamed seas. After he'd drowned in a gale, village folk expected her to return to England with her brood, the youngest still a babe in arms and the oldest no higher than a beer barrel. But she didn't leave.

'This is my home,' she'd said in her odd English accent. 'The land of my husband and one day the home of my sons.' And she'd asked her husband's brothers, the ruddy-cheeked Blad and the leather-skinned Bjorn, to teach her sons the seafaring trade, and thus she'd settled down to tend her herbs and love her four boys and let them roam as free and wild as bear cubs. I loved her garden, filled with its wealth of herbs and grasses and medicinal weeds, and I loved her fragrant cottage scented by dozens of bunches of herbs hanging from the rafters to dry. Where our cottage had the bleak, wintry smell of starch, her cottage was rich in mystery, layering the scents of hundreds of herbs. She spent her evenings experimenting with different strengths and mixtures of herbs, and folks said that if one of her potions failed to cure you, then it was a sign that God had marked your soul for death and there was nothing to be done.

It wasn't so much her work that I craved, but, if I had to stay in our village when I came to be a woman grown, I'd much prefer to be the Herbwife rather than Myg. The Herbwife had a strange, wild beauty, while Myg was as plain as a knuckle. The Herbwife had seen something of the world beyond our small patch of Denmark, while Myg had never ventured farther than an hour or so in any direction. The Herbwife's cottage was filled with wonders shut away in hundreds of little jars, while Myg's house was scoured clean of all mystery or romance. When the weather was too rainy to play out of doors, I'd go to the Herbwife's cottage and help her sort and preserve her herbs while she taught me English, a much more slippery language than Danish and one that had stolen many of our good Danish words.

Most of all, I envied the Herbwife's four sons. They were all reckless, dark, bold, and kind. By my eleventh year, the oldest already sailed a ship and had set up a trading base in England in his mother's old town. He was often gone for months at a time, but when he returned his ship was crammed with spices and silks and fabulously woven cloths that he traded first to the castle folk and then to the local merchants. He and his brothers planned one day to own the biggest merchant fleet in the world.

The middle brothers were already apprenticed to their uncles in the shipbuilding and merchant trades, but the youngest brother, Ragnor, was just a little older than Piet and me. I longed desperately to get him in our plays. He was strong and self-assured to the point of cockiness, and he'd make a villain strong enough for the Flying Catgirl to let loose her full strength without having to hold back for fear of frightening him. To my disappointment, although Ragnor loved to watch our plays, he refused to take part. He was already sea-mad, and he had a tiny boat of his own that he'd built with his brothers. He'd built it in the style of the old-time Viking ships, flat-bottomed and swift. Most of his days were spent exploring the coast or seeing how far he could venture out into the open waters before he had to turn back to beat the night home. Myg and other village women thought it scandalous that the Herbwife would let such a young boy take to the sea, but the Herbwife understood that if she tried to rein in her wild colt of a son, he'd just sneak off and do the same thing without her permission, so she kept her breath for arguments she could win, and the village grew almost accustomed to seeing Ragnor skim across the water, the wind pulling his long dark curls until they stood straight out from his head. I often wondered what it felt like to skim across the surface of the sea so swift it looked like flying.

Still, I never gave over coaxing Ragnor to act with me.

'A play needs those to hear it as well as players to perform it,' he always said. 'I am better cast as audience than actor.'

In truth, I suspected he was so comfortable being himself that he had no longing to play anyone else.

I myself longed desperately to be anyone but the person I was. Only when I played the Flying Catgirl did I feel I came near to living in my true nature.

My transformation into someone else began the afternoon that Hvalp came running down the beach, screaming for my aid.

2

'Girl! You must come. The miller's son is doing dreadful things and I don't know how to stop him.'

Piet and I dropped our baskets into which we were collecting driftwood for kindling and dashed after tiny Hvalp up the beach to where the miller's son and his three loutish cronies squatted, a bony stray hound cowering in front of them. It cringed and pawed against the ground and made little whimpering sounds. The miller's son held out a strip of dried fish. It was clear that the poor dog was hungry and longed for the food but didn't trust men enough to come too close, until hunger won out over judgement, and the poor pup crept near enough to seize the fish in his teeth. The miller's son shouted, 'Grab him,' and his cronies each grabbed a leg. They threw the writhing hound over on his back, and the miller's son took a large knife out of his belt.

'Now we'll have fine sport,' he said, raising his knife. 'Two strokes, and I slice the hamstrings clean in two. You'll find it better than a fair to watch the silly creature drag itself around on its bottom, scooting this way and that and never being able to rise up and walk. How it will make us laugh.'

The knife flashed down and the hound gave a squeal of pain. It was as if the knife stroke cut something free in me, for I was screaming like a Valkyrie in the old tales and rushing full tilt at the boy, and then I slammed my body into his and began to pummel him with my fists, over and over. Even though he could have made two or three of me, he was startled and dropped the knife. His cronies, equally startled, let go of the poor pup who dragged itself out of their reach. Piet had run in after me and butted the next biggest boy in the stomach, but I called to him, 'Help the poor dog,' and I had a dim memory of Piet gathering the dog up in his arms.

I had the advantage only for a moment or two, and then the miller's cronies laid hands upon me and dragged me away. Piet hesitated, unsure whether or not to abandon the dog and run to my aid, but I screamed, 'Get the dog to safety.'

'Well, now,' the miller's son said, looming over me with a leer on his face. 'What a little spitfire we have here.'

I kept screaming and writhing in anger.

'What a little cat indeed. Since she's ruined our sport, perhaps we should do to her what we planned to do to that worthless bitch. Slice her hamstrings and watch her crawl!'

He raised the knife above me and leered some more. I was too caught up in anger to be scared.

'Turn her over on her belly,' he commanded, and I was flopped over onto my stomach so hard that the breath was knocked out of me.

Dimly I hoped that Piet and the pup had made it to safety.

I felt rough hands pulling up my gown into a bunch above my waist, and the miller's son ran the knife lightly across the top of my thighs, a scratch deep enough to draw blood but not deep enough to slice the muscle.

I'd regained enough air to lift up my head and scream out, but he gave a hard blow to the back of my head, driving my face down into the sand.

'Wildcats must be tamed,' he said. 'After we've hobbled this spitfire, we should cut out her tongue as well so she can tell no one of our deed.'

Then, all of a sudden, he gave an 'ooof' sound as if the air had been knocked out of him, and I was free. I scrambled to my feet. The Herbwife's three younger boys were beating the miller's son and his companions with sticks while small Hvalp stood there, his eyes shining. I launched myself against the miller's son, kicking and biting. My four assailants began to blubber.

'It was only a jest,' they sobbed. 'Myg's Girl knows we'd not have truly harmed her.'

'Look!' called out small Hvalp in his shrill little voice. He pointed to the crotch of the miller boy. 'You have wet yourself!'

Then the Herbwife's sons roared with laughter, and my assailants pulled themselves free and staggered off toward the village, blubbering all the while.

I thanked the boys who rescued me, and we all took ourselves off to where Piet crouched behind a sand dune. The Herbwife's third son crouched to examine the pup. One leg dangled uselessly behind him.

'He can live with three legs,' said the oldest of the boys. 'It will not be a pretty sight, but he can get himself around like a walking tripod.'

So we carried the whimpering dog to the Herbwife who examined it with an expression of great concern.

'The leg will have to come off entire,' she said, and she showed us which herbs to use to brew a tea that put him into a deep sleep, and we watched with great interest as she sliced off the dangling leg and then sewed the wound back up with elderbark thread.

She kept the crippled pup until he was well enough to lope around, and by that time he'd grown so fond of her that she didn't have the heart to send him away. It didn't occur to any of us children to tell any other grown folk about this adventure. No one could have stopped the miller's son from the cruelty of his ways, and I feared that if Myg heard the story, she'd curtail my freedom and force me to stay as close at hand as the crippled dog.

A week later, the miller's son got his revenge.

The other children and I had prepared a particularly good play about the Flying Catgirl and her adventures with the evil Dragon that Swallows its Tail and the Ravening Wolf of Hell. We spread the word that on Sunday after church, we'd perform the play in the clearing in the stand of trees that served as our stage. Of course the miller's son and his cronies caught wind of it. Before the play began, they hid themselves up in the leafy branches of a tree that formed the canopy for our playing area.

The play went along quite well. Our audience (and some of my fellow actors) lustily cheered the heroic speeches of the Flying Catgirl and hissed those of Loki as he gave his orders to the Dragon and the Wolf (played by two boys who were particularly well-suited to these roles since they were quite handy in fighting scenes but were too shy to speak any lines above a mumble). Just before the final fray, when I called up to Heaven to unloose its favour and drench me in courage, there was a whistle, and the miller's son and his cronies dumped down onto my head the contents of the chamber pots they held.

For a moment all was silent, and then they began to laugh and then the audience began to laugh and finally my fellow actors began to laugh until I was the only one not laughing. I burned with shame, my best gown ruined, my best play ruined, and all that was dearest to my heart laid bare to mockery.

'While low comedy is caviar for the groundlings, the heroic heart knows the action of the play must go on to its end,' a new voice called out.

It was a voice that would have done credit to Michael, the warrior archangel, a voice that was both golden and fierce at the same time. Its accent wasn't that of our villagers. It was as if our village accent was mud, and the speaker's accent was clear water from the very source of the spring.

The audience grew quiet. My eyes were still shut against the piss that ran down my face, but I pried one open to see who was speaking words so fair.

'If none of the "dreadest apparitions of hell itself" can daunt the valiant Catgirl, then sure it is that she'll not be slowed by the contents of a chamber pot or two.' To my amazement, I saw a young man – more beautiful than any angel – step into the flat dirt clearing that we used for our stage. I'd never before realized that any human being could be that beautiful. This one had a face like a virgin saint, and his body was both rounded and delicate as if he was carefully carved out of soapstone while the rest of us were merely slopped together from slabs of clay. His skin had the subtle tints of the inside of a shell, and his hair shone like a beacon of the palest gold.

He smiled at me. His smile was slow but it filled his whole face, especially his eyes, till there was no space for anything but joy in his entire visage. 'You prayed to heaven for aid,' he said. 'And heaven sent me.'

He was tall, taller than most of the men in the village, and his clothes were wondrous fine. His doublet was velvet, dark as a midnight sea and thicker than the costliest carpet, and all about the neck it was embroidered with gold thread in a pattern of leaves and vines. The sleeves were black silk, with regular slashes, each about a hand's-span apart, through which gold cloth gleamed. His gloves were a wonder. Cream-coloured leather with wide cuffs embroidered in green, crimson, gold, and a tawny brown.

He put his hands on my wet shoulders and drew me to him as if it were rain and not waste that had befouled me. He showed not the least care for protecting his fine, pale gloves. Then, with his own silk sleeve, he wiped my face dry.

I could hear the audience murmuring, but I was too enchanted to make out what they were saying.

My saviour pushed a damp hank of hair back off my forehead. 'I'm yours to command, Catgirl,' he said, sweeping me a deep bow. 'What is your will?'

For a moment I couldn't think what to say, and then I said, 'Sire, there be demons crouching in the branches above, highwaymen along my path to heaven. Can we not teach them not to trespass between me and my ends?'

He gave a yelp of laughter as if he was both surprised and pleased that I could so quickly think of a plan. 'I like it well, Catgirl. Shall we teach those ruffians better manners toward a lady and a hero?' He peered up into the tree. 'Ahh, I spy four fat plums ripe for the shaking.' He reached up and began to shake the tree.

'Please, my lord,' the miller's son called down, 'we mean no harm.'

'But harm you did, and it was harm as mean as if you'd meant it, so look you, arm you now to demean yourself before this lady and restore the harmony of the afternoon.' He shook the tree harder. 'For if you haven't the means to beg pardon, then I'll harm you all the way to Elsinore and back again.'

The four miscreants leaped to the ground. They grovelled, muttering, 'Beg pardon, your lordship.'

'Beggars!' he said, knocking them to the ground with his foot. 'Do not beg pardon of me, but address yourself to this lady that you've mightily offended.'

They scrambled to beg my pardon. I didn't wish to forgive them, but I cared more about impressing my saviour with my graciousness than nursing my grudge, so I finally told my tormentors that we need say no more about the matter.

'Be off, then, and sin no more!' my saviour commanded them. They scampered toward the village as he called, 'If I hear ever again that you've caused this lady the least bit of worry, then I'll have you whipped to within an inch of your life and locked in the pillory to be made the laughing stock of all the country round. Shut yourselves in your houses, so now only these folk know what fools you be, but if you transgress again, then all folk near and far will know that we have here the four greatest fools in all Denmark.'

The crowd cheered as the miller's son disappeared.

For perhaps the first time in my life, my words deserted me, and I could do nothing but stare at my rescuer in wonder and love.

'Yours is as brave a play as ever I did see,' my saviour said. 'Brave in writing and brave in the heart of its hero. Right glad am I that I was riding past and could rein up in time to see some of it.'

'We play a new one each month,' I said boldly. 'It would give us much joy to have you hear our next one. We will decorate a seat of honour for you should you favour us with your presence.' An idea filled me and I quickly croaked out before I could lose my nerve, 'Or I'd pen you a great part if you'd prefer to be one of our company.'

He gave a long laugh, but I thought he was pleased. 'Naught would give me greater joy than to be one of your company of players.' Then his face grew a little wistful. 'It would be bliss indeed, lass. Could I be a player instead of a prince . . .'

I caught my breath. A prince. This must be one of the two sons of King Hamlet who lived much of the year in Elsinore Castle. I was talking to a prince! More than that, what bliss indeed it would be if he were to perform with us. What a fine villain he could make, finally a player strong enough to battle with my Flying Catgirl.

Then he gave himself a little shake. 'But such a state of affairs is not to be, my heroic lady. I regret that I must be off on the morrow to Wittenberg to return to university.' Then he took my hand in his glove that was soft as the flesh of an infant.

To my amazement, he kissed my fingertips, never caring that they might still be mucky from the dumped chamber pots.

'Farewell, fair lady,' he said. He leaned close and whispered, 'Keep faith with your own nature, Catgirl. Never let anyone divide you from your true self.'

Then in a twinkling he was back up on his horse and riding away. I watched until he disappeared, although the sun shone direct in my eyes and blurred my view.

Once or twice during the weeks following the prince's intervention, the miller's son leered at me, but well he knew that if I were to tell the tale of his misadventures, it would reflect no credit on him, and so finally he gave me a wide berth.

'Tell me about the prince!' I begged Myg.

'That was young prince Hamlet,' she said. 'The king's second son.'

But she knew no more about him, nor did any of the other folk I questioned. Whenever I could grab enough time, I'd walk to Elsinore Castle and stare at it with longing, trying to picture Prince Hamlet within its walls. I'd crouch for as long as I dared, watching it as a hunter might watch his prey, willing the prince to appear, but I never saw Prince Hamlet or any of the other royal folk.

Spring turned to summer and then slid into autumn as I waited eagerly for the prince's return from school. Surely he'd come to our village to watch another drama. He'd spoken favourably of my play. I had no doubt but that he'd want to see another of our performances. Perhaps he'd even invite my band of child players up to the castle to entertain the royal folk.

But one year passed and then another, and still Prince Hamlet didn't return.

Oh, life in our village went on as it always had, but even though the form was the same, the flavour was different entirely. It was as if I'd spent the first part of my life shut up in a cave but I'd never realized it was a cave until the prince had stepped in and lit it up with the golden light of his presence. That light had been brief as lightning, but now I was aware of how very dim my cave-life was. I craved his brightness, but I couldn't figure a way to crawl out of the cave. As my thirteenth year edged nearer, I grew even more frantic. Soon I'd be a woman, but I hated most of the women in the village, so dull and so worn. There were three of us girls in my band of actors, me, the barrelmaker's daughter, Hilde, and skinny Snefnug whose father was a not very successful fisherman. They didn't have my boldness or imagination, but we all three had ten times the fire and life of the older women around us. It seemed to me that womanhood was actually a walking tomb for our childhood, a place in which we became pale ghosts of our ardent girl-selves. I liked the me that I was. I didn't want her to die into adulthood, but I didn't know how to save her. I had a pirate heart, and I couldn't stomach the thought of settling down and patiently starching collars day after day after day. If I'd been born a boy, I'd have sailed to adventure upon the seas, but since I was a girl, the whale road was closed to me. What kind of life could a girl with a bold heart lead?

And still the days marched on like condemned prisoners toward the time I would be officially made Myg's apprentice, starched and crucified upon the cross of ordinary village life.

Until a single visit changed everything.

3

On the day that my life changed, Piet and I had gone gathering mushrooms. We returned well before dark, so we were startled to see Myg waiting impatiently for us in the doorway. Piet and I looked at each other, bewildered. We'd done our chores before leaving, so we could think of no other reason that she might want us.

'Girl,' she called to me, making shooing motions like someone whooshing her chickens back into their pen. 'Get yourself in here, quick as catch can, for there is one who wishes to see you.'

This bewildered me further, but she grabbed onto my shoulders with her bony red hands, and she swatted my hair several times as if she thought to smack it into order and obedience. She spit in her hand and rubbed it hard against some stains on my bodice, and she sighed loudly when they didn't rub away. She gave me a sharp push with her hand in the small of my back, and I stumbled into the house.

As always, it took several moments for my eyes to adjust to the dimming of the light. Then I saw a young woman there dressed in the finest clothes I'd ever seen apart from the garb of the prince. Her gown was a pale green, halfway between the white of an apple's flesh and the green of its skin. Across the breasts was a golden web like a net with tiny seed pearls sewn at each intersection of the gold threads. A cap of the same golden web sat on her head, almost obscuring her thick brown hair. The sleeves of her gown hung full and wide as the wings of an angel.

'Is this the girl?' she asked. Her voice was rich as cider, but she had a foreign accent that I couldn't identify.

I said nothing in reply but cast about in my mind to see if I'd committed some mischief without being aware of what I'd done, trampled some flowers or spoke overloud after failing to notice the lady nearby.

'This is the girl,' Myg said, and her voice sounded heavy next to the delicate tones of the lady, like a whale leaping into the brine after the splash of a little silver fish. 'I had long thought someone would fetch her 'fore now.'

'To tell truth,' the lady said, 'her father forgot all about her till a remark of mine chanced to remind him that he had a daughter.'

I was bewildered. About whose father did they speak?

Myg sighed. 'For all that, she was a good worker and not much trouble about the place. I'd be willing to keep her for aye.'

'For always?'

Hope, like a trapped bird, began to struggle in my breast. I didn't quite follow this conversation, but it sounded like this unknown lady was offering me the chance to leave Myg, to leave the village, to leave my life. I hardly dared breathe for fear of upsetting this delicate opportunity.

Myg inclined her head. 'I have no daughters to follow me in my trade. I'd fain keep this girl, for my husband is dead, and it's unlikely that any more babes will tumble from my womb.'

Don't make me stay here. Don't leave me here. I tried to will the visitor to take me with her, but she only said, 'Provided, of course, that her father continue to pay for her upkeep.' Her lips twisted in a wry smile.

'But of course. The child is small but she eats like a seal.'

In her most pious voice Myg added, 'After all, I teach her a trade for free. Most apprentices have to pay dearly to gain knowledge like mine.'

But the lady shook her head till her dark hair bounced like aspen leaves before the storm. 'That's kind of you, but I would have her as a companion about me. It's lonely, in truth, up in that stone pit there, and I long for a little daughter of my own.'

Please take me with you. All you martyred virgins in heaven, have pity on me and grant me this one boon. I'll never ask you for anything else, will you only grant me this.

Myg clucked her tongue. 'I doubt not but this baggage can leave me without a second glance, but it will go hard for her to be parted with Piet, for they've been like brother and sister since they were but a single day old.'

The mention of leaving Piet caught my attention. I wanted to move out of Myg's house, but it hadn't occurred to me that I could be parted from Piet. I grabbed hold of his arm. 'He must come with us!' I shouted. 'We stay with each other.'

'Hush,' said Myg, and her voice sounded as scandal-struck as if I'd pulled off my shift and paraded naked through the streets. 'Hush, girl. You weren't brought up to be such a prickle-hook.'

'Hush,' said the lady in milder tones, but she looked amused.

'I'll not leave Piet,' I shouted, loud as the roar of a wounded bull.

We went at it for a time, they hushing me and me shouting all the louder, till the visitor said, 'I don't know how all this is to end.'

Nor did I. There were but two things I wanted – to go wherever this lady meant to take me and to make sure I wasn't parted from my foster brother. Piet was as much myself as my arm or leg. 'Take us both!' I wailed.

Piet, as usual, said nothing.

'I have an idea,' Myg finally said, and her eyes glittered greedily. 'My Piet has been training to 'prentice in the kitchens of the castle. I hadn't thought to send him there for three years more, but he's as skilled as a man full grown.'

'What does he do?' asked the lady, and I, my attention caught by this new ploy, stopped my wailing. Piet waited silently, placid as an oyster in the sun.

'He is skilled as a subtler,' Myg said. 'He can make bread dough into any shape that can be imagined, and his likenesses can almost be mistaken for the true thing. I doubt not that his fingers would be even nimbler with pastry.'

The lady looked doubtful. 'His majesty is a man of most sparing habits when it comes to his food,' she said.

Myg looked a little daunted, but she quickly countered with, 'But surely his majesty wishes to impress all guests to Denmark with the majesty and luxury of the Danish court. Piet's skill will go far to amaze all guests of the Dane.'

Astonishment froze me into uncharacteristic silence. The lady had mentioned the king. Did she wish to take me to the castle itself?

The lady turned her dark eyes to Piet. 'Is this true, little fellow?' she asked.

'Show the lady some of your carvings,' Myg said quick as the beat of a wing.

Piet walked over to his little wooden chest and threw back the lid. As well as shaping bread dough, he liked to whittle figures out of wood. He surveyed his treasures carefully, debating what to bring out.

I couldn't bear his slow caution. I ran across the floor and thrust my hands into the chest. 'Look!' I crowed, as proud of Piet as if he were my own son. 'Look and marvel!' I snatched up as many of the carvings as my little hands could hold, and I toddled back over and threw them into the lady's lap.

For a heartbeat she was struck dumb, and then her peals of laughter rang out.

'Are they not beautiful?' I called out. 'Are they not treasures indeed?'

She smiled at me with her eyes. 'I think there are many treasures in this room.'

'Then you will speak with the cook?' Myg asked eagerly.

The lady shook her head and sighed. 'I regret that I haven't the rank to direct the cook. Should the opportunity arise, I'll mention Piet's skill to the queen, but it will likely be a long, slow business if he come to the castle at all.' She rose gracefully to her feet and shook out her silken skirts. A faint scent of lavender wafted through our cottage and disappeared in the raw smell of the starch. 'It grieves me much to leave this girl here, but I haven't the power to force her from you, and, in truth, my husband hasn't the interest.' She reached a soft hand out to stroke my cheek. 'Farewell, child. I am sorry that you cannot come with me.'

I was cleft in twain. My soul danced with joy at travelling to the castle, but my heart reached toward Piet as if he were the moon and my blood a tide. I peeked at Piet's face. Never before had I seen him so stricken. While I knew he regretted losing his chance at the castle kitchens, I also knew his regret was greater at losing me.

'I cannot come with you unless Piet goes with us,' I said firmly.

Neither the lady or Myg paid us any mind. It was as if I hadn't spoken or as if little puffs of silence came out of my lips instead of words. The lady looked at me and then slid her eyes over to Myg. 'I don't even know her name.'

'Didn't her father tell you?'

'In truth, her father cannot recall it. He said in the flurry of her birth and her mother's death which followed hard upon, he cannot call to mind what they named the girl.'

'No more can I!' Myg said. 'I was never told. A rider came down from the castle and hammered against the shutters of my hut. "Open up," called he. "I seek the woman who has just given birth to a boy." My husband, God give him peace, oped the shutters for I was still sprawled bloody across my birth bed and the midwife's seat was still warm. "A lady in the castle gave birth and died," the swaddled rider said, "and we need someone to nurse the poor babe or she'll travel the same road her mother has passed. A guard said there was a woman just gave birth down in the village, and I rode down straight to find you. It's no more trouble to nurse two babies than one, and you shall be well-paid for giving shelter to this little one." And he thrust a damp bundle in through the window. The bundle contained the babe. It was ten years ago and more since that night, and each quarter day a sack of coins is faithfully delivered, but no one has shown any interest in the child until this very day.'

'Was I that child?' I asked.

'Hush,' Myg said. 'A wise child listens much and speaks little.'

'You were that child,' confirmed the lady. She eyed me thoughtfully and I eyed her right back.

Myg saw that look. 'Take her!' she cried. 'I'll trust you to try to gain a place in the kitchen for my Piet, but take her and may you have good fortune with her.'

My heart gave a leap of hope.

The lady smiled and inclined her head. 'I'll speak with the queen about your son at my first chance.'

'I am not going to the castle without Piet,' I said, but my voice sounded less firm. I wanted Piet with me, but I was more frightened that this might be my single chance to escape the life of a starch wife. The lady's hands were smooth and white, and perhaps if I went to the castle, I need not someday have raw hands like Myg's.

'You will be my own little daughter,' the lady said, 'for your dear mother has been with our Saviour these many years, and I am married to your own father.'

Her words made no sense. How could it be that I had a father all these years and no one had whispered a single word to me. I couldn't fathom what she had to say, so I turned to familiar meat. 'Piet must go with us!'

The lady wrinkled her brow. 'I'll speak with the queen and perhaps it can come to pass. But even if he comes, he'll sleep in the kitchen and your life will be above the stairs. You will see little of him.'

The distance couldn't be as far as all that.

The lady tossed a heavy pouch to Myg. 'Here's for your pains.' Myg clutched the purse eagerly, and I could see on her face that she was impatient for us to be gone so she could count the coins. Then the lady smiled at me. She was easily the prettiest lady I had ever seen. I doubted she'd yet reached her twentieth year. 'We must hurry if we wish to be back home before dark.' Her eyes flickered up and down me, and she frowned. 'Do you have any other gowns?'

I felt the colour rise in my cheeks. Next to this lady I had felt shabby already, but now I felt like a veritable ragpicker. I did in fact own a second gown, but it was too small, and I doubted it was cleaner than the one I wore.

'I'll fetch it,' I mumbled, wishing I could magically change it into a fresh new one.

I pulled it out of the chest while everyone waited in silence, and I held it up for the lady to see. She wrinkled her nose and thought for a moment. Finally she said, 'Perhaps we can pin up one of mine for you to wear when you meet your father. Leave it. Leave all your things. If you find there's something you truly need here, we can send a servant for it.'

I didn't tell her that in truth I had no things other than the clothes on my back and that one sad gown.

'Come then,' the lady said and walked like a queen out the door.

I began to follow her, but Myg stopped me. 'You ungrateful girl,' Myg snapped. 'You will leave me and your dear brother without a word of farewell then?'

I ran to Piet and threw my arms around him. He smelled of wood shavings and grass with a tang of damp earth. Suddenly my heart was too full and I could find no words.

He awkwardly folded his arms around me, too. We weren't in the habit of behaving so, and I could tell he too was uncomfortable because he let me go all of a sudden and hurried out the door as if he couldn't bear to see me depart.

I then moved over to Myg, but I couldn't bring myself to hug her. For a moment we looked at each other warily, and then I dropped a quick curtsey and scampered to the street where the lady waited.

'Let us go to the castle,' I said.

She looked a little amused.

In the castle I'd meet the father that I didn't know I had.

In the castle I'd be waiting for Prince Hamlet when he came home from school.

4

Judith, as the lady was called, was my father's seventh wife. On the way to the castle, she told me all that she knew of my own story.

It seemed my father gobbled down wives the way a glutton crammed down sweetmeats. Later, after I got to know my father well, I privately concluded that his first six wives chose death over continuing to live with him.

'Your father,' Judith said, lowering her head against the wind, 'married his first wife when they were both little more than children, but she died in childbirth and the child died with her.'

This didn't surprise me. Well I knew from life in the village how many pregnancies ended in the death of the mother or child or both.

'His second wife was from Norway. They say she was mad for flowers of every kind. They also say that one day she climbed up into a tree over a brook to gather some flowering vines, but the branch broke and she plunged into the water. She cried out for help, but the few folks on the bank couldn't find a pole long enough to reach her, and there wasn't a person there who could swim.'

That, too, made sense. I myself didn't know anyone who could swim. Sailors in particular scorned learning how to swim since many captains refused to hire men with that skill, feeling that a sailor who learned to swim lacked faith in his ship and his captain to bring him safely to the shore.

Judith continued, 'Her heavy skirts let her float for a while, but before she could be helped, her skirts grew soaked with water and dragged her down to her death.' We walked on in silence for a while in respect for this poor girl.

'His third wife, the youngest daughter of a Danish knight from over in Jutland, provided my husband with his only son but then a wasting sickness overtook her and she faded and faded until she was no longer there.'

'Did the baby die of the same sickness?'

Judith stopped walking and stared at me. 'No, your brother is very much alive.'

A brother! Not only did I have a father and a stepmother, but I had a brother as well! This was almost too much to swallow. 'Is he at the castle?' I managed to croak out.

Judith shook her head. The gold threads in her hairnet glittered in the dimming light. 'No, he's away at school.'

'With Prince Hamlet?' I asked, my heart thumping with eagerness.

Judith laughed. 'Oh, they're as different as chalk and cheese, your brother and Prince Hamlet. The prince is a scholar, and so he's been studying in Wittenberg these past ten years and more. That's where all the best scholars go. Your brother has gone instead to Paris to school himself in the arts of pleasing and advancement rather than the lore in books. Your father wishes him to be an important man at court, and he feels a Paris polishing will make him shine.' Judith sighed. 'I myself would dearly love to see Paris.'

I felt a little shy, but I said, 'So would I.' She smiled at me. I suddenly didn't mind as much that she'd turned up her nose at both my gowns.

'Was my mother the fourth wife?'

'No. The fourth wife was a lusty girl from Spain with an eye for the soldiers. One day after eating a sauce made of foreign spices, her belly swelled and burst and she died. Some of the folk whisper that my husband poisoned her so she wouldn't betray him with other men.'

This shocked me more than anything else that had happened on this amazing day. 'Is my father a murderer?' I whispered.

'No!' Judith's reply was sharp and swift. She followed this, though, with a comment in low tones. 'And even should he be so, we'd never say such a thing out loud where anyone might hear it.'

Now it was my turn to laugh. 'There's no one but us around. Not unless you reckon the gulls and the fishes to be secret agents of the king.'

'You will soon learn, child, that the court is a garden for spies. Remember always to set a guard on your tongue to strangle any careless remark stillborn before you can deliver it.'

I didn't say so to Judith, but the possibility of my father's being a murderer made him much more interesting than he'd been before. What would it be like to have a murderer for a father? I grew increasingly eager to meet him.

'Your mother was the fifth wife,' Judith said.

'Was she foreign born?' If so, that might explain the restlessness in me.

Judith's answer dashed my hopes. 'She was of good Danish stock, they say, stretching all the way back to one of the heroes in an epic.'

I was thrilled. The way I was drawn to act out the adventures of the Flying Catgirl . . . I must have known there was heroic blood flowing in my veins. 'Which hero?'

Judith laughed at my eagerness. 'I don't know which one. Folks have said that she traced her descent to "some hero or other," but I haven't heard anyone say which hero it is. I doubt anyone at court knows.'

'Perhaps my father knows.'

I felt Judith grow silent. 'It would be best, child, if you didn't discuss your mother with him.'

'Why?'

I glanced at her face. It looked worried. 'Perhaps I shouldn't have told you so much about your father's history. One of the wisest sayings at court is "Let the past rest safely in its grave."'

In the village folks had said, 'Do not water the past,' which is much the same thing. 'Why doesn't my father like to talk of my mother?'

'She came from an island far to the west, an island called Bornholm. It's many days' sailing.'

That thought intrigued me, that I might have relations living on this island far to the west. Still, Judith had sidestepped my question. I repeated, 'Why doesn't he like to talk about—'

'They say she lived in a castle perched on a cliff high above the sea.' I shivered. I'd always believed myself to be an abandoned princess, but now that it was perhaps true, I felt more frightened than comforted.

Judith tilted her head to look at me. 'I fancy you have rather the look of her. She left no portrait, but people say she was as fair and slender as moonlight.' A smile seeped into her eyes. 'You know what they say about the folk of Bornholm, don't you?'

I shook my head.

'They say that they have elven blood mixed in their veins.'

I was taken aback, but then Judith laughed and I understood she was but making fun.

'And she died in childbirth, is that right?'

Judith walked on in silence. I thought perhaps she hadn't heard me, so I repeated my question.

'No, not childbirth exactly.'

I could tell there was something amiss in this answer. I

pressed her farther for information. 'What, then, happened to my mother?'

'Perhaps this is something better asked of your father. It was, after all, before I came to the castle, so I know only what the gossips say.'

Another mystery. But this was one that concerned me more nearly than the fate of my father's fourth wife.

'How do they say she died?'

Judith shook her head until her bundled hair bounced. 'Oh, there are many fevers and such that go about. She grew ill with one of them, she sickened, and she died. It does no good to stick your finger in that wound.'

Why was she being so evasive? Then an idea hit me. 'Did my father perhaps poison her as well as his Spanish—'

Judith stopped short. 'Child, don't say so! Your father poisoned no one. Heed me well. He poisoned no one. Especially not your mother. She died of a fever, and now we must put that cat out and shut the door behind her.'

'But I want to know—'

'The sixth wife,' Judith said firmly, walking again, 'was a young widow. Her family was naught but farmers, but her father snared a match with an elderly knight at court. Then what must her new husband do, but up and die not three months after the wedding. By this time, her father was determined to have his family tied to gentlefolk, so he cast an eye over all the old men at court and approached your father who had been several years without a wife. They were married at once, only three months after her first husband's death, which set the tongues wagging, but both your father and hers were concerned if they gave her any more time, she'd dig in her heels and balk at taking another old man to her bed. So they waited the three months to make sure she wasn't carrying the child of her first husband, and on the first day of the fourth month, she was dragged to the altar.'

'Was she really dragged?' That would make a good play, the young girl bound and carried to the altar, forced to marry a doddering old man, and then the Flying Catgirl could swoop in and rescue her just in time and take her off to . . . take her off to . . . in truth, I didn't know a place where women could live free to write the stories of their own lives. Then it hit me. I'd no longer be performing any Flying Catgirl dramas.

Judith laughed, a little breathless from our brisk pace. 'I don't think that her body was dragged to the chapel, but while her flesh was obedient, her spirit was in rebellion.' She stopped again and motioned me close. She whispered, 'It was put about that Rosmarin, as she was called, died of black fever when she'd travelled to France with your father to visit your brother in school, but there are rumours that she didn't die but ran away with a travelling player instead.' She sounded pleasurably scandalized, but that made sense to me. I couldn't imagine any woman preferring marriage to an elderly gentleman to the chance to travel with the players.

Judith picked her way over a sand dune. 'So I am the seventh wife.'

A thought hit me. 'Judith, if that last wife is not dead, then how could my father be free to marry you?'

She gave a peal of laughter. 'I am quite convinced that poor Rosmarin is dead, for all that I never heard tell of her until after I was wed to your father. In fact, your father told me of only one wife, the mother of his son, before we were married. It was only when he brought me to Elsinore that I learned I was but the latest in a long procession of brides.'

'Do you too hate being married to an old man?'

For a moment her face looked wistful, and then she looked brisk. 'My dear father was a laird in a land called Scotland.'

I hadn't heard that word before, so I repeated it to engrave it on my memory.

'It's a beautiful land,' she said. 'Not at all like Denmark. It's a land of hills and mountains and roaring streams. Beautiful waterfalls—' she caught my blank look. 'Water comes tumbling straight down from a great height, and rainbows dance all around it.' I wondered if she was making sport of me. In Piet's book of foreign places, there had been no pictures of waterfalls. Judith turned her head in both directions and sighed. 'This land is so flat.' I didn't know what to say to that, so I trudged on silently until Judith began to speak again. 'I was even younger than you when my father died. My older brother gave me over to the nuns for keeping. I hated it. My father had let me run as free as a fox, and it felt like prison to be shut up in a cloister. I spoiled in their care like a cheese in a damp cellar, and then I grew wilful and angry.' She chuckled at this memory. 'So the good sisters sent me back to my brother who had become an advisor to the Scottish king. My brother was negotiating to send me to a different order of nuns when your father came to the court as an ambassador for the Danish king. When my brother learned that he'd take me sans dowry, he leaped like a trout swallowing a fly at the chance to pass me along.'

'Were you sorry to leave your home?'

Judith thought about this for a moment. 'I find Scotland more beautiful than Denmark, but my brother would never have brought me to court, and I didn't relish spinning out my days in a small estate that was all hills and sheep. My old nurse had taught me Danish, and I was glad of the chance to move to the court of Elsinore. An hour or two a night with an old man seemed a small price to pay for the chance to spend my days at a royal court.'

Then her face flushed as if she felt she shouldn't have said those last words, and she began to talk of the different folk I'd meet in the court.

Soon we spotted the little town that crouched at the foot of the castle the way a greyhound might press against the skirts of its mistress. Elsinore stood above it on a cliff above the sea straits. I'd spied on the castle times beyond counting, but now I saw it with different eyes. I was going to be one of the castle folk. I was going to live with the kings and princes.

Quickly I learned that the inside of the castle was much larger than I'd realized when I'd stared at it from afar. I despaired of ever finding my way around. The inner courtyard was a warren of small sheds and buildings – the stables, the scullery shed, the brew house, the kitchens, the laundries, the blacksmith's, and on and on and on. Then there was the castle itself, huge with corridors and passageways that twisted about, moving up and down levels, till I was dizzy with all the turns, as tangled as a dropped skein of yarn.

My father had his chambers at a great distance from those of the royal family and from the Great Hall.

'It's a fine honour to be housed in the castle proper,' Judith told me. 'So many of the folk at court live in one of the outbuildings, but the king harbours the highest respect for your father's advice, and therefore wants him near at hand.'

Our chambers consisted of three whole rooms.

'Compared to the rest of the court, they're not very grand,' Judith said in an apologetic tone.

I didn't understand why she spoke that way. I was dazzled by how fine these chambers were. They weren't overlarge; that much is true. Taken together, they were no larger than Myg's cottage. But there were soft rugs upon wooden floors instead of a floor of pounded dirt, and there were more rugs draped over chests and table tops. I'd never seen so many candles all together in one place. Even though night was falling, the blaze of the candles made our chambers at least as bright as dawn. There was my father's bedroom, an antechamber where visitors could wait, and a tiny room to the side.

'This will be your bedchamber,' Judith said.

What unthinkable luxury, a bedchamber of my own! Myg's cottage had been but one room, so we'd all slept together. A few of the richest cottages in the village had had separate sleeping closets for the husband and wife, and a couple of the richest merchants had had besides a sleeping chamber for all the children, but I knew no one who had an entire room to themselves, a room not used for any other purpose. True, my bedchamber was tiny. Standing in the middle, I could touch both side walls at once without even stretching my arms out full length, but a bed had been laid over the top of chests along one wall, plump with piled featherbeds and coverings. There was even a fine fur coverlet on top of all.

'Is this the girl?'

I whirled about to the source of that unknown voice. A stout woman stood there, her arms folded across her chest. She had a red face and, like most older women, was missing several teeth. She was dressed much like the women in our village with a tightly-laced bodice, an apron, and a wimple tight across her forehead.

'Yes, this is the girl. Do you think she has the look of her mother?'

'Her mother was before my day,' the red-faced woman said in her flat voice, 'and from all I hear tell, a good thing that is.'

Judith smiled at me. 'This is Gret. She serves us here in the castle, keeping our chambers clean and tending to our care.'

I gave Gret a nervous smile that drew forth no response. Did she find something lacking in me, I wondered, or did she just not want another body in the chambers? Or was there some other reason that she didn't want me here?

Judith said, 'Will you fetch us some water, Gret, so I can wash the girl before dressing her in one of my gowns?'

'I should think so, lady.' I'd thought it impossible, but Gret's face grew even sterner. Her brows pulled together, and she added, 'Forgive me if I'm impertinent, my lady, but time is short. Might it not be better to take this young person down to the laundry shed and wash her off there? It will take a good two hours to fetch enough hot water to fill a tub, and supper will be long over by then.'

'A very good idea!' Judith said, clapping her hands in delight.

The idea of the laundry room sounded ominous. I half-wondered if they planned to beat me with sticks the way you beat soiled clothes to make them clean. Still, after Judith gathered up her smallest gown and filled a pouch with herbs, I followed her meekly out of the room and through the warren of corridors back down to the courtyard. I was amazed by how many folk we passed on the way. From their dress, I guessed that most of them were servants, but some wore very rich raiment indeed. A few wore outlandish styles that looked very different from anything I'd ever seen. I reckoned that some of them were from foreign parts, ambassadors and such to the king, but several wore garb that reminded me of the gowns worn by figures in the stained glass church windows and paintings on the church wall. I'd have thought them servants, for the styles worn by peasants had the simple lines of the olden-times gowns, but these gowns were of sumptuous velvets and silks trimmed with ribbons and fur. Judith spoke to a few of the folk we passed, but she didn't address any of the ones in the old-fashioned gowns.

The laundry room was steamy and warm. I was most impressed by its stone floors slashed with large cracks to drain away the water, the rainbarrels, and huge fireplaces to heat as many as six cauldrons of water at once. Judith led me to a tub in one corner. Several girls working there stared at me curiously, but they said nothing as they scrubbed tubfuls of sleeves, collars, cuffs, and other small clothes. Judith sprinkled the water in her tub with a mixture of herbs in which I could make out only rosemary, rose petal, lavender, and comfrey. She bade me step in, and she scrubbed me all over. She used handfuls of a soft white soap that smelled of almonds, not the harsh yellow stuff that Myg made by the vatful. Then she had me stand up on the stone floor while she poured several buckets of clear water on my body and hair to rinse the soap away. She tossed my gown to the nearest laundry maid. 'Keep it or toss it away, for we have no more need of it.'

Judith turned back to me. 'I'll cut down some of my own gowns to fit you,' she said, 'but tonight we'll make do with this one.'

It was the finest thing I'd ever put on, the cloth as soft as petals. The shift was so white it nearly burned my eyes, and the skirt and bodice were a silky peach. There were brown velvet ribbons to lace up the bodice both in front and behind, and Judith showed me how to twitch the top of my shift so it showed above the top of the lacing. She laughed as she tied the ribbons.

'Most girls want to lace their bodices too tightly to show off their breasts beneath, but you are such a slip of a thing that even laced as tight as can be, your bodice hangs loose.' She considered it for a moment ruefully. 'Well, it must do for tonight, and and I'll fix you a proper gown for the morrow.' She tied on close-fitting sleeves of ivory satin cross-ribboned in black. Her slippers, laced tightly, were a good fit although it felt strange to walk shod in warm weather.

Then she led me through the maze of hallways back to our chambers. Even Gret looked a little more approving.

'Cleans up better'n I reckoned she would.'

Judith made me sit on a stool so she could comb my hair. Even at the best of times, my hair was an unruly cloud, and she grew cross as she struggled to bring it to order. Before she'd made much more than a start, a deep bell rang and the entire castle seemed to shiver from its sound.

'Shall I stay with the young person while you go to supper?' Gret asked.

Judith shook her head.

'The king doesn't take kindly to those who refuse to take their meals in the hall,' Gret told her.

I could see Judith struggling to answer civilly. 'We don't intend to make a common practice of it. Now be off and fetch us some supper for here in our chambers this one night.'

It was a long while before Gret returned. I'd expected some sort of wondrous meal, but she brought only a tray on which were two bowls of bread and milk and curds. There were two tankards of beer, and two dried herrings laid on a small loaf. I was hungry and ate heartily, but the food was no better than that served by Myg.

'Will I meet my father soon?' I asked as we ate.

Judith rolled her eyes. 'He said he'd try to stop by to greet you, but the king does keep his revels tonight, and the men drink deep. In truth I don't expect to see him before the dawn.'

In fact, it was well after my first castle middag before I met my father, well after midday.

If the first night's supper had disappointed me, the Great Hall surpassed all my grandest imaginings. I'd never dreamed that any indoor space could be so big. We could have easily fit three of our village churches into it and still had room for a cottage or two.

'Some folk say it's the largest hall in any castle in the world,' Judith whispered to me.

At one end was a raised platform on which stood a table draped in gold cloth. 'The royal family sits there,' Judith explained. The rest of the room was filled with long trestle tables draped in white cloth. Judith showed us our places, about a third of the way toward the dais. People were hurrying into the huge hall.

'No one is allowed to enter after the king or queen,' Judith explained. 'If you don't make it here before them, then you go hungry.'

Just then a horn blared forth a trill of notes, long as a bird's song, and two people strolled to the dais and took seats there. Like her son, the queen was tall and fair, but while he was all golden, she was pale as frost. Her hair was tucked under a cap the colour of snow in the late afternoon, and her dress was of the same colour, striped with silver ribbons. The man with her was also tall, and his hair was scattered with grey, but he was shaped much like Prince Hamlet with broad shoulders, long limbs, a self-assured tilt to the head, and a humorous mouth, although he was more like a Prince Hamlet smudged by age and fat. They were joined by a third person, a tiny man with a twisted shoulder in the brightly-coloured clothes of a jester. He sat at the far end of the table at the dais, with the lady in the middle and the tall man next to her. They were an odd trio – the men so bright and vivid and the lady pale as a ghost between them.

'The king and queen make a handsome pair,' I whispered to Judith after the meal had started.

She looked scandalized. 'That isn't the king, although he has much the same look of the king. That's the king's brother, Claudius. He will become king if the present king dies.'

'But what about Prince Hamlet? Why can he not take the throne?'

'Custom is that the throne goes first to the brothers of the present king, then to the sons of the old king in order of his birth. To gain the throne, Hamlet must outlive his father, uncle and older brother. They are hearty men of excellent health, so it isn't like that the throne will ever come to Hamlet.'

'Accidents happen,' I whispered back, never dreaming how

prophetic my words were. 'Unexplained sickness can fell even the strongest among us.'

'Hush!' Judith looked truly angry, so I turned my attention to the food.

We spent the rest of the day in cutting down two of her gowns for me and instructing me in the manners of court. There were so many things to learn that it made my head buzz. There were new ways to eat, to walk, to curtsey, to bow. Everything was arranged according to birth rank. As my father's daughter, I outranked all the servants, but I was balanced on the very bottom rung of the gentlefolk. This meant that I had to give way to all of them should I pass them in the hallways and we stood toward the rear of the courtiers in every public audience.

'I reckon the queen will take a fancy to you,' Judith said. 'It would please her greatly to have a little girl about the place. There are men a-plenty in Elsinore Castle, but until you came, I was the youngest woman here.'

Already I'd seen many girls about my age working about the place, and I said this to Judith.

'Servants,' she said. 'They don't matter. But I've always felt that the queen has hungered for a little daughter of her own, and so she may raise you to a special place. At least, that's what your father hoped when he agreed that I might fetch you here.'

'She has only sons, then?'

Judith nodded and bit off the thread from the hem she was sewing. 'They say the king's blood is so powerfully male that he cannot father female children.'

'When do you think I can meet Prince Hamlet?'

She looked amused. 'What is this worry about Prince Hamlet?'

'He passed through our village once. I'd like to see him again.'

Her smile grew broader. 'Yes, he's handsome as the sun, that one is. He will break many hearts before he's through.' Then her smile faded and her eyes grew soft. 'It's such a shame that . . .' Her voice trailed away, and she bent back over the gown on her lap.

'When will I meet the prince?'

She didn't look up. 'He is away at school. Like your brother.'

'Is he not old, though, to be away at school?'

Judith hesitated as if she'd say more, but then she just pressed her lips together and continued to sew.

'Folk reckon he must be in his twenties at least.'

Without looking up, Judith said, 'Twenty-six or twenty-seven.'

I was shocked. He'd seemed years younger. 'Why has he not yet begun a family? Does he study to be a priest, then, that he's so long at his studies?'

She paused and looked as if she was trying out words in her mind before she spoke them aloud. Finally she said, 'This is a road that we'd better not travel. It isn't our place, child, to question the customs of kings.'

'Is his brother married?'

'He was. When he was but fifteen, Prince Holger married the daughter of the Duke of Naples, but three or four years ago, when she sailed to her brother's wedding, her ship was caught in a storm and all were lost.'

How horrible. I'd always thought that being royal would keep you safer than the rest of us, but it seemed even high birth couldn't protect you against the sea. 'Was the prince heartbroken?'

Judith paused briefly, her needle poised above the cloth. Then it plunged back through the material like a ship bobbing in and out of view on the waves. 'Prince Holger has found his consolations,' she said in an even tone.

'What—'

'Child!' Judith slammed her small hands down on her lap. 'Let me give you the best advice that you will ever hear. Don't delve too deep into the ways of princes. If you wish to live a happy life, grant them the respect you'd accord flame or tempest, but don't draw too near.'

'But—'

'They are stars who rotate around other earths than ours, child. Marvel at their light, but only a madwoman would try to come close. They aren't for the likes of us.'

They may not be for the likes of you, I thought mutinously, *but they are for the likes of me.* Chance had opened the castle to me. Was this not proof positive that I was intended for a grander future, a future that would include Prince Hamlet? Even at that young age I knew that Fate doesn't dribble out her bounty evenly as a farmer might carefully drop a line of seeds. No, Fate doesn't often bestow her blessings, but when she does, it is in the manner of a prince tossing a handful of coins into a crowd of beggars. You must be alert so you can scrabble up and seize the coin when it comes flying in your direction. No matter what Judith said, now that I'd been brought so close to Prince Hamlet, I didn't intend to fall back into the crowd. While I didn't have the blood of the Flying Catgirl in my veins, I had her spirit in my heart, and no matter what it took, I'd see my life was one of soaring rather than grovelling.

If Judith wouldn't help me come near Prince Hamlet, I'd employ my father.

As if cued by Fate, he came to us late that afternoon.

5

I must confess that when he did appear my father was a sore disappointment to me. He was, first of all, old, terribly old. He had a sprawling round belly but thin little arms and legs, and he wore a beard that was scraggly and white, like the tufts on the chin of a goat. The top of his head was bald as an egg, but thin yellow-white hair dribbled down his back in rats' tails. His eyes were a little bulging and flickered back and forth like a nervous sheep's.

'So this is the girl?' he asked. He looked me up and down like I was a cargo that had been dumped salt-stained on the beach.

I wouldn't let him cow me. I tilted my chin up and regarded him steadily.

'She's pretty enough, and she looks to have some wit,' he said, still not addressing me.

'I find her both pretty and bright, my lord,' Judith said.

'Time will tell, time will tell. Even the reddest apple can conceal a worm, so we must not yet puff up our hopes. What is her name?'

Talk to me, I wanted to shout at him, but even though I was fuming inside, I stood obediently silent.

'She doesn't know.'

My father looked impatient. 'Did you not ask it of the wet-nurse?'

'She said you never told her a name.'

He patted the palms of his hand against his belly as if he

was tamping down dough. 'Perhaps I never gave her one. As I recall, she was so weak and sickly that I didn't expect her to live.'

'You told me as much, my lord.' Judith's eyes flickered over to me to see how I took this news, but I kept my face blank. I hated these callous words, but I was determined not to leave the castle, and I feared that if I let my father know my true nature or feelings, he might deem me too troublesome and send me away.

'I haven't thought of her in years,' my father went on in his peevish, thin voice. 'I suppose I'd thought she'd died.'

'Your man of accounts has been sending money for her keep all these years. That's how I learned she was there.'

My father waved an impatient hand. 'Those were minor accounts. A few coins only. Not anything that needed my attention.' He patted his belly again. 'I suppose we must call her something. Perhaps a good Latin name. Latin names are all the rage now. Latin names give a respectability that birth sometimes denies. What about Polonia?'

I hated it. Judith must have seen that in my expression because she quickly said, 'What about Filia, sir. I believe it means daughter.'

'Filia? An apt name, that will serve. Still, I'd like her name to have more distinction. A name is our shield; a good name and a good shield will both protect you from the world and announce our rank. Filia is an ill name for peacocking my status to the world. Any man's daughter might have such a name, at least any man who knows Latin. My daughter must have a name that will give us both more distinction.'

'Shall we add a preface to it, sir? What think you of Perfilia?'

'Perfilia? No. A misbegotten preface. Purr me no *per*'s. *Per*chance, such a name might bring *per*fidy upon both our shoulders.'

I wanted to scream out, *Leave the name alone and look at me. Talk to me. I am your daughter. You haven't seen me since my birth. I've gone ten years without a name, so a few moments will not matter a whit more.* But it was as if my father couldn't see me unless I had a name, that his brain would only regard things that could be neatly pegged and stored.

'Refilia?' Judith suggested. I think she sensed my frustration. 'One who has returned?'

'No, Refilia is an ill thing, for it rhymes with grief, and one who invites grief into her life has sorrow as a lodger. We must think further, wife.'

'Oh, let it be for the present,' she snapped.

To my astonishment, his eyes lit up. 'O?' he said. 'Yes, let it be O. Ophelia. O for Octavia, the sister of Augustus and wife of Mark Antony. Yes, O has a full, rich, distinguished sound. O echoes my own name: Polonius. We shall call her Ophelia, daughter of distinction.'

Judith's eyes began to dance with a wicked merriment. 'Yes, O comes before P, so Ophelia shall come before Polonius in all things.'

'That she shall,' he said gravely. 'Well-spoken, wife. Before Ophelia does aught, she must come *before* Polonius her father and beg his permission.'

How could Judith bear such a windbag for a husband?

My father then turned his eyes to me. He examined me solemnly now, as if I were a slab of meat delivered for the royal table. He still didn't speak to me. Instead he said to Judith, 'I still worry that it may have been misjudged to bring her here. She may be a great bother, and we cannot be sure that she'll contract a marriage that will help our advancement. I'll have to scrape a dowry together. I do hope she doesn't cost me more than the profit she'll bring. Her own mother left me nothing. You know that.'

'I don't fear on that score, my lord. One day our Ophelia will be a beauty.'

My father looked at me sceptically. 'She shows no sign of it now. She's plain as a post, and there's something defiant about her wanton hair. Her eyes and mouth are over-large. Her skin is too brown.'

Judith said serenely, 'Great beauties are seldom the prettiest children. They must grow into their looks. Trust me. Ophelia will be a rare beauty someday.'

My father gave a little snort. 'Let us hope. For the present, train her to be meek and biddable. Let us hope you're right and we may be able to marry her off profitably in a few years.'

He said no words of welcome to me nor did he address me direct. He just turned on his heels and waddled out of the chamber.

Judith let out a little gust of air. 'Well, that's over with. I think it went well.'

I was outraged. 'Went well? My father said nothing kind, and he treated me as if I was dung dropped upon his carpet.'

She grinned. 'Do not take so much to heart, Ophelia. He didn't send you back. To my mind, that's as good as a victory.'

I was too offended to answer. I stalked over to the window bench and threw myself down on it.

Judith laughed. 'Now that your father has acknowledged you, I can present you to the court. Then all the fun will begin.'

But it wasn't fun that began when I went to court the next day.

6

'Remember, follow me in everything I do,' Judith cautioned me. I could tell from her voice that she too was worried about how I'd be received at my audience with the king and queen.

My father inspected me. 'Can you not smooth her hair down? They will think I've fathered an unruly beast instead of a meek little daughter.' He gave a few hard swipes to my head, but I could tell from his irritated expression that my hair sprang right back up again.

'The rest of her looks seemly,' Judith offered, adjusting the net that had been knocked askew by my father's ministrations. 'She will be fine.'

I was dressed in a blue-green kirtle the shade of a summer-time sea overlaid with an ivory tunic halfway between white and butter yellow. The gown was more costly than anything that I'd ever worn, yet I'd still have preferred something with more flash and glitter for my first foray to court. When I said as much to Judith and my father, they both tut-tutted me.

'You aren't the daughter of a noble,' my father protested in a voice as shocked as if I'd suggested stripping naked and prancing before the Virgin herself.

'You are a maid,' Judith said. 'Your task in these years is to look pure and simple. Save jewels and such until you're safely wed.'

I hated waiting and I hated safety. I wanted to sparkle now.

Judith wound a white cord about my hair. It kept the cloud off my face, but she looked at it in exasperation. 'I could plait it,' she said doubtfully, 'but then your daughter will look more like a serving maid than the child of a trusted advisor to the king.'

'Leave it,' my father squeaked and tugged at his own raiment, a black velvet gown embroidered about the cuff with violets.

Although my father's dress was costly, I thought he looked silly in it. Judith, however, looked regal in her blood-red velvet gown under a tunic as blue as a June sky. Her coif was velvet entwined with blue and gold. She looked taller and grander than her everyday self.

'Costly let your apparel be,' my father said, 'but not extravagant, for the clothes often—'

'"Proclaim the man,"' Judith interrupted. 'You have told me such before.' She gave another tug to my hair and added, 'Many times.'

'"Women, be subject to your husbands,"' my father said. 'Saint Paul tells us that—'

'You have also often told me that as well.' She winked at me. 'Time to meet the king and queen.'

I was stunned by the number of folk standing around the Great Hall, folk enough to fill the village five times over. My family stood close to the dais. We were there early and watched most of the people filter in. There were few women, no more than a handful, and most of them were elderly and plain. Most of the men were warriors, cold-eyed and stern-faced, not looking bored exactly, but as if they would endure this trial only so they could pass to the real business of their lives.

We all stood for a long time with nothing happening except new people trickling in. Without the tables, the hall looked even bigger than it did at mealtimes. As we waited, I studied the decorations in the room. I admired the carved rafters in the shape of dragons and other fantastical beasts. I studied the hangings on the wall, but I failed to recognize the story behind a single one of them. I grew intrigued with a little window up above the dais. There seemed to be a tiny room up there with curtains to open and close. I nudged Judith and tilted my chin upwards. 'The minstrel gallery,' she whispered back. 'Musicians used to sit there and play, but I've heard that the stairs to it have crumbled and—'

'Hush!' hissed my father, and we fell silent again.

I shifted to another foot.

Among the band of warriors and nobles, I began to spot a scattering of folk dressed in outlandish fashions, much like the folk I'd passed in the corridors on the first day. I was amazed to see one burly man draped all in skins, bearskins I guessed by the thickness of the pelt, and he carried a rough-hewn club. I was astonished that they'd let an armed man come before the king. Another man was tall with a long face and long blond hair that fell halfway down his back. On either side of his face hung a thin braid, no thicker than my little finger. He wore a long gown, almost like a priest's, and just as plain. He caught me looking at him and gave me a little wink.

I winked back.

Then I began to see folk line up behind the dais, behind the two chairs of the king and the queen. One figure was burly and wore chain mail from head to toe. His face was cruel, and he kept his hand clasped tight around the hilt of his sword. I figured he must be a special guard to the king. Another man was tremendously fat in a gown spattered with cooking grease. He carried a haunch of venison in his left fist, and from time to time he'd bite into it and rip off an enormous strip. What audacity, to eat here in the court! I twisted back and forth to see if anyone else was disconcerted by this rude behaviour, but no one else seemed to pay him any notice. I figured they were probably used to his antics by now. Another man was small and bent over like the husk of an insect, his head at a twisted angle as if he could see behind him. His lips moved ceaselessly, but no sounds came out. There was also a young man, pale and tall and as twitchy as a cat's tail, who kept his hand on his sword hilt, whirling around at any sound as if he expected an assassin to attack at any moment.

'Who are all those folk?' I whispered to Judith. She looked at me blankly, but before she could speak, my father leaned past her to glare at me.

'Hush!' he said in the sternest tone I'd yet heard from him.

I opened my mouth to respond, but someone whispered in my far ear, 'Your father is right. Say no more for now, and I'll explain it all to you after.'

I turned to the speaker. There stood the gnome of a man in striped green and purple and yellow who often sat at the end of the dais. A jester. I saw there were tiny bells sewn to the points of his cap. He had merry eyes and surveyed the company with lively interest.

I was grateful for his offer. I nodded to let him know I'd heard him, and then I too lapsed into silence.

Soon there was a blare from horns that made me jump, and then the people began to ripple down to their knees from the far side of the hall to the front like grain flattening underneath a wind moving across a field. Just behind the roll of the flattening came a procession of royals, the king, the queen, the king's brother, and Prince Holger, the king's oldest son. I was so stunned by seeing them up close that I forgot to sink to my knees, and Judith had to grab my hand and jerk me downward like a calf at the butcher's block.

Once the king and his family had taken their places upon the dais, we rose back up. I had an excellent view of the whole royal family. I'd now been in the castle for more than a week, and I'd seen them all several times at meals, but they did look different close up. The king looked remote and the prince was clearly bored with all this ceremony while the queen smiled a lot as if to make up for the lack of attention shown by her male kinfolk.

The first part of the reception involved a lot of ambassadors being presented to the king by my father and everyone gobbling a lot of empty courtesies. Even to me it was clear that all of them talked out of both sides of their mouths. I was impressed, though, by what an important personage my father was in the court of Denmark. Several times he echoed the king's words of greetings to the foreign visitors, and the king seemed willing to have him do so.

During this first part, I was bored, so I passed the time studying the royal family, looking for resemblances to Prince Hamlet. His father had darker colouring and was leaner, but his shape was very much that of his second son's. About the face, though, Prince Hamlet bore more the likeness of his mother. Oddly enough, Prince Holger looked less like his brother than did the three older people, including his uncle Claudius. Prince Holger's colouring was similar, but where Hamlet's body was supple, the older prince's body was thick and hard. He had a soldier's body, lacking Hamlet's easy grace. Where Prince Hamlet's face had contained an open-eyed friendliness, Prince Holger looked both arrogant and peevish. I thought I detected a little bloat to his skin and a bleariness in the eyes as if he'd caroused too long and hard the night before. The clothing of both the king and the prince was plain, containing more of an army captain's efficiency than the elegance of Prince Hamlet's.

The greetings to the foreign emissaries droned on and on. From time to time I shifted from one foot to another just to keep my legs from going to sleep. Each time Judith gave me a little swat, hidden by the folds of our skirts.

My attention was caught when the king said, 'And now, Polonius, we understand that you wish to present to us a newcomer to your family?'

'Good, my lord, that I do, for new she is to my family here at court, but to say new may be to mislead, for she's not new to the world. New she is to my presence, but not by birth, for the present of her birth she achieved ten years ago or more, although to call it an achievement is to suggest that it is something she laboured to bring to pass, but the labour of her birth was her mother's, and—'

The queen leaned forward and interrupted him. 'Is this your daughter?' She smiled at me.

Judith's hand in the small of my back gave a little push, and I stumbled forward. The momentum almost made me fall, but I changed it into a kneeling pose.

'She's welcome to Elsinore,' the king said. His words were polite, but his voice lacked warmth. His eyes flickered away from me before his mouth had finished with his words.

The queen said, 'Stand up, child.'

Up till now I'd thought the queen less handsome than Judith, but up close I saw that she had a finer-drawn beauty. Everything about her was clean and smooth. Her skin was very white, and her bones looked as delicate as those of birds. 'I've always longed for a little daughter,' she said. 'We shall do well together, you and I.'

'If all our business is concluded,' the king said, his voice overbearing hers like a walrus might smash down a butterfly, 'we shall take our leave.'

The trumpets sounded again, and we all knelt once more as the king and his party swept out. As the queen passed Judith, she paused and said, 'Come to my closet later and we shall talk of women's matters.' Then she too passed along.

The company followed the royals out of the hall, leaving it to the kitchen staff to set up the trestles for middag.

My father turned to me and rubbed his plump hands together.

'A very good start. Very auspicious indeed. This daughter of mine has caught the favour of the queen.' He turned to Judith and put a hand on her shoulder. 'I think we've done well, wife. Very well. I know you're a bosom-bow of her majesty, and now it looks as if our daughter will pass along the path you've carved. Although to say you've carved the path—'

'You did well, Ophelia,' Judith said. Her eyes smiled approval.

'Just what I say,' my father began, 'but while it is easy to begin well, it is harder to continue well along the—'

'Ophelia and I will withdraw now, sire, to make ready to obey the queen's summons.' Judith swept me out of the hall.

In the passageway, I saw the gnome in the brightly striped clothing. Judith ignored him. He put his finger to his mouth to caution me to silence and then motioned me to follow him.

'I'll join you in our chambers presently,' I said.

'We can go together,' Judith said. 'Come.'

'First I must visit the necessary,' I lied. 'I'll come to you directly.'

As soon as she was gone, I turned to the man in the motley cloth.

'I've much to ask,' I said.

He pressed his finger against his lip again and set off at a pace surprisingly brisk in one so bent and gnarled. I trotted after him. He led the way up a winding stairway to the battlements.

In my delight at the view up there, for a moment I forgot all about him. Never before had I been so high up in the air. The Danish countryside wasn't rich in hills, so I was used to looking at everything straight on, but now I felt as high as heaven itself. I could see the whole countryside round, and what a beautiful countryside it was. Our village appeared in the distance, a barnacle clinging to the land just above the sea line. There were fields and forests, dunes and springs, and the beautiful, treacherous sea herself. The sea by the peninsula on which the castle stood is very narrow, squeezed between Denmark and Sweden, so I could see clear into Sweden itself.

To my disappointment, Sweden looked very much like Denmark. I wanted it to be more exotic, more strange.

The voice of my companion pulled me back. 'You wondered about the odd folk in the hall.'

I turned my eyes back to the gnome in motley beside me. 'Who were the ones garbed in these peculiar fashions? I am new here at court,' I told him. 'I don't know all the folk yet.'

'There's no one here at Elsinore who knows all the folk,' he said. His voice was a little thick as if his tongue was too big and his mouth too small for a perfect fit. 'And Elsinore is a place where even folk who are known aren't known to the core.'

'You speak in riddles,' I said. 'Your speech is as twisted as—'

'My body?' he said quickly.

'As my father's,' I said firmly. 'Elsinore seems a place where folk prefer riddles to plain speech.'

He grinned. 'You are quick-witted, lass.'

'Spit the sand out of your words,' I said, 'and speak direct. What do you wish to tell me?'

'You saw the folk behind the dais? You saw them plain?'

'They were as plain as the stripes on your tunic.'

'You found them remarkable?'

'It amazed me greatly that no one else took notice of them. That man with the haunch of meat, for instance. Why is he permitted to eat in the king's presence? And the fellow draped in the bearskin. I fail to understand—'

He gave a little sigh as if the air had been punched out of him. 'No one else here at the castle sees these things, lass.'

How could that be? 'Are folk at Elsinore then blind as well as riddle-mouthed?'

'It's not that . . .' He hesitated and then he plunged on. 'There are two sorts of folk here at Elsinore. The ones in normal garb are the normal folk.'

'And what are the folk in the outlandish garb?'

'Ghosts,' he said slowly. 'Elsinore is thick with ghosts. But you're the only living person who can see . . .'

His voice trailed off. I stared at him in stunned wonder as the understanding of what he'd just told me sank in me like a boulder in a bog.

7

I blinked at him. 'I don't believe you.'

Since he was the king's jester, doubtless this was his idea of sport, to spin a tale to the credulous country girl fresh come to court.

'Why should I lie?'

'I am but green here in Elsinore. My guess is that you play with me and use me as your fool. Feed lies to the newcomer to see how much spit she can swallow.'

He laughed, but his laugh sounded kind. 'Nay, lass. With this twisted body of mine, I've faced enough cruel sport that I wouldn't make sport of anyone else.'

'Yet you'd have me think I see ghosts in the hall?'

'This castle is thick with ghosts, child. Many living folk witness one or two of these shades, but for some reason, you've been chosen to see them all.'

His words startled me. 'Chosen? What do you mean, chosen to see?'

'Ghosts don't appear willy-nilly. Ghosts choose who can see them and who cannot. For some reason, you have the power to see every one.'

I shuddered. It was fantastical to think of ghosts crowding the castle, but it was more fantastical to think that folk had dressed in those strange costumes and sworn the whole court to secrecy just to play a joke on one green girl. 'But why would I be chosen to be the ghosts' witness?'

His eyes narrowed. 'That's what intrigues me the most.'

Just then the bell began to ring to signal middag.

'Hell and damnation,' I said. Judith would be angry that I hadn't returned to our chambers. 'I must go.'

'We will talk further,' he called after me.

Yorick, for such was the jester's name, and I spent many long afternoons puzzling out the mystery of why I was given the power to see the ghosts. Yorick was right about one thing. The castle was indeed thick with ghosts. During my first year at Elsinore, I couldn't tell the ghosts from the real people, but gradually I learned that there was a slight thinning of the light around the outline of the ghosts, the tiniest bit of shining like a glint off the side of a pan. The ghosts paid me no special attention, although the merry-faced king would always wink when he caught sight of me. The ghosts were mostly mum, drifting silently in and out of rooms. They shared little else in common. Some of them seemed avid to follow the affairs of humans, peering at our little dramas as if they were starving and the interactions of the living was their only meat. Others moved about with eyes as muffled as smoke, often looking quite surprised as if it was only by accident that they found themselves among us.

By my second year, within a dozen heartbeats I could usually tell a ghost from a living person, although I was occasionally fooled from time to time.

That afternoon after my first audience with the king, the queen sent a messenger to invite Judith and me to visit her in her closet. Judith wetted down my hair and gave it a few tugs. 'It will have to do,' she said.

The queen's closet was a marvel of silks and velvets with thick white furs thrown across the tops of chests and an embroidered bed covering in white satin stitched in silver thread. Her bed looked like a vast snow plain, and I longed to throw myself on it and roll around to see if it was soft as it appeared. The queen sat on a small stool near the window filled with tiny leaded panes of amber, rose, and pale blue. The coloured panes dimmed the light so that the room was dark, but candles stuck in holders along the wall made it bright enough to see. Judith sat on a three-legged stool at the queen's feet, and I sank down on a gold velvet cushion on the floor.

The queen welcomed me again to the castle and asked how I was getting on.

Before I could answer, the door to her chamber flew open with a bang and Prince Holger strode into the room. He ignored Judith and me, addressing himself directly to his mother.

'Look at this,' he snapped in an accusing tone. He held up a leather glove whose cuff had come unravelled. 'I haven't worn these above a dozen times, and now I am late for falconing. You must mend it straight away.' He threw the glove down onto her lap the same way a man might toss down a gauntlet to start a war.

'I have guests,' the queen said quietly. 'Elspeth is in the antechamber, and she'll mend it for you.'

His face grew pettish. 'Elspeth is old and more than half blind. I doubt she can see to thread the needle, and even if by chance she got the thread through the eye, the seam she'd stitch would wander across the cloth like a drunkard fumbling his way home from a tavern. I need you to mend it for me.'

'You shouldn't speak of your nurse so. That woman tended you and loved you since the day of your birth.'

'For the which I am grateful, Madam, but now she serves no purpose in my life.' He threw himself onto a chest, one foot propped up as he lounged there. 'I have heard tell that in the old days of the heroes, when the old sensed they were a burden to the whole community, they'd drag themselves alone off to the snows and let themselves fall asleep, dying peacefully so they wouldn't tax the resources of the young.'

The queen looked troubled. 'I trust, my son, that you wouldn't wish your own dear nurse to drag herself off to an ice floe to die.'

'Of course not,' he said. 'Besides, I doubt that she would do it should I ask.'

Most afternoons after that, Judith and I spent with the queen. Hours upon hours passed as we devoted ourselves to stitchery. The queen was a wizard with a needle, and Judith did passable embroidery work, but I never did master the art. 'Your work is slapdash,' Judith would say. 'You want to bang through everything at a neck-or-nothing pace. To succeed at needlecraft, you must take pains and work slowly.'

I never argued with her accusations because she was right. I simply hated all the tiny, precise little stitches resulting in tiny little pictures of unimportant things.

'I'd rather carve statues than do needlecraft,' I told them once, and they exchanged amused, condescending glances. They didn't even bother to remind me that women couldn't be sculptors. Finally they left me to work on small clothes to give to the poor on holy days, figuring rightly that the poor would be so glad to have anything at all that they wouldn't object to my crooked seams and irregular stitches.

I liked the afternoons best when I could coax the queen to tell stories of the princes. Holger was soldier mad, loving everything to do with warfare and weaponry. He was much fretted that Denmark had been at peace for more than twenty years. 'I am glad that Claudius will be king before Holger,' the queen often said, 'for time will cool his warlike flame. Should he come to the throne at present, he might attack some country or other just for an outlet for his martial desires.' It also vexed her that Holger was foolhardy in his courage, scorning to refuse a challenge. Once he had almost drowned, trying to swim far out to sea like his ancestor, Beowulf, and another time he had broken his collarbone by riding a horse so hard that the poor beast had fallen dead beneath him. 'I fear for him,' she'd whisper, and her lips would flutter in a brief, silent prayer.

She talked more often of Hamlet, and it seemed to me that he was her favourite son. Her stories of his childhood were just what I expected. He'd been a bookish, imaginative boy, loving to his mother but terrified of giving offence to his father. 'They are very different from one another,' the queen said carefully. 'My husband and Holger are two peas of the same pod, but Hamlet . . . my husband is bewildered by his second son.'

'Still,' I said one time, 'I imagine Prince Hamlet has never caused you a day's trouble.'

I was surprised to see the queen stiffen. There was a moment's silence, and then old Elspeth who had been nurse not only to the princes but to the queen as well, began to talk loudly of a quarrel that had broken out between two laundry maids and how one had pushed the other into a vat of dye and how both of them now were as green as new grass, and the talk drifted in a different direction.

After that the queen would no longer talk about her sons.

I kept prodding Judith, so a few months after I came to the castle, she asked the queen about Piet.

'His mother fancies he'd make a skilled subtler, and, in truth, I saw some of the things he fashioned and it seemed to me that he had a nimble touch.'

One of my chief delights at Elsinore had been at mealtimes, seeing the ingenious marvels that the kitchen fashioned to send to the high tables. On feast days in particular, all manner of miracles were carried to the Great Hall. One time there was a pie as big as a washtub, and when the king cut into it, dozens of doves flew out and went flapping about the hall. Another time there were huge bowls of a blue jelly on which stood pastries shaped and painted to look just like the old Viking ships of the days of glory. Frequently a platter of fruit turned out to be made of marchpane, and oftentimes roasted swans or peacocks appeared on platters, upright with all their feathers on them just as if they were alive. Judith explained to me that the kitchen folk had plucked the birds, roasted them, and then sewed every feather back in place to dazzle the eyes of the jaded royalty. Especially when foreign visitors were present, did our tables fill with one amazement after another.

'Please,' I begged the queen, 'please let Piet work as one of your subtlers.'

'The lad would be well-apprenticed to your master subtler,' Judith said, gently moderating my words.

The queen had agreed to speak with her subtler to see if he'd take on a pupil, and within two days all was settled. Judith and I were allowed to return to the village and tell Piet of his good fortune.

I was surprised to see how much smaller the village had seemed to grow during my weeks at the castle. I myself was as much a wonder as a two-headed calf at the fair. Folk stood in the doorways to their cottages and gawked at me as I passed by. A few of the children who had been my playfellows called out greetings, but most stood silent, merely tugging a forelock or giving a curtsey. Even Myg seemed a little shy of me in my fine new clothes, and after Piet scrubbed himself within an inch of his life, the three of us set off. For the first time in his life, he looked a little nervous, but he voiced not one word of complaint.

The castle kitchens looked bigger than the entire village. The subtler was a hugely fat man, pale and rounded like a pan of dough risen to the bursting point. Silently he studied the samples of shaped pastries that Piet had brought, and then he broke into smiles. 'I think you have the skill, lad,' he said. 'But you look half-starved. Have you eaten yet today?'

Piet shook his head, so the master subtler sliced off three slabs of bread, slapped a mound of orange cheese on top of each, and then fished out some pickled onions and plopped them on top. He handed these offerings to me, Piet, and Judith. I liked the strong smell of this food and its even stronger taste. The food in the Great Hall was always well-spiced, but at times I yearned for the simple fare of my childhood. I saw that Judith had quietly handed her share to the smallest of the kitchen lads who was wolfing it down behind a barrel of salted cod. I groaned inside. The rest of the afternoon, I'd have a breath like a dragon. I'd have to beg some fennel seeds to chew in order not to offend my table companions.

Quickly I discovered how correct Judith had been in her words that day in the cottage. In the castle, I almost never saw Piet. Servants were even more invisible than ghosts. Still, at meals when we were served a cunning confection such as a pastry treasure chest filled with beads made of roasted beets and onions or a herring pie fashioned to look like a castle, I always smiled to think of Piet working away on it down in the kitchens.

When I'd been at Elsinore several months, the queen asked one day if I was lonely.

'I like it here,' I told her.

'Do you miss the people in the village?'

I thought a moment. I missed making the plays with the village children, but I didn't miss most of the village children themselves. 'I miss the Herbwife and her sons,' I said finally.

The queen then granted me permission for Piet and me to go back for a visit once a week. Judith would accompany us. Friday was chosen for our excursion. Because Friday was the day our Lord hung on the cross, the queen thought it wrong to indulge in fancy meals on that day. Middag consisted of bread, cheese, curds, and porridge, and supper was dried fish on flat bread. There was little work for Piet to do on those days, so it was no great hardship to grant him a few hours of leave.

In truth, it wasn't so much the time in the village that I craved as the chance to walk there and back. Some days in the castle I felt like a bird who was too large locked in a cage that was too small. Before our return to the castle, we'd stop by the house of the Herbwife for a cup of ginger tea. Usually before we left, her sons would come in, smelling of salt spray. After Piet and I gulped down our tea we'd wander down to the shore with Ragnor. The middle sons would drift back to work, but the eldest often stayed until we had to leave. Sometimes he'd even walk partway to the castle with us. He was a pleasant fellow, with the same dark curls as Ragnor, but Torvald wore his cut neatly and close to his scalp. Piet and I would stride ahead while Judith and Torvald paced in a more stately fashion behind us.

'What do you find to talk of?' I asked Judith once.

'Torvald is a man of big dreams,' she said. 'He plans to make his family very rich. He has opened two shops in England already for trade, and he questions me to learn all he can of Scotland. He thinks perhaps to open a post there as well.'

In a way, these few hours of freedom each week made me feel all the more confined the rest of the time. I'm not proud of the bad habits I began to develop. My life didn't provide me enough fodder for my spirit, and Prince Hamlet still didn't return home, so I began to amuse myself by spying on other folk around the castle. In a way I was like some of the ghosts, feeding on the lives of those who were more active. I found Elsinore the perfect place for playing spy. There was a wealth of crannies into which I could slip and overhear all manner of conversations. I learned from my father that one of the kings who built Elsinore had feared that he would be betrayed by his own folk, so he'd ordered his Italian architect to create a lavishness of spy holes, secret passageways, and leagues of curtains and hangings behind which a girl could hide and watch the scenes unfolding before her. I wondered if my drive to spy on others was a legacy from my father because he, too, made much use of these secret places. 'I am the eyes and ears of the king,' he told me. 'And how should the body survive if the eyes and ears are derelict in their duty? Conversely, how shall the eyes and ears survive if the body is slain?'

To puff up his importance, my father showed me many of these passageways and hidey-holes himself. 'We aren't noble-born,' he said, 'and so we must compensate as we can, for, as I always say, be guarded by wits if not by birth, for he who has not a bloodline as a shield must weave his armour out of his own brain.'

My father, as I quickly learned, liked to have an aphorism for everything. He carried with him a small tablet on which, throughout the day, he set down any sayings that might occur to him, and at night he'd refine them, pacing our chambers and mouthing variations over and over until he fashioned one that he liked. He took great pride in having a saying for everything.

'He brings the tablet even to bed,' Judith whispered to me, rolling her eyes. 'Sometimes when we are in the midst of a marital embrace, a saying will pop into his head, and with one hand he fumbles for his pencil while with the other he fondles me. A most disconcerting habit.'

Much of the time, Judith and the queen struggled to train me to be a lady. I was hard-pressed to reduce my walk to a lady's mincing steps and wrestle my voice to a lady's quiet, flavourless tones, but I did like learning the various dance steps. Judith and I passed many afternoons romping up and down the length of the Great Hall while the queen plucked out melodies on her lute and called out corrections to my lively moves.

Best of all, the queen taught me to read. In turn, I spent the Friday visits to the village teaching Piet and Ragnor to read as well. Instead of roaming the hills and seaways, we'd stand along the shore while I sketched letters and words in the sand. It became quite a game to see which boy could name the letters first before the swirling tide wiped it into oblivion. We progressed from that to sounding out Piet's picture book about the different lands.

'I'll travel one day and see all these places with my own eyes,' I announced.

Piet frowned.

'What's amiss?' I demanded.

'Folk like us don't wander the world. Folk like us were planted by God in one particular place to grow and flourish there.'

'Not me. Already I've travelled from the castle to the village and then back again. I'm one of the folk made for walking the world.'

Piet still looked doubtful but said nothing more.

'I'll go to Egypt one day,' I said loudly.

'I'll go to Egypt, too,' said Ragnor and grinned at me. Sometimes he seemed to understand me even better than Piet did.

The queen had two entire shelves of books, each chained to the wood with a small silver chain. She liked best to have me read the Bible to her, but while I liked the stories of Delilah and Jeptha and Judith's namesake who drove a nail through the head of an enemy king, the queen preferred the boring passages in which Paul or one of the other dead prophets blathered on and on about how to live, speaking in preachy aphorisms like those of my father. Better than the Bible were the thin manuscripts of tales of the old days, heroic epics about Danish heroes like Beowulf Dragonslayer and Hald Long Hand, bold hearts who sailed unexplored seas.

One time when we were looking through a book of Ovid's tales, a book that neither of us could read because it was written in Latin but one that had beautiful pictures, several leaves of paper tumbled out. I scooped it up and handed it out to her. She looked at it and laughed. When she laughed, she looked as young as a girl.

'That book is Prince Hamlet's,' she said. 'When he was six or seven, he asked me to read him this book, but I explained to him that I couldn't because women aren't taught to read Latin. So that very day, he began to work on a translation of the tales into good Danish so that I could read them as well.' She laughed again. 'The poor fool didn't finish even one tale, but he laboured manfully for several weeks or more to bring this gift to his mother.'

She slid his translation back into the book, but when I put the tome back on the shelf, I twitched one sheet of his translation out and, hiding it with my body, tucked it into my girdle and carried it to my closet. I drew the curtain across the doorway and sat on my narrow bed, the piece of paper spread out before me.

'This is *his* handwriting,' I whispered, smoothing my hands across the page. Then I shut my eyes and imagined I was smoothing my hands across his face in just such a fashion.

When he'd appeared in the orchard, Prince Hamlet had called the miller's son a ripe plum, but it was I who had been indeed the ripe plum. When he shook the tree, it was I who fell into the hand of his affection as surely as shook fruit tumbles into the fist of the harvester. I treasured every bit of knowledge about the absent prince, and from that moment forth, I slept with the page of his translated Ovid either under my pillow or pressed close to my heart. In the daylight hours, I kept it folded and tucked in my bosom.

It was two whole years and one heartbreak, though, before the prince returned for a visit.

8

It was about Michaelmas which many of the village folk called by its old name, Hay Sunday. I'd spent the morning with the queen, struggling to learn to play the lute. I must have been a sore trial to her, for while I dearly loved music, my fingers turned to sausages when it came to plucking out a tune. Then I helped her dress and coil her hair into elaborate braids. It seemed a waste to me to spend so much time fooling with her hair since most of it would be hidden beneath her cap, and I told her as much.

'What is hidden in us matters as much as what is seen,' she said, but there was laughter in her voice. 'Perhaps more.'

Although she seemed quite old to me, the queen's hair was lovely, like sunlight on drifts of snow. 'If I had hair like yours,' I said, 'I'd never hide it. I'd flaunt it for all the world to admire.'

'Married ladies must not unveil their treasures to any man but their husband,' she replied.

'Why not?'

She thought a moment. 'I suppose people fear that it would enflame the lust in other men's hearts.'

That made no sense. 'Virgins go about with their hair uncovered. Do they enflame lust, then?'

'Sometimes,' she smiled. 'That's why you must quit your hoydenish ways and stay close at hand.'

Never, I decided. Rather than quit my ways – which weren't at all wild compared to those of the Herbwife's Ragnor or the queen's own first-born – I'd shave my head slick as a gull's egg and paint myself blue all over. Instead I pushed argument further. 'If men can control themselves around virgins, then why do folk think they wouldn't be able to control themselves around married women?'

She looked at me steadily, and I could tell she was thinking. Finally she said, 'Give over this, do, Ophelia. I should have said that it is a thing of custom for married ladies to veil their hair and leave it at that.'

'But—' I began.

'Pick me out a robe for the feast,' she said and made a noise that was part laugh and part groan. 'If your fingers could be as nimble as your brain, then you'd be the chief musician in all Denmark. Carry on in this fashion, and you shall be the death of me.'

She spoke truer than either of us could know.

That day's meal was to be a true feast indeed. Years and years earlier, the country had been at war with Norway over an island that lay between our two countries like a rich piece of fat surrounded by two strips of scrawny meat. The seasons had been lean, and this island supported many plump cows and farms abundant in crops. For generations, the folk on the island had thought themselves Norwegian, but in truth the histories of Denmark, Norway, and Sweden were so entangled that it was like the bloodliness of some of those feckless peasant families in which fathers and daughters and brothers had lain together so often that there was no sorting out which child belonged to which man. Besides, the peasants on the disputed island cared little whether the profits from their labours went to the king to the north or the king to the south. It made no difference to the unceasing toil of their lives. But in lean times, a country has need of any profit it can find, and in this case, it wasn't national pride alone that fuelled the fight. Instead, both countries had just ended the hardest summer in generations, and with so many of the menfolk gone to war and the sun being too generous with his gifts and the rains being too niggardly with theirs, the winter looked bleak indeed. Neither country seemed to make any advance in the war that was gobbling up so many men, so our present King Hamlet – then a young man – had proposed a way to break the stalemate before the fighting pounded the island into waste.

'We will battle as in the olden days,' he proposed to King Erik Strong Arm of Norway. 'Just us two. When we've finished, there will be but one king standing, and that king will claim this island for his own use.'

I imagine that Erik Strong Arm didn't wish to agree. In truth, war is much safer for kings than for foot soldiers, so no doubt he'd hoped to get through this war with a scarred land and an unscarred body. Now, however, he dared not lose face in front of his men. Although both kings were mighty warriors, most folk gave the palm to Erik Strong Arm who was younger and more agile than Hamlet the Dane.

'Be it so,' Erik Strong Arm had said, and then both kings made their followers swear that even should their sovereign die, they'd follow the wishes of their lord and fight no more.

The fight between the kings was terrible and bloody, lasting through the entire morning and all the way to the dregs of afternoon.

'Was it horrible to watch?' I asked the queen.

She'd just shaken her head at me. 'I didn't witness the encounter, child.'

'Why not?'

She laid one slender hand across her flat belly. 'On the very day that my lord fought, I was brought to bed with the birth of my second son.'

'What a pity it should happen just then and prevent you from watching.'

Her eyes had grown wide with horror. 'Child, child, I'd never have watched it. I can conceive of nothing that would make me watch someone I love fight to the death.'

'I'd have watched it, my lady.'

She brushed my cheek with one knuckle. 'You think so now, but wait till someone you love is forced to fight. Like me, you will lock yourself away to pray for his safety.'

In the end, King Hamlet had triumphed, whittling away at Strong Arm with small slashes until Strong Arm was bloodied and battered and couldn't get off the ground. Then with arms trembling with exhaustion, King Hamlet had lifted his heavy sword up high above his head and plunged it through the heart of Strong Arm just before he, completely spent, collapsed to the ground that was sticky with their blood.

The feast on this day was to commemorate that victory. Each year Erik Strong Arm's son – also called Erik Strong Arm – came to our court to deliver Denmark's profit from the island. In the ceremony Strong Arm knelt to King Hamlet and called him his liege lord and handed over a pouch of gold. I could tell by the tightness in his voice and jaw that Erik Strong Arm hated having to abase himself this way, but his uncle, the present king, was a man who honoured the compact. Doubtless he knew that Prince Holger was spoiling to fight, and that he'd take to arms if Norway so much as snapped a straw in the wrong direction.

From the look of Erik Strong Arm, I imagined he, too, was being kept tightly leashed. I doubted that when Strong Arm came to the throne, he'd keep his father's pledge.

This was our most shining ceremony of the year. The king wanted Denmark to glitter down all other royal courts. He insisted that Queen Gertrude make herself as beautiful as possible on that day, wearing her finest jewels and robes. All the courtiers vied to outdo the other in the lavishness of their own apparel. All the villages within a half-day's travel sent a representative to this feast, and they competed with each other to make their own man look more prosperous than the rest. Nothing was more important to King Hamlet than for Erik Strong Arm's eyes to be dazzled by the wealth of Denmark.

Erik Strong Arm always looked as if he'd prefer to have salt rubbed in his eyes than to spend time in the Danish court, but he seemed a young man of iron control, and he said only what was right and proper. He scared me, though. The tightness of his muscles bespoke rage underneath, and his eyes were as cold as pebbles embedded in ice. I didn't think it would bother him a whit if all of us in the Great Hall were to fall down dead at his feet. On the contrary, I suspected it would give him great pleasure.

I chose for the queen to wear that day my favourite of her clothes, an underskirt of satin red as a rose or fresh blood and an overmantle made of cloth of gold striped with black. The queen seldom wore this outfit on her own, and, to speak true, her delicate beauty did get lost in the bold colours of her apparel. But the king loved this outfit. Like me, he favoured strong hues and clothes that rang out, and in her red and gold and black, she'd outshine all others at the feast. As I helped her into her robe, I noticed bruises around both her upper arms, almost like the bracelets warriors wore in the days of old. I realized the queen often sported bruises which struck me as odd in one of such sedentary habits, but at the time I assumed that they happened only because someone with such milky skin must bruise at the slightest touch. The queen had given me a wondrous tunic to wear over my shift of elderblossom white. The tunic was a web of pale green silk threads and tiny pearls like something that might be worn by the queen of the merfolk under the sea. Just as I favoured clothing that was overbold for the queen, she favoured clothing that was underbold for me, but the clothes were by far the prettiest I'd ever worn, and I was grateful.

I couldn't wait for Judith, Piet and Yorick to see me in my new gown and admire both it and me. At the feast I caught the eye of Piet trotting around with a great platter of pies. On most days he didn't serve at table, but on feast days he, like almost all the kitchen folk, was pressed into service. When he saw me, his mouth made an O-gape of amazement, and I waved back merrily. Yorick lounged at the end of the dais. It broke my heart to see him there. The king never took any notice of him, but Yorick was like an elderly sheepdog who had served his family faithfully but was now ignored as being of no more use. Judith had told me that it was no longer fashionable to have a fool at court. It saddened me to see how he still clung on, long past his days of favour. I tried to catch his attention, but I couldn't tell if he'd seen me. I knew it wouldn't be proper to address him in the squeeze of people. I'd have to wait until after the revels to ask him if he saw my fine new clothes

What surprised me most, though, was that Judith didn't appear at the feast. The seat between me and my father stayed empty. He worried over the problem like a dog with an old bone.

'Where can she be?' he whispered to me. 'She knows how important this day is. I gave her ten silver pennies to have a gown made specially. Have you not seen her today?'

I thought back. I hadn't seen her since we parted after supper the night before. It was often thus in the hugger-muggery of the castle, easy to go an entire day without seeing your own kin. There had been no middag meal. The men at court had gone out hunting for sport, and the rest of us had grabbed food catch as catch can. It wasn't like Judith to miss such a grand occasion.

Worry about her robbed me of my enjoyment of the celebration. The kitchen folk had laboured for weeks on this feast. There was all manner of meat, nearly forty different kinds of fish, smoked swan in a dried cherry sauce, entire pigs encased in pastry covered with silver leaf and propped upright so they looked like fat knights riding on chargers made of roasted oxen. There were platters of turnips and swedes whittled to look like eggs, in baskets woven of strips of carrots and parsnips. My favourites were the jellies made in all the colours of a cathedral window, the spun-sugar flowers, and the almond milk custard whose surface was painted with gold-leaf dragons. Still, I was glad when the king signalled for the ladies to withdraw so the men could carouse in the hall until morning, drinking honey beer and swapping tales, gambling and betting on contests of strength.

Eager to find out what had happened to Judith, I hurried along to our chambers and threw open the doors. 'Judith, we missed you at the feast.'

I didn't find Judith there.

I found something else instead.

9

In my closet, atop my little couch lay a folded leaf of paper with my name on it.

This bodes no good.

With trembling hands, I unfolded the letter.

My dear daughter Ophelia,

My Heart does break that I must write this letter to you, but I could not leave without I wish you Farewell. We have but one life upon this earth, and while Happiness is to be sought in Heaven and not here, I cannot believe it right that we should suffer needlessly. You and I are both Women who like to grab hold of Life and ride it no matter how it bucks and brays. I cannot choose to shut myself in the Prison of Suffering that is Elsinore when Happiness beckons with both hands. As you doubtless suspect, I have Fallen in Love with Torvald the Merchant and I have lately learned that he loves me in return. Your father is a good man, but he is too Dry and Shrivelled for me. My Temperament must have Heat and Water or I perish. With Torvald I am alive to the very Ends of my Hair and Fingertips, but with your Father I could just as easily be the Dust on the Floor of a Marble Tomb. My Best Chance for Escape would be on this Feast Day when I might not be missed until Late into the Night, so I have run away with Torvald. By the time you read this, God willing, we shall be Far out at Sea. Henceforth my Home will be in a Distant Land. Please beg my forgiveness

*of the Queen, your Father, and of anyone else I have
Wronged. Know that I will love you always and would have
taken you with me if I could, but I suspect your Destiny lies
in Denmark. Tell your father he can get an Annulment and
marry again, for when I said the Words of Wedding in the
Church, in my Heart I was saying the opposite, and that
when he lay with me, I did take Medicines and Potions to
prevent Conception. Say Anything you will so that he can
get the Annulment for I do not wish him ill for all that I
was a Bad Wife to him. I am Presently so full of Joy that I
have it in my Heart to Wish Happiness to the Entire World.
Grow well, little Ophelia and try to think Fondly of your
Stepmother who loves you, Judith.*

It was as if someone had punched me in the stomach and
knocked out all my air. I sat down on the couch and stared.
Then I wanted to howl like a babe in arms. Judith, gone. I'd
never see her again. I'd never know where she dwelled or if
she lived or died. I couldn't think. The person who, next to
Piet, loved me best in the world, and now she was gone. I was
furious. I wanted to rip worlds apart with my bare hands.

*She could have waited. She could have waited until I was
grown and married.*

It was as if Piet had taken his knife and scraped me hollow,
leaving only the shell. My head felt thick as if my thoughts
couldn't push through to my awareness. I felt hot and cold
at the same time and very, very weary.

She will never see me in this mermaid gown. I curled up on
the couch like a child, wanting to be as small as possible.

I kept Judith's secret as long as I could. I left our chambers at
first light so that I wouldn't encounter my father when he tottered back from the men's revels. I went to one of my favourite
places to be alone, the minstrels' gallery that looked down into

the Great Hall. It was true that the steps up to the gallery had begun to crumble, but I was light and could pick my way up the nubs that remained. The gallery floor itself seemed solid, but there were little cracks in the wall through which I could spy on folk down below in the hall. Depending where they were standing down there, I could sometimes catch bits of conversation. As long as I stayed low, no one could tell I was hiding up above. The worst of it was that the minstrels' gallery was a favourite perch for a few of the ghosts, especially a very thin lady with very long, very fat yellow braids, but the ghosts and I'd studiously ignore each other the way, when you're travelling, you ignore your companions when they must squat by the roadside. Sometimes there were as many as five or six ghosts in the gallery with me, but on this morning there was only one, a glowering young warrior who had something of the look of Erik Strong Arm. I paid him no mind, but lay down on the floor and closed my eyes. I wished I could close my mind as well, for I ached at the thought of all the years stretching before me without Judith as my guide and companion.

The men went hunting again in the afternoon, so it wasn't until that night's feast that I had to tell my father about Judith's desertion. I was glad I'd been able to delay the news for so long. By now there was no chance that my father could catch up with the fleeing lovers. She'd given me so much, given me an entire new life, and I'd given her nothing. I could at least give her this gift of time to escape.

My father didn't take the news of Judith's desertion very well. 'Let me see this *letter*,' he said, 'for *let her* go I will not. Has she no concern for how this will make me look in the eyes of the court? What ill have I done her that she leaps to crown me in the horns of the cuckold and make me the butt of every joke? Show me the strumpet's letter.'

'She wrote the letter for my private eyes.'

'A young girl hasn't the right to conceal anything from her father. Let me see it now, Ophelia.'

'This is a private matter,' I protested, but he wouldn't give over his commands, although it wasn't until he was about to call for the guards that I retrieved the letter from under my pillow and permited him to read it.

As he read the letter, he seemed to grow smaller and more frail, looking less like a man than like a copy of a man made from old dry sticks and a handful of cloth. For the first time ever I felt sorry for him. His hands trembled slightly as he folded the paper and handed it back to me.

'Now I'll be the stockfish of the castle,' he said. His voice, too, trembled slightly. 'The old cuckold. The pillow with double horns.' I saw the pain in his face. 'Now all the castle folk will pull faces at me behind my back and mock me just beyond my hearing.' He tottered for a few steps about the room and then turned back to me. 'Daughter Ophelia, remember this well and lock it in your heart. The parsons say that what matters is who we are in our soul, but souls count for little in this world. Heed me. It matters not who we are but who we seem to be. Who we are is a private matter between ourselves and our God, and sometimes it seems God doesn't give a fig about any of us. Who we *seem* is a public affair, and, think you, our most important moments are the public ones. Who gives a rat's tail for the moments alone in our chambers? All that counts in life are what we do under the eyes of others and for others. Just as we wear a suit of clothes when we go forth, we must also wear our *selves*. As we embroider and decorate our clothes, we must embroider and decorate our selves for show. In both clothes and selves we do well to choose good cloth, but cloth means nothing without a good cut and fit and copious decoration. Fashion yourself to please the world because if the world withdraws its notice, you are nothing. Appearance is all.'

How could Judith do it? To love a common-born boy so much that she'd throw away her place at court, her adopted land, her rank among the gentlefolk? How could love ever be heavy enough to tip the scales against all else that you had or were in the world?

I could never be lost to love in that way.

No, now that I'd found a home in the castle, I'd never return to the mire of village life, no matter what it took to keep me here.

I was more my father's daughter than I'd previously suspected.

My father was right. Behind his back and just out of his hearing – which was growing a little deaf – folk at court found much merriment in his predicament.

The queen, however, took pity on me and was kinder than ever. I think she too was lonely. Few folk went visiting during the winter, for dark sneaked in early and crept away late, and the wind roamed the countryside like the hungry souls of the damned. Folk preferred to be safe at their own fireside during the winter months. Yet as November bled into December, I grew more and more restless. The queen's tame pursuits didn't suit my rough-hewn spirit, but that was a winter of heavy snow which barred me from visiting the village. I loved the queen for her kindness, and I loved lame Yorick for his fellowship, but both of them were old and sedentary. Their blood was slow and made even slower by the cold. Me, I wanted to dance and burn, not nod away by a meek fire that couldn't even banish the chill from the corners of the room.

As was their custom, the king and Prince Holger kept their distance from the queen. The king was proud of her in front of company, much the way he might be proud of a rare jewel purchased at great price or a scrap of the Virgin's robe won after great daring, but he kept apart in their private life.

I said as much to Piet one Friday afternoon when I crept down to visit him in the kitchens.

'I don't think the king loves the queen with the love a man feels for a woman,' I said. We sat apart from the other kitchen folk who were gambling before the great hearth. The kitchen was blessedly warm, and smelled pleasantly of the ropes of onions and garlands of herbs hanging from the rafters. Piet was making a wooden chess set with each of the pieces carved like a figure in the old legends. He planned someday to present the set to the king or one of the princes and so perhaps win advancement. I took up one of the delicate pawns in my hand. 'Perhaps our king doesn't have the urges for a woman that most men have.'

Piet's hands paused. He thought for a moment before he said, 'He is a man. Our king has urges enough.'

I looked at him in surprise. Piet had grown older in his time at court, but it shocked me to hear him talk of such things.

He lowered both his head and his voice. 'Only it is not the queen who satisfies his craving.'

By all the old gods, I hadn't thought of this. 'What do you mean?'

'I shouldn't be telling you this.'

'Tell me!'

'Such things are not seemly for a maiden's ears.'

I pinched him hard. 'Tell me, Piet!'

He continued to whittle without saying anything.

My hand shot out and shut over his. I cut myself on the edge of his knife, but I cared not. With my other hand I jerked the little figure, a pawn in the shape of a dwarf, away from him. I held it just out of his reach. Back in Myg's cottage he'd have wrestled me for it, but here I was a lady and he but a serving boy, and he dared not lay even a finger on me. 'Tell me all that you know of this, or I'll throw this wooden piece into the fire.'

He looked at me, shocked, and I dangled the piece back and forth to drive my threat home.

'Let go, let go, I'll tell you all. Just have a care with my dwarf, for it has taken me near a month to carve him.' He held out his hand for the manikin.

'No,' I said. 'First you tell me. Then I'll give you back your little man.'

Piet looked as cross as ever I've seen him. 'All that I know is that the king takes his pleasure with the scullery maids and the laundry maids, not with his wife.'

I was aghast. 'He sleeps with the peasant lasses instead of his beautiful queen?'

Piet nodded. 'Both he and the prince prefer servants to fine ladies in their beds. Girl, it is common knowledge that Master Cook and the Laundry Wife have been ordered to select especially handsome girls to work down here. At least, that's the talk below the stairs. Now give me back my pawn.'

'Not yet.' I wanted to get this straight in my head. I tried to remember any scullery lasses I'd seen. Most of the time, only the lads from the kitchen serve in the hall, but on feast days the entire kitchen staff, scullery lasses included, brought in the food and waited on the tables. Now that I thought about it, the lasses had all been pretty enough. Then I remembered something else. 'Piet! At the Feast of Saint Helgreth, one of the lasses was great with child. I remember thinking that she looked ripe to the bursting point. Could that have been the king's own child?'

'Hush!' Piet looked around to make sure that no one was listening. 'It's not safe to talk of these matters.'

I whispered, 'Do these lasses ever carry in their bellies the children of the king or the prince?'

Piet hesitated.

'Tell me!' I tossed the chess piece from hand to hand.

Piet finally nodded.

I couldn't believe my ears. 'Why did our king then marry our queen, if his heart flies to the common girls?'

Perhaps it was a trick of the gloomy light, but I thought I saw pity in Piet's eyes. 'It is not *love* that he feels for these girls.'

Of course I knew that lust could drive people to foolishness, but whenever I saw him, the king looked so cold and controlled, no more impassioned than a stone statue. I tried to picture him burning with lust, but even with my grand imagination, I couldn't envision such a thing.

Piet seemed to warm to his tale as if he was glad for once to know more than I did about a subject. 'In truth, our girls down here aren't even allowed to talk to him when they're in his chambers. They say he goes about his business in the same way he might go to his water closet, relieving himself as quick as possible.'

I was shocked, but still I pressed on. I wanted to know all. 'How does a girl know that he wants her? Does he come to the kitchen to fetch her?'

Piet's voice was equally shocked. 'This is not a seemly subject—'

'Tell me.'

After a few moments he said, 'He sends Osric.'

Osric was the king's messenger, a prissy little man barely taller than me. Many courtiers mocked him behind his back, calling him the lapdog of the king, but his devotion seemed absolute to the royal family.

'How does Osric know which one to choose?'

'The king and the prince don't care. They leave the choice of woman to Osric. Folk down here say that to them one of our girls will do as much as another, so long as she's spring lamb rather than mutton.'

I pressed on. 'What happens when one of the girls finds herself with child?'

'Ophelia!' He jerked his head to look at the rest of the folk close to the fire, agonized lest one of them overhear.

'Tell me.' How many of his girls had borne a child to the king? Or to Prince Holger? Did Prince Hamlet, too, prefer to lie with kitchen maids? Had any of them given birth to his offspring? Did a son of the king and a peasant girl have a right to the throne? It made me dizzy to think that there could be dozens of the king's children running about Denmark. 'Tell me something,' I begged.

Piet grabbed my arm and hustled me out into the snowy courtyard where no one could overhear. 'I'll tell you only because this knowledge concerns you as well.'

I felt a thrill that could be either excitement or fear run through my veins.

Even though no one was about, he spoke in low tones. 'If the child is a girl, the serving lass is given money to raise the child.'

'And what if it's a boy.'

Piet hesitated, then said, 'The king has decreed that it is not safe for a country to have by-blows of the king running about. He says that it imperils a nation to have pretenders to the throne.' He lowered his voice still more. 'If the child is a boy, then the king has one of his attendants take the child away as soon as it's born, even before its mother can see it.'

'What if the mother refuses to permit her baby to be taken from her?'

'All his bedfellows understand that this loss of their babes will come to pass. They know this before they go to the king's bed. Folk say that he sends his servants to snatch the baby boys as soon as they spring forth from their mother's bodies.'

'Where do they take the boys?'

Piet leaned his head close to mine. 'The babe is given to a foster mother in another country, Norway or Poland or such. Neither he nor his mother has any knowledge that he was sired by a father with royal blood.'

'And the mother never more sees her child?'

Piet shook his head.

We both stood for a moment, shivering from the cold, in silent contemplation. Then I recalled his earlier remark. 'Piet, why do you say that this concerns me?'

He nibbled his lip for a moment as if he was debating whether or no to say more. I pinched him. Finally he said, 'The man in charge of taking the babies from their natural mothers and delivering them to their foster mothers is your very own father, Polonius.'

It took me a moment to digest this. My father, smuggling babies out of the kingdom! That did explain a lot about my own past. If my father was used to taking the king's bastards to foster mothers to raise, no wonder he'd thought to get rid of me, his own daughter, in the same manner. Still, it bothered me to think of the arrogant Prince Holger and the wrinkled, elderly king callously relieving themselves with various young serving maids, girls of about my own age, and the men probably never even bothering to ask their names. One thing in particular still troubled me. 'And what of Lord Hamlet? Does he, too, seek his pleasures below?'

I thought with yearning to that golden prince and the courtesy he'd shown me the one time we'd met. In his eyes, I'd been the same as these serving wenches, and yet he'd treated me as if I was the finest lady in the land. Did he, too, order Osric to herd some poor female or other to his chamber?

Piet shook his head. 'Folk say that as far as they can see, he lives like a monk, taking his pleasure with neither servant nor lady.'

I felt a rush of longing to hear him talked about. 'What else do they say of Prince Hamlet?'

'Folk down here have a high opinion of him. They say he has the common touch, that he knows the name of everyone who serves him. They deem it a great pity that he's not the first-born son, that he'd make a better king than his brother for all that his brother is the better soldier.'

Inside I felt a glow of pride for Hamlet. Then another thought hit me. 'How does the queen feel when she sees the serving maids and laundry lasses with bellies swollen by her husband's get?'

Piet shrugged. 'They say she keeps her own counsel. They say she takes no notice, just as a highborn lady should. After all, folk claim that it is common for great men to seek their pleasures outside their own wives' chambers.'

I knew Piet was right, but I didn't like it. How humiliating it must be to know that your husband turns to other women. I doubted that Osric kept his actions secret, so doubtless the whole court knew as well. At banquets when the queen caught sight of these serving girls with swollen bellies, did she ache, knowing that they carried her husband's child inside? Or if it wasn't her husband's child, it was her own grandchild. Perhaps it was my lowly village origins, but I wouldn't like to be betrayed in such a fashion by my husband. 'If I were queen and my husband played me such an unfaithful trick, I'd take handsome serving lads to my bed to pay him back in his own coin.'

Piet shook his head. 'That she cannot.'

'The broth for the hen serves as well for the cock.'

'Infidelity in a queen is treason, girl, but infidelity in a king is less than nothing at all.'

Perhaps it was because these close winter days left me with so little else to occupy my mind, but for the next week, when I was with the queen, I kept studying her for signs that she was angry with her husband for his wanton behaviour. At mealtime I studied the king and Prince Holger, both of them so proud and stern, and I tried to picture them with the rosy, laughing serving maids. It didn't fit. Finally, one afternoon, when Yorick and I met for a few stolen moments up on the battlements, huddled out of the wind behind a column of stone, I asked him about Piet's tidings.

'All true,' he verified.

'The king is a bad man.'

Yorick gave me his twisted smile. 'But he's a good king. There's the rub. Good men aren't always good kings, and vice versa.'

I was outraged. 'How can he be a good king if he's a bad man? It makes no sense.'

'It takes different skills to rule a country than to rule one's own nature.'

'That makes less sense.'

Yorick gave a tight little laugh. 'We live in a world of paradox, not sense.'

Then we both fell silent while the ghost of a lady all in white furs drifted past, almost indistinguishable from the snows through which she moved without leaving any track.

Nevertheless, I burned to do something to right the scales, to avenge the patient queen. How could a man be so faithful to his country and not to his wife?

And then I did something that shocked even me.

IO

On the day my disgraceful behaviour began, when I came to the queen's rooms, all the curtains were drawn and one candle only was lit. Her chamber was as dim as a deserted chapel.

'My eyes hurt,' she said in her soft voice. 'We will not read or do needlework today.'

Yet even in the grey light I saw a large bruise across her cheek.

'You've hurt yourself, majesty!'

She hugged her elderly little lapdog. 'I tripped over my poor Blanche and hit my cheek against my clothespress. Grant me three or four days until I'm better, and then we shall resume our lessons.'

Elspeth took my elbow in her hand and eased me from the room without a word. Elspeth had a face like a starved frog, and her shoulders bowed forward as if a drawstring between them had been pulled tight. One eye was hard and fixed, but the other eye whirled on its own, knocking about the socket like a dried pea rolled around in a cup. She was a tiny woman, not much bigger than me, and she spoke with the thick accent of the Laplander. I knew that many Laplanders had magical powers, so I wondered if Elspeth could be a witch.

'I don't see how the sharp edge of a chest could make that broad bruise,' I said to her once we were in the hall and out of the queen's earshot.

She gave a harrumphing snort but added nothing else.

'In my village,' I ventured, 'the chandler's wife drinks too much honey wine in secret. When she is tipsy, she'd trip over her own benches so that we never see her without she is covered with bruises and scrapes.'

Elspeth looked outraged. 'I've never seen our majesty one hair's breadth the worse for drink, and I've served her since she was a child.'

It was unsettling to think about the queen being a child. *Once she'd been as young as me and younger.* It was a terrible thought to try to picture old folk as young. My *head* knew that they'd been children once, but my *heart* could never believe it. Older folk seemed so solid, so hard, and it passed understanding to believe that they were ever juicy and lithe with the suppleness of youth. It was as if the middle years were so powerful they could smother all trace of childhood in a man or woman. 'What was she like, the queen, when she was young?'

Elspeth considered for a moment, and then a smile split her huge froggy mouth. 'Oh, she was a little devil, was our Gertrude. A spitfire about the castle, she was. Afraid of nothing and lively as the day was long.'

Surely she couldn't be talking of the same queen. 'I cannot envision her majesty thus.'

Elspeth made a clicking noise. 'To look at her now, you wouldn't credit it. I don't marvel at your disbelief. But Gertrude was a headstrong hellion, but so pretty and so warm-hearted that we forgave her everything. She was the apple of her father's eye, her mother's darling, the pretty poppet of the entire court.'

'Until she was forced to marry the king?'

Elspeth's loose eye spun even more wildly. 'Forced? Forced? There was no forcing there. Her father even cautioned her against it, I warned her against it, but Gertrude was hellbent for the pretty young prince who came a-wooing.'

'So it was a love match, then?'

I'd gone too far. She peered at me suspiciously. 'It is not meet we should gossip about our betters. Back to your own chambers you go, girl, and come back in three days.'

As I trudged back to my chambers, I marvelled over what Elspeth had said. The queen had once been spirited . . . too high spirited. Was it age alone that had watered down her essence to make her the diluted figure I knew? Was it having a husband who cared for her only as a public monument?

Or was it something else entirely?

Looking back, I blame my disgraceful behaviour in part on my hunger to make sense of the lives of Prince Hamlet and his family. If we're to stay sane, our world must make sense, and to my thirteen-year-old self there was too much in the lives of the queen and king that made no sense at all. In part I blame my bad behaviour on my boredom. Yes, it was glorious to live as a lady in the castle, but I hadn't realized how tedious such a life would be. Servants did all the work, and except for a few hours of schooling each day, I had nothing but sleeping and eating and grooming myself to fill my time. The gentle-born boys of my age had hawking and hunting and riding and training in the arts of war, but girls were expected to wait patiently until they were given in marriage as brood mares for their husbands. Perhaps if there'd been other girls of gentle birth in the castle I'd have had playfellows and not become so corrupt, but I was mostly alone. Piet's duties kept him from me, and, in any case, my father, the queen, and the kitchen staff as well frowned on my visits below stairs. Certainly it was in part my age that drove me to do what I did. At about thirteen the blood begins to boil and a dark sap in us begins to rise. I suspect even the most chaste among us begin to be haunted with lewd thoughts and dreams. I do know that in the beginning, my fantasies of Prince Hamlet had centred around acting in plays together, but now I began to have fantasies of a baser nature. Certainly in the village I had, from time to time, caught glimpses of lusty couplings. Folks tried to keep them private, but there was little privacy in the village, so sometimes you'd stumble upon such a thing unawares. Every year, Piet and I had been ordered to lead our she-goat to Farmer Othger's ram, and we'd watched with great interest as the two beasts coupled. But it was only now, as my thirteenth birthday approached, that I felt a curiosity that was both dreamy and feverish to understand this madness in the blood.

Or perhaps I merely play the moral coward, seeking to shift the blame from a defect in my own nature, attempting to make my own depravity seem a common fault. Perhaps in this first transgression I should have spotted the seeds of the murderer I was to become.

Whatever the cause, I began to spy on the king and his trysts with the serving maids.

I've never liked to sleep. It seems to me a cheat and waste of living. The night after I'd been sent away by the bruised queen, I crept out of my bed as soon as the castle grew quiet. In the corridors I passed a ghost or two who looked at me strangely, but I didn't see any other live folk. In my earlier prowls about the labyrinth of corridors, I'd found a cranny in a passageway through which folk travelling from the kitchens to the king's chamber would have to go. This cranny was covered by a tapestry of a knight being stabbed by another knight as he knelt to drink from a spring. Behind the tapestry was a tiny secret room – no wider than a large trunk – with a narrow window and a little curved window seat underneath. This niche seemed completely abandoned and forgotten. I wondered if anyone besides me knew any longer that there was the little seat inside. The masking tapestry was old and slightly rotted. I widened a small tear in the hangings so I could peek out at the passageway. That night, as I kept vigil, I saw several new ghosts, including a bald man who carried his head in his hands and a thin, sad-eyed boy who walked the passageway with a dagger hilt sticking out from between his shoulder blades. The only one who worried me was a plump woman dressed like a servant who drifted up and down with the body of a babe carried in her outstretched arms. I was ashamed of myself. But inside me was something hard-packed, like a hand made of a substance a thousand times more dense than iron or rock, and that inner hand relentlessly pushed me toward the action I took. It was as if, with all my being, I *had* to understand what would drive a girl my age to lie with an elderly king. I felt depraved beyond all salvation, but I was mad to see beneath the elegant surface of royal life. I wanted to know everything.

That first night I saw nothing of interest, only Elspeth passing with a steaming mug that probably contained a soothing draught for the queen and, just before midnight struck, two fresh guards to replace the ones outside the king's door. It took three nights before I saw what I sought. Osric, the king's oily messenger who was rumoured to feed off the droppings he licked from the king's behind, escorted a girl down the passageway. She was dressed in the russet homespun favored by the scullery maids. She had a sturdy peasant body and looked to be barely older than I. It was too dim in the passageway to tell for certain, but I thought she walked like someone who was scared, but Osric's body was between her and my hiding place, so it was hard for me to see her clearly.

It was no more than twenty minutes before she returned, this time alone.

I slid out from behind the hanging as soon as she passed and grasped her wrist with my hand. She gave a little squeal of surprise.

'Who are you?' she asked.

'Speak in a whisper,' I commanded, and she looked at me with scared eyes. 'I'm a waiting woman of the queen's,' I told her. Although the girl had sprinkled herself with rosewater, I could smell onions and bacon grease underneath her perfume. 'She wishes me to question you, to find why you progress along the passageway to her bedchamber at such an unseemly hour of night.' I figured this lie would do well enough.

The girl hesitated. I didn't see in her any beauty beyond the natural handsomeness of youth, but she had all her teeth, always a powerful attraction in a woman.

I gave her arm a little shake. 'What are you doing here?'

She jerked her arm away and gave a defiant toss of her head. 'I am about the king's business, so tell your lady this is not her affair.'

My fingers itched to slap her, but then I saw she looked scared – as if her defiance was only a front. 'And what business of the king's are you about at such an hour of night?' She didn't answer, so I added, 'I can guess what your business was with the king.'

She chose to brazen it out. 'I have no doubt, lady, that your guess is true. This night I've shared the bed of a king.'

What a fool! 'Do not puff yourself up with fine airs. It's not you in particular, girl, that our king desires. Any warm body would do when these urges blaze.'

'But it was me he chose!'

I couldn't believe how smug she sounded. 'He has sent for dozens of maids in his time and he'll send for dozens more. Do not think that this makes you special.'

'I *am* special!' Her voice was sharp as the edge of a shattered pane of glass. 'I've been in the bed of a king. No other girl from my village can make that claim.'

'Hundreds of girls could say the same thing.' In truth, I didn't know how many peasant girls he'd taken, but he must be all of sixty years old, so it could easily be even more than I'd stated.

'I've been in the bed of a king, and my whole life long, nothing can take that away. A king desired me.'

'You are nothing to him.'

'I am a girl who slept with a king.'

'Did he speak to you with soft words? Treat you fair.'

At that she looked a little lost, but she rallied. 'I've slept with a king and that's all that matters.' Her voice curled into gloating. 'My bride price will go up, for many village boys will desire a woman who has slept with a king.'

'Did he give you gifts of love?'

In answer, she uncurled her fist. Several copper coins lay there.

I said, 'That makes you a whore, not a fine lady.'

Her fist snapped shut. 'He didn't have to give me anything.'

'If you carry his child, they'll take it away at birth,' I warned her.

'What care I about a child?' she asked, her voice now as scornful as mine. 'I've this night slept with a king, and that's honour and glory enough to last me my whole life long.'

Then she swept out of the alcove and I could hear her bare feet slapping their way down the stone corridor.

Three days later, when we resumed our lessons, I regarded the queen with special tenderness, but I noticed no difference in her manner. Her bruise had faded, but it wasn't entirely gone. That day was bitter cold. We sat close to the fire, Elspeth, the queen, and I, and Blanche huddled beneath the queen's skirt for warmth. Yule was approaching, and I served as scribe to the queen, writing down on a tablet a list of Yule gifts that she'd give the entire household, all the way from the princes of blood to the lads in the stables.

'I've asked the king to join us,' she said in her mild voice.

'I'd have my lord approve my accounts before I begin to make up the offerings.'

I was eager to see the king at close quarters, to study this lover of peasant lasses.

Toward the tail of the morning, both the king and Prince Holger appeared. I rose to make my departure, but the queen waved me to resume my seat. The king bowed to the queen in deep courtesy, and then he gently kissed her cheek. 'Lovely as always, my lady,' he said. 'Though I don't fancy that shade of yellow against your skin. It makes you look too haggard.'

I pictured his hands fondling the scullery wench from the corridor, his mouth crushing against hers.

'I'll not wear the gown again if it displeases you, my lord,' the queen said.

He flicked his hand. 'Wear it in private if you wish, wife. Just don't wear it out where other folk might see it. Remember, your beauty is one of my treasures, and I'd have all my treasures well tended.' He looked over at the prince who was lounging in the doorway. 'Come make your bows to your mother, sirrah.'

The prince slouched his way over to the queen and swept a bow, then he folded his arms about her and kissed her on both cheeks. 'My dearest mother,' he said, sounding both sleepy and bored, but her eyes shone with pride.

She pressed one of her palms against his cheek and said, 'My dear, dear son.'

'Gertrude, you wished me to overlook your list of Yuletide remembrances?' the king said, holding out his hand.

The queen stretched forth the list, and as the king stepped to get it, he trod on little Blanche who gave a yelp and then snarled. She popped her head out from under the queen's skirt and snapped her teeth again at the king's boot.

'By God, bite a king, would you?' the king roared in anger, his face turning red. Then he pulled back his foot and gave a mighty kick to Blanche, sending her halfway across the floor, her head smacking against the stones of the hearth. She yelped again, and then, with more energy than I fancied such a tiny body could possess, she sprang back growling toward the king.

The queen had risen to her feet and was screaming, 'Stop, stop!' although I didn't know if she was talking to the king or to the little dog.

The king raised his boot again and kicked Blanche over and over, until she began to whimper with pain. Finally she dragged herself over to cower under a stool. Prince Holger was laughing and slapping his thigh. 'The battle of King Hamlet and the ancient bitch!' he roared. 'Before God, Father, an epic worthy of one of the scops of old.'

The queen was giving little coos of alarm, and the king turned to her, breathing hard. His frosty grey eyes were now as cold as January ice. 'Madam,' he said, 'if I visit you in future, make sure that this thing comes not within my sight or hearing, or I'll skewer it on my own sword and roast it and make you eat of it for middag.'

Then he flung into the fire the list that we'd laboured over the whole morning through and swept out of the room, the laughing prince at his heels.

I'd been too shocked to move throughout the encounter, but as soon as the king had gone, I dived over to the stool and gently lifted the whimpering Blanche up into my lap. It was clear that she was grievous hurt. Blood ran out of one ear and a back leg dangled, broken in at least two places.

'My poor Blanche,' the queen said, kneeling beside me and burying her face gently against the dog's shivering flanks.

We washed the blood off Blanche's fur, and the queen carefully wrapped the broken leg against a bit of kindling, but I doubted that the leg in such an old dog would be able to heal overmuch.

'He didn't mean it,' the queen said to me. 'He was startled, and he acted without thinking. He will come back this afternoon and be very contrite. You will see.'

I didn't say anything because everything I wished to say was treasonous.

We spent the rest of the morning reconstructing the burned list of giftings. We didn't speak further of the king's tirade, although Blanche's occasional whimpers made certain that his cruel behaviour was never far from our minds. The queen's thin fingers caressed the dog's curly fur without cease. When we were summoned by the bell to middag, the queen laid Blanche in the middle of her own bed, and afterwards she smuggled back several slices of roast meat and hand fed them to the dog.

We still didn't talk of the incident. I knew nothing I could say would please the queen or grant her heart's ease, and I suspected she knew that nothing she could say would dampen the blaze of my anger. Halfway through the afternoon, Osric appeared at the door to her chamber.

'My lady,' he said, giving her an oily bow, 'my lord the king desires an audience with you and begs permission to wait on you in your chamber.'

Refuse him, I wanted to shout at her. *He behaved like a lout and a bully, so treat him as you would any lout.*

'Tell him that I await the pleasure of my lord,' she said.

I was rigid with disapproval, and, although she said nothing, I fancied Elspeth felt the same way. The queen looked back and forth between us several times, then said, 'I told you that my lord would be contrite. Poor man, he has so much to stress him and vex him and he's always had the devil's own temper.'

I refused to meet her eye.

She glanced nervously at Blanche who had been lying listless on the bed ever since we'd returned from middag.

'Ophelia, perhaps it would be for the best if you'd take Blanche to your chambers until the king is gone. I wouldn't like to trespass on the king's present good humour.'

Without a word, I swept the poor dog up in my arms and marched out of the room. I carried poor Blanche to my own closet and lay cuddled against her on my bed. The rest of the day, I didn't return to the queen's chambers. I didn't care if she became angry at me because I was so very furious with her. Not as furious as I was with the king, true, but she should have confronted him with his behaviour and refused to let him treat a defenceless animal so. I spent the rest of the afternoon curled up with Blanche, stroking her and telling her stories of the Flying Catgirl. Only, to please her, I pretended it was a Flying Dog-girl instead.

Several times at supper the queen looked toward me with a troubled face, but I refused to acknowledge her.

That night I didn't spy on the king. I tended Blanche instead.

Blanche grew worse through the night. The kicks had seemingly broken something inside her. The next day I returned her to the queen, and all through the following week, the two of us worked to tempt Blanche back to health. Instead she grew weaker and weaker. She refused to eat or drink, even when the queen took the food and milk to her and tried to feed her with her own hands.

'Send for the castle doctor,' I suggested.

'He will not treat a dog.'

'You are the queen. Command him to do so.'

She shook her head. 'It would anger the king.'

Finally I offered to consult the Herbwife for potions to mend the little dog.

The snows were deep and thick, and I had to struggle to clear a path down to the village. It took twice as long as usual to fight my way there, and by the time I reached the

Herbwife's hearth, both my cloak and my skirts were sodden with snow.

It was good to be in her house that smelled so sweetly of herbs. She brought me one of her own gowns to put on and hung my clothing next to the fire to dry. As soon as I'd changed out of my clothes, she wrapped me in a clean blanket and handed me a cup of hot, fragrant tea.

I explained my business. She asked many questions about the condition of the dog, but when I'd finished my account, her face looked troubled.

'I can make up a tincture that might dull the pain,' she said, 'but I fear the curing of the dog is a matter beyond my skill.'

'But you must,' I said, 'for the poor little creature suffers most dreadfully.'

The Herbwife sighed. 'An old dog, in winter, who doesn't eat or drink. I doubt that she'll get better. I doubt even the most skilled doctor alive can coax the poor creature back to health. In truth, the most we can do is pray for her recovery because if she's to recover, it's in the hands of our Lord Himself and not in the power of any earthly agency.'

'Blanche's pain never stops,' I protested. 'I'm not content to leave it to our Lord who has so many calls upon His attention and aid. I must do something myself.'

She tapped her finger against the arm of her chair several times and then said in her clotted English accent, 'Child, the kindest thing would be to put Blanche out of her misery for I feel certain she cannot recover from these blows.'

My voice rose like the wind in a gale. 'Kill her, you mean? Murder that poor dog? Finish the work that the king started?'

She looked at me sadly. 'When a creature cannot be healed, kindness prompts us to ease their way to gentle sleep. There's no virtue in the suffering of animals.'

'No!' I leaped to my feet and took several agitated turns about the room. 'Just because something suffers, it's no reason to kill it.'

'No,' she agreed in a mild voice. 'Not if it can recover. But sometimes recovery is impossible. This is your decision, child. Yours and the queen's. But if Blanche were my dog, knowing that she'll die in a few days or so, I wouldn't draw out her time with suffering. I'd let her go easy, not hard. Such is the only gift we can give the wee creature.'

For several minutes I railed against what she'd said, but at last I calmed down. After a while I asked, 'If I did want to ease her toward her eternal rest, how would I do it?'

She rose and went to her mantelpiece. She shook a little key out of a blue flowered jug and unlocked a large wooden cabinet. Inside were thirty or so small jars and pouches.

'These are potions that can bring sleep,' she said.

'Poisons?'

'Some of them. Some are just strong potions to bring on natural sleep or vomiting or such. They are all powerful medicines that I wouldn't have fall into careless hands. The poisons are meant, of course, to work on animals only, or to be applied onto to the outside of folk where they can cure rashes and such.'

'Have you ever used them on a person?' I asked, fascinated.

She shook her head. 'I'd never use them on a human being.'

'But if a person were suffering and couldn't get better . . . ?'

'I'd never make that judgement about a person. That judgement is God's alone.'

'But if the person himself asked you for it, would you let him make that judgement about himself?'

She frowned. ''Twould be against the law of God. Animals don't understand why they suffer, but God gave man the gift of understanding. The price of that gift is that we cannot choose the hour of our own death.'

'But—'

She held up a warning hand. 'These conversations are dangerous, child. We will continue this one no more.'

She surveyed her store of poisons. 'This one,' she said, tapping the top one with her fingernail, 'is a mixture that, dissolved in wine, will stop the heart and breathing, but often causes great cramps in beasts. I'd use something gentler on poor Blanche.' She took the next jar off the shelf, pulled out its stopper, and shook some of its contents onto her palm. She held them out for me to examine. There were little pellets, the colour of swirled cream. 'This too needs to be dissolved in a liquid, and death is very rapid. One single pellet can kill an ox, but I worry that Blanche couldn't drink enough to do her any good.' She shook the pellets back in the jar and stopped it back up. She reached for a little bottle on the bottom shelf. 'This one is liquid. It needs to pass directly into the blood. You could dip a knife into this tincture and then make one quick cut of her skin, not deep but just enough to draw blood. Within a minute or so, it leaps into the blood, and then no force on earth can stop its deadly spread.'

'Is there naught else?' I interrupted. 'She has been so hurt already, I don't want to pain her more.'

The Herbwife picked up a squat jar. 'If you shut her in a room and sprinkle this in the fire . . . but you must leave the room as quickly as possible without breathing any of the smoke. Keep the room sealed for three days—'

'No. I don't wish her to die alone.'

The Herbwife nodded. 'Then you will probably not wish to use this one either. You soak a cloth in it and hold it over the nose and mouth of that which you wish to kill.'

I pointed to a green jar on the top shelf. 'What about that one?'

She smiled. 'In cattle, it eases labour. But it's a most curious mixture. Sprinkle it in a drink for a human being, and a few minutes after you consume it, you will give every appearance of death. No breath can be detected on a feather, no heartbeat can be felt beneath the hand. But in three days, almost to the hour, you will wake as if from a deep sleep.' She laughed. 'I gave it once to a pregnant woman. I thought I'd killed her. Luckily, she swallowed it on a Friday with the priest gone from the village, and he returned after sundown on Saturday, too late to lay her in the ground. We were all gathered around her body on Monday, ready to consign her to the grave, when she woke, bright-eyed as you pleased and as refreshed as if she'd slept for a week.'

'And her babe?'

'The babe had come quickly and easily after she drank the tincture, so it was doing fine and glad to be restored to its mother's breast.' She laughed again. 'I had God's own luck then, and never again will I give that potion to aught but labour-strangled cows.'

I was glad that story had turned out so well, but I needed to focus on my present errand. 'Is there nothing, then, that can be given to Blanche while she sleeps?'

The Herbwife's eyes lit up. 'The very thing!' She took down a small bottle of crimson glass. 'You will need only a few drops. While Blanche is sleeping, drop some into her ear. She will die without ever waking up. Her body will be stiff like one who had been bit by a serpent, but she herself will feel nothing.'

I reached for the poison.

The Herbwife didn't hand it over at once. 'Use only a few drops on Blanche and pour out the rest. There's enough in this bottle to kill a dozen men, and I wouldn't have it misused.'

'It will not be misused,' I said.

I had no suspicion then that I was lying.

11

The poison worked just as the Herbwife said.

All that afternoon, as I fought my way back to the castle through the leg-clinging snow, the wailing wind that scourged my face with little whips of ice, and the thick winter darkness, I argued inside about whether or not to ask the queen for permission to put Blanche out of her misery. I arrived too late for supper, and, to tell true, by then I cared only about shedding my freezing clothes and wrapping myself in my fur coverlets. After I warmed myself back to human state, I dressed in my thickest wool gown and went to the kitchen in search of food for by then I was hungry enough to eat an entire school of herring. Piet found me some pickled beet root and cheese, but he was busy working on the contents of a pie for the next day's meal, a pastry ship that, when cut open, would reveal a wealth of Noah's animals, two of each kind. He had no time to talk.

I seldom visited the queen after supper, but my concern for Blanche drew me thither. The queen herself looked frayed to breaking, her pale hands stroking the dog's little head. Poor Blanche lay whimpering from time to time, but for the most part she looked too worn even to cry.

That made up my mind. I would *not* let Blanche continue to suffer, and I would *not* involve the queen in my plan. I would not inflict upon the queen the pain of being the one to decide to kill her little dog, but, more than that, I would not make poor Blanche suffer just because the human beings around her were too reluctant to act quickly.

I had to wait a long time for the queen to leave me alone with Blanche, but when she left to visit the water closet, I slipped my hand through the slit in the waistband of my gown and pulled the vial out from the pouch beneath. I looked deep into Blanche's eyes. Like most dogs, she had beautiful eyes, but now hers were bruised with pain.

'I am going to give you rest,' I said. 'The pain will disappear.' I kissed her on the top of her soft little head, and I turned her to her side. She gave a little cry as I eased her over, but then she settled down as if she could sense what I intended. I turned back her fat, fluffy flap of an ear, and I uncorked the vial. I held her down with one hand while with the other I poured six drops of the liquid into the chamber of her ear. She twisted a little bit when the first drop plopped down and gave a soft yelp, but then she seemed to relax. I held her for just a moment longer, and then I felt all her muscles ease. I let go and corked the bottle and slipped it back into the bag between my skirt and my first petticoat. Blanche's breathing grew slower. I began to stroke her, murmuring, 'Sleep, little one. Sleep.' Then, I began to croon a lullaby that long ago I'd heard the Herbwife sing to Ragnor at the end of the day.

> *Men must sail and women must weep*
> *And all small things come at last to sleep.*
> *Sail forth then in dreams, but come to no harm*
> *For I hold you forever now safe in my arms.*

When the queen returned, I was still stroking the dog and singing to her. 'See,' I said, 'Blanche sleeps peacefully at last.'

Only then did I realize tears were running down my cheeks.

The queen sank down onto the bed beside me and put her

thin hand against Blanche's chest. She looked startled, and then she enfolded me in her thin arms, and we both wept together.

Two days later, the queen showed me a new emerald neckband that the king had given her.

'His heart is sore that he kicked the little dog,' she said.

I gave a scornful snort.

'Men are often like that, Ophelia. Especially men of high-born estate. They never had to learn the self-control that women do. Understand, dear Ophelia, that when most noble-men were growing up, their underlings would never dare say them nay, so they never learned how to govern their impulses or tempers. The firstlings of their minds became the firstlings of their hands. Sometimes therefore they do things in a rage, but then they repent of them. If you wish to be a good wife – and both your father and I have great hopes of finding you a husband of high birth – you must never blame a man for what he does in the fury of a moment.'

I could swallow this stone soup no longer. 'Majesty, it is true that I've had little experience of men, but well I know that most men don't behave in such a fashion. If Piet or the Herbwife's sons had kicked one of our dogs to the edge of death—'

'Hush!' said the queen, looking about wildly to make sure I wasn't overheard.

'—the rest of us would have refused to stomach such an excuse. We would have swiftly cuffed the miscreant into more seemly behaviour.'

'Forgive me, Ophelia, but those were common folk. I speak of lords and such.'

'Forgive me, Majesty, but I see no reason to let a king behave worse than a commoner.'

'You cannot hold a king to the same customs as a peasant, child.'

I certainly could, but all I said was, 'I don't believe that Prince Hamlet would behave in such an ungentle way.'

A worried expression that I couldn't interpret flitted across her face. 'You're right. My son Hamlet is very different from his father.'

Two days later the queen received a gift that pleased her even more than the emerald neckband. The king's brother, Prince Claudius, brought her a tiny white puppy, as round as a snowball.

'I've searched hither and yon to find this scamp,' he told her as she laughed and kissed the wriggling little creature.

She smiled up at him with a shining face. 'I'll call him Trey because he's the third dog that ever I owned.' There was more colour in her face than usual, and I fancied I could see within her expression the ghost of the beautiful girl she once had been. She stretched out a hand to Claudius. 'As ever, you're much too good to me, brother, Claudius.'

He kissed her fingers lightly. 'As ever, I live to serve you, my lady and my queen.'

A wash of pink colour arose in her white cheeks, and I was shaken by a new thought. When the king was about, the queen was prim and a little desperate to please, but when she was alone with Claudius, she blossomed like a rose in the sun and seemed to shed many years and a load of worries. She was almost girlish with him. Could she be in love with him? As soon as the notion flew into my head, I dismissed it as indecent. The queen and Prince Claudius were old. They had to be fifty at least. Of a certainty, women that ancient couldn't fall in love like chits of marriageable age. Still, I began to study Prince Claudius more closely. All in all, he was a puzzle to me. He wasn't often at court. The king sent him on missions of ambassage to many nations. He also oversaw all the king's castles.

My father approved of Claudius as a sensible man who

kept good accounts and governed well in the name of his brother.

'Had we not been graced with good King Hamlet,' my father often said, 'Prince Claudius would have made a fine ruler himself.'

He didn't add, 'Better than either of the king's sons,' but there were others at court who did so. For all that Prince Holger was a skilful sportsman and swordsman, folk increasingly whispered that he was unbridled and impetuous, prone to reckless actions and long past the age to settle down and start a family. I noticed the king never trusted him with anything of importance, not the way he trusted Claudius.

'Has Prince Claudius a wife and family?' I asked the queen one afternoon when I was working on my hated embroidery. I was trying to stitch a rose, but it looked instead more like a cabbage on fire.

A little smile flickered across the queen's lips and again her cheeks grew faintly pink, but she said only, 'No. He never married.'

I wanted to draw her out. 'What a pity that such a valuable man has never set up a nursery of his own.'

The queen made no answer to this, only tangled her long fingers into Trey's fur. 'I think that's enough embroidery for one morning, child. Run to the kitchen and fetch some meat for Trey.'

A few days later, the king came again to call on the queen. I shrank back into the shadows by the bed, but I didn't withdraw altogether because, frankly, I wished to see how he treated her.

He was in high spirits, and he even took a cylinder seal out of his pocket and tossed it across the floor for Trey to fetch. Both he and the queen laughed to see the snowball waddle after the seal and trot back again. The king called the queen his little swan and his mouse and he asked her if she'd like to go with him in the summer when he paid a state visit to Sweden.

The queen, matching his good cheer, then opened her chest and took out a robe that she'd embroidered, a fine surcoat of cloth of gold with ivy embroidered down both sleeves and tiny white daisies worked across the hem and collar.

'What think you of this,' she asked, 'as a Saint Nicholas gift for our son?'

The king examined the handiwork. 'You have done well, lady. You were ever clever with your needle. No one at court embroiders half as well as you.'

The queen glowed with pride. 'It will become our son, will it not, my lord?'

He nodded. 'Holger will look very handsome in it.'

The queen's smile faltered. 'I hadn't meant it for Holger. This is a gift for Hamlet.'

'Hamlet?' The king snorted. 'It will be wasted on that boy. Fine stitchery like this shouldn't be buried in some school, marvelled at only by monks and eunuchs. Give the surcoat to Holger instead and have done with it. Let it be an ornament of our court for such it well deserves.'

The queen looked nervous. 'Perhaps, my lord, if our Hamlet could come more often to court, he could wear it here.'

The king blew out his breath in disgust. 'That cannot be, and well you know why, lady. Give the coat to Holger.'

'I've had letters from his good friends, Rosencrantz and Guildenstern both, and they write that Hamlet is much improved.'

'Much improved, but I doubt he's improved enough to risk at court. The boy does well enough in Wittenberg, lady. He is happy there. We are happiest when he's there. Leave all that's well, well alone.' He scooped up his seal from the floor and dropped it back into the leather pouch on his belt.

'I miss our son,' the queen said. Her voice was tight and nervous.

'Holger is a prince to delight any mother's heart. Be content with that. Let us not stir up the waters and rouse the sleeping monsters beneath.'

The queen's hands twisted the cloth back and forth. 'Have you forgotten, my lord?'

'Forgotten?'

'You did give him permission to join the Christmas revels at court.'

'By Jesu's beard! I'd forgot!' The king took several agitated paces, and then turned back to the queen. 'If I knew you less well, lady, I'd think you'd played me false, for that lad is no true son of mine!'

'He is a fine boy, my lord.'

'Boy! Near thirty if he's a day. Holger is the better son in every way.' He looked down at the surcoat. 'This is your handiwork, wife, and therefore yours to waste as you see fit. Waste it on Hamlet if you will, but the fine clothes cannot turn eels to angels. Deal with him as you choose, for I've done with him!'

I didn't understand the king's anger, but I was thrilled to my last drop of blood and beyond.

Prince Hamlet was finally coming home!

When next I saw Yorick, I complained to him of the king's treatment of his wife and his attitude toward his second son.

'It's not fair! It's not right! He prefers that lout Holger who does little but sport and guzzle too much beer and ravish the serving wenches, and he ignores Prince Hamlet who is a scholar, a man of the arts, a man—'

Yorick interrupted my tirade. 'Young Hamlet was ever my

favourite, but this issue is more complicated than you yet know, Lady Ophelia.'

I stamped my foot in frustration. 'People call things complicated when they're too cowardly to face the simple truth. The king is a bully, and he gets away with his bad behaviour because he's a king.'

'He is a good king. One of the greatest, perhaps, that Denmark has ever known.'

'That still gives him no right to play the tyrant with his family.'

Yorick swept me a mocking bow 'And what would you, O Champion of all that's down-trodden? How is he to be stopped, my Lady of Lost Causes?'

In spite of myself, I gave a laugh at his foolery, but I wasn't to be turned from the matter at hand. 'Someone must call the king to a reckoning.'

'And who can do such a Herculean task? He is the supreme ruler. No man in Denmark has authority over him.'

'Then let it be a man of the church, for the state is subject to the church.'

'The king of Denmark also rules the church in Denmark. Besides, no churchman would risk his neck criticizing the private life of the king.'

'But it's not fair. It's not right. Why should a king have leave to break the laws of God and man that his subjects must follow?'

Yorick chuckled. 'If you cast out every king who failed to follow the ten commandments, then would you have no rulers in all of Christendom. Often, I'm told, we wouldn't even have the Pope himself.'

'It's not fair.'

'Ophelia, child, fight the battles you can win and do not throw your heart over the moon. Let it go. Such is the way of the world, child.'

I wouldn't be mollified. 'Then it is a *bad* way.'

Yorick ruffled my hair. 'You will have folks think you as prudish and pinched as a cloistered nun.'

I jerked away. 'I will not let those I love be hurt.'

Still, as Yule approached, I grew more and more excited about again seeing Prince Hamlet. Would he remember me from that day in the orchard more than two years earlier?

Then, one day, toward the middle of December, I got a shock.

At middag, my father prattled to me and the rest of our table of a dispute with Sweden over fishing rights. I paid him little heed. Even with its huge fireplace blazing, the Great Hall was cold. In their thin slippers, my feet felt like blocks of ice, and I couldn't wait for the meal to end so I could hurry back to the fire in my own closet. There were no foreign emissaries at court on this Friday, so our meal was particularly pinched. At the best of times, meals in Advent tended toward the scant side of the larder, and this day those of us at the lower tables had only a thin broth of dried pease and some thick, sour black bread.

Osric's voice startled me.

'The king craves an audience with you.' He was standing between my father and me, looking at us both. 'He bids you come to the high table when folk leave the hall.'

My father preened. He liked that our table companions heard that he was being summoned to the king. 'I'll take pains to come to him right away, although to say truly, to come to the king gives no pain and gives much pleasure, for anon and anon and ever and anon it is my pleasure to—'

'He commands the presence of both of you,' Osric said. 'You and your beauteous daughter.'

I was shocked. What in the world could the king want from me?

'Both of us?' my father asked. He looked as shocked as I felt. For once words seemed knocked out of him.

Then Osric bowed and was gone.

'Both me and my daughter,' my father said, his brow wrinkling. 'What mischief have you been about now, Ophelia, that the king would call you forth?'

I shrugged, but inside I was swirling with worry. Had someone overheard me complain to Yorick about the king? I knew Yorick was the king's man, but I couldn't believe that he'd betrayed my confidences. Had the queen somehow learned how I'd poisoned her dog? The poison was safe in my dressing chest, and I didn't see how anyone could have found it there. Did the king know I spied on the maids who crept to his bedchamber?

My father continued to fuss about this unexpected happening, pressing me as to why the king would demand my presence. I kept insisting that I didn't know what this was all about, but my father kept asking the question in different forms as if he could trick me into giving a straight answer.

Then he switched over to my appearance. He grieved that I couldn't go back to my chambers and make myself more tidy. In all honesty, there was some foundation for these laments. I'd been careless in arranging my hair that morning. I didn't like dragging the heavy ivory comb through my tangle of curls, so I'd just tied a blue ribbon around them and patted them into place. Since this wasn't a formal meal, I was wearing the simplest of all my gowns, a blue woollen kirtle plain enough for a milkmaid.

Finally the queen rose and departed, signalling that everyone else could leave the hall and return to his own affairs. Once the queen left, the rest of the company had to stop eating whether they were finished with the meal or not. Usually the queen was kind and, even though she was herself a sparing eater, she'd tarry long enough for even the brawniest of the guards to eat his fill, but every once in a while she forgot and would hurry out after only a few mouthfuls, so most of the folk at the board shovelled their food in with great rapidity in case the queen took early departure.

My father and I tarried at our places till Osric returned to escort us to the high table.

In spite of myself, I had to admit the king was still a good figure of a man. His face looked more worn than his body. Like most men of court, his face was paler in winter than summer. Once Piet had pointed out to me that all people wore a colour under the outermost colour of their skin. The undercoats of some people were pink, some were golden, some red, and a few folk had a kind of bluish-white undercoating. This was true of the queen, but now I saw that the undercoat of the king's skin was a tawny yellow like that of old gold.

My father and I made our bows. 'What is your majesty's will?' my father asked. 'For will what you will, I *will* carry it out. My only will is to do your will, and I will—'

The king turned his blue-grey eyes to me. He studied me hard, as if he were going to draw my portrait. I wouldn't be cowed by this brute who attacked tiny dogs and tumbled kitchen maids without the power to tell him nay. I drew myself up tall to show him I wasn't afraid.

He gave an appreciative smile, his yellow-white teeth glinting through his yellow-grey beard.

'She has spirit, this daughter of yours.'

'She's a good girl,' my father said doubtfully, as if he couldn't decide if the king's comment was a compliment or a veiled insult.

'She's very pretty,' the king said. 'Near as pretty as the queen.'

But it was the king's next remark that made me nearly fall to the floor in shock.

'What would you say to being a princess, girl?'

12

As the village folk say, I'm sharp enough to tell a hen from a hacksaw. I'm not as educated as a clerk, but I can recognize a question with a trick as its hook.

Cautiously I answered, 'Many think it a fine estate, sire.'

He gave a bark of laughter. 'A careful remark, as befits the daughter of a careful man.'

My father broke in. '*Tend* the tree and you will *tend* yourself *tender* fruit, I always say. Indeed, I'm *careful*, and I'm most *full of care* for anything that involves your majesty, but I do *care* most *fully* for all that falls—'

The king ignored him. 'A careful remark, but not, I think, an answer.' His eyes were glazed with a rime-frost of amusement.

'I don't know how I should answer you, my lord.'

The corners of his thin lips curled into the hint of a smile. 'Oh, I think you do. Such a cool surface, but I suspect there are fires banked beneath your snow.'

Did he flirt thus with his serving maids? 'What would his highness like me to say?'

He seemed amused by me in the same way the queen was amused by her new puppy. 'His highness would like the truth.'

'As a true subject of the king's, I will say to his face whatever he wishes to hear.'

'And as a true and obedient daughter, I have no doubt you grant the same favour to your father.'

'That she does, my lord,' my father broke in. 'For often have I told her that just as a child must be obedient to his parent, a loyal subject must be obedient to the king. And therefore it behoveth for a child to be doubly obedient, both to the father and the king, for the king is the father of a country . . .'

My father prattled on, but I regarded the king more closely. For all his faults, he was a clever man who had heard the words behind my words. Cleverer than the queen, I thought with a pang of disloyalty.

'Polonius,' the king said, 'you have a pearl beyond price.' He turned his eyes to me. 'Leave us. I have a matter to lay before your father.'

I made a deep curtsey and scurried out of the hall. Quick as I could, I hurried up the winding stairs to the minstrel gallery and slipped beneath the hangings and peeked out its spy hole at the top of the stairs. The king and my father were deep in conversation. The one handicap of this place was that I could either see what was going on in the hall through the spy hole or I could crawl on my hands and knees into the actual gallery and hear what was taking place, but I couldn't both see and hear. Now I chose to listen, so I fell to my hands and knees and carefully crept into the little balcony that stood above the dais. One of the ghosts, a mournful-faced matron in a purple gown, was leaning against the rails of the balcony. She turned her prune face to watch me crawl in, and then she turned back again to look down on the king.

'I don't know,' my father was saying doubtfully. 'She's not of royal blood.'

'Her birth is not high enough for her to be queen. No, for Prince Holger we must look to one of the other royal courts. I had great hopes for Navarre, but, even to gain alliances with a great kingdom, one cannot expect my boy to stomach a butter-toothed hag of a wife. I'd thought by now this whole business would be concluded, but France says the two little princesses are still too young, and Flanders still hopes for the alliance with Castile. Still, we can afford to be patient there.'

'Then, sire, forgive me for playing the fool, but do you not wish Lord Hamlet to also make a splendid match?'

'Lord Hamlet!' The king's voice sounded as if something bitter had been slipped under his tongue. 'If he were my heir, then certainly, he'd have to make a good marriage. But it's unwise for the peace of a kingdom to permit second sons to marry too high. No, Prince Holger must marry into one of the other great houses, but we must keep Lord Hamlet from an alliance that could give him ambitions of overthrowing his elder brother. Should Hamlet marry into a powerful foreign family, they might use him as a pawn to take over this country and fashion it into a button for their cap. No, it would mean disaster for Denmark if the heir to the throne didn't bring a strong foreign ally into his bed and it would be equal disaster if his younger brother did just that thing.' After a bit of silence, the king added, 'More important, we must keep Denmark's secrets safe in Denmark.'

'Need he marry at all?'

The king sighed. 'His letters pepper me with a request for a wife. He has imbibed too much of the monk's moral brew, I fear. He will not take a common wench to his bed and have done with the business, but he keeps himself pure for a wife!'

My father made sympathetic clucking noises.

The king continued before my father had a chance to speak. 'I've been in despair over where to look for a suitable bride, and then the queen suggested your pretty daughter. I've been watching her, and she may do very well for Lord Hamlet.'

I felt as if my blood had turned to fire. I expected my father to leap at that suggestion like a toad at a gnat, but his voice sounded doubtful. 'She is very young, sire, and Lord Hamlet—'

The king's voice was irritated. 'Yes, yes, we know all that. Perhaps I've talked before the idea had a chance to properly ripen, but I wanted to give you a hint of what is in my mind.'

'My lord—'

'All I ask of you is that you let your daughter meet him and afterwards sound her out.' You and I both know that his is an unusual situation. We both know that the woman he takes to wife must not be one who will turn town crier when she learns what he is.'

What secret were they hiding about Lord Hamlet?

'I've spoken too much,' the king said. 'Let events play out how they will. Come with me. I wish to inspect the custom sheds before dusk.'

They left. Although the minstrel gallery was near as chilly as the great hall, I scooted into a sitting position, my back against the wall and my knees hugged to my chest. I felt if I stood up, I might tumble back down again. I felt giddy with the possibility in front of me. The king was thinking of me as a proper wife for Lord Hamlet. A future beyond my fondest dreams. Always I'd been eager for Hamlet to return, but now I burned with impatience.

Finally I could sit still no longer. I raced up to the battlements. The wind whistled around it, scouring the stones with tiny flecks of ice. The chill lashed through my gown as if it were woven from moonbeams instead of wool, and my skin felt glazed with ice.

'Where is your cloak?' Yorick stepped out from behind one of the stone turrets.

'The king wants me as a wife for Lord Hamlet!' I shouted, and then I began to dance about the battlements, the wind whirling me around with unseen hands, stirring my dance to a feverish pitch.

'Stop it!' Yorick's voice was as icy as the wind. I stopped short in amazement. Never before had he spoken to me in such a sharp tone.

He hobbled over to me on his bowed legs and laid his little hands on my shoulders. I couldn't feel his touch at all, only two icy weights. In spite of myself, once I stopped moving about, I felt frozen inside and out.

'Listen to me, Lady Ophelia, and pay heed. I have two things to say.'

I began to shiver.

'First, what the king says and what the king wants are two things entirely different. Do not be a baby and take his words at their surface meaning. Delve deep and discover what he truly intends.'

I didn't like it, but Yorick's comment made sense. 'What game do you think he might be playing here?' I stammered out between teeth that were chattering with the cold.

'It could be that he's somehow testing your father, his loyalty, his ambition, or something else entirely. Or it could be that he's testing you.'

'Or perhaps he's testing the queen,' I ventured. 'It was her notion.' I shivered more violently. Underneath the wind, the cold seemed to be squeezing me to death.

Yorick nodded. 'That could indeed be the case. The king is a man of so little honesty in himself that his own villainy has veiled his eyes, making him see dishonesty whenever he looks at others.'

'Two things. You said two things.'

'This second one comes hard to me.'

I'd grown so cold that I could barely listen. 'Let us go inside because I'll perish out here if we stay another minute.'

He gave me a little shake. 'What I have to say, I dare not say indoors. It would be treason of me to speak and, more importantly, treason of you to hear.'

'Then tell me quick for I'm near frozen to death.'

'Lady Ophelia, be wary of Lord Hamlet.'

I broke away from him and took a couple of tottering steps backwards. 'How dare you! You have always told me you loved him well.'

'It's because I love him well that I warn you thus. Lady Ophelia—'

'No! I'll not listen. How can you betray him thus?'

'Lady Ophelia, true love doesn't blind us to the faults of those we love. And it's because I love young Hamlet that I—'

I'd listen no more. I clapped my hands over my ears and ran toward the door. I had to jerk at it twice before it creaked open, and then I fled back to my chambers, to the warmth of both the fire and my dreams.

To my fury, that night my father, too, spoke to me about Lord Hamlet's visit.

'I hear Lord Hamlet joins us for the Yule revels, Ophelia. You haven't met him, I think.'

I sidestepped his implicit question. 'I saw him once when he passed through the village. Truly I found him a glorious prince.'

My father made a sour face. 'All that glisters is not gold.'

'Are you saying that Lord Hamlet is not gold?'

He hesitated, and then he said, 'Prince Holger is gold indeed, but there are some who deem young Hamlet . . . or who might deem if they knew the bent of our conversation . . . fool's gold.'

'Do you call Lord Hamlet a fool, then, sir?'

'No, no. You mistake my meaning. It's simply that . . .' His voice trailed off as if he couldn't follow his words.

'Yes?' I asked, feeling a challenge rise up in my heart.

'I've wandered afar from the matter, child. I don't call Lord

Hamlet a fool, for he's a clever young man indeed, although perhaps more clever in mind than in deed, but he's indeed clever in mind. No, his mind is as nimble as a candle-leaper's feet, but, mind you, there's more to a man than his mind, and a man's wit can be lacking though his mind be sharp, and—'

'Are you calling Lord Hamlet a lackwit, sir?'

'No!' He looked scandalized. 'No, Lord Hamlet is a witty young man, although one's wits can be sharp and one's sense may be—'

'Then what is it, sir, you wish to say about him?'

His eyes bore deep into mine. 'Treat him with courtesy as befits the daughter of the king's chief advisor. But don't make free with your time or favours. See him only in company. Better than that, make yourself scant of time while he is about.'

What was he saying? This ran directly contrary to what the king had commanded. I'd never known my father to do anything contradictory to the king. What about Hamlet could be grave enough for my father to defy the wishes of the king?

He frowned at me. 'Do you understand me, Ophelia?'

I didn't understand him in the least, but empty words of obedience oiled the machinery of our relationship, so I cast my eyes down and murmured, 'I hear you and understand you, my lord.'

Lord Hamlet arrived four days later.

13

The morning of his arrival, it snowed again. Fat, fluffy flakes as big as baby chicks. Folks kept muttering that never had Denmark seen such a bitter winter. I fretted that the roads would be too packed with snow to let a traveller pass.

I'd taken extra pains with my appearance, weaving the hair on either side of my face into two long plaits with a silver ribbon woven in them and then catching them at the back of my head. I longed to wear my new Christmas gown of silver embroidered with gold, but since this wasn't a feast day, I knew to dress in such a showy fashion would occasion unwelcome comment. Instead I wore my third-best gown of a blue so pale as to appear almost white.

The queen laughed when she saw my hair.

'Here, child, let me do that for you.'

I was a little hurt. 'I thought it looked pretty.'

She sobered immediately, although her pale eyes still danced with amusement. 'So it does, but sometimes it can be hard to tidy your own hair. It's a task best done by others.' She shook my hair free and wove it again. Then she let me look at myself in her glass, and, in spite of myself, I had to admit that her version was much more attractive.

Never had a morning dragged on so long. Each time I fancied I heard the clatter of hooves down in the courtyard, I raced to the window to see if Lord Hamlet had arrived. In preparation for Christmas, the queen had me read to her from a book of days, a tedious volume with lessons to ladies on how to win their way to heaven. I suspected the queen had me read the book as an attempt to tame me and make a pious Christian of me. Lord knows she herself didn't need the lessons. I wanted to shriek with frustration, and, after a while, I wanted to shriek just for the pleasure of shrieking. But I dutifully sat at her side and let my voice drone on and on while she stitched on and on until finally the door to her chamber flew open.

Lord Hamlet stood in the doorway.

'My dearest mother!' he cried, and in four steps he'd covered the distance from the door to her chair. He scooped her up in his arms, sweeping her feet right off the floor. 'My dearest mother! My own true love!' Then he whirled her around in a circle while she laughed with delight.

'Put me down!' she gasped, half laughing and half scolding. 'Is this a proper way for a prince to behave?'

'It is the proper way for a loving *son* to behave,' he said, but he set her down gently on her feet.

She laid one of her long thin hands against his cheek and then pressed a kiss onto his lips. 'I am heartily glad to see my ramshackle son.'

'I'd think in this snowstorm, any kind of *sun* would be welcomed.' He laughed at his own pun. 'How does my mother?'

'Better now that you're here,' she said, stroking his cheek.

'Then I'm content to bring *sun*shine into my mother's room.'

He was even more beautiful than I remembered. Tall, although not quite as tall as in my memory. His hair was still a pale white-blond like the feathers of a snowbird, and any lady would envy his long dark lashes over his heavy-lidded eyes. There was a quickness of understanding in his face that made it more attractive than his brother's coarser features. His travelling cloak was sober in colour but of finely tanned leathers, soft as a baby's skin and lined with thick sables. He had a particularly beautiful voice, deep but musical and more supple than the skins of his cloak. He had a way of caressing every word he spoke as if it was something cherished and dear that he hated to give away.

'Now where's our good Elspeth?' he demanded, looking around.

She'd been huddled in her usual corner by the fire, but she'd risen when Lord Hamlet had entered the room, and in one giant stride he was at her side. He threw his arms around her and lifted her off the ground in a bear-hug.

'Now leave me be, master, do, for I'm too old for your antics and you're no longer a schoolboy,' she scolded in a fond tone.

He set her down and looked down at her, his eyes twinkling. 'Not you, dear Elspeth. I vow, you grow younger every time I set eyes on you. You must be a sorceress to be able to travel backward in time the way you do. By my next visit, I expect to find you weaving your hair with primroses and dancing around the Maypole with all the other village maidens.'

'Leave off, Master Hamlet,' she said. 'Be not so daft.'

There was the barest flicker of silence, as if a ghost had passed through the room or as if time itself had given a little shiver. Or perhaps it was just a mad fancy of mine, because the moment vanished before my mind could lay hold of it and puzzle it out.

Trey trotted up to sniff at Lord Hamlet's boots. He caught the puppy up and lifted him gently. 'Now who is this pretty fellow?' he asked. 'My mother's newest admirer? Should I turn jealous and fall into a green and yellow melancholy at thus being supplanted in my mother's favour?'

'Hamlet, meet Master Trey, the newest member of my household.'

Lord Hamlet nuzzled the puppy's belly, and Trey waved

his stubby little legs in delight. 'I command you, sirrah, to be my mother's faithful knight and watch over her well when I'm not here to champion her.' He set Trey down and laid a gentle hand on his mother's shoulders. 'As I wrote you, Mother, I'm heartily sorry about Blanche.'

'She was only a dog,' the queen said, but she slid a hand up and squeezed her son's.

His glance flickered over to me, and his face lit up. 'By all that's marvellous, who is this nymph in your chambers? Has Diana herself forsaken the wood and come to shelter here out of the snows and bitter weather?'

I smiled up at him. 'I'm the second newest member of your mother's household.'

He squatted down and lifted the puppy up so it looked as if Hamlet were talking into his ear. 'Forgive me for saying this, Master Trey, but I fear you're not the prettiest member of the household.'

'This is Ophelia, Lord Polonius's daughter,' the queen said. 'Ophelia, meet my slippery-tongued son.'

I began a curtsey, but his hand shot out and pulled me upright. 'It is I who must bow before you,' he said, and he touched his knee to the ground in obeisance. 'For ever must nobility bow to beauty. And in truth, lady, saving only the queen my mother, you're the fairest thing I've seen in many a year.'

I laughed. 'I'd be flattered, sir, but I haven't heard tell that Germany is bereft of beautiful maidens. Or have I been misinformed?'

He squeezed my hand a little tighter. 'I'd be glad to take the time to inform you of anything you would know, lady.'

I inclined my head in a little gesture of pleasure. I was of two hearts. Part of me was glad that he found my present beauty appealing, but the other part sorrowed because it was clear that he failed to recognize me as the Flying Catgirl of the play.

'Have you come alone?' the queen asked, and Hamlet let my hand drop.

'I've brought Rosencrantz and Guildenstern with me.'

The queen smiled. 'They are most heartily welcome. It eases my heart to see such good friends.'

He caught up her hands in both of his. 'Oh, Mother,' he said. 'I've brought you such gifts.'

'My son, your presence is gift enough.'

'You say that now, but see what treasures I shower upon you.'

He let go of her hands and clapped his three times. Suddenly the room filled with servants lugging huge flat pieces swaddled in white cloth bindings. Most were the size of a chessboard, but some were as big as a table cloth.

'O look and see!' the prince called out and clapped again.

The servants began to unwrap the pieces. I drew close to look at them. Elspeth cast him a disapproving glance.

'What bee up the tail have you taken this time, my boy?'

He just laughed.

Each package contained a painting. Never have I seen art such as this. All other painted pictures in the church and the castle were of the holy family or Bible scenes, but these pictures showed ordinary people at ordinary tasks. Each surface was crowded with all manner of folk, peasants tilling the fields and nobles riding past with hawks on their wrists, and down in one corner, monks making merry around a cask of wine. The colours were rich and earthy. I could look at each one for a week entire and still not see everything there was to see in it.

'Do you like them?' With a start I realized he was talking to me.

'They're glorious,' I said. 'The most beautiful work that ever I've seen.'

His eyes shone. He lifted my hand in his. His hand was surprisingly warm. He raised my hand to his lips and kissed it. 'They're the second most beautiful works that ever I've seen,' he said, looking at me in a way that turned my winter stomach to a garden of butterflies.

At the evening meal, he sat on the dais next to his mother. On her other side sat two newcomers that I hadn't previously seen, a squat, burly man with a red-gold beard and a thin fellow with a pinched face and a scar at the lower corner of his left eye that dragged the whole eye downward. I assumed these were the prince's two school companions. The queen was almost rosy with pleasure, dividing her conversation between her son and his friends and looking equally delighted with each. Although the king sat on Prince Hamlet's other side, only twice did I see him exchange a word with this son, although he talked steadily to Prince Holger.

We ate sparingly, for this was the night of the winter solstice celebration in which all the folk in Denmark welcome back the sun. A double homecoming, for both the sun in the sky and the son in the castle. The custom was to drag logs out to the shore and build a huge bonfire. The kitchen staff would haul out sleds crammed with cauldrons of steaming stew and hot spiced honey beer with melted butter floating on top. There was something particularly comforting about this celebration. In the village we'd celebrated the same way with exactly the same foods. I liked knowing that all folk, high born and low, were doing exactly the same thing on this particular night.

After the stew and honey beer, the older folk would withdraw to their beds, but the younger folk, well-bundled and mittened, would dance and sing until the sun returned in the morning. In the ancient days when folk were less knowing about the ways of the world, they actually did believe that the fires and celebrations would call the sun to return to the world and saw as proof of this that each day now grew a little longer than its elder brother in the line of days. We now knew that this wasn't the case. The days would grow longer even without our celebration, but, good Danes that we were, we saw no reason to forsake a party just because it wasn't needed to coax the sun's return.

My father liked to be there on shore from the very beginning, bustling about and making sure that the brawny working men who piled the wood did so just right, but he ordered me to remain in our chambers until the queen and Elspeth joined the company, just before midnight. The past two years the queen hadn't stayed long. She never had much appetite for revelry. I'd hated that when she'd returned to the castle, my father had made me accompany her. Back in the village I'd been permitted to stay at the midwinter fires for the whole night long.

Because the cooks were busy preparing the cauldrons of midwinter stew, everyone therefore put up with the meagre supper of brown bread and dried fish. In any case, I was too excited about the return of Prince Hamlet to swallow even a portion of my supper. I kept feeling the press of his warm, soft lips against the back of my hand. I hadn't known that a man's lips could be so very soft, or that a hand could tingle afterwards in just such a way.

Several times early in the meal, I saw Hamlet's eyes searching the hall as if he'd lost something and thought if he cast his gaze just once more about the place, the missing item might turn up. Then he spotted me. We looked at each other steadily across the long distance, and then he lowered his eyes down to his plate, a little smile playing about his lips. After that, his eyes swept the hall no more, but each time came direct to mine as if my eyes were magnets and his made out of tin. Or perhaps I was confusing the gaze of our eyes with the feeling in my heart, for I felt as implacably pulled toward him as the tides are pulled toward the moon. I'd hoped that the king might call my father forth to let him greet Prince Hamlet, but as soon as the queen arose, my father hurried me off to my room, there to await her summons to go with her down to the shore.

I was certain that Lord Hamlet would join in the festivities, and I felt almost as certain that he'd seek me out. He'd *recognized* me. Not as the girl in the play, but as someone important to him. I spent my waiting time in my chamber in a despair of trying to tidy myself up. Oh, how I hated that I'd been such a headstrong child. I should have spent this past year trying harder to be a fine lady worthy of such a prince. My hair was a wilderness, and my hands were rough with jagged nails. Whenever the queen moved, she seemed to float above the ground, but my feet were firmly on the earth. I walked quickly and lightly enough, but it was as if all my limbs burst with energy, and I was always throwing myself around like a hoyden or an unbroken filly. How I wish I'd learned to move in the delicate, half-alive way of the queen and the other fine ladies. I moved like a peasant girl, all fire and sass, and not with the dreamy drifting of a would-be queen. *Don't let that put him off me*, I prayed.

My clothes, too, were a disaster of a different sort. I favoured the hearty wool gowns that let me tramp all over the castle. The queen's clothes were thin and fine. This meant she never dared move too far from the fireplace for fear of freezing to death, but it gave her the elegance that now I suddenly craved. I pawed through my chest of clothing, but suddenly all the gowns that had once seemed so grand looked coarse and homely. Tomorrow I'd beg my father to have some new ones made for me.

I nipped down to the kitchen and sought out Piet. The kitchen was hot with all the roaring cook fires. I couldn't imagine hell itself being much warmer. All the kitchen folk and all the laundry maids and stable lads, too, bustled about in a mad frenzy of activity. I found Piet counting out dried juniper berries to put in each cauldron of spiced honey beer.

'I need some sheep fat,' I said to him, 'to rub into my skin.'

'I cannot leave this task,' he said with a frown, not at all glad to see me. 'Come back day after tomorrow.'

I stamped my foot. 'Then will be too late.'

'Too late for what?' He scooted one little pile of the black dried berries to the side and began to count out another. Such work would have driven me mad, but was well suited to Piet's careful temperament.

'I expect to dance with Prince Hamlet tonight at the festivities, and I must soften my hands.'

He snorted. 'You will be wearing gloves, so he'll never guess whether your hands are soft or no. Come back day after tomorrow.'

'No!' I was sure the prince's hands were sensitive enough to feel the roughness of my own hands through the leather of my gloves. 'I need sheep fat now!'

He gave a cross sigh, but he knew I could be a spitfire when my fixed will was opposed. 'Down in the undercellar. In the room full of barrels. In a brown barrel against the outside wall.'

I thanked him and made my way through the press of people to the winding stairs that led down to a low-roofed chamber underneath the foundations of the castle. The room was thick with barrels. Many of them were brown, even against the outside wall. I opened three of them before I came to the one I sought, a barrel two-thirds full of a thick oil skimmed from the water in which sheep's fleeces are washed. Men who wash the fleece from sheep have the tenderest hands in the kingdom. There's a greasy substance that clings to the fleece that softens the hands. I wondered how much my hands could be softened in a single night.

There were some empty flasks on a shelf on the wall, and I dipped one into the gooey liquid and filled it full of the stuff and then I threaded my way back through the kitchen. In a corner was the girl I'd first seen go to the king's chambers. Now she sullenly stirred a pot over the fire, mopping her sweaty forehead and cheeks from time to time with the sleeve of her gown.

Back in our chambers, I went first to my father's cabinet. It was locked, but I took a hairpin and worried the lock until it opened. Inside I found a small sack of salt. In the Danish court, folk still took their own salt with them to the meals. I half-filled a little purse, and then I shut the lock again. I hurried into my bedchamber. First, I sprinkled some of the thick brown-white salt onto my hands and rubbed hard until some of the roughest skin flaked away. Then I poured just a little of the sheep fat onto my hands, rubbing until it all melted into my skin. I stroked both my hands against my cheek. They felt a little smoother, although not nearly as smooth as I hoped.

I changed into a cherry-red gown. It was perhaps over-bright for my complexion and would have better suited a dark-haired woman like Judith, but it would be covered with my cloak so the red wouldn't be seen against my skin and the skirt would look very appealing in the dancing, swirling brightly underneath my brown cloak. The memory of Judith hit me with a pang. How I missed her. I wished she were here so I could confide in her about Prince Hamlet and what the king had said about marrying the two of us.

A little before midnight, Elspeth appeared at my door, inviting me to join the queen for her progress to the bonfires. I bundled myself into my cloak and mittens and wrapped a long scarf around my throat. I hoped Hamlet would be in the queen's chamber and so travel down to the fire with us, but the queen was alone, looking beautiful and tall in her thick ermine mantle. She smiled. 'Ophelia, your eyes are bright as starshine.'

Oh, how I loved the sight of the huge bonfires on the shore, roaring defiance to the dark, spreading night. I loved the ferocity of the flames, the way they held nothing in reserve but went after life full force. I loved their violent slash of red and orange against the dark sky, as if the fire was shouting over long distances to its faraway cousins, the stars, 'Come home, come home.' I loved the smells: the salty sea air crisp and cold in my nostrils, the dark and savoury odour of the stew, and the thin, sharp scent of the hot honey beer. I loved the tune of the pipes and the thud of drums, creating night music in a place where music was seldom heard. I loved the jumble of folk, blacksmiths pressed cheek to jowl with knights and laundry maids bumping into the noble ladies.

To my disappointment, I didn't see Prince Hamlet. I saw the king and Prince Holger seated on upturned logs and talking with some fishermen. My father was busy getting in the way of the kitchen folk, spying on them with an eye so sharp that you'd have thought my father himself had paid for all the food. I saw Piet ladling up mugs of fragrant stew, but I didn't see Yorick at all in the throng. This surprised me. I'd have thought the king's fool to be in the middle of all this merriment.

The dancing hadn't yet begun, so I consoled myself that certainly Prince Hamlet would join us by that time.

The queen laid a hand on my shoulder. 'Ophelia, these gentlemen are Lord Rosencrantz and Lord Guildenstern.' I saw she was standing with the two strange men from supper. 'They have come from Wittenberg for our Yule revels.'

Lord Rosencrantz was the one with the scarred eye. Up close I saw that his face wasn't pinched at all, just too long and a little sad. I couldn't tell for certain in the flickering light of the bonfire, but I thought that his scarred eye was blind and he could see only out of the other since he turned his face slightly to that side to look at me. Lord Guildenstern had hair red as a fox although his beard was a little darker than the pelt on his head. He was shorter than I'd realized at supper. His torso and head were that of a normal man, but his legs were undersized so that he wasn't much taller than Yorick and half a head shorter than me. They seemed odd friends for Prince Hamlet. As beautiful as he was, I'd have expected him to choose handsome friends, not this ill-assorted pair whose looks were almost as damaged as those of the king's fool.

'You have travelled from Wittenberg with the prince?' I asked.

Lord Rosencrantz bowed. 'It was our privilege and our pleasure.'

Lord Guildenstern said nothing. He just stood there, looking a little bored.

'Have you known the prince long?' I asked.

'Since we were first crawling,' Lord Rosencrantz said.

I wondered if they, too, were younger sons and that was why their fathers could spare them for such long study at Wittenberg.

'Where is Prince Hamlet?' It wasn't my place as either a woman or a subject to ask this question, but I wanted the information and I didn't know how else I would get it.

Luckily the queen echoed my question. 'Yes, indeed, where is my truant son?'

There was just the briefest pause, and then Lord Rosencrantz said, 'I have no doubt he'll join us presently, your majesty.'

'But where is he now?' she asked. One of her hands curled into a fist and the other closed over it and kneaded the base of her fingers.

The two men exchanged a glance. This time it was Lord Guildenstern who spoke. 'He said he had a plan to enliven the festivities, Madam.'

'Enliven? How enliven?'

But before she could question further, a murmur of amazement rippled through the crowed, and several people pointed back toward the castle. I turned to look, and I felt just as amazed as the rest.

The whole top of the castle was ablaze with lights. Torches had been carefully placed along each of the turrets on the battlements, and then the whole had been lighted, so it was as if the castle itself was crowned with a halo. The sight was beautiful beyond all imaginings.

The queen let her breath out in wonder. 'Is this, then, the work of my clever son?'

I didn't need to hear the answer. Of course it was. Of course it was Prince Hamlet who had envisioned such a possibility and created such beauty. He was a wizard, transforming solid, stolid, flat Denmark into a shimmering bauble.

Lord Rosencrantz answered her in surprisingly careful tones, 'I doubt not but that it is, Majesty. Your son has a fondness for such fancies, turning things into what they're not.'

Then, at a corner of the battlements, I saw Yorick, his head and shoulders barely topping the stone wall. He was gesturing frantically, gesturing to me to return to the castle. All at once I realized that this could be my chance to speak with Hamlet alone. The queen was busy talking with her sons' friends, so I slipped through the crowd and hurried back up the path to the castle.

Never before had I seen the castle like this, all dark and silent. Few ghosts glided through the hushed hallways. I suspected that even they'd roused themselves enough to drag to the casements to watch the festivities. Yorick met me just inside the gates.

'Lord Hamlet wishes to see you,' he whispered to me.

I followed Yorick up the narrow winding stairs to the battlements. The glory on the roof was even more beautiful close up. It was as if each turret and abutment blazed with its own inner fire, and all the torches had turned the night to day. Overhead arched a sky sprinkled thick with stars and one fat shining globe of a moon, dangling like a pearl worn at the throat of God Himself. The snow on the roof glittered as if it weren't snow at all but powder made of ground diamonds. There was music playing, a slow sad tune. My heart ached with beauty and longing.

Yorick inclined his head to the figure of the prince who stood with his back to us, looking down to the bonfires as if trying to gauge how his subjects liked his treat.

'My Lord Hamlet!'

He whirled around, his black cloak swirling about him even darker than the night sky. His face lit up with pleasure when he recognized me. 'Lady Ophelia! By all that's marvellous!'

'This fairy kingdom of light is what's marvellous, sire. Never have I seen anything so beautiful.'

He bounded over to me. 'But you've brought a gift of such beauty that puts all my torches to the blush.'

'A gift, sire? I don't fathom your meaning. I bring nothing but myself.'

'And so my case is proved.'

I felt a blush rise in my cheeks. I hadn't yet learned the game of flirtation, but I did know better than to take his words as true coin. To change the subject, I asked, 'Do you hear the music, sire?

'I hear the singing of my heart.'

'The other music, Lord Hamlet. Do you mark it?'

'The only other music I hear is the plainsong of your gentle voice.'

'Sire, I hear a tune comes out of neither your heart nor my mouth.' This music played a soft dance tune, all strings and one mournful reed. At first I thought it must be the pipes and drums from the bonfires, but surely they were too far distant with their sound too thin to float all the way up here. Besides, there were no strings in the bonfire band. This music was soft as falling snow and a little sad. All the bonfire ditties would be hearty and lively. 'Can you not hear it, my lord?'

'Between my heart and your voice, I need no other music. Perhaps, child, in your chastity and innocence you hear the music of the spheres. Scholars often say that in the season of our Lord's birth, the stars themselves do croon carols of joy, but most mortals are too corrupt to hear the purity of the celestial airs.' For a moment his face grew wistful. 'I wish I could tune my ear to catch those tunes, for it is said they're the most wondrous melodies.'

Impulsively I snatched up his hand and pressed it to my heart. 'My heart keeps step with the music, sire. Can you now feel its beat?'

The music did indeed keep the same beat of my heart, and even with his hand as a barrier, I could feel the beat-thump, beat-thump, beat-thump of my own rhythm through his hand. All of a sudden his eyes lit up. He threw back his head and started to laugh. He grabbed both of my hands in his and he began to spin me around in a wild circle. 'I hear it,' he cried, laughing and spinning more wildly. The wind scraped against my cheeks, but I was gasping and laughing too. 'I do hear the music.'

And then, right on top of the battlements, surrounded by the hundreds of torches, he spun me into the first steps of a pavane. The music kept time with our steps. Lord Hamlet was a wonderful dancer, graceful and strong. Each time we moved together for a lift, he thrust me high into the air, so quick and free that I felt as if I was about to take flight. We didn't speak as we danced, but gradually, slyly, the music grew faster and faster till my breath felt like a sword thrust into my chest. All at once he spun me in till I was pressed against him, breast to chest. Through his cloak his body felt as warm as a brazier, and his clothes gave off a marvellous scent of dried orange peels and cloves. I tilted my chin up to look at him, and his brown eyes looked deep into mine, and then he began to lower his face and I knew he'd kiss me. In spite of myself, I tilted my head back a little more. The music had stopped, and our breaths were harsh in the night like rasps scraping back and forth across unplaned wood. As his face came closer, I could even smell the rich spiced wine on his breath.

My knees felt wobbly and I was glad he held me so firmly because I was sure that if he let go of me, I'd tumble to the ground. Time itself seemed frozen, as if we'd been lifted right out of the world and plunked down in a place where the only sounds were our breath and hearts and Lord Hamlet himself was as vast as the sky. I felt wrapped in the heat of his body the way a martyr would be wrapped round and round with flames. I felt that I'd die if he didn't kiss me right now, and I felt that I'd die if he did.

Then he gave a little shake of his head and pulled away from me. I stumbled, but I caught one of the stone outcroppings to hold me upright.

His breath was harsh and laboured. 'Lady, get yourself down to your chambers, because I'm not safe here with you tonight.'

He took several steps, backing away, but still kept his eyes fixed on me.

I stepped toward him. The snow squeaked beneath my feet. 'My lord, my only pleasure is to bring you pleasure.'

His face darkened. 'I am indifferent honest, lady, but I would not imperil your virtue for all the swords in Denmark, and yet, if we linger in this magic dream any longer, I dare not answer for the honour of either of us.' A rueful smile swept over his mouth. 'I doubt not but we're both a little drunk on the beauty of the night and too caught up in the spell of the music that's not music. Get you to your chamber, Ophelia, and on the morrow we'll both rejoice that we let this danger pass.'

I couldn't bear to leave the magic of the night. 'My lord—'

He stepped farther away. 'Lady Ophelia, tomorrow let us meet and talk of these things. It's not prudent for either of us to follow where this night does take us.'

I took one step toward him and stretched out my hands. 'I have no wish to be prudent, my lord.'

'Then I must be prudent for both of us, lady.'

'No, my lord. Throw prudence to the winds, for I'll have none of it. Give me magic.'

He smiled although he continued to breathe as hard as if he'd been running a long distance. 'Lady, you're too innocent to play duenna to your chastity, so I must be the dragon at our gate.' He touched the tips of his fingers to his lips and then turned the fingers toward me as if he'd kiss me without touching me. 'Sleep well, my Ophelia, and dream of all the wonders of fairyland. On the morrow, we'll talk.'

I wanted to fling myself at him, but my head recognized the wisdom of his words even if my heart wanted to break the bonds of reason and tumble him into madness, evil, hell itself. *There will be other nights and lots of days*, I reminded myself. This would be the first of many pleasures. I didn't need to gobble down everything all at once.

'Till tomorrow, my lord.' I swept him my best curtsey and headed across the parapet to the curving stone staircase. I felt as if a fire had consumed all my insides and left nothing except a yearning for him. I tottered as I went, and it wasn't that my footing was made slippery by the snow. No one in the history of the world had ever felt such a gigantic yearning, for most people would never be strong enough to survive this hunger, this fever of the blood, this madness.

Just as I reached the steps, I spotted the source of the music. There, huddled in a corner out of the wind, was a small group of minstrels holding a viol, a lute, an oboe, and some tiny silver bells. They'd played that sublime, sad music that had grown wilder and wilder until both Lord Hamlet and I were aflame.

The musicians were all ghosts.

I'd never particularly minded the ghosts before, but for the most part they'd kept themselves out of my life.

Things had changed this night.

I wondered why ghosts were nudging me toward Lord Hamlet.

14

He didn't talk to me the next day.

For the entire court, middag was a rather sullen affair. Since most people had stayed awake until dawn (which had come only an hour or so earlier), few folk had bothered to go back to bed, preferring to wait until after their midday appearance in the hall. Most weren't hungry, and many were in the dregs of drunkenness, that gloomy state in which the sweet frenzy of the liquor had departed leaving only sour stomachs, aching heads, and dry mouths. Although I'd retired to my chamber as Lord Hamlet had ordered me, I'd not fallen asleep for a long time, and so my own eyes were heavy and sore. Most of the folk at table didn't speak at all, and those that did converse chose to grumble rather than chatter. We Danes love revelry, but in the winter darkness we can be a heavy-hearted lot, and the day after the solstice celebration tended to show us at our worst.

The king glowered at the whole company, and Prince Holger sulked. The queen drifted through the meal looking more ghostly than any of the ghosts I saw about the castle. I didn't see Yorick, and even my father seemed subdued. Lord Hamlet wasn't at the high table, and his empty place looked as obvious as a bruise. I had no stomach for the rich venison stew, choosing instead a few pickled beets that had been carved to look like roses. Piet's handiwork and very well done, but I frowned to think how his hands would look as bloody as Herod's soldiers for days afterwards, stained with the juice of the beets. When I lifted a morsel to my mouth, the sweet-sharp smell of the vinegar made my stomach flop, and I lowered the food untasted. I felt too excited, too much on fire to eat such a squishy food, so I made my entire meal of a few bites of the flat bread and a few sips of beer. Perhaps the thing I missed most about living in the castle was sweet water drunk fresh from a stream.

Where was he? Last night he'd said we'd talk this day, and I felt like I'd burst into flames if I couldn't see him soon. At least the queen didn't dawdle over her meal, and as soon as she rose, I threaded among the crowd to Lords Rosencrantz and Guildenstern, waylaying them before they could depart from the hall.

I knew I should employ my father's diplomatic skill, but my words popped out of my mouth with no bark on them.

'Why is Lord Hamlet not at table?'

The two men exchanged worried looks. The scar on Lord Rosencrantz's eye seemed heavier than before, tugging his lower eyelid down almost to his cheekbone. Both men looked tired and a little threadbare.

'Lord Hamlet keeps to his room this morning,' Lord Rosencrantz answered in a cautious tone.

'He is sick and so cannot come to court,' Lord Guildenstern said in a tone even more cautious.

It was as if there was a meaning wedged between their words, but I couldn't make it out.

'What ails him?' I asked.

The men looked at each other again as if their eyes were speaking a language that didn't need their tongues. Finally Lord Guildenstern said, 'Too much revelry last night.'

'He drank too deep and must sleep it off today,' Lord Rosencrantz said. 'At school he partakes sparely of wine, and so he wasn't accustomed to the libations of solstice.'

This didn't ring true. There was more to this mystery than

the words made out. 'I'd hoped to talk with Lord Hamlet today,' I said.

Out of the corner of my eye I saw Lord Rosencrantz's fingers flicker nervously against each other, but Lord Guildenstern remained as stolid as a lump of February butter. 'I don't think Lord Hamlet will be joining the company today. If the matter cannot wait until the morrow, perhaps you'd best share it with us and we'll see what may be done.'

There was no way I'd confide in anyone else.

'It will wait,' I said in what I hoped was a lofty tone.

Unexpectedly Lord Rosencrantz said, 'Has my lord Hamlet done anything . . . anything that he shouldn't do?'

'Hush!' said Lord Guildenstern, looking like a ruddy thunder-cloud.

'I meant only—' began Lord Rosencrantz, his fingers wildly plucking at his doublet, but Lord Guildenstern hushed him again. Lord Rosencrantz looked abashed and sank into silence, but Lord Guildenstern took me by the chin.

'Girl, perhaps you'd best go to the queen with these matters.'

I jerked away from him. 'These aren't matters worth taking up her majesty's time,' I snapped. I turned and marched out of the hall.

I could feel the two men watching me as I left.

I'd planned to spend the afternoon in sleep, but I was too intrigued by the mystery in front of me. Why did his friends claim that Lord Hamlet was too drunk to come to middag. The courtiers were all hard-drinking men, and on the day after the solstice, no one would take offence at a drink-sotted prince. On the contrary, all at court would regard it with good humour, indulgent toward the prince who'd come home on this Yuletide visit. No, it had to be something more than that to keep him from the assembly.

Had he perhaps departed court and for some reason those at the high table were concealing this fact? Had the king been disapproving of his liberty in dotting the roof of the castle with those glorious torches? Had he confined Prince Hamlet to his chambers in punishment? As soon as those thoughts occurred to me, I dismissed them. Lord Hamlet was a man grown. He wouldn't be punished like a child.

Puzzle the matter as I would, I couldn't unravel its mystery.

Finally I gave it all up and tumbled into a dreamless nap.

Lord Hamlet wasn't present at supper either.

I couldn't eat. I worried about him. I wanted to find out what was wrong, but I didn't know where to go for aid. I looked about for Yorick, but he wasn't present. My best guess was that he stayed closeted with the prince. I didn't want to approach his two friends again. They'd given me no information at noonday, and I had no reason to expect them now to be more forthcoming. Finally I whispered to my father, 'I wonder at Lord Hamlet's absence from the table.'

'The affairs of the mighty aren't your concern, girl,' he whispered back, and he scooted his body around to turn his back on me.

Why was Lord Hamlet avoiding me? I spent the meal playing again in my mind the wondrous comedy of the previous night, but I could detect no misspeaking, no misstep that would have driven him away.

I longed to go directly to his rooms, to bang on the doors and demand an answer, but the hall outside the chambers of the royal family was dotted with guards, and while they looked with indulgence on my visits to the queen, I doubted they'd let me approach the prince.

That was it! I could go to the queen. If anything ailed her son, she'd know it.

I was in a fever of impatience for the meal to end. As soon as we were dismissed from the hall, I ran to the queen's chamber, anxious to put this mystery to an end.

I knocked hurriedly on the door, and when Elspeth eased it open, my words tumbled out in a breathless cascade. 'I'm here to visit the queen.'

Her wrinkled face creased into a pucker of concern. 'The queen doesn't feel well tonight, child,' she whispered. 'She will have no visitors this eve.'

'But I want to see her.'

Elspeth shook her head, but her voice remained kind. 'Come back tomorrow, Ophelia. Tonight the queen is closeted with her family only.'

'But—'

She shut the door firmly in my face.

I stamped my foot with fury. I didn't like being shut out.

I saw one of the guards looking at me with amusement, and I glared back at him. What was going on?

I glowered at a serving lad who passed me with a basket of kindling in his hands. I felt like a cat stroked the wrong way, as if my skin gave off sparks of impatience. I didn't like these mysteries one little bit. I stomped back to my closet and plopped down on my bed. I felt angry enough to beat something, but when, unable to sit one moment longer, I snatched up one of my waist-girdles and began lashing it against the bed-clothes, slapping them over and over, I felt foolish rather than relieved. Finally I just sank to my knees and pounded my fists against the bed until I'd skimmed the top off my worry and anger.

Lord Hamlet didn't appear at middag the next day.

I felt furious enough to bite the heads off live salmon. Where was he?

It was Juleaften, the day before Christmas. The servants were busy hanging long ropes of greenery about the hall and preparing for the Christmas Feast the next afternoon.

When the meal concluded, my father said to me, 'Be sure to return before nightfall.'

I looked at him in bewilderment.

He thundered, 'From the village, girl! I wouldn't have you caught out in the darkness for this evening promises to be bitter cold.'

For a moment I couldn't think what he meant, but then I remembered that every Juleaften, I took bottles of wine down to Myg and to the Herbwife to celebrate the season.

Part of me balked at leaving the castle without seeing Lord Hamlet, but my mind knew that if he wasn't present at middag, I'd be unlikely to see him during the rest of the afternoon. Another part of me relished the walk down to the village, using up my excess energy to carve out a way through the opposing wind and snow.

I went to the kitchens to fetch the bottles of spiced wine. With all the preparations for the next day's feast, Piet couldn't accompany me, but, in any case, my mood was so dark that we both would be better off for me to travel alone. It was a more difficult and longer journey than I'd expected with the deepest snow drifts that I'd ever seen. Darkness was already staining the edges of the sky by the time I reached the village. Both Myg and the Herbwife begged me to stay until the morrow and not endanger my safety battling my way back to the castle after dark, but I wouldn't risk missing Hamlet at the festivities of Juleaften evening, so I paid no heed to their requests.

'I can follow the track I broke on my journey here, and so my return will go all the faster,' I assured them, although I wasn't sure that once darkness fell I could see any of my previous path.

The Herbwife lent me a lantern and fixed up a jar of extra oil, and so I set off, ignoring the troubled expression on her face. I wasn't more than two field's lengths out of the village, when I felt a touch on my shoulder. It was Ragnor. I hadn't seen him since the previous summer.

'You've grown so much taller,' I said. I wouldn't be surprised to find that he was now the tallest of the Herbwife's tall sons. I could see little else of him except his merry dark eyes.

'Mother doesn't like you to wrestle the wind all the way back to the castle alone, so she's sent me to keep you company,' he shouted over the roar of the wind.

I was privately glad of his company, although I was indignant that the Herbwife didn't trust me to find my way back to the castle myself. Something of my inner conflict must have shown in my eyes, because Ragnor let out a roar of laughter that seemed even to silence the wind.

'Do not eat me, Cat,' he said, using the nickname that he called me throughout childhood. 'I'm too much at sea these days, so grant me the Yule gift of letting me spend company with a pretty playfellow of my younger days.'

That made me smile. I knew that I didn't look at all pretty just then with my cheeks scoured scarlet by the wind, my eyes red from the gritty bits of ice, and the rest of me wrapped as thick as a bear against the winter cold. He grinned back and fell into step beside me.

Going back was indeed easier than the trip down for the wind was at our backs, pushing us along, and my track through the snow was mostly still visible. Shouting over the wind, Ragnor told me about his life at sea. He claimed to be a trader, but I'd heard rumours that he and his brothers had turned pirate, and finally I confronted him with this charge.

He didn't say yea or nay, but only, 'It would be in the tradition of the Northmen of Denmark to seek our fortunes on the high seas, would it not? For if we're pirates . . . and, mark you, I don't accept that name, we'd never touch a Danish ship. Call us instead patriots and have done with the matter.'

'Patriots? No, I cannot go that far. Adventurers, rather.'

He laughed at this. 'Then adventurers let it be.'

We travelled perhaps a quarter of a mile in silence before I asked, 'Do you kill people, then, upon your adventures?'

He was quiet for a few more paces, and then he said, 'We aren't murderers, Cat. No treasure is worth the life of men, and despite all the stories, sailors would rather give up their cargo than their lives.'

I didn't know whether or not to believe him, but as if he sensed my doubt, he said, 'You have known me nearly all my life, and you've known my brothers, too. Can you think us murderers, Cat?'

I couldn't. The boys were wild, but they had good, noble hearts.

'Do you see foreign lands?' I asked wistfully.

'Not many. Not so far at least. England. We know England well. Mother's people have helped us find safe harbour there. Scotland we visit, and Norway and Sweden and sometimes France and Ireland. Once a year we sail to Spain, Portugal, and Italy. Next we hope to open a trade route with Morocco.'

I let out a sigh loud enough to be heard over the wind. 'How I do envy you.'

His next words almost knocked me over. 'Come with us.'

I stopped so abruptly that he bumped into me and we both tumbled into the snow. He pulled me to my feet and swatted against my cloak to knock off all the clinging snow.

'What did you say?' I asked.

'Come with us.'

'I am a girl.'

'Girls can sail as well as men.'

'I thought it brought misfortune to have a woman aboard a ship.'

'Not our ships.' His eyes warmed into a smile. 'We have built them very solidly, you see.'

For a moment my imagination soared at the thought of sailing the world, but then I collapsed back down into myself. 'I cannot.'

'Why not?'

'My father would never let me go.'

'This is your life, not his. Run away.'

Lord Hamlet's beautiful face flashed into my mind. 'It cannot be. I've chosen a life in the castle. It cannot be.'

He glanced down, and when he looked back up at me, his eyes glinted as cold as the snow itself. 'Cat, I don't like the girl that the castle is changing you into.'

'It's making a lady of me.'

'Then I'm not sure I like ladies.'

I stepped back away from him, and he reached out two gloved hands and pulled me close enough to hear his words. 'Cat, as a child you shone brighter than the sun. You had such spirit, such energy. You gave off light. But now you're letting your light be dimmed.

I jerked my hands away from his and set off for the castle. I wanted no more of his silly words. I wasn't being reduced by the castle. I was being refined.

'Cat—' he called after me, but I pushed my way onward, paying him no attention. He ran and caught up with me, but one glance at my stormy eyes must have warned him to keep silent. We spoke not another word all the way to the castle, and I went inside without a word of thanks. I didn't even offer him a bed for the night or to let him warm himself beside a fire before he set off back home again. I wanted to hear no more of his nonsense, his mean-spirited judgement of me.

To my great relief, Lord Hamlet was at supper.

15

All through our meal of spice breads and herring stewed with nuts and dried berries, Hamlet didn't speak to me, although his eyes often slid over toward me. Whenever I glanced toward him, he looked away. He seemed pale and tired, although that might have been because he was dressed all in black, which drained the little colour from his bleached face and made him look as if he were in mourning even though we'd had no recent deaths at court. He toyed with his food, but he spoke with much animation to his father who ignored him, favouring the remarks of his older brother Holger. After supper, as was the custom of the night before Christmas, we listened to Father Jan read the story of Jesus' birth and then gathered around a sizzling pot to see whose nimble fingers could snatch the flaming raisins from the punch. The king sprawled on the dais, drinking deep of the hot spiced beer, but Prince Holger had quick hands as did his uncle, Prince Claudius, and it soon began a competition between the two of them to see who could collect the most raisins. Neither of them liked the taste of sweetmeats, but each seemed determined to triumph in the contest. Soon all the folk around them were making extravagant wagers on the match, each side cheering on its champion as one more raisin was filched from the steaming pot.

I stood toward the back of the crowd, and all at once I felt hands seize me about the waist.

'Do not turn,' a voice instructed me. 'Keep your eyes straight ahead.'

Lord Hamlet.

He'd sneaked up behind me while I was watching his brother and his uncle.

'We float through a magical night,' he said, his breath tickling my ear and making me want to squirm with pleasure. I could smell the faintest trace of almonds on his breath, and his clothes had the same orange and clove smell I'd noticed before. 'The moon is fat and full and beams down on the earth like a tipsy friar. Lady, will you drive forth with me?'

'I'd travel to the ends of the world with you, my lord.' A prudent girl wouldn't let him know what was in her heart. A modest girl would never leave this company to place herself alone with a young prince. I was neither prudent nor modest. *Give me life rather than virtue.*

'Keep your voice low. Look straight ahead. We want no one to tumble to our private game.'

It was exciting to indulge in this secret commerce in the very heart of the court. I pitched my voice as low as I thought would carry to his ears. 'What means your lordship?'

'I've ordered my sledge made ready. It stands at the gate with four fine horses. Lady, shall we travel across the snow and welcome Hecate, the empress of night?'

I knew my father would forbid it, and I knew that no gently-raised girl would go forth in such a reckless fashion. None of that mattered. All I cared for was another adventure with the prince. 'When shall we leave, my lord?'

He gave my waist an approving little squeeze. 'Wrap yourself warmly and sneak down to the gate.'

It was easy as anything to slip away from the crowd that chanted encouragement to Claudius as he plunged his hand back into the cauldron. I saw no one, not even ghosts, as I padded down the dark hallways to my chamber and there swathed myself in my thick fur cloak, still damp from my afternoon's excursion, and pulled its deep hood over my hair. I ran quickly down the stairs and out the door toward the gate, but something made me glance back to the castle. The battlements were thick with ghosts, more ghosts than I'd ever seen at one time, all staring down at me. I couldn't make out their expressions, but they were as still as a flock of birds you might see assembled on a single bough.

As I approached the gate, I heard voices raised in anger. Lord Hamlet sat in the driver's seat of a grand sledge trimmed with gilt, the reins in his hand. A groom stood holding the bridle of one of the four horses, but next to the sledge stood Lords Rosencrantz and Guildenstern.

'It is folly to venture forth on such a wild ride in the middle of the night,' Lord Guildenstern was saying.

'It's *dangerous* folly,' said Lord Rosencrantz. 'Without a groom, with only the chit of a girl beside you. If you should pitch into a drift, there's no one to pull you and your sledge out, and the ground is treacherous underneath the snow.'

'Even with a full-stomach moon, it's reckless to drive at night,' Lord Guildenstern said.

I slipped past them and wriggled into the seat beside Lord Hamlet. He looked down at me, devilry dancing in his eyes. 'My friends say it's foolhardy of us to set forth, Ophelia.'

I kept my voice prim, although I was sure my eyes were dancing as much as his. 'They are sensible men, my lord.'

'We would be wise to listen to them, would we not?'

'We would indeed.' I gave a loud sigh. 'What a pity that neither of us is wise, is it not, my lord?'

He threw back his head and laughed, his pale hair a silver flame in the snow-blurred night. 'Lady, where should I take you?'

'To the ends of the earth, my lord.'

'Too far.'

'To the edge of madness, then?'

He gave a wry smile. 'That path is too familiar. To the beginning of moonlight perhaps?'

'Too unsteady, my lord. To the doors of death?'

'That journey would be too long for me and too short for you. Pick some other destination.'

I laughed. 'My lord, I care not where we go, but the horses will freeze if they're left to stand much longer, so let us away.'

He gave a shake of the reins, and the groom sprang back from the horses' heads. I felt the sledge shake, and, turning my head, saw that Lords Rosencrantz and Guildenstern had flung themselves onto the back of the sledge, belly down, the way boys might throw themselves into a summer pond. The ground raced away as we flew over the snow. Guildenstern and Rosencrantz scrambled to right themselves, and, past them, I saw the flock of ghosts watching us as we dashed off.

The moonlit world was silent and just as magical as Lord Hamlet had promised. Trees were mere slashes of darkness against the softer black of the night. Once or twice we passed shapes that might have been deer, and once in the distance I spotted a wolf tearing at the body of his prey, but for the most part we were the only living creatures in the entire landscape.

Conversation was impossible. The rushing wind tore our words away before they could battle their way to the ears of the others. After a while I began to sing tunes I'd learned down in the village, and Lord Hamlet grinned. He knew one or two of them, and he joined in on those songs, but mostly my voice drifted alone in the silent night air. A few times I glanced back at Rosencrantz and Guildenstern huddled beneath some fur blankets in the back of the sledge. They looked cold, baleful and miserable. Part of me laughed to see them thus, for they hadn't been invited to come and were thereby well-served for their audacity, but another part of me pitied their discomfort and understood that it was good for my reputation to have them accompany us.

Soon, like a battalion of spies, the cold crept under our fur lap robes and my cloak, and I began to shiver. Lord Hamlet glanced down at me and turned the horses back toward home. I hadn't seen this part of the country before and was amazed to find myself travelling along the shores of a huge lake. Lord Hamlet reined the horses to a stop so we could admire the view. The waters had frozen, and the surface glowed like a black opal or a sullen pearl.

Lord Guildenstern leaned over the seat. 'We should go back,' he shouted. 'Or this cold night will be the death of us all.'

Ignoring him, Lord Hamlet smiled at me. 'It would be a wonder indeed to race our sledge above the waters of a lake,' he said. 'I fancy it would be as near as one could come to flying in this earthbound life of ours.'

Lord Guildenstern gave a squawk. 'My lord, the night is miserable cold, but I doubt me that it's ample cold to freeze the waters solid enough to support horses and a sledge.'

'Jesus travelled atop the water. Can a prince do any less?'

Now Lord Rosencrantz leaned over the back of the seat. 'My lord, you must not!'

'You will kill us for certain,' said Guildenstern.

Hamlet looked deep into my eyes. 'Death comes to us all. Could there be any more glorious way to leave this earth? A race that feels like flying, and then a plunge into the embrace of beautiful black waters.'

Both men chorused, 'My lord!'

Lord Hamlet looked only at me. 'What says my lovely lady? Shall we risk it or no?'

'Hamlet, you dare not!' Guildenstern shouted, his voice shredded to tatters by the ferocious wind.

Hamlet's eyes didn't budge from mine. 'What say you, Ophelia?'

I was torn in two. Part of me was terrified, but part of me was wild to soar across the smooth surface of the lake. Perhaps the biggest part of me wanted desperately to please the prince.

'Do you think the lake will hold our weight?' I asked Hamlet.

'No!' shrieked the two men in the back seat.

'I'm certain it will,' Hamlet said.

'I've always longed to fly,' I told him though my teeth chattered with cold.

'Hamlet, you must not!' Guildenstern shouted.

Lord Hamlet twisted around to his friends in the back. 'Let me propose a course of action. I'll drive down to the shore—'

'No, my lord,' they chorused in perfect unison.

'Hear me out, friends. I drive down to the shore, and then you both climb out and test the ice. Tell me whether you think it solid enough to serve as our road. I'll let you judge before we set out.'

They didn't seem happy but they finally fell in with his suggestion. I was surprised by how tame a plan it was. Lord Hamlet drove us carefully down to the shore and again pulled the sledge to a stop.

'Judge the thinness of the ice,' he said, and Rosencrantz and Guildenstern hopped off the sledge and scurried over to the lake. The shoreline ice was thick and hard, but the two lords hadn't gone very many steps before they turned back to us.

'It's not safe,' Guildenstern said.

'Only a fool would risk it,' said Rosencrantz.

Carefully they began to pick their way back to land.

Because my hood was so deep, I had to turn my head halfway around to see Hamlet. 'Are you a fool, my lord?'

He gave a shake to the reins. 'All men are fools, lady. Now if you haven't the stomach for it, tell me quick, for I too long to fly.'

'Then fly away, my lord, for I'll not say you nay.'

Hamlet rippled the reins and headed the sledge out onto the ice. Perhaps it was my fancy, but I thought I heard it give a deep groan.

Guildenstern shouted, 'Hamlet, stop!'

'You said you'd listen to our judgement,' Rosencrantz called, scrambling after the sledge. Then his feet flew out from under him and he sprawled onto his knees on the ice.

'I said I'd listen to your judgement, but I never said I'd follow it,' Lord Hamlet called over his shoulder, and then we were far past the point of hearing.

We hadn't gone very far when I heard a loud crack, and just ahead a large piece of ice the size of a cart broke away from the rest, exposing the dark waters beneath. There was another crack, and I felt the ice under the sledge start to buckle. I gave a scream and clutched Lord Hamlet's arm, and one of the horses reared and another shrieked, but Lord Hamlet was turning the sledge around, and then we were racing back toward the shore. Louder and louder I heard ice cracking all around us, and behind us one crack seemed to race toward us as if we were its prey. But our sledge reached the shore just before all the ice broke into dozens of pieces above the hungry black water.

Prince Hamlet and I dissolved into a paroxysm of relieved laughter, leaning against each other and gulping down mouthfuls of air so cold it burned out throats. Guildenstern and Rosencrantz marched up to the sledge.

'Your foolishness almost killed you both,' Guildenstern scolded.

I was laughing like a madwoman. I told myself to be quiet, but I couldn't stop.

'I humbly crave your pardon for all my sins,' Lord Hamlet said meekly, and then he joined back in my laughter.

Guildenstern gave a snort of disgust and flung himself back onto the sledge. Rosencrantz didn't say a word, but he squeezed in next to me. We were crowded on the front seat, but it was much warmer to be wedged between two bodies.

'I'll drive,' Rosencrantz said. Hamlet winked at me and handed him the reins.

When we drove back into the courtyard, I noticed all the ghosts were gone.

Rosencrantz pulled the horses to a stop. 'Help the lady Ophelia out, my lord, and hurry her into the castle for she must be near freezing.'

Lord Hamlet climbed down and held out his hand. I took it, but my own hand was so cold that I could barely feel his. 'I can get me in the castle fine,' I told him. 'Get your horses to the stable quickly, for they'll catch a chill if they stand about.'

Lord Guildenstern too popped out of the sledge, but he was charging away like a bull back to the hall without a backward glance or word to anyone.

Hamlet nodded. 'Then I'll take the horses back to the stable, for well have they earned their rest.'

Rosencrantz offered him the reins, and Hamlet kissed my hand although it was still too cold to feel even the touch of his lips. 'Good night, sweet lady, and pleasant dreams attend your slumbers. Never will I forget this enchanted night.'

By this time, Lord Rosencrantz had slipped out of the sledge. 'Lord Hamlet, I'll escort the Lady Ophelia back to the Great Hall.'

I stood shivering until the sledge had disappeared into the stables. Then I followed Lord Rosencrantz out of the yard. As we trudged along the corridors to the hall, Lord Rosencrantz scolded me. 'You might have been killed. Young as you are, you well know it to be dangerous to encourage him in his wildest fancies. Hamlet needs prudence, and if you cared for him, you'd help steady his ship with the ballast of sense, not join him in tossing the rudder overboard.'

'I like Lord Hamlet just as he is. I see no need for him to change.'

'You like him well, then?'

There was no way I was about to discuss my private feelings with Lord Rosencrantz, so I parried with, 'He is a most affable young man. Everyone must like him. You do, do you not?'

When he didn't answer at once, I sneaked a look up at his face. It was very red, whether from cold or embarrassment, I couldn't tell. When he did speak, his words surprised me. 'If the need arose, I'd give my life for him.'

He sounded sincere, so I ventured, 'Then why do you seek to criticize him thus?'

He fumbled for words. 'Sometimes . . . when these mad passions seize him . . . sometimes my lord Hamlet is not . . . sensible. My concern is ever to keep him safe, even if it means keeping him safe from himself.'

How silly! How could he claim to care so much for Lord Hamlet and yet want to change him into something different? That wasn't love. Surely you loved people just as they were, wholecloth, or else you turned your affection to someone else. More than that, I had no great respect for safety. I'd choose passion over safety in a heartbeat.

When we reached the Great Hall, I saw Lord Guildenstern standing next to the king, whispering in his ear. I had no doubt but that he was filling him with poison about Prince Hamlet's behaviour. The king looked like a thundercloud, growing darker and darker, and indeed, when Prince Hamlet strolled into the hall, his normally pale cheeks ruddy with the cold and his eyes bright, the king stood up and bellowed in front of the whole assembly, 'What mad scheme was that?'

Everything came to a halt. Music and conversation stopped,

and all eyes flickered back and forth the length of the hall between the king and his second son. Out of the corner of my eye I saw Prince Holger lean forward, as if he were a snake and the king's scolding a dish of milk, an unlooked-for treat.

I hated him.

I hated all who would hurt Hamlet.

Prince Hamlet grew pale. 'Sir, this is not the proper place to—'

'*I* am the king, sirrah, not you, and *I* will decide what is the proper place. Besides, tonight you've shown yourself a witless fool! To risk so much out on that unstable ice. You could have killed that girl as well as the best horses in my stable, not to mention your foolish self!'

'Father—'

'Silence! You have no sense, and therefore anything you say would be senseless. Perhaps you'd be better suited to play the court fool than the brother of the king to be. Had I not known my queen to be a pattern of virtue, I'd have thought she'd played me false with Yorick the jester, for you seem more suited to be his son than my own.'

The queen spoke quietly but her words were clear. 'Not here, my lord. These are private matters, and therefore are best discussed in private.'

The king ignored her. 'Look at this sad spectre of a son. More monk than man, less warrior than witless. We should have done better to drown him at birth.'

Prince Hamlet's eyes blazed. Prince Holger began to laugh, but there was no other sound in the Great Hall. Then Prince Hamlet turned sharply on his heel and left.

I longed to run after him, to comfort him, to whisper to him that his father was a bully and mean-spirited, but I knew that wasn't my place. Everyone continued to stand stock still. No one knew what to do in the face of such royal fury.

Then a log cracked in the fireplace, breaking the spell. The king roared, 'Bring me some more wine. The rest of you, back to the revels!'

The musicians struck up another tune. I saw my father winding through the crowd toward me, so I hurried out of the hall. I was in no mood for his longwinded lectures. I was equally in no mood for celebration. I burned to avenge Prince Hamlet's humiliation.

I climbed into my bed, but even the thick pile of covers couldn't warm me. I lay for a long time, shivering, remembering the exhilaration of the nighttime ride.

At Christmas mass the next morning, Prince Hamlet didn't show himself. In the winter, Father Jen hurried through the services at a clipping pace because the chapel wasn't heated. There was a single brazier by the queen, but the rest of us stood quivering with cold. At the feast afterwards, Prince Hamlet still didn't make an appearance. The queen looked tired and heavy-eyed. The king and Prince Holger looked worn as if they'd drunk too much wine the night before. A wealth of fine food was set before us, including cakes carved and iced to look like tiny crowns and dozens of roasted geese, but I had no stomach for the feast.

I missed Lord Hamlet.

He didn't appear for seven days.

For that entire week, I held myself apart from Lord Guildenstern. I would never forgive him for exposing Hamlet to his father's wrath. Several evenings, when he asked me to dance with him, I refused. With so many nobles visiting the court, I could dance as much as I chose, for there were many more men than women. I even danced nightly with Prince Holger who was lithe but careless with his steps and apt to stop in mid-figure if he grew bored. For the first four days, I also would neither speak nor dance with Lord Rosencrantz, but on the fifth night I relented. He hadn't been the one to betray Hamlet. I agreed to partner him in the rondelet, a vigorous dance much favoured by the young men at court.

Lord Rosencrantz wasn't a skilled dancer; he was stiff and clumsy. I marvelled at Hamlet's having such misshapen and ugly friends as these two. Next to him they were like trolls surrounding an angel, or apes trailing after the king of the elves. Lord Rosencrantz at least seemed to have a good heart and a genuine friendship for the prince, so once our dance was finished, I ventured to ask him about Hamlet.

'He keeps to himself.' His voice sounded sad. 'He says that the harsh words of his father have exiled him from the celebrations.'

'I wonder he doesn't return to Wittenberg.' The thought of his leaving was a stab in my heart, but I couldn't see why he'd stay only to be shut up in his rooms.

'He has asked permission of his father to depart, but the king told him he must stay until Epiphany, so he holds himself alone, counting down the days.'

I cast a glance of loathing at the king who sat with wine goblet in hand, listening to his brother, Prince Claudius. My father sat on his right hand, a panting lapdog snuggled beside his master, and Osric fluttered around them all, eager to be sent on any errand or do any service, no matter how small or mean.

I hated them all.

'I feel his magic, too,' Lord Rosencrantz said unexpectedly. His eyes were sad and kind. 'I well know how easy it is to fall beneath his spell.' He sighed and looked down at his hands. 'Life is better for him at Wittenberg. When he's away from this court, he's—' he searched for the proper word and settled on '—safer.'

'Safer?'

'From himself. From others. Guildenstern and I keep watch over him, keep him from harm. We share a good life there.'

I couldn't bear the thought of Prince Hamlet's being gone for good. 'He is a prince. His rightful place is here.'

'He has an older brother, an uncle, who will assume the throne when death comes to his father. It's doubtful that our prince will ever rule.'

'He is a better man than all three of them, and he should be the next king.'

'He is a good man,' Lord Rosencrantz agreed, 'but good men don't always make good leaders.'

What nonsense men have let themselves believe. 'Of course they do.'

He smiled at me. In spite of his ugliness, he had an attractive smile. 'Sometimes being a good man is enough,' he said.

Before I could reply he excused himself. 'The queen is beckoning, and I must go to her.'

The next morning my father told me that the king had ordered me to keep my distance from Lord Hamlet.

This confused me. 'I thought the king had wanted me wed to the prince.'

'He has since come to his senses, girl.'

I lifted my chin. 'I should very much like to wed the prince.'

'It's not to be, Ophelia. And to say true, even if the king still desired it, I myself wouldn't wish to swallow that match.'

I was amazed. 'It would make you father-in-law to a prince. Brother-by-marriage to the king himself.'

My father passed a nervous hand across his brow. 'We speak of vain fantasies, Ophelia. It will not come to pass for the king now is firm that Hamlet shall never wed.'

He would say no more about it. For perhaps the first time since I'd known him, my father chose silence over speech even though, for once, I wanted him to talk. What had caused the king to change his mind so abruptly? Had he found a match more fitting, perhaps one with a princess or a woman with a wealthy father? Or was there something else?

What also didn't make sense was that he seemed to relish the recklessness of his elder son, yet he used the excuse of the same quality in Hamlet to cast him off.

On the eighth night, Lord Hamlet returned to court. He didn't look crestfallen or sullen. In fact, he glittered with energy. He didn't dance, but he conversed with his entire family with sparkling vigour, and after the food was removed, he passed about the court, affably greeting the nobles and even the servers.

He didn't speak to me.

Nor did he even cast his eyes in my direction. It was as if I'd become invisible, had dissolved into one of the court ghosts.

The same thing happened on the next two nights.

The only reason it didn't happen in the days as well was that Prince Hamlet didn't attend middag.

I didn't even have the comfort of my customary visits with the queen, for she'd sent Elspeth to tell me that our lessons would resume only after Hamlet returned to school.

In the evenings, the queen glowed under the attentions of her younger son and the harmony in the family. One afternoon Yorick and I watched from the battlements as the two princes rode out together.

'He ignores me,' I told Yorick. I could feel no more forlorn if God Himself died and left me an orphan of the universe. 'It's as if I didn't exist.'

He sighed. 'Prince Hamlet has always blown hot and cold with all those he loves. Fear not. His wind will change, and he'll sail back to you in time.'

I didn't see how I could survive the wait.

On the eleventh night of Christmas, I felt someone shaking me awake.

Alarmed, I opened my mouth to cry out, but a hand

clamped across my mouth. I smelled the familiar scent of oranges and cloves, and I stared up into the face of Prince Hamlet.

'I have a surprise just for you,' he whispered. 'If they knew I'd come to you, they'd stop me, but I want to show you something before I depart on the morrow.'

He slid his hand off my mouth and eased me to a sitting position. 'Can you dress yourself without attendants?'

I nodded.

'Do so quickly, and bundle up well and come with me.'

My gown from the previous night lay just where I'd tossed it across the top of the chest. I pulled it on over my shift, but my fingers were stiff and fumbled with the laces. Lord Hamlet saw my struggles. He took the laces from my fingers and did up my bodice himself, tying it tight. Then he picked up my stockings and motioned me to sit down so he could slide them up my legs. To my shame, there was a small hole in the heel of one of them, but he paid no heed even to this slovenliness. My legs were warm from the bedclothes, yet as he slid my stockings up my legs, I shivered and gave an involuntary gasp. His hands were hot as fresh-baked bread. As he tied the ribbons of my garters clumsily around my thighs, my breath quickened and my heart banged wildly against my chest until I feared that I might faint from pleasure. He kept his head lowered, but his breath rasped the air like a file against silk. My cheeks blazed. He slid my slippers onto my feet, then plucked my cloak from its peg and wrapped it around me without a word.

Inside I was ablaze with longing and excitement, but I didn't say anything. I didn't want to break the spell.

He motioned for me to hang back as he opened the door to the passageway. He looked it up and down, and then he beckoned to me to follow him. I couldn't think what was about to happen, but I trusted him with my entire being. I don't approve of half-hearted measures or holding back. Like God, I choose to spit the lukewarm out of my mouth.

Hamlet led the way down the stairs to the courtyard. New-fallen snow blanketed the cobblestones. He eyed my slippers dubiously. 'I wouldn't have you chill your feet, lady,' he said, and then he picked me up in his arms as if I weighed no more than a bolster. He carried me over to where four saddled horses stood waiting. Two of them already had mounted riders, but they were so muffled in scarfs and cloaks and wrappings that all I could make out was that they were probably servants rather than nobles. A stableboy stood next to the third horse, and Lord Hamlet set me onto the saddle of the fourth.

'Sire, I don't know how to ride,' I whispered.

He patted my hand. 'I didn't think you did. I shall have to teach you, come summer, but for now will you share a horse with me?'

I grinned back at him and tried not to shiver from either elation or cold. He leaped up in front of me, and I wrapped my arms around his waist. He felt blessedly solid and warm. We bounced our way across the cobblestones to the gate.

The sleepy porter growled after us, 'You will catch your death if you be gone long, young master, so see you get back here before the Swan rises above the horizon, or I'll be sending off the guard after you.'

Lord Hamlet ducked his head in assent. Once outside the gate, we broke into a gallop. My head was pressed against his back, my cheek firm against the leather of his fur-lined cloak. I thought he said something as soon as we were out of the porter's earshot, but I couldn't make out what it was.

It was different seeing the world from horseback rather than sledge. On this evening, the moon wasn't as bright, but there was a lantern affixed to the stableboy's pommel, casting a yellow glow just ahead of us. Except for that little orb, the rest of the world was all dark shapes and pale snow. Everything was as silent as if all noise itself had frozen.

We rode for a long time, perhaps half an hour, and then Lord Hamlet stopped the horse. He slid to the ground and held up his arms for me and lifted me down to my feet.

'What do you think?' he asked.

16

In front of me stood a tiny palace made all of snow. It was a jewel of a dwelling with turrets and crenellated battlements no wider than the span of my hand. The whole thing was about the size of a small cottage, but it glowed from the inside like silk screening a fire.

'It's beautiful,' I breathed.

He laughed, pleased. 'Pray you, walk in, my lady, my dove.' He gestured one gloved hand toward an archway, then turned to whisper something to the stableboy.

I had to stoop to go through the arch, but what I saw inside made me blow out my breath in wonder.

I stood in a little antechamber made of polished ice. Small niches had been carved along the wall, and each niche contained the base of a candle that jutted out toward the centre of the room. The candles were all lit, and the ceiling and floor and walls glittered as if they'd been carved from sanded diamonds. At the far end of the antechamber was another arch, this one draped with a heavy curtain of tawny fur.

'Do you like it?' Lord Hamlet had stepped in beside me. The ceiling barely cleared his head, and if there'd been a feather in his hat, it would have been squashed flat.

'It breaks my heart with its beauty,' I whispered, afraid that if I spoke out loud, the whole enchantment might vanish.

'Step into the next chamber,' he said, reaching past me to hold the fur curtain open.

Without a moment's hesitation, I stepped through and then clasped my hands in delight.

Here was another chamber, a little bigger than the first but smaller than my bed chamber. It too was carved from ice, but the floor was covered with piles of soft bearskins. The room glowed golden from the lights of perhaps thirty tapers stuck in small crannies along the walls. At the far end was a seat carved into the ice and heaped high with throws of many kinds of furs, velvets, and heavy silks as well as piled silk cushions.

'Pray you, lady, be seated,' he said. 'I welcome you to my palace of dreams. I have spun this wonder for you, for you, and only for you.'

I sank down onto the fur mounded deep on the ice seat. The room was amazingly warm, sheltered as it was against the wind. Lord Hamlet made sure I was comfortably enthroned on the softest of the cushions and tucked several of the throws around me until I was snug as a tabby cat on the hearth. Then he rummaged around in a little box in the corner and brought forth a dish of candied cherries and another of amber and emerald jellies edged in gold leaf. He produced a flask and two goblets netted with silver.

'I play your humble serving man tonight,' he said. 'Command anything you will, and I must obey.'

'Do not return to Wittenberg,' I said.

There was the briefest pause, and then he said, 'Anything but that.'

Just then music began to play from the antechamber. There was the sound of two pipes, sweet and mournful against the night, their two plaintive voices winding together as if in a dance of love.

'With all my soul, I do regret that I put you in danger that night on the lake,' Hamlet said, lowering himself to lounge next to me. 'It would be criminal indeed to drown your brightness in black and deadly waters.'

'I didn't mind,' I said truthfully. 'I enjoyed it.' I wanted to tell him that it had been the best adventure of my life, but something inside me cautioned me not to say too much.

'I was so caught up in the night and the excitement of being with you that I forgot how frail a thing is a woman and how easily she might be hurt or lost. I beg pardon, I beg pardon, and a thousand times more I beg pardon.'

'I'm sturdier than I look, my lord. You cannot harm me or break me so easily.'

He reached out and brushed an errant strand of hair off my cheek. 'It was my duty to keep you safe, and I failed in that. But what think you of this fortress I've built for you? Is this place safe enough?'

My mouth fell open in amazement. 'You built this, my lord?'

'I did, my lady. I've worked here every afternoon since Christmas. I wanted to create something befitting your beauty, lady, for ever since we first met in my mother's chamber, you've haunted my heart.'

I was touched. No, I was more than touched. I was dazzled by his grand gesture. I knew my father would find it foolish to make a palace all of ice and snow, but in Lord Hamlet's act I saw the Danish tradition of the flyting, the practice of our seafaring ancestors in which they'd set their life at a pin's fee to risk some grand, glorious, futile gesture. They might fight naked in battle like the berserkers, or leap onto a promontory, chest exposed, to hurl an insult down on the attacking multitudes. Folk often said that we in Denmark were at our best when things were at their worst, and a rash, glorious thumbing the nose at fate was a way to shout out that while Death might get us in the end, we could live defiantly free rather than as slaves under his yoke. I loved the audacity of making a castle of ice, the way it cried out, 'Life may not last, but we can enjoy it while we have it.'

'This is the most marvellous place I've ever seen,' I said, and his dark eyes shone to put all the candles in the shade. 'But,' I added, 'that afternoon in your mother's chambers wasn't our first meeting.'

He looked puzzled.

'Three years ago, when you were going back to school, you stopped to watch a play in an orchard outside a village.'

There was a moment of stillness, like the silence before the furious attack of a storm, and then comprehension broke over his face.

'You were the girl in that play,' he said.

I nodded.

'The one who played a sphinx.'

'Sphinx?' I didn't know that word.

'The woman with wings and the body of a lion. Wasn't that the creature you pretended to be?'

I tried the word out in my mind. *Sphinx. A Flying Catgirl is a sphinx.*

'Sphinxes are wise,' he said. 'Often they come to you with riddles. You may choose whether or not to answer the riddle, but if you unravel it correctly, they'll grant you great fortune.'

'And if you don't?'

'They kill you.'

I liked that. It would make a good play, one that told the story of a Flying Catgirl – a *sphinx* – who fell in love with a man and who offered him a riddle. If he answered correctly, she'd take human form and be his wife, but if he gave the wrong answer, she'd have to kill him.

All at once part of me wanted to be back in the village so I could perform my plays.

Lord Hamlet held a sugared cherry to my lips and I gobbled it as if I were a baby bird. 'You look very far away. Have I said something to offend you, my sphinx?'

'Oh, no.' I told him about my idea for the play, concluding, 'but there's no one at court to join with me in an acting company.'

'Then you too like plays?'

I nodded vigorously. 'More than anything.'

Except you, I added in my heart. *More than anything except you.*

'What are some of the favourites you've heard?'

I confessed that I'd heard very few. 'But since I've come to court, I've beheld neither hair nor hide of a player.'

He looked shocked. 'What? Since you've been here, no travelling troupe has come to Elsinore? Very shabby indeed. Why, at Wittenberg most weeks we can choose from three plays or more.'

Three plays in the same week! What riches! 'Oh,' I breathed out reverently. 'I hadn't before realized that there were places in the world where you could hear one play every single week.'

He laughed. 'In cities such as Paris and London, I doubt not but you can hear a different play every single day.'

Such luxury nearly made me swoon. He smiled at my enthusiasm. 'When I go back to school, I'll cast out my nets to see if I can catch a travelling band of players to send to you.'

I felt transfigured with joy. What a treat it would be to see a play performed again. 'So you like the theatre, sir?'

His eyes lit up. 'It's the favourite pastime of my life.'

I sighed. 'If I were a man, I'd turn player.'

He smiled. 'I wouldn't like you as a man, fair Ophelia.' He held another cherry up and I took an obedient bite. 'But you do know, do you not, that in some parts of the world, there are women players as well as men?'

It was as if the walls of our ice room had suddenly turned

to fire. I sat upright and seized his wrist. 'Women on stage? Truly?'

He leaned forward and gave my wrist a little kiss. 'Truly. In Italy and France there are wandering players that employ women to play the women's roles. I myself am more comfortable with the tradition of our good North where—'

'Sir,' I interrupted, my words tumbling head over heels like a schoolboy rolling down an embankment, 'oh, let us run away, you and I. We could become players together. We could leave the castle and take to the road—'

Now he interrupted me. 'Ophelia, Ophelia, this cannot be.'

'But you love to act, and so do I, and if we—'

'We cannot. It would be madness.'

'Then let us be mad. Let us be mad together.'

For a moment his face grew wistful, and then he patted my hand like a kindly uncle. 'It's a fair dream, but it is naught but a dream, child. Ours would be a life full of hardship and struggle. We wouldn't be on stage every moment, and we'd sleep in mean places and eat meagre food—'

'What does that matter if we're living our dream? I've lived in mean places and eaten meagre food. That's not so hard, my lord. It's much easier to bear the stings of this simple life than the sword slash of living a life you don't love.'

'No!' He threw off his coverings and rose to his feet, his head only inches from the glassy ice ceiling. 'You paint me a pretty fantasy, but let us put an end to it before longing takes away our ease. We must put off these notions as we'd put off our childhood clothes.'

I wasn't ready to give up the thought, but I could see at this moment he wasn't to be swayed. I temporized. 'We will talk further.'

'We will talk of such matters no more,' he said firmly, but I thought I'd give this notion time to gnaw privately at his heart like a worm at a bud. With luck the idea of turning player would burrow its way into the innermost chamber of his heart and there lay the eggs that would crack open our two lives.

For the present, though, I left that sea change to time and said meekly, 'I wish you'd tell me of some of your favourite plays.'

Joy flooded his face. He began to talk of different plays, and then he began to act out the parts. It was as good as a show. He could capture all the characters, and he could recite long passages without a stumble or hesitation, although I didn't know if he was actually mouthing the passage word by word, or if he merely remembered the gist of the matter and glossed over it with his own words as I'd have done. He gave me the story of a jealous princess who killed her own children and served them on a platter to her unfaithful lover, of a god who was chained to a rock after he stole fire and brought it to human beings, of a musician who followed a god all the way to the underworld to rescue his dead wife, of a girl who could see the future but who was captured as the spoils of war by an enemy king and then stabbed by the jealous queen. His taste in drama ran to the bloody and treacherous. All my old dramas about the Flying Catgirl had been stories of high adventure, but I could see that these stories with their twisting plots and tragic endings were much superior.

Although his energetic words showed no sign of flagging, the music stopped, and one of the musicians poked his head through the curtain.

'I beg pardon, sire, but my fingers and those of my companion grow too cold to stop the holes of our pipes.'

Hamlet was immediately remorseful. 'You are good fellows and have given me yeoman service. I beg pardon that I lost the thread of the time.' At once he invited them both to step into this inner room and have some treats while he summoned the stableboy to return with the horses. 'Ophelia, will you play hostess?'

I nodded, and he ushered the two musicians into the room. I made them both wrap up in some of the throws, and they gobbled down the rest of the cherries and jellies. I heard Hamlet whistle outside our little ice palace, and, quicker than I cared for, the stableboy returned from wherever he waited with the horses.

I knew this was set down as the last day of Hamlet's visit, so I pressed myself tight against him as we rode back to the castle, part of me thinking that if I could press hard enough I could dissolve my body into his. As we rode, a rosy-gold dawn was just tinting the sky. It was probably close to the hour of ten. The ride back to the castle seemed much too short. When Hamlet lifted me off the horse, I saw his eyes were dark with misery.

'Ophelia, I don't know when I can return,' he said.

My own eyes were heavy. I felt as if I was made of nothing but sorrow.

He leaned forward and kissed me on the lips. To my disgust, my lips were so cold that I could feel nothing but the press of cold flesh to cold flesh. It was like the kiss of two corpses. I began to cry.

'Remember me, Ophelia. Please remember me.'

Then he tore himself away, and I ran to my chamber, blinded by tears.

To my amazement, Ragnor awaited me in my chamber.

'How did you get here?' I asked.

He looked completely at his ease, perched on my bed. 'The castle was in such a hubble-froth over the Twelfth Night festivities that I simply walked in, bold as a lord. If I'd been a Swedish soldier, we'd all now be in the suds.' His eyes narrowed and he leaned forward to study me. 'Are you crying, Cat?'

I blinked back my tears and shook my head.

He looked unconvinced. 'Is there anything I can do to help?'

I shook my head again.

'Then perhaps this will turn your sorrow to joy.' With a little flourish, worthy of any player, he reached into his doublet and pulled out a folded sheet of paper. 'Here.' He held it forward.

I couldn't imagine what it might be, but I took it readily. It had been sealed shut, but I broke the wax and smoothed out the page. I looked first at the signature.

It was a letter from Judith.

17

To my Beloved Daughter, Ophelia,

*I am living in England with Torvald. Here they think us
Man and Wife. I regret leaving you in such a hugger-mugger
way, but I did not want to place you in the awkward place
of having to lie to your Father or keep Secrets from him,
and so I crept away all alone. I was very sorry to leave you,
for although you are not the Daughter of my Body, you
are certainly the Daughter of my Heart. Torvald and I are
now the Parents of a Boy, a Lusty Lad whose cries could
Startle the Thatch off a Roof. If you would write me a note,
Ragnor will see that it reaches me. If you do not care to do
so, I understand. Forgive me, Ophelia, but Life with your
Father was driving me mad, and I was not Willing to spend
the Coin of my Life to purchase Unhappiness. My Thoughts
often turn to you, and I Hope you get on well. Know that I
will love you always, and that I am*

Your doting Mother, Judith.

I threw the letter down in disgust. I hated her. I still hated
her for deserting me. I begrudged those months of wasted
worrying whether she was dead or alive. How dared she say
she loved me when she'd left me as she did, without a spoken
word, without even a gesture of farewell?

I glared at Ragnor. 'Have you known all this time where
she was?'

At the sight of my fierce expression, his own face grew sober. 'My brother swore me to secrecy. I helped Judith board his ship and watched them sail off. I wanted to tell you, but I couldn't, you know. I couldn't break my word.'

I hated him as well as Judith. At this moment, I hated the whole world. Most of all, I hated Prince Hamlet for going back to Wittenberg and the king for not wanting him here at court and the queen for being such a namby-pamby that she dared not defy her husband, even for the well-being of her much-neglected younger son.

'Get out!' I ordered Ragnor. 'Take your promise of silence and leave my chambers at once.'

He looked puzzled. 'Will you not write a note for me to take to Judith? She's sick with longing to hear how you go on.'

'Then let her die of her sickness. If she can keep silent, then so can I.'

To my amazement, Ragnor burst out laughing and clapped his hands together.

'What is so comical?' I asked crossly.

'The last few times we met, Cat, you were such a watered down little creature that I couldn't stomach it. It does my heart good to see the piss and vinegar back in you.'

I suddenly remembered our last conversation in which he'd told me how he disapproved of me now that I was becoming a lady. I snapped, 'Take your sneaky cat ways and your vow of silence and you leave my chambers at once, or I'll call the guards on you and have you thrown in the dungeon until the flesh rots from your lazy bones!'

When I threw a pillow at him, he scampered grinning from the room. The letter from Judith was still lying on my coverlet. I tore it into little pieces and threw them in my chamber pot. I didn't know what the serving maid would think when she saw the small bits of paper lying like sunken crafts at the bottom of the sea of piss, and I didn't care.

The day didn't get better. My father hadn't noticed my absence, but when I told him I wanted to cry off that night's feast, he threatened to pull me off my bed and dress me himself.

'It will give much offence if you absent yourself from the Twelfth Night revels,' he twittered like a fox-worried hen, and so I made a half-hearted effort to dress my hair and pulled on my second-best gown. I consoled myself that I'd at least have one last glimpse of Hamlet, but in the hall, Lord Hamlet didn't look at me once. It was as if none of our adventures had ever been. To make my pain worse, several times I caught sight of Piet all the way across the hall. Most of the time he was grinning like a noddycock at a thin, kitchen girl in a mustard-brown kerchief and a hazelnut brown skirt, and each time she saw him grin at her, she gave him a shy little smile and blushed. It shocked me that Piet too might have fallen in love. Then I grew sodden with envy that Piet's beloved would work alongside him here in the castle while the man I loved was going far away. By the end of the feast, I was half-mad with self-pity. Not only was I losing Lord Hamlet, but I'd always been the most important person in Piet's life and now I'd lost him to this kitchen slut. Doubtless even Ragnor now had a sweetheart as well, and after my tantrum of the afternoon he'd never again speak to me. I drank glass after glass of hot wine, dredging my memory for every sorrow of my past till I half staggered to my bed where I curled up and wept for Hamlet, for my dead mother, for Blanche, and for a future that seemed as bleak here in the castle as it had back in Myg's cottage.

Prince Hamlet rode away at dawn.

I'd been awakened by a scratching on my door. My first thought was that Hamlet had again come for me, so I'd leapt from my couch to greet him. Instead, Yorick stood there.

'Prince Hamlet's horses are saddled and waiting,' he whispered. 'I thought perhaps you'd want one last glance before he disappears.'

I'd tumbled to sleep in my gown, so it was but the work of an instant to snatch up my cloak and slip my feet into my boots. I was so impatient to see Hamlet that I ran ahead of Yorick up to the battlements. In silence we watched him mount his horse, kiss his mother who had come to see him off, and then ride through the gates – and out of my life – with Rosencrantz and Guildenstern just behind him. My heart didn't feel as if it was breaking as much as it felt as if God had plunged His hand right through my chest and was now pulling out my heart, roots and all.

'You have no idea how much I too hate to see him go,' Yorick murmured.

There was no way his misery could be even a patch on mine. 'Why don't you then go with him,' I snapped.

Yorick sighed. 'I would if I could.' He looked away and added softly, 'But I cannot leave Elsinore.'

It was as if all light had drained from the castle, and for two days I moped, refusing even to go to the queen when she summoned me. On the third day I went to her chamber.

I had a plan.

18

If I were to marry a prince, I must become a wife fit for the son of a king. Until now, I'd been half-hearted in my attempts to become a lady, content with only a handful of shallow changes. I'd fooled myself into thinking that I could polish my looks, my voice, a few habits, but I could cling to the self that was inside me. Now I saw that if I truly wished to win Hamlet's love, I'd have to sacrifice the person that I was in order to become the person he'd love. Doubtless I'd driven him away because I was too loud, too big, too full of life. I'd set to work in earnest to alter myself into someone more like the queen, someone soft and soft-spoken, neat and neatly held back, the kind of woman with polished manners and polished edges, gentle and womanly. Only in stories did kings marry hoydenish Flying Catgirls. In life they wanted meek, beautiful maidens.

So I spent the next two years taming myself. Some of it was easy, like playing a role on stage. I blurred my speech into the mush-mouthed phrases of the queen and the ladies who came visiting from time to time. Most of the time, I had no trouble with it, but if I grew passionate, I had to expend much energy to keep my voice gentle and low. I hobbled my stride, no longer loping along like a she-wolf but prancing about with teeny-tiny steps that almost looked like a rope-bound filly. I harnessed my wild hair, trapping it firmly in ribbons or under a net and cap. No matter how much the out-of-doors world called to me, I penned myself inside with the queen so that my complexion would stay pale and white as a maggot. Despite my most earnest efforts, I never managed to take joy in stitchery, but I disciplined myself to sit for endless hours with needlework, reminding myself of how Leif Giant's Bane kept going while he was chained for twelve years in the ogre's dungeon. To tell true, sometimes I thought I'd have preferred to be imprisoned in an ogre's dungeon to needlework, but I then reminded myself that the prize I sought was a life with Prince Hamlet, and if this was what I needed to do to bring that life about, then it was a small but necessary price.

Day by day I domesticated the wildcat that I'd been. After a while, the whole court began to regard me with approbation, and even my father began to take delight in me. Once the king called me forward and told my father that I was much improved.

'She's becoming everything a woman should be,' the king said, his words a little slurred by wine. 'Modest, docile, demure, quiet, compliant.' Then he gave my father a wink. 'She will make someone a fine wife.'

I prayed that he'd think again of marrying me to his younger son.

I no longer went to the village. The sun and wind during that long walk would wreak havoc on my face and skin, and, more than that, I didn't want to be reminded of my village days.

In late April, a servant appeared and said that there was a man in the courtyard who wished to speak with me.

Curiously, I made my way down there, grateful for something to vary the monotony of my days. My heart gave an odd leap when I saw Ragnor waiting for me. The passage of time hadn't tamed him in the least. His long dark curls wove about his face like those of a young marauder in Denmark's days of glories, and his skin was already dark from the sun. His tunic was a little dusty with a small tear at the elbow.

He smelled of the sea and the sun-warmed earth, and for a moment I longed just to take big whiffs of him to strengthen my blood, but I let that silly notion pass.

He looked at me critically. 'You have become mighty fine.'

A lady doesn't show anger. 'Why do you wish to see me?'

He cocked his head. 'Two reasons. First, my mother is hungry to see you and learn how you go on. She misses you.'

I felt a pang. I missed her too, but I needed to trim away my previous life the way you slice off a seam that's too generous so you don't ruin the lines of a skirt. 'Tell her that I love her well, but I haven't had time to come to the village. I will do so when I can.'

He set his hands against his hips and looked at me with disfavour. 'Last time I was here, you were ripping into Judith for deserting you, but now you desert us in the village and you claim—'

'This is not the same thing,' I blurted out, horrified to hear my voice slip toward the accents of the village.

'Then tell me the difference.'

For a moment I couldn't think of anything, and then I said, 'You aren't my family.'

I expected him to counter with a remark about Judith's being my stepmama and therefore not my family either, but he didn't say anything. After a long silence I said, 'You spoke of two reasons for coming?'

He pulled a sealed letter from his doublet. 'Judith has written to you again.'

Part of me longed to grab the letter, but just in time I remembered that I was now a lady and a lady always moves slowly, as if she's moving through salt water or through a vat of mashed turnips. I stretched a languid hand out, and Ragnor put the note into it.

'You may go,' I told him in my most queenly manner.

He looked at me, hard. 'This place has been the undoing of you.'

Forgetting my queenly manner, I snapped back, 'This place has made me a fine lady.'

'That's just what I mean.'

Then he turned and left without another word or bow. For a while I stood there staring after him, not knowing what to think. Then I stared for a long while at Judith's sealed letter. Finally I walked over to one of the wells and dropped the letter in, unread. Ragnor and Judith were too costly an extravagance for the life I intended to lead.

And so the wheel of time turned slowly as another year passed and my fifteenth birthday rolled around.

Girls in the village usually don't marry until they're twenty or so, but fifteen is a marketable age for noble ladies. By this time I'd turned myself into a pattern card of virtue. Every day I took shorter steps and smaller bites and spoke in more muted tones. I'd traded the large, dramatic words that I'd loved for more malleable words, words as harmless as raindrops in a brief summer shower. There were times that I wanted to stand on the walls of the battlements and scream out frustration, but I hamstrung my wild nature to win what I wanted. After all, everyone except Ragnor approved of the way I'd broken my basic nature to the bit and bridle of court. In truth, I didn't know if Piet approved or not, because we seldom saw one another, and when we did, we had little to say. Some evenings I'd glimpse him walking out with his undersized serving wench. Leaning on the walls of the battlements, I'd watch them wander hand in hand across the fields or wind their way down to the shore where the tangled wild roses grew. Sometimes I'd wonder, *Has the king or Prince Holger taken her to their beds?* Then I'd wonder, *Could Piet take her back after one of the royals had used her in such a fashion?* Most of all, though, I wondered how it would feel to wander hand in hand through the warm summer evenings, picking wild roses along the beach.

When my envy threatened to choke me, I reminded myself, *One day that will be Lord Hamlet and you.* When he sees how fine you've become, he'll no longer be able to resist you.

He finally came on Midsummer's Day a year and a half after he'd left.

19

It was the custom to spend the time from sundown on Midsummer's Eve to sundown on Midsummer's Day as much out
of doors as possible. Like the winter solstice, Midsummer's
Eve was celebrated with bonfires and dancing, these huge fires
blazing to tempt the sun to tarry before beginning his journey
back to the dark. Most folk remained out of doors all through
the short night and the following day, but I'd accompanied
the queen to the bonfires, and we'd stayed only long enough
to sip a cup of the green wine.

I felt wistful as I watched the dance, and asked her, 'Do
you never long to dance, Majesty?'

She sighed. 'The king doesn't like me to dance with other
men, even at Midsummer revels.'

Several of the knights asked her permission to dance with
me. By now many of the men at court looked at me with
warmth in their eyes, and my father rubbed his hands with glee
over the six or seven marriage proposals that he'd received on
my behalf, but he thought I could aim higher and I knew that
Hamlet was my true fit in the world as if I were a lock and he
was its only key.

The queen gave me permission to dance, but after an hour
or so, she led me back to the castle.

It was the tradition in the Danish court for the royal family
to take the Midsummer middag atop the battlements. Servants
carried up trestle tables and set them on the roof. Garlands of
flowers were twined around the legs and down the length of

each one, their surfaces scattered in the petals of violets and wild roses and white columbine. On Midsummer's Day we ate cold foods only, fat strawberries in bowls of thick yellow cream, tiny green apples that puckered the mouth, a porridge made of breadcrumbs, curds, and sour whey that was sprinkled over with white sugar. There were pickled shrimp, each as small as a baby's curl, and chewy herring in brine. Bowls were heaped high with the first lettuces and newly-picked greens. All up and down the table was a wealth of butter carved to look like wild swans floating serenely on a sea of ruffled spinach. My favourites were the pastries, some round as the sun and others stuffed with nuts, plump as baby hedgepigs. I particularly liked the marchpane flowers that dotted the table, shaped and painted to look as real as the ones whose petals had been scattered about.

We were a small assembly – the king and queen, Prince Holger (who was heavy-eyed and quarrelsome after indulging too freely in the revels of the previous night), Prince Claudius, my father, Elspeth, the fawning Osric and a handful of older knights. Some musicians played as we ate, but afterwards the king waved them away, so the only sound was the distant drumbeat of the sea. The men, except for Claudius, played at dice, and the queen took out her stitchery while Claudius read to her from a book of French fables, but I was too restless to dole out the afternoon in tiny, measured stitches, so I leaned against the sun-warmed battlements and lazily watched the goings on of all the folk far below on the shore.

Early in the afternoon, I saw a small company of horsemen gallop across the fields. I thought about alerting the king to their approach, but he was caught up in the excitement of his dice, and I didn't want to risk his bad temper at being disturbed. I knew the porter was more than up to the task of sorting out any visitors, so I swallowed my words and waited.

As the horsemen approached, I made out four riders, but it wasn't until they were clattering up to the gate that I caught sight of a head of gilt hair, shining as bright as a helmet.

They reined in directly underneath me as they addressed the porter so I could see no more, but I ran to the other side of the wall and peered down into the courtyard, scarcely daring to breathe. In just a few moments, the riders passed into the courtyard proper and dismounted.

Lord Hamlet had returned.

I started to tell the queen, but I slowed my steps to a walk. He'd come to surprise her, and I didn't want to rob him of that treat. Instead I made certain that my hair and clothes were tidy, and I went to stand next to her, too excited to sit down.

She glanced up from the altar cloth she was embroidering. 'Do you feel well, Ophelia? Your face is flushed and you seem to be breathing hard. Do you wish to go in?'

I'd thought I'd learned to school all my emotions, but some renegade eagerness was slipping between the fence posts of my control.

'I'm fine, your majesty.'

Quiet, calm, controlled, maidenly. I kept repeating this chant to myself.

She looked unconvinced. 'Perhaps you've been too much in the sun today. Why don't you step into—'

But the rest of her words disappeared into a little squeal of joy, for her second son appeared at the top of the stairs. She cast her handiwork aside and hurried over to him, only to be caught up in a crushing embrace.

'My dear, dear Hamlet! How good to have you home.'

The king and the other men looked up at the sound of the queen's little shriek. At the sight of Hamlet, the king looked annoyed, and Prince Holger looked downright peevish. My father announced, quite unnecessarily, 'Look, Majesty. Here is your son, the good Prince Hamlet, come to celebrate the Midsummer with you and your family.'

Hamlet pushed his way past his mother and stood before his father, his arms stretched out as if he'd embrace him. 'Father?' he said, a question in his voice.

The king didn't rise or offer to return the embrace. 'I didn't know you were coming.'

'I thought it good to surprise you, sir.'

The king's eyebrows drew together. 'It's a shabby business to surprise a king.'

Prince Holger gave a yelp of laughter that he tried to turn, unsuccessfully, into a cough.

'I meant no harm,' Prince Hamlet continued. He looked crestfallen. 'I've missed you, Father. And you, too, brother. I've been overlong at Wittenberg.'

'You should have written to request my permission before setting off on your travels,' the king said.

Hamlet regarded him nervously, doubtless trying to will some words of welcome from the king's mouth.

But all the king said was, 'I suppose it too late to send you back now.' Then he turned back to his game and picked up the cup of dice.

Hamlet's face turned pale.

I wanted to push the king and Holger off the roof for their heartless welcome to the returning prince.

'Welcome home, nephew,' Prince Claudius said, moving toward the prince. Although Hamlet greeted him politely, his eyes strayed toward his father.

'Since you're here, we might as well celebrate,' the king snapped. 'Polonius, have them bring up a cask of brandy and some fresh mugs.'

I stepped forward. 'I'll go, sire, and save my father the trip.'

It wasn't so much that I wished to run the errand, but I

did want to draw the prince's attention to my presence. I was much pleased to hear him draw in his breath sharply when he noticed me.

'Angels and ministers of grace preserve us! Is this young Ophelia?' he asked, and I fancied his tone was gilded with admiration.

'Let your father go, girl,' the king said, 'for he'll know how to choose the best butt of wine in the cellars.'

'His majesty does me too much honour,' my father said, 'and while it's honour enough to serve the king, it's a greater honour indeed to be trusted, and so I trust that my deeds—'

'Oh, leave off talking and fetch the brandy,' the king said.

I hadn't yet lifted my eyes to Lord Hamlet's face, but I did so now, and saw him smiling at me, his eyes hot and eager.

'I'd been weary from riding,' he said, 'but one sight of you and now it's all May morning with me.'

'His highness is a welcome sight back at Elsinore,' I said as primly as I could. 'I know the queen is very well pleased to have you back again.'

'And you? Are you well pleased, Ophelia?'

I kept my voice level although inside I was turning cartwheels of joy. 'Anything that pleases the queen pleases me.'

The queen's voice broke in. 'I don't believe that I've previously met your companion, son. Will you present him to me and to your father so we can make him welcome in Denmark?'

The man standing behind Hamlet was a stocky, sober-faced man in the plain doublet of a guardsman. He reminded me a little of Piet, both of them having the same steady gaze, compact body, and quietness in their movement and stance. Prince Hamlet waved the man forward.

'This is Horatio, a new friend of mine from Wittenberg.'

The queen welcomed him and the king echoed her greeting. I'd often seen the king distempered but he never showed any displeasure to a new-arrived guest. The tradition of hospitality was deeply felt in Denmark.

Horatio returned the greeting in a level voice.

To steady my excitement, I sat down next to the queen and took up my own stitching. That day my needlework was more miss than strike, but it calmed me to push my needle in and out of the cloth. I keep stealing peeks at Lord Hamlet who sat down across from his father and was regaling him with an account of the journey home. Once, when I glanced up, I saw Lord Hamlet's eyes fixed on me, and my heart began to struggle wildly like a rabbit in a snare.

The long afternoon stretched into the long evening. Servants took away the remains of middag and brought up bread, dried fish, and a pudding of berries and cream for our supper.

'You catch us not at our best,' the king explained to Horatio.

The queen quickly explained that we took a simple supper on Midsummer's so that the servants could attend the revels.

'I have no stomach for rich foods,' Horatio said. 'Enough is as good as a feast.'

I itched to address Lord Hamlet alone, but he stayed at his father's side. All through the afternoon he played at gaming and drinking with the other men. They finished off the cask of brandy that my father had escorted up there, and they sent him to capture a second and then a third. At supper the queen chatted courteously with Horatio, drawing him out about his home in south Jutland and his own family while I fretted about the chance to talk with Lord Hamlet out of the hearing of the rest of the company.

He was almost as beautiful as I remembered him, like an archangel come to earth, but his hands were restless, and he grew a little less beautiful as he became flushed with wine.

It was late indeed when night finally stained the sky. The bonfires on the beach had long since burned to embers. The queen announced she was off to her chambers and would leave the men to their games. 'Shall we go, Ophelia?'

I couldn't bear to be cloistered below when Lord Hamlet was up here, so I said, 'This is a fair evening, your majesty. I'll remain here a little longer with my father if I may.'

My father, his face ruddy with brandy, and shadowed by the torches that the servants had lighted, said irritably, 'Oh, go below, girl. I'm no nursemaid, and there's naught for you to do here.'

'I pray you, sir, grant me leave to stay a while.'

'There's naught for you to do up here, girl. Go below with the women.'

I frantically cast out the nets of my mind to capture a reason to let me stay up here with Lord Hamlet and fished up a memory from my time in the village.

'Good, my Father, village folk say that if you wish on the last star of Midsummer's Night, then you might have your heart's desire all through the coming year.' Actually, it was supposed to be a wish on the *first* star, but I doubted that my father knew that particular bit of village lore.

'Tosh,' he said, his voice a little slurred from drink. 'You live here in the castle and serve the queen. What more could you wish for? Leave off these carp-brained peasant superstitions, for if a lady let herself be governed by the words of yokels, then she will *yoke* herself to—'

Unexpectedly, it was the king who came to my rescue. 'Oh, let the chit stay if she doesn't trouble us, and come you, Polonius, back to the game for the throw sits at your elbow.'

I pulled back into the shadows of one of the turrets and made myself as small as possible as my father bustled back to take his turn.

Lord Hamlet didn't glance at me again, but I was well content to sit and watch him. The torchlights cast dancing gleams across his golden hair as he drank with the other men, talking of homely subjects such as crops and the catch from the sea and the duties levied from the ships that wished to pass through the straits below us. The men griped about the nephew of the king of Norway, Erik Strong Arm, who was said to be grumbling about taking back the lands his father had forfeited in single-arm combat to our king. They speculated at length about our chances of going to war with Norway.

I sensed someone behind me. Yorick stood next to me. 'I see Prince Hamlet has returned,' he whispered. Then we turned in unison to watch him.

After a while I dozed a little, and when I blinked myself awake, Yorick had drawn close to the table. A sizable pile of coins stood in front of Prince Claudius. I could see the men were far gone in drink, all save Horatio who seemed as steady as ever. One of the king's guards had even fallen asleep, head down on the table, snoring faintly.

'No,' the king thundered. It had probably been the sound of his angry voice that had snapped me awake. 'Denmark is not the land that she was in her days of former greatness.'

'No, no, sire,' my father said, 'for I doubt me whether there ever reigned a king more able than you. Even the tales told of the long departed King Holger, while heroic enough – and I wouldn't impugn his memory, although there be not folk alive who remember him other than from the old tales, and, as we all know, old tales cannot be disproved, but neither can they be proved, and his tales may prove—'

The king ignored his words as if they were the mere buzzing of a gadfly. 'This younger generation, they haven't the fire in the loins or in the heart to equal the men of days gone by.'

Prince Hamlet said pleasantly, 'That is, I believe, sir, the complaint made ever by the elders about the younger ones. Socrates himself, it's said, grumbled that—'

'It is certainly true that there are those among us who substitute book learning for knowledge and the rapiers of the mind for the swords of war,' Prince Holger said in a nasty tone, much blurred with drink. 'Some of us lack the fire of our forefathers.'

Prince Hamlet scooted his chair back from the table. 'Do you talk of me, brother?'

'Take them as you will, brother, but if the words fit, then you had best take them to heart.'

Prince Hamlet took several angry little breaths before saying, 'And have I then missed hearing tell of your deeds of valour, Holger? Remind me again, what enemies have you conquered? Tell me once more what coffers of riches you've brought to our people. Have you hidden the corpses of the dragons you've slain so as not to awake envy in the hearts of us lesser mortals?'

Prince Holger staggered to his feet. 'At least I don't drive a sleigh across the ice, thinking I can walk on water just because I've read a few books and live like a eunuch.'

'Nephews, please!' Claudius said, but no one paid him any mind.

Hamlet rose to his feet to glare at his brother. 'True, brother, I've conquered many books, but just what have you conquered, brother, other than a few unwilling serving wenches?'

'Come,' growled the king, 'enough of this. Come sit you down and return to the play.'

Prince Holger ignored his father. 'It makes me sick to think that you bear my father's name, for you're but a weak shadow of your namesake, not fit to call yourself—'

'Whereas you've surpassed the glory of your namesake, King Holger, who is known far and wide as the saviour of

Denmark. Tell us all, glorious Holger, just what you saved Denmark from.'

'We are fortunate indeed,' said my father, manfully trying to distract the angry brothers, 'that old King Holger himself is buried underneath the stones of this very castle, for legends say that in Denmark's days of greatest need, he'll rise back up and save her. Many have sought out his tomb, though, but all have failed, so perhaps it is naught but—'

'Enough of this foolishness,' said the king. 'Make peace, both of you.'

I hated Prince Holger for making sport of Hamlet.

'I believe that it's easy to drape the deeds of the past in great glory for when there are no live witnesses, anything is possible,' said Prince Claudius from behind his great mound of coins, faithfully supporting my father's efforts to turn the quarrel around. 'I myself believe that men of the olden days were no more valiant than men of today—'

Prince Holger interrupted him. 'And thus we hear from another weak copy of my father. Uncle Claudius, you and my scholar-brother are two peas in a common pod.'

Claudius said, 'I'm no scholar, nephew, like your brother.'

'No, but you and my brother are both men of words rather than men of action, flapping your mouths rather than flailing a sword.'

The king gave a bark of laughter.

I hated him, too.

I expected Claudius to chastise his drunken nephew, but he didn't show the slightest sign of irritation. Instead he seemed even more jovial than before. 'And so you believe all the tales they tell of the valour of the olden days?'

'I doubt them not.'

Prince Hamlet snorted. 'Then it's I who has a fool for a brother, one who lends a credulous ear to every nursery tale of dragon and ghost, wizard and—'

Prince Claudius's placid voice cut him off. 'Hamlet is right. We cannot place credence in some of the old tales that make the men of yore so very heroic and all folk of today puny in comparison.'

Holger shouted, 'You say that only because you're a coward who hangs on my father's sleeve, deeming the exploits of the past as false coin only because neither you nor my monkish brother have the courage to attempt anything that smacks of glory.'

'Oh, come now, brother,' Hamlet said in a scornful tone. 'You may not be bookish, but surely you're not such a blockhead as to believe all the old stories.'

'Just because you yourself are hen-hearted, you need not disparage the heroes of the past.'

'I don't say there were no heroes, but even you cannot swallow all of their deeds.'

Holger tensed his hands into fists. 'I dare you to name me one tale that names an impossible deed.'

'Gladly,' Hamlet said. 'Let us take your namesake, King Holger, whose body is said to sleep beneath our dungeons.'

'It does!' Holger shouted back. 'The tale says he's buried there, and that I believe.'

'I don't dispute that,' Hamlet said, 'but the old tales claim he'd regularly overleap these very battlements to plunge into the sea for a swim, yet you and I know this is not possible. Even if you missed the rocks below, the shock of the impact of the waters would kill you dead. Therefore that story at least—'

'I doubt it not. If it's told of King Holger, then it's the truth, and only scholars—' he said the word as if it meant moneylenders or panderers '—like you and my uncle would question its veracity.'

'Come, come. No one would be foolish enough to do something so reckless,' Claudius said.

'It was the nature of our ancestors to have courage even

to the point of recklessness,' Prince Holger said. 'We inherit that courage in our very blood.' He turned his face to Prince Hamlet and let his eyes slide up and down him. 'At least some of us do.'

'Indeed?' said Prince Hamlet, his voice unsteady with drink and anger. 'Have you such courage, oh brother of mine?'

'This is a foolish argument,' the king said. 'Leave off.'

'I do indeed,' said Prince Holger. 'Not for nothing do I bear his name.'

'Then show us, brother. Leap off the battlements into the flood.'

There was an ugly silence. The two brothers glared at each other, each breathing hard. Then the king and Horatio spoke at the same time.

'Leave off this foolishness and return to the table.'

'Lord Holger, I believe the dice are at your elbow.'

Prince Holger hesitated, and then he moved back to the table.

Prince Hamlet gave a bark of laughter. 'I thought not. Easy indeed to be pot valiant, brother, but—'

And then the events moved so quickly that even now they're a blur in my mind.

Prince Holger gave a yelp, and then he was running toward the battlements. Several people cried out, and Horatio took several steps after him. Quicker than breath, though, Prince Holger sprang up to balance on the battlements wall next to the sea, and in the next moment he was gone.

20

It took three days to recover his body.

The king ordered all ships out to look for what remained of the prince. They floated loaves with lighted candles across the water, for it's well known that a drowned body will rise up and come to a candled loaf. The king, ashen faced, ordered Prince Hamlet out of his presence, and no matter how often Prince Hamlet sent a messenger to beg pardon of the king, he refused to see him. The queen spent the three days in prayer in the chapel, white as winter snow, and most of the time I stayed with her. Twice Prince Hamlet joined us and begged his mother for forgiveness.

'Your brother's death is not your fault, for my older son was ever headstrong and would go his own way, willy-nilly,' she said in a faint voice, but her eyes slid past Prince Hamlet as if he were a ghost.

Finally a fisherman found Prince Holger's body which had floated south into the Baltic. I didn't see the body myself, but Elspeth later told me that it bore little resemblance to the handsome, bold prince.

'After three days in the water,' she said, 'a body puffs up like an infected wound, and the flesh turns slippery as soap and slides from the bones.'

As soon as the funeral rites were concluded, there in the rainy graveyard the king ordered Prince Hamlet back to school. 'Do not come back until I send for you.'

'Father, I—'

'Do not call me father,' he said, 'for you do not feel like a son of mine. Let us both hope that time will soften what I feel for you.'

'I'd do anything, anything at all to wind my way back into your favour, Father. Command me to complete any task, no matter how hopeless, and I'll do it, even unto my own death.'

'For now, get back to school, for I'm sick when I do look upon your face. I don't know why my worthy son was taken and my unworthy one, a son capable of killing his elder brother, was left to walk among us. I don't know what sins Denmark has committed for such a wrong to come to pass. Perhaps one day I'll give you a task to regain my love, but at this moment I cannot feel that you're any son of mine.'

Prince Hamlet looked so white and so miserable, that I longed to run across the damp graveyard and take him in my arms. His father was unfair. Prince Hamlet hadn't made his brother attempt that brainless feat.

'Father—'

'As far as I'm concerned, it was the wrong son who died! So get you to your university, for I love you not.'

The queen stepped forward. She looked as threadbare as if this tragedy had rubbed the fibres of her being so thin that you could peek right through her, but she said to her husband, 'My dearest lord, do but consider—'

He pulled back from her as if she were a viper spitting poison. 'Nay, Madam. Do you but consider. How have we offended God that he took the good son and left us with the rotten one?'

Her mouth gaped in a little O, but she said nothing, as if his last remark had punched all the words out of her. Prince Claudius glanced at her and then moved in front of her as if he could shield her from her husband's anger. 'Brother, when all the eggs are broken, then it's time to make a sauce. We cannot raise our dear Holger from the grave, but—'

'No more!' thundered the king. 'I can bear this no more.'

He gave Prince Claudius a shove that sent him staggering back into the queen. My father moved forward to steady him. Prince Claudius showed an inclination to speak, but I could see my father gentling him and tugging his clothes to rights. For once my father knew enough to hold his tongue in the presence of the king, for King Hamlet didn't seem willing to listen to any man. Nor to woman either. I wanted to fly to Prince Hamlet's defence, to point out that Prince Holger had been a lout and a bully, but I held my tongue.

Horatio laid a soothing hand on Prince Hamlet's shoulder, but Hamlet shook him off and began to move toward his father. The king deliberately turned his back to his remaining son and faced the assembled mourners.

'Hear your king and heed us well,' he called out in his loudest voice. 'This day we have buried the brightest hope of all Denmark, but he's dead and will come to us no more. Therefore we proclaim that no one in this kingdom shall mention his name again. On pain of death, his name is not to be spoken. Since he's dead, it will be as if he has never been. His clothes are to be burned, his sword broken and buried, his horses slaughtered and their flesh given to the hounds. Why rub our wounds with the salt of memory? Anyone who speaks of him or remembers him is henceforth a mortal enemy to Denmark, hated by its king above all creatures on earth, and we shall deal with him as we'd deal with the foulest traitor. See that you observe the word of your king and dread lord!'

Then he turned sharply on his heel and marched back through the drizzle toward the castle, his back stiff and straight. When I looked at him face to face, he seemed powerful as the tempest, but in spite of my intentions, the sight of his back in the rain tugged at my heart for I could see now that he was an old man and all his warrior training wouldn't turn back the tides of age and make him young again.

Back in our chambers, once we'd changed into dry clothing, my father had much to say about the funeral.

'An ill business, an ill business indeed, this whole tangle. As he is my liege lord, I owe him obedience, yet we cannot but find it a havey-cavey business to order matters thus.'

'Yes,' I said, pleased that my father and I finally agreed on something. 'To cast off Prince Hamlet—'

'Think of the waste!'

'Indeed, for Prince Hamlet has the best mind—'

My father continued as if no words were coming from my mouth. 'His horses slaughtered and fed to the hounds. Why, the prince who must not be named, he had a whole stable of horses. Enough for their flesh to fill our tables for a month or more if the cook was careful to use that meat well. To think of all that good meat being given over to a pack of hounds.'

I wanted to shake him. 'But, Father, what of the king's treatment of poor Prince Hamlet? To order him away, to claim that he's no son of the king's and to cast him aside like a rind of cheese! How can you countenance such cruel treatment? Can you not go to the king and counsel him to—'

My father looked scandalized. 'Tut! You speak like a green girl! The word of our king is law in Denmark, and my life would be worth no more than a pin's fee should I defy him thus.'

'But if Prince Hamlet is to be our next king, then it is madness to exile him thus to the nether regions of his father's life.'

'Our next king?' My father looked astonished. 'Prince Hamlet to be our next king? Who fed you this grass?'

Now it was my turn to be astonished. 'I don't understand your meaning, sir. Since Prince Hamlet is the king's remaining son—'

'Go to! Go to, Ophelia! Why should the throne descend on young Hamlet?'

Something was amiss. 'He is the son of the king.'

My father rolled his eyes and lifted his hands to heaven as if he were asking them to look down and marvel at his having such a foolish daughter. 'In Denmark, son doesn't succeed father as night follows day. No. When a king dies, a council convenes to select the next ruler. I myself, as chief advisor to the king, will be head of that very council. And I tell you now, girl, that there's as much chance of young Hamlet's being chosen as king as snow falling on Midsummer's Day.'

I was outraged. 'How can that be? Prince Hamlet is a brilliant man, a good man, an educated man—'

'He may be schooled in the sciences and arts, but he's unschooled in the way of diplomacy and war.'

'There are no wars these days in Denmark. We don't need some brutish warrior as our king.'

'True, true, we're at peace now, but peace is a fragile thing, no more substantial than the ice that glazes the top of a washbasin in the morning. One tap of a finger shatters the ice to a hundred bits, and it takes as little to shatter our delicate peace. We have held our present peace for nearly thirty years because our neighbour countries fear our king's fist. Should the milky Prince Hamlet sit on the throne, then Norway, Sweden, Poland, even England, perhaps, would come roaring down upon us, boar hounds ready to savage the meek little rabbit that rules us. No, no, Ophelia. Besides, Hamlet is too changeable ever to rule.'

'Lord Hamlet is *not* changeable.'

'He is no more steady than a feather floating on a lake.' My father plucked an invisible hair off his doublet and let it flutter to the floor. 'One day he's with the angels, and the next he's plunged into the lowest pit of hell. On Monday he might commandeer a squadron of carpenters to build him a palace, and on Tuesday he keeps to his bed the livelong day, his curtains drawn against all light, drowning in melancholy and his whole plan for the palace forgotten. I tell you, girl, a country cannot be ruled by such a noonday dreamer as that.'

My father was wrong, of course. Hamlet was a fine young man and would make the most glorious king that Denmark had ever known.

That night Prince Hamlet came to me in my bedchamber.

21

As was the custom after a funeral, my father stayed below with the king, drinking, even though the name of the young man buried was never to be mentioned again. I lay in bed, mulling over the events of the past week, when I heard my door creak open. I could barely make out a shape in the pitch darkness, but then I smelled the mixture of orange peel and spices used in Hamlet's clothing chest to keep the lice and fleas away.

We'd not talked privately since he'd arrived back for his Midsummer visit, and we didn't talk now. As silent as a ghost he moved to me, and as silent as a ghost I scooted to the edge of my bed and held out my arms. He sank down onto his knees next to the bed and buried his head against my chest, and I wrapped my arms around him, my cheek resting on the top of his head. He felt warm like a sleeping cat, and he drew his breath in and out in little shudders. When I'd been small, Piet and I had shared a bed, and on cold nights we'd slept with our arms wrapped about each other in this same way. I'd forgotten how good it felt to hold someone in your arms, to feel the touch of a living, breathing human being.

For a long time we sat thus. After a little bit, I began to rock gently back and forth, humming a little wordless tune.

I don't know how long we sat thus, perhaps an hour or more, and then I felt him pull away. I let him ago. I'd never hold him against his will. He stood up, and I felt him bend down and plant a gentle kiss on the top of my head. Then I saw him feel his way out the door again.

I didn't fall asleep for a long while after that.

The next morning, when I went to the queen's chambers, I learned that Prince Hamlet and his friend Horatio had left at first light to return to Wittenberg.

I felt bereft, as if Hamlet had stolen my soul the night before and smuggled it away with him. I'd waited a year and a half for him to return this time. How long would I now be expected to wait?

Then at Elsinore, things slid swiftly from bad to worse.

Each day the queen grew more frail. She was as thin as a wisp of dust that hides under a bed. She couldn't bear the taste of food. The only thing she'd take was a crust of bread that Elspeth soaked in warm milk and wine, and even then, more likely than not, she'd leave it half-finished. Sometimes when she was talking, she'd quit in the middle of a sentence as if the thread of her conversation had unravelled leaving her only with silence. I myself mourned Prince Hamlet's absence, but she grieved over both her sons, so I shouldered aside my private pain and tried to cheer her up. She had no more interest in her needlework, and, to tell true, I didn't regret this because embroidery felt to me like carrying away the beach one grain of sand at a time. There was a fine chess set in her chambers carved of alabaster and onyx. I coaxed her to teach me the game, and I found I quite enjoyed it although I had to hobble my play so that I didn't triumph too quickly over the sad queen. More satisfying were my daily games with Prince Claudius. He had a quick mind for chess, and never did I beat him, but I preferred a challenge even if it meant defeat to a victory that came too easy. I didn't feel guilty playing with Claudius, for the queen would draw her chair near and watch our game with more interest than she showed in anything else in her present life.

It was Claudius only who could occasionally tease a smile out of her. He treated her with tenderness, and I wondered anew what exactly passed between them in the realm of feelings.

Each day I badgered her to go out walking with me. She didn't wish to leave the castle, but in this matter Elspeth intervened on my behalf, scolding the queen and telling her that we both needed fresh air. I no longer worried about turning my skin brown. My concern for the queen trumped my vanity. Most days that we went walking, I led her down along the shore. I loved the strong salty smell of the sea and to watch the ships out on the waters. Ships of all nations passed through the strait in front of the castle, and it was a delight to me to try to identify the flags they flew. Each time we walked along the beach I'd return with my arms filled with the fragile wild roses that grew in profusion there.

Other days we walked through a patch of woodland into a glade we'd discovered. A deep stream cut its path through the glade in its headstrong dash to the sea, and the banks above the stream were thick with wildflowers. Usually I could rouse the queen to enough interest to gather a handful of the blossoms, and I'd tell her their names and their properties which I knew thanks to the Herbwife's teachings. I liked to slip out of my shoes, gird my skirts up above my knees, and wade through the tumbling cold waters, but I could never persuade the queen to join me. She seemed content enough to watch me, calling out every once in a while a warning to be careful or not to go too deep. There was an old tree whose branches hung over the brook, a giant of a tree with its lower branches as wide as the back of a horse. Sometimes I'd crawl out onto the limbs to collect the flowering vines entwined in the branches over the stream. I could then pinch off those blossoms right at the bottom of the petals and carefully draw them off their base, releasing a single drop of sweet nectar that I could lap up with my tongue. It was almost as sweet as honey, and carried the spicy scent of the flower. It always terrified the queen to see me creep along the overhung branch above the water. Each time I returned to earth, she breathed a sigh of relief and said, 'Ophelia, you must not do that again. You might have been killed.'

I also gathered the tender shoots of sour grass, no longer than a baby's finger, that could be chewed for hours, giving off a pleasantly green and mouth-puckering taste. Sometimes I found young nettles that hadn't yet begun to prickle. When their skin was pulled off, they were delicious to eat, tender and a little bitter and flavoured like a wind from a distant place. In the shady places I found a wealth of mushrooms, some gnarled as sea sponges, others red and dotted with grey; translucent brown ones that were fluted and delicate as any petal; and squat white shells that popped up overnight in battalions. There's nothing more tasty than a mushroom hot from the fire, and this was a taste I missed in the castle, for by the time it reached the Great Hall from the kitchen, our food was never more than faintly warm, and mushrooms aren't good keepers, turning leathery and flavourless once they cool. So I kept a little pan in the queen's room, and when we returned with a basket of mushrooms, I'd beg a lump of butter from Piet in the kitchen, and then I'd cook a mess of mushrooms over the queen's fire, browning them till they were tender as the flesh of a newborn babe and offering up their particular flavour of smoke and soil and wildness. Even the queen relished the fresh-cooked mushrooms, and Elspeth, Claudius, and I wolfed them down greedily.

Prince Claudius remained a regular visitor. The queen preferred his company even to mine and Elspeth's. He made no demands on her, just talking easily of this matter or that. In truth, I sometimes ran out of conversation because most days very little happens of interest in a castle. Village life offers many more diversions. Claudius, though, never seemed to run out of things to say to the queen. We both read to her. I didn't especially enjoy the reading matter she handed to me, long homilies or passages from the Bible. Claudius read her French fables and romances, and every so often they surprised a laugh out of her, and sometimes she swatted at his hand and called him naughty for bringing such things into her chamber.

Even though the king's rooms were next door, after Holger's death, the king and queen lived at a great distance from each other. More and more she sported cruel bruises on her arm, and twice her eyes were blackened. Once Elspeth turned me away for three days running, and when I finally saw the queen, bruises encircled her neck like a collar, as if someone had tried to strangle her, and her wrist was bandaged around a splint of wood.

'Majesty!' I breathed, fiery with wrath.

She gave me a weak smile. 'I grow short-sighted and it makes me clumsy. I fell several days ago over my good dog Trey, and I'm keeping myself apart from the court until I've healed.'

Recklessly I said, 'A fall could never put those bruises about your neck.'

'This fall did,' she said in the firmest tone I'd heard her use since Holger's death.

Later that morning, when Claudius was reading to her, I drew Elspeth aside. 'Tell me true – was it the king who injured her thus?'

Elspeth's lid drooped down like a turtle's over her whirling eye. 'This does not bear talking of.'

'If the king is harming her thus, she must not stay here.'

'And just where can she go?'

'Away. Anywhere.'

Elspeth grasped my hand in her clawlike one and squeezed it hard. 'Her father is dead, and there's no kin to take her in, not if it means the enmity of the king of Denmark. I like this no more than you, but a man has a right to school his wife thus, so neither law court nor royal court would take her side in this matter.'

'Then let her go away on her own, for he'll kill her surely if she stays.'

'She has no place to go.'

'Then let her buy a place and live there all alone, for loneliness would be preferable to this.'

Elspeth threw my hands aside. 'You prattle like a child. She has no money with which to buy a castle. All that she owns belongs to her husband, even down to the clothes on her back. Good or bad, she's the king's to make or mar. All we can do is counsel her to do nothing that will trigger the anger of the king, and that's more and more difficult to do in these dark days.'

For a moment I hated them all. I hated the king for doing this to her, but I hated Elspeth more for advising the queen to accept it meekly, and I hated the queen most of all for letting him turn her into this spineless creature who drifted about her own life.

'I wouldn't suffer him thus,' I said.

Elspeth gave a huff of impatience. 'The queen is not you.'

'She must have been like me once!'

Just then the queen returned and so put an end to our talk. I was angry on the queen's behalf, but I was also a little frightened for myself. Someday, could I become such a cowed and beaten creature? I hated it that we know what we are, but we know so little of what we might become. I worried the matter, turning it over and over in my brain, but I couldn't puzzle our way to a happy ending.

The king grew worse in other ways as well. He'd always been a heavy drinker, but now by midday he was often drunk. He and the queen made a sad pair sitting in their throne chairs on the dais, neither of them eating, the queen as faint and pale as a star in a daylight sky, and the king brooding like a cauldron about to boil over. The whole court grew thin because the queen usually forgot to sit at her place long enough for regular folk to finish their food, so when the queen rose to depart, it almost made me laugh to see the nobles grabbing at hunks of bread and blocks of dried fish to stuff into their pockets to gnaw at once they were safely alone.

Summer sank into the autumn, the season of the gathering of eels. Most years the fisherfolk needed only to dangle their nets in the waters to fill them heavy with migrating eels, but this year the schools were scanty and far between. It was as if a curse had been laid over the whole of Denmark. Then, as nights grew longer, the king grew even more morose. His drinking bouts lasted longer and longer, sometimes two or three days at a throw. Seldom did my father return to our chambers before dawn, and soon all the men about court grew heavy-eyed and snappish. The king himself seemed to need little sleep, although a few times he fell into a deep slumber at table. Once his head bobbed forward until he plopped face first into a tureen of beet soup, and I had to choke back a laugh when he lifted his head up, his whole face stained a deep pink.

As far as I could tell, though, no one else found it funny.

Once, when a courtier forgot the king's edict and mentioned the dead prince, the king had him flogged to death right in the middle of the hall. No one dared stop the beating for fear of incurring the king's wrath.

Ragnor's next older brother brought me a third letter from Judith. I read this one. She'd been delivered of a hardy girl that she'd named Ophelia in my honour. For the first time I considered penning a note to her. How she'd stare to hear about all the changes here at court, although to me it was beginning to feel more like a prison than a court, particularly since there was no word from Prince Hamlet.

One night I was roughly roused from a deep sleep. My father and two guards stood beside my bed, one of the guards holding a taper. I blinked to see them there, and my sleep soaked brain could make no sense of this encounter, but my father ordered me, 'Rise up at once, Ophelia.'

'What is the clock?'

One of the guards rumbled, 'The king has sent us to fetch you to him.'

This made no sense. 'Has something happened to the queen?'

The other guard grabbed at my elbow and pulled me out of bed. The stone floor was cold beneath my feet. 'Come with us, lady.'

'Prince Hamlet? Has something—'

'Come!'

I jerked my arm away. 'Step out so I may put on my gown—'

'The king doesn't wish us to tarry. Come at once.'

'Father!' I looked at him, alarmed, so he could tell the guards to leave me alone, but he cast his eyes downward and mumbled, 'It will be to the best if you just come along, daughter.'

One of the guards again grabbed my arm and was pulling me forth, even though I was clad only in my undershift. I snatched up a coverlet and wrapped it around me. I was frightened. Had Elspeth told the king how I wished the queen to run away?

The guards hurried me down the dark corridors to the Great Hall. We passed several ghosts, and I thought they watched with unnatural avidity. For once the Great Hall was empty and dark, save for a single candle burning on the high table. The guards hustled me up to the dais where the heavy-eyed king sprawled on his throne.

'Here is my daughter as you ordered,' my father piped

up from behind me, and I could hear the nervous flutter in his voice.

The king's eyes slid up and down me, as impersonal as cold stones. I drew myself up a little taller. I refused to be cowed or shamed by him. I matched him stare for stare, and something that might have been amusement flickered for a moment in his eyes. Then he said, 'Pull the damn blanket away.'

My God, was he going to rape me right here in the Great Hall? Surely not. After all, I wasn't one of his sheep-brained serving maids. Besides, my father was privy to this scene, and while he was a loyal servant to the king, certainly he wouldn't let the king violate his daughter.

At least I didn't think he would.

Still, it wasn't fitting for me to stand in my shift before the king like a strumpet. I pulled the coverlet more tightly around me. But both of the guards tugged on it and, unwilling to play pull-the-blanket with them, I disdainfully let it fall. I felt naked in just my thin shift, but I wouldn't let the king shame me. I could hear my breath moving in and out of my pinched nostrils, a sign that I was angry to the very marrow of my bones, but I stood stock still.

'By our lady,' the king muttered, 'but she's a pretty one.'

Then he straightened up and leaned close to me. I smelled his sour breath, reeking of stale wine. His body had an unwashed smell, and I began to breathe through my mouth so I wouldn't have to endure his stench.

He laid his thick hands on my hips. Through the thin fabric of my shift I felt first the heat of his hands and then the coarseness of their surface.

'Wide hips,' he said. 'This one can bear many children and still go out the next day to till the fields.'

The guards guffawed as if he were a great wit.

Hope flooded my brain. Did he mean to announce my betrothal to Hamlet? Was that the matter behind all of this?

Still I stepped back away from his hands.

He gave a bark of laughter. 'I like them to have a little fight in them. No man wants a corpse in his bed.'

Even if this was a bizarre prologue to marriage with his son, I wouldn't endure this treatment. I summoned up my courage and demanded, 'What means your majesty by all this show?'

The king hooked one arm over the back of his throne and grinned at me. 'Tell me, Ophelia, what think you of being queen?'

I was right! He intended me to marry with Hamlet. I wanted to explode with joy, but I also wanted to show that I had dignity enough to fit my new position. In my steadiest voice I said, 'I don't know what your majesty means, for presently there is a fine queen upon your throne.'

I expected him in turn to say something about how after his death, Prince Hamlet and his consort would rule Denmark, but he didn't say what I'd expected. Instead he remarked, 'I have a fancy she'll not be queen for long.'

22

I blinked to clear my head. 'I don't catch your majesty's drift.'

His eyes crinkled as if we shared a joke.

A jumble of thoughts flew about my head trying to sort themselves into sense. The only way the queen would step out from her rank would be death. I gasped. 'Is her majesty secretly ill?'

The king yelped with laughter. 'Yes, that's it. Her sorrow is an illness that gnaws away at her heart.' He looked past me to my father. 'A king should leave a pack of sons. Not one mad eunuch who is more hermit than hero, more monk than man. Your girl looks like she can deliver up sons enough, and she's a pleasant salve to the eyes as well.' He looked back at me. His face was as stern and inhuman as a carved stone. 'What say you, pretty Ophelia? Will you have me as a husband?'

I couldn't believe my ears. I had thought he'd marry me to Prince Hamlet, but now he talked of marriage to himself instead. Was he testing me in some way, trying to gauge my faithfulness to his remaining son?

'You have a wife,' I said, and to my disgust, my voice trembled, 'and she's as fine and fair a lady as ever ruled a Christian kingdom.'

'She's old,' said the king in a voice that sounded close to a snarl. 'She can bear me no more children. She's of no further worth to me. Denmark is doomed if I don't leave a strong son to rule.'

'Nevertheless, sir, the queen is your wife in the eyes of both the law and of God.'

He thundered, 'I am the law in Denmark.' I met his glare and didn't look away even though my knees trembled. Finally he sank back in his throne. 'I don't think my wife will last for long.'

'She's healthy, sir. No sickness inhabits her, nor does she waste away.'

'Still, she grieves overmuch.' Amusement crept back into his voice. 'I hear she paces back and forth atop the battlements, often leaning over the parapet from which the prince perished, and she's been known frequently to whisper, "My son, my son, would to God I'd died with thee."'

'This is not true, sire! I am her companion nearly every day, and never—'

'I believe,' said the king, 'she goes up there each day after you've departed from her.'

He was lying. The queen never went near the parapets. It even terrified her to see me climb a tree. More than that, she had no more will or energy than a piece of damp seaweed washed upon the shore. It took all my coaxing to get her to walk with me in the afternoon.

He said softly, 'Have you not heard these whisperings, Polonius?'

There was a long pause, and then my father said, 'Yes, your majesty. Indeed, your majesty, I've heard all this and more.'

At that moment, if I could have disowned my father, I would have. I'd always known him for a king's man, but I'd never dreamt he'd sink to slandering the queen.

The king leaned back. I've noticed that many people lean back just before they tell big lies. 'They tell me that she bends over the parapet, staring down into the flood. I've ordered my attendants to watch her carefully, to keep her from all self-harm, but I much fear that one day she'll give my attendants the slip and throw herself off the wall and into the sea.'

My blood froze to ice. *He's going to kill the queen.* He wanted to father more sons, and so he was going to murder his wife and replace her with a girl of childbearing age.

Me.

I longed to scream, to fly at him and pummel him with my fists, to kick and bite and gouge. But just then I heard a soft cough. I looked upward, to the minstrel gallery. Yorick stood in the shadows there. He held up his hand in a warning gesture, shook his head, and then pressed his index finger to his lips.

He was right, of course. For once I was glad of the discipline that my training as a lady had given me. What I wanted most to do was to grab a sword and plunge it into the guts of this evil king, but I didn't know how to handle a sword and I doubted not but that one of the guards would stop me before the tip of my blade even scratched the king's doublet. No, there was nothing to be gained and much to be lost if I indulged myself in a show of my true feelings. After all, I was my father's daughter. I could use a waterfall of words to disguise my heart.

For a moment I held Yorick's eyes with mine to let him know that I'd heeded his message. Then I slid my eyes back to the king. Trying to look and sound as innocent as possible, I said carefully, 'I don't think her majesty is likely to harm herself.'

The king smiled. If a serpent could grin, it would have a smile identical to this one. 'Her majesty is mad with grief. I much fear what that grief could prompt her to do.'

'But her majesty is a good God-fearing woman. Well she knows that should she harm herself thus, she cannot be buried in consecrated ground and her soul will wander in hell forever.'

He sighed heavily. 'Grief and madness can overpower reason. We all pray that the queen stays in her right mind and far from the sickness of overmuch grief, but a king must be prepared for all that might come to pass. It's a pity that she bore me but two sons, but my queen – good woman though she may be – has watery blood and hadn't the stuff to bear many children.'

'You still have a living son, my lord.'

For a moment our eyes met and held like the blades of two swordsmen pressed firm against each other, but when the king spoke, his voice was surprisingly mild. 'There's much you don't know about my remaining son, Ophelia. Take comfort in that.'

I ignored him. It was fruitless to argue tonight with his irrational dislike for his remaining son no matter how superior Hamlet was to his dead brother. 'What of Claudius, my liege? He could take a wife and produce heirs that would carry the blood of your family into the next generation.'

'I want my sons to rule!' the king shouted, his face reddening. He fumbled for his cup and took a long drink. Then he slammed the cup down onto the table so hard it fell to its side, dark wine spilling across the surface and dripping to the floor. My father sprang forward to right it, but the king muttered, 'Leave it,' and my father moved back. There was a dark patch on the king's beard where the wine had spilled. He said softly, 'Ophelia, you do know that it's high treason to refuse the will of your king.'

'Even when he's wrong?'

My father gasped, 'Ophelia!' but I stood my ground.

To my surprise, the king didn't seem displeased. He kept his eyes on me even though he addressed my father. 'Your daughter has a strong will.'

'Forgive her, your majesty. She's young and she doesn't know what she's saying, but she'll be brought to understand that the will of the king, willy-nilly, is the will of his subjects, and a wilful woman will bring—'

The king gave a slow smile. 'I don't mind. It may be amusing to see how quickly she can be broken to the bridle. Her body is strong and healthy, and perhaps her strong will can help her produce strong sons.'

There was so much I wanted to spit out at him, but I used every bit of my strong will to hold my tongue.

As if he sensed my struggle, he gave me another of his serpent smiles. 'No more tonight. But think on it, Ophelia. Let yourself be schooled by your father. Remember your duty to Denmark and your king. It would be pity indeed should we have to put you to death.'

My father began one of his fluttery speeches, but I let my voice top his. 'God grant your good wife many more years of life.' My voice rang harsh like a knife dropped onto paving stones.

'So say we all,' the king said. He looked mighty pleased. 'But think over what I've told you.' He waved his hand in dismissal and picked up the jug of wine.

I forced my trembling knees to curtsey. My father was mouthing a speech about all the honour that the king was doing to our house, but neither the king nor I paid him any heed. My father kept talking as we backed away and backed out of the hall. As soon as we reached our chambers, he clapped me to his chest in a strong hug. Then he held me at arm's length to examine me as if I was an unexpected gift.

'A very great honour, a great honour indeed! I never dreamed of so great an honour! Just think, Ophelia, I will be father to a queen! God willing, I will be grandfather to a line of kings.'

I hated him. 'Father, he talks of murdering the queen!'

'Hush!' He looked all around, even though we were alone in our chamber. 'You have mistaken the matter, Ophelia. Our king would never do such a thing, and even if he did, it would be dangerous folly for us to talk of these matters.'

I made a most unladylike sound.

He gave my arm a shake. 'There is the taint of madness in the queen's blood, Ophelia. Who knows what she might do in her unruly grief?'

I must have looked as mutinous as I felt, for, to my shock, he slapped me hard. 'Give over that mulish look, girl, for our great day has arrived. Have you no sense? Are you not proud? Are you not jubilant for this great honour? You are to be queen, girl! Queen of all Denmark! I never dared hope that a mere girl could bring such honour to our family.'

'Have *you* no sense, Father? In order to make me queen, he plans to murder his present wife. Honour indeed!'

My father slapped me again. 'Treason! Treason even to think such a thing!'

'How can it be treason if it's true?'

His face grew red with anger. 'Our king is a great king, and the welfare of the state is his only concern.'

'He is a murderer, Father.'

'He serves Denmark. Sometimes we must all do things that we'd prefer not to do in service of a higher cause.'

'Like murder?'

'Sometimes one person must die to save an entire country.'

'And tell me, pray, how the death of the queen can save this country?'

'The king must leave a strong heir.'

'He has two heirs already, his brother Claudius and his son, Hamlet. How many heirs does he need?'

'Claudius, like the king, is not a young man, and he leaves no children.'

'Prince Hamlet is young and strong.'

'Prince Hamlet hasn't the temperament to rule.'

'Then let the king name one of his bastard sons to the throne.'

My father looked stunned. 'What? What is this foolishness?'

I pressed my advantage. 'I know, Father. I know all about his romps with the kitchen girls and such. I know that he's sired a passel of bastard brats. Let our poor queen live, and let him gather his bastards around him and train them to be the defenders of Denmark when he's gone.'

My father's face grew blood red. 'There are no bastard sons.'

How I wished I could slap him in return. 'You lie! I know that there have been many peasant girls who have given birth to the king's sons. Do not lie to me about that!'

'I don't deny, Ophelia, that there have been serving girls who've given birth—'

'Then do you claim that all their children are female?'

'No, but—'

'And do you deny, Father, that you yourself took the babes away at birth?'

'That much is true, but, Ophelia—'

'So why can you not go to where you left the babies and bring them back to court to be raised as true sons of the king? God in Heaven, I reckon he's sired enough bastards to fill half an army. Fetch them back.'

'I cannot.'

'Can not or *will* not, sir?'

'*Can* not!'

I couldn't stomach his foolishness. My angry voice topped his. 'And just why can you not bring these babies back?'

'I cannot bring them back because I didn't deliver them to foster mothers. When I took the babies away, I took them away not to be raised, but to be killed.'

23

My knees began to tremble, and I had to lean against the wall for support. 'You killed all those babies?'

My father took several nervous steps away from me. He picked up a seal from the table and began to turn it around in his plump fingers. 'Not me, no. I wasn't the one who did the deed. But, on the orders of my king, I did deliver the newborn male by-blows over to be put to death.'

I thought of all the small, helpless babies I'd seen in my days down in the village. 'They were innocent babes. How could you kill them?'

'My king had commanded it.'

'But, Father—'

'Ophelia, it's our part to serve our king, to do whatsoever he demands. It's not our part to question. Besides, Danes have always taken pride in absolute loyalty to their king, even unto death.'

'But to kill his own sons! What danger could those defence-less things have represented?'

He put the seal down on the table. 'Babies grow to be men. And more than one kingdom has been pulled all to pieces by a usurper, a king's bastard who claims the throne. Sometimes a few people must indeed perish in order to insure the good of the multitudes. For the good of Denmark, the king couldn't take the chance of leaving a usurpation as his legacy. If that meant that a handful of children had to die in order to buy peace and prosperity for the entire kingdom, then that's the price we must pay.'

I took a deep breath. 'Could you not have left the baby with some peasant to raise, never telling her that he was the king's child? Would it not have been enough to let the babe grow up ignorant of his heritage?'

'Those weren't my orders. The king had commanded—'

But I could bear to hear no more of this. 'Stop it!' I shrieked, my hands pressed over my ears.

My father's mouth opened, but I wouldn't stay to listen. Even though I was dressed only in my shift, I ran from the room out into the hall.

Two ghosts stood like sentinels outside our door, as if the kingdom of the unseen had placed an honour guard to watch over me. I paid them no mind as I dashed up to the battlements, my refuge, perhaps the one place in the entire castle that I could hope to be alone.

It was raining. Almost at once I was soaked, but I didn't care. I began to cry, but my tears were those of rage rather than anger. Where could I go for rescue or aid? I could tell the queen what had passed, but I doubted the knowledge would make her any safer. Indeed, it might in fact hasten her death. If I didn't wed the king, he'd quickly find another girl to marry, so my defiance and death would make no difference. I could see no way out of this maze.

'This is bitter weather,' Yorick said, 'yet I thought I might find you up here.'

'It's more bitter than you know.' I quickly told him all about the king's slaughtered babies.

'The gods of history eat children for breakfast,' he said.

'You must help me, Yorick. You are my single hope. King Hamlet plans to kill his queen.'

Yorick looked away and sighed. 'Poor lady.'

I took a step away from the wall. 'We must stop him, you and I.'

Yorick slowly shook his head. 'There's nothing we can do.'

I refused to accept that. 'We will stop it.'

Yorick's face looked very tired. 'How?'

I pawed through my mind for a plan. All things could be changed, even the schemes of a king. 'We could tell someone,' I suggested.

'Who?'

'I don't know. Some of the soldiers.'

'All the soldiers serve the king, Ophelia. They've sworn absolute fealty to him. They swore to live and die by his word. For them to go against their king would be the death of their souls.'

'But if they don't, it will be the death of the queen!'

Yorick moved a little closer, but there was no warmth from his body to help shelter me against the chill of the rain. 'We will get no help from them.'

'Then we must go to the queen and warn her.'

Yorick cocked his head. 'Will she believe you?'

'Yes.' I hesitated, then repeated, 'Yes.'

Yorick said nothing.

'She must,' I said, as if by my passion I could turn my words true.

There was a moment's silence. I heard the raindrops patter against the stones of the walls. Then Yorick said, 'Even if she believes you, what will she do?'

'She will stand up against the king.'

'Has she ever done it before?'

'She will do it now.'

Yorick shook his head. 'She doesn't say him nay, even when he beats her. What can she do now?'

'She can run away.'

'And go where?'

'Anywhere.'

'She has no family, no money. What can she live on?'

I was sick of his objections. 'She can learn a trade and take to weaving.'

Amusement flickered in Yorick's eyes. 'I don't think a queen can throw over being a queen and take to a trade.'

'Better than to stay here and let one of the king's loyal soldiers toss her over a parapet to her death in the sea.'

'In the eyes of the law and the church, she's the king's property, like his hounds or his boots. She cannot leave him.'

Oh, for the wings of an eagle to fly far from this coil.

'I could write to Prince Hamlet,' I said suddenly. 'He could come back here and be his mother's champion, defend her from his father's evil.'

Again Yorick shook his head. 'The prince idolizes his father. He would do anything at all to gain his father's love.'

'Even betray his mother?'

For a moment Yorick considered this, and then he said, 'I don't know for certain, but I suspect that the young prince would even cast his mother away if it meant he could finally win his father's approval. He has been hungry for his father's notice his entire life.'

'Then I myself will keep watch over the queen to protect her—'

'You cannot watch her without cease night and day.'

'No!' In frustration, I slammed my fist against the stone wall. There had to be something I could do if only I could think of it. 'I'll not let this happen. You and I must puzzle out what must be done to stop the king.'

Yorick put his hands on the stone balustrade and stood looking out over the rain-veiled sea. He looked very small and thin against the wide dark sky. 'This is a hard truth, Ophelia, but there's no way to stop the king once he's set his mind to murder.'

Suddenly something came clear.

'Yorick,' I said in my gentlest voice, 'it was King Hamlet who murdered *you*, wasn't it?'

24

For a moment Yorick looked stricken, and even though he was small of body, he seemed to shrink into himself even more. I could hear the keening of the sea in the distance and the lonely cry of the birds. Finally he whispered, 'Hamlet killed me.'

'I knew it!' I said, my blood boiling with fury. 'King Hamlet murders and murders, and he'll murder again, and nothing is done to stop him.'

Yorick gave me a queer look. 'You don't understand.'

God's blood, but I was sick unto death of folk telling me that I didn't understand! I banged my hand against the ledge. 'Yorick, the difficulty is not that I don't understand, but that I understand much too well.' A sudden gust of wind lashed me with a sheet of cold rain. 'You and all the others tell me that the king cannot be stopped, but, listen to me well, for I now tell you not only *can* the king be stopped from his frenzy of murders, but that he *will* be stopped.'

Yorick gave me the kind of pitying look folk might give a cripple who announces she plans to dance at the Midwinter Revels. 'Ophelia, your heart means well, but how can you stop King Hamlet?'

'How can I stop him? How can I *not* stop him?' Suddenly my memory flew to a story from the Apocrypha. It was one that the queen hadn't cared for but that I'd loved best of all. 'Judith!'

'Your stepmother? How can she—'

'No, Yorick. In the Bible. She invites the enemy general

into her tent, and when he's sleeping, she slices off his head.' I'd need to get a weapon, but I didn't see that as an insurmountable obstacle. 'It's probably more difficult to slice off a head than the Bible made it seem, but the story implied that Judith had had no previous experience with decapitation either, so if she could do something like this, then surely I can too.'

'Lady Ophelia—'

'I need to get me a sword. Then I need to figure out how to hide it. That will be a challenge. On the other hand, it should be easy to get the king to invite me into his bedchamber. Perhaps if I don my cloak when I go to him—'

'You don't know how to wield a sword. The king would have it out of your hands in an instant. Besides, as I know well, violent death is seldom as swift or clean a matter as the living suppose.'

There was an emptiness behind his voice. Doubtless his death had been neither clean nor easy. I burned to know just what had happened, but while the queen had taught me a wealth of manners, she hadn't instructed me whether or not it was proper to ask the dead about the manner of their death. I suddenly remembered the way the king had kicked and damaged the little dog who'd annoyed him. No doubt he'd done something similar to his court fool.

'You must cast off these fancies,' Yorick said, 'for the king is a fortress that cannot be assailed.'

'No.' By now the idea of killing the king had taken hold of me. I didn't relish killing for its own sake, but there seemed to be no other way to stop the murder intended by the king. 'The way I look at it, Yorick, is that I don't have a choice whether or not to commit a murder.'

'Of course you have a choice.'

'Hear me out. If I do nothing to stop the king, then he'll murder the queen, and it will be on my hands, and I will be damned by the sin of omission. If I am to be consigned to hell, I prefer to be damned through a sin of commission. Someone is going to die whether I do anything or not, so let it be the king who is the one responsible for so many murders himself and not the innocent queen.'

'Go to the queen. Tell her all.'

'To what avail? She will not believe me. Even if she did, she can do no more than you to escape the power of the king, her husband.'

Yorick pressed his hand to his brow. 'Believe me, Lady Ophelia, you've plunged in seas too deep and cold for you to swim.'

His attitude surprised me. 'Of all folk, Yorick, I'd think *you* would want King Hamlet killed.'

'Oh, I want Hamlet killed.' There was a note in Yorick's voice that I'd never heard before . . . a kind of snarling savagery.

'Then kill him.'

'We haven't that power. Ghosts cannot kill. That's a privilege reserved for the living.'

A new thought hit me. 'Yorick, Prince Holger, is he a ghost here now?'

Yorick shook his head again. 'Not just any dead person can become a ghost. Only the murdered can still walk the earth. We don't know what happens to the souls of those who die peacefully in their beds or by simple accident. Prince Holger wasn't murdered. Therefore he's not one of us.'

I wasn't sure I understood him aright. 'Do you mean that all the ghosts who walk this castle have been murdered?'

He nodded.

'By King Hamlet?' I asked. 'But that can't be right. Some of them wear antique garb.'

Yorick's words confirmed my thought. 'Most of my fellow ghosts were murdered long ago.'

Perhaps it was indelicate, but I longed to know more. 'How long are you condemned to walk the castle?'

A blank expression drifted into his eyes. 'We don't know. Some of us believe that we have a fixed number of years upon the earth and then we will disappear, but I don't share that belief. As long as I've walked, not one of the others has passed to a life beyond. He absently reached for a gull feather that had landed along the stone parapet, brushing against it as if he'd flick it away, but the feather didn't move. 'Others believe that our only hope of passing beyond the bonds of the earth is to persuade one of the living to avenge our death.'

'So if I kill King Hamlet, I'll aid you as well!'

Immediately, though, I felt a pang. It was selfish, true, but I didn't want Yorick to pass beyond. He'd been a good advisor and, along with the queen, my best friend since I'd come to the castle. I wanted him to stay here until I myself had to leave. Before I could give any voice to my thoughts, he said, 'Lady Ophelia, face the harsh truth. There's no way to kill the king.'

'You are wrong, Yorick! He can be killed and I'll find the way to do it.'

Through the rest of the morning and well into the afternoon, I tugged and nipped at the matter like a dog worrying a bone, but I couldn't think of a plan. I didn't trust my face to hide my thoughts, so I sent a servant to tell the queen that I was indisposed and couldn't attend her this day. I couldn't settle to anything, and once I was halfway to the kitchens to confide in Piet before I realized that my news might put him in danger, so I turned back again, my errand incomplete. I was so agitated that I was surprised that when I touched anything, my hands didn't flash out sparks. My body suddenly felt much too small for my spirit, and I wanted to fight, wrestle, scream, flog, *anything* that might siphon off the fury inside.

Instead of going to middag, I went to the chapel to pray, but I couldn't bear to stay long motionless on my knees, so I gave that task over and walked out of the castle instead, even though I was now a young lady and shouldn't be walking about the countryside like a servant or peasant.

I walked to one of my childhood haunts, the ruined monastery. It was more crumbled, more overgrown with vines than ever. I broke a branch off a sapling and strode about the graveyard, whipping the monuments and gravestones. The action brought me no nearer a solution, but it did tap off some of my wildness.

The best plan I could come up with was to consult Prince Claudius. I knew he treasured the queen, and he had the king's ear as well. Perhaps he could find a way to stop the king's mad plan so that I wouldn't have to resort to murder. In fact, on my long walk back to the castle, I began to think that I had – out of lack of sleep and shock at discovering how my father had routinely slaughtered the king's bastard sons – allowed my imagination to gallop away with me.

I slipped into the hall for supper just before the doors were shut. I had no appetite, so I toyed with my food until the queen withdrew. I lingered in the passageway to the royal chambers in the niche from which I'd once spied on the king, slipping out only when I saw Claudius approach.

He was startled to see me. 'Lady Ophelia!'

I swept him a curtsey. 'My lord, I'd have some words with you.' I looked pointedly at the two men who accompanied him.

'Go wait for me in the hall, and I'll join you there,' he told them. 'Now, Ophelia—'

I pressed a finger to my lips and tilted my head to his companions, not speaking until a turn of the passageway took them out of sight. 'Prince Claudius, I must speak to you of a delicate matter and I dare not risk anyone else hearing. Will you go with me up to the battlements where we may speak alone?'

I couldn't read his face, but he bowed and stepped aside, gesturing me to precede him. We traversed the warren of corridors and climbed at last up to the roof. A flock of ghosts sat perched along the walls like birds come home to roost, Yorick among them. I made sure there was no one else up there to overhear us, but Claudius fixed his eyes on the Swedish shore.

'My brother is inclined to dismiss the rumours about young Erik Strong Arm, but I wish he'd post a watch on the Swedish coast so that Erik doesn't sneak over like a thief in the night and so attack us in a foolish attempt to win back the lands forfeited by his father. Better to waste toil to be safe than to lose all by being sorry.'

I seized the opening. 'Prince Claudius, it's of your brother that I would speak.' I poured forth the story of the night before.

When I'd finished, he stood in silence. I couldn't tell if he believed me or not. Then an idea hit me with such a force that it made me dizzy. *What if he's in league with the king?* If he was indeed his brother's confidant, then perhaps this confession of mine had been enough to seal my own doom.

Fear seized my throat, so it took all my strength to croak out, 'I cannot let the queen be killed.'

The falling shadows didn't allow me to see his face clearly. 'Tell me, Ophelia, if the queen could be put aside by some peaceful means, would you then be willing to marry my brother?'

An image of Prince Hamlet's face rippled across my mind. 'Never. I'd die sooner than marry him.'

When he didn't respond, I added, 'But, forgive me, my lord, but I don't think that the king will choose peaceful means when foul ones serve his purpose much more quietly and swiftly. Indeed, I fear he'll act soon, for the farther time travels from the death of his son, the less likely will people be to believe that the queen would kill herself from grief. I don't know what is to be done, but the queen has been more a mother to me than any other I've known, and I'd do anything in my power to ensure her long life.'

Claudius pressed closer, his body tight against mine, almost as if we were lovers. I heard the rasp of his breath and felt the heat from his skin. 'Would you, Ophelia? Would you indeed?'

Words spilled from me like beer from an overturned tankard. 'He hits her. Although she's his wife and his queen, he strikes her the way he strikes a dog.'

Claudius gave a moan and released me. 'I know. I know. At least, I suspect as much, although even to me she'll not tell the whole truth. And I'm powerless to prevent it.' He struck himself across the chest. 'Powerless!'

Lord above, did everyone in this kingdom throw up their hands and prefer wailing to action? 'I don't believe in powerlessness,' I said harshly. 'There's always a way, although sometimes it takes a while to find it.'

'What can I do?'

'You are a man. You are a prince. Surely you can find a way to stop him from his present mad course.'

'He will not listen to me! He has never listened, always judging himself the stronger and wiser.'

'He must be stopped.'

The ghosts slid off their perches and drew nearer, attracted by the passion of our words. Did they feed off human feelings the way we humans fed off bread? They seemed more eager than I'd ever seen them, almost panting with desire. For the first time, they scared me.

Oblivious to the ghosts crowding around us, Claudius said, 'If my brother is not stopped, he'll kill her indeed.' His hands groped to his sword, and he fingered its hilt. 'When you ended your tale, I had at first half a mind to kill you in order to protect her, but I realize that if you're not here, he'll simply choose some other young woman with whom to breed sons.'

'He has a remaining son. Prince Hamlet—'

'Prince Hamlet—' Claudius opened his mouth to say something, but then he shouldered the words aside.

I broke in. 'The king has set the queen's life at a pin's fee, and we must find a way to save this good lady.'

'Only the death of the king can save the life of the queen,' Claudius said.

Those were my very thoughts, but it seemed madness to have them so baldly stated. All around us the ghosts throbbed with eagerness.

'The king is old,' I said, ignoring the treason implicit in his words. 'Yet is he hale and hearty and shows no disposition to oblige us by dying on his own.'

'I can get near enough to stab him,' Claudius whispered, 'but his guards would kill me all of an instant, and even to protect the queen, I wouldn't leave my country in the hands of her son.'

I didn't understand why he'd say that, but he continued before I could object. 'Do you not agree that in order to save the queen, the king must die?'

God spits the lukewarm out of his mouth. I nodded my agreement. 'But I don't see how this can come to pass.'

'No more can I,' Claudius said with a groan and buried his face in his hands.

'We cannot let him continue in his present course,' I said. 'If he doesn't have her pushed off the ramparts, he'll kill her when he beats her like he beat her poor dog.'

I stopped short. In the silence I could hear the sea, but I also fancied all around me I could hear the ghosts panting.

I remembered back to the death of Blanche and what was locked in my closet.

Carefully I said, 'I have a poison. Pour it into the ear of a sleeper, and he'll never wake.'

ACT TWO

Treason

25

King Hamlet died the next afternoon.

I wasn't the one who poured the poison in his ear. That was Claudius. I could never have come close enough to the sleeping king to do the deed, but Claudius had unhindered access to his brother. I was the one, though, who gave Claudius the vial of poison and explained to him exactly what to do when he caught the king asleep.

It was Chance the next day that made the afternoon unseasonably sunny and warm. Chance sent the beer-sodden king staggering out to the orchard to nap after the heavy middag of salted beef and stewed calf's brains.

It was Claudius, though, who made certain that the king would never wake.

The story given out by his guards was that while the king was asleep, a serpent bit him. Folk knew that snakes grew bold in these waning days of autumn, jealous of any sunny spot, so it made sense that the king could be bitten as he lay helpless on his sun-warmed stone bench.

Before the message of King Hamlet's death had time to reach Wittenberg, his Council of State met and decided that Claudius should be our next king. I was angry at the slight done to Prince Hamlet, but I consoled myself that Claudius had no legitimate heir, so on his death the throne would almost certainly pass to his nephew. Unless, of course, Prince – *King* – Claudius decided to snatch a page from his brother's book and take a young wife of childbearing years.

To my surprise, the queen seemed genuinely to grieve the loss of her bullying husband. I didn't remind her of her husband's many cruelties, nor did I tell her that he himself had been plotting her own death.

According to Lord Rosencrantz who accompanied him, Prince Hamlet rode night and day to reach home as quickly as possible. Six days after the king's death, when I was keeping vigil in the chapel with the queen and much of the court, the door clattered open, and Prince Hamlet strode down the aisle, his hair standing wild on his head like a tempest cloud, his eyes flashing wildly. Without even a look at his mother or me, he flung himself on the king's coffin. He clutched the lid, sobbing wildly. I ached to go to him and comfort him, but it wasn't my place, so I watched him as sympathetic tears ran down my own cheeks.

For a while he was left to cry in peace, and then King Claudius hauled himself stiffly to his feet. He held out a hand to the queen, and she sprang up, almost nimble as a girl. She moved forward to her son, and she stretched one white, thin hand to his shoulder. He leapt away as if he himself had been bitten by the serpent said to kill his father.

'My dear Hamlet, let us comfort one another,' she said.

'Comfort, Madam? How can there be comfort when my father is dead? The very heart of Denmark has been stopped, so I fail to understand why the rest of the body bothers to keep on living. My only comfort, good mother, is to be with my father in the grave. Save your comfort for women and those who are too weak to feel their grief like a man.'

He gave an exaggerated bow and swept out of the chapel without one glance at me. Oh, how I longed to go after him, to try to gentle his tortured face and coiled body. His words had been cruel, but I knew he didn't mean them but spoke all hugger-mugger out of sorrow for his father.

Neither the queen nor Hamlet attended supper, so as

soon as the meal was concluded, I hurried over to Lords Rosencrantz and Guildenstern who sat alone at the high table.

'How does the prince?' I asked.

'We feared he'd tear himself apart in the throes of this great sorrow,' Guildenstern said. 'He hardly eats or sleeps.'

'We rode day and night to reach here as quickly as possible,' said Lord Rosencrantz.

'Where is the prince?' I asked. 'Shut up in his chamber?'

The two men looked at each other, and something seemed to pass between them.

'Out of the castle,' said Guildenstern carefully. His stubby fingers pulled against his beard.

I wouldn't be fobbed off. 'Out where?'

Rosencrantz made a face and scratched the back of his neck uneasily.

'Tell me,' I insisted.

'He has been seized with the notion—' began Rosencrantz, but Guildenstern interrupted him.

'If you tell her, then let the prince's fury be on your head.'

'Tell me,' I said, 'or you will feel my fury which is infinitely more cruel than that of the prince.'

Guildenstern shrugged his way to his feet. 'I must pay my respects to the queen.'

'She's in prayer,' I said. 'She will not look favourably at being disturbed.'

Guildenstern slapped a small hand against his stocky chest. 'She will see *me*,' he announced.

'Should I tell her?' Rosencrantz asked him.

Guildenstern shot him an irritated look. 'Do as you will.' He took two steps away, then turned back. 'She will find out soon enough. Tell her, don't tell her, it's all the same to me.'

As soon as Guildenstern was gone, I leaned over the table

toward Rosencrantz. His scarred eye seemed to droop even further. 'Tell me where Lord Hamlet is.'

'You will not like the sight. Wait until morning.'

'Tell me now.'

He blew the air out of his nose and said, 'Go down to the shore. There you will find our young lord.'

It was already dark. I knew that I shouldn't be wandering about the countryside alone after dark, but I was desperate to see the grief-stricken prince. I've never liked the sea at night. It's too vast, too empty, too lonely, too indifferent to the struggles of human beings. The sea wouldn't care in the least if every man and woman were wiped off the face of the earth.

At first I saw nothing different, and then far down the shore to the west, a huge bonfire glittered. I made toward that.

I didn't know what to expect, but I own that I was surprised by what met my eyes.

Next to the huge bonfire was the skeleton of a new-made ship, turned upside down and supported by the frame of logs. It had the sleek lines of one of the old ships of our ancestors, one of the flat-bottomed boats that helped Danes once rule the world. Five or six men – stripped to the waist even though the air was chill – bustled about her, laying boards in place and hammering pegs in to attach them. Why would anyone be building a ship this late in the night? Why build one of the old ships? These days men wanted bigger ships, big enough to carry huge loads of merchandise or fish.

Of course, the modern ships lacked the beauty of the sleek Viking vessels, graceful as wooden swans or floating dragons. Ragnor's boyhood ship had been made to the old design, and this ship promised to be even more beautiful.

Its curved prow stood propped up by two sawhorses. The completed ship would have the head of a dragon. Already the dragon was half painted with gold leaf scales that glittered in the firelight, huge pitiless black eyes, and red teeth tipped in gold. With a start I realized the workman painting the dragon head was Lord Hamlet himself.

Before I could speak, a firm hand slid against my waist.

'Come to join in the madness?'

I pulled away and saw Ragnor standing there, clad only in his leather breeches and with a strip of leather holding back his tumbled black curly hair. He looked like the picture of a pirate. He lacked only a knife between his teeth.

Then I recognized the other workmen, his ship-building brother and some other lads from the village.

'Why do you build a second ship in the old fashion? To keep your childhood craft company?'

He laughed, and his teeth gleamed white in the firelight. 'This one is a beauty, isn't she?'

I looked up and down the lovely little boat. 'She's a beauty,' I said softly. 'But why do you build her?'

Ragnor gave a bitter laugh. 'We build her to burn.'

That sounded uncomfortably like a riddle. 'Then will she not sail?'

'This little beauty is built for one brief voyage only, and then she'll be turned to ash.'

'No!' It would be sinful to burn this lovely ship. 'She's too beautiful to burn.' In my agitation, my voice slipped back toward the twang of the village. 'It would be downright cruel to destroy something so perfectly wrought.'

Ragnor inclined his head toward Hamlet who was still busily painting. 'Then tell that to his lordship, for he's hired our labour for this task.'

The sight of Hamlet filled my eyes, shining down everything else. I liked Ragnor and was relieved that he seemed to have forgotten the rancour of our last meetings, but he was no more than a mote on the magnificence of his lordship. Hamlet was a man, while Ragnor was still partly a boy. Hamlet was the golden sun, eclipsing Ragnor's dark handsomeness as the daytime sun shines down all the stars in the sky.

Forgetting Ragnor, I flew to Hamlet as the soul of a saint flies to salvation. 'My lord,' I breathed.

He didn't seem surprised to see me. 'What think you of my handiwork, Ophelia?' he asked, not pausing in his brush strokes.

'It's glorious. The whole ship will be glorious.'

He nodded. 'Worthy of a king.'

'Worthy of *you*, my lord.' Did he intend this as a gift for the new king, Claudius? I didn't recall that he'd ever seemed overly fond of his uncle.

'I hope it's worthy of my father.'

My knees suddenly got shaky, and only an act of will kept me from sitting down right on the sand. Had grief deranged his mind? Had he forgotten that his father was no more? 'My lord,' I said in my most cautious tone, 'you do recall, do you not, that your father is dead?'

And it was my poison that killed him. My stomach lurched like a bear in a trap.

Anger flashed in his eyes. 'Of course I know my father is dead.'

Then why are you making a ship as a gift for him? I forced these words back from my mouth and waited. After a moment he laughed.

'Do you think me mad, girl? Do you think that I expect my father to rise from the grave?' He slapped his brush against the prow. 'I do think my father the greatest man to walk the earth, but even I don't expect him to rise from the dead.'

'Then I don't understand, my lord, why you're making this elaborate gift for your father when he's not here to accept it.'

'Silly puss,' Hamlet said, his tone as jovial as if it were a feast day. 'This will be his funeral ship, of course. We will lay his body atop it, set it alight with fire, and then shove it out to the sea to let it float where it will.'

This news didn't reassure me in the least. 'My lord, that was how they sent off a king in the olden days, but in the modern world—'

'My father was a great warrior and so he deserves the old rite,' he said. 'I want his departure to be the most resplendent ceremony in Denmark's memory. Never again will the world witness such a man, and so I want even the very seas to blaze with his taking off.'

I thought back to the man who tumbled the uneducated serving girls and killed their bastard sons.

'He was the perfect husband to my mother—'

I remembered her bruises, the way he kicked her dog to death, his plan to kill his wife by having her thrown from the top of the castle so that he could marry me.

'A father beyond price.'

Now my mind was flooded with memories of the king mocking his younger son, comparing him unfavourably with his brother or the Norwegian prince, Erik Strong Arm. I remembered how he'd called out the complaint that it was the wrong son who had died.

'My father wasn't only a great king, but a great man as well.'

Did Hamlet even know that he was lying? True, it's common to say only good things about the dead, but surely Hamlet was carrying this custom too far.

'He was a good father to your brother,' I began cautiously, but he interrupted me.

'My father has forbidden us to speak of my brother, and I choose to carry out his wishes. I'll devote my life to carrying out every one of his wishes.'

'But he's dead, my lord. What he wished no longer matters.'

Hamlet leapt to his feet. 'It matters all the more now that he's dead. Now more than ever it's vital that I do nothing at all that would have displeased my good father.' His eyes shone, and there was a reverent tone to his voice as if he were a blessed martyr and his father the faith for which he'd die.

'We all have faults,' I began, but he again interrupted me.

'My father had none.'

I said nothing, but my face must have expressed my inward thoughts, for he gave a laugh.

'I see you think I protest too much, but truly, Ophelia, my father was a man without compare. Perhaps Hector or Holger the Great or Harold Bluetooth or Aeneas might have been my father's equal, but he was truly peerless among all men who walk this world.'

Already he'd rewritten his own history. His father's own orders had erased Prince Holger from the family history. The dead king was now a saint, and Hamlet had transformed himself into the much loved son. *Houses aren't the only things that can be haunted and ghost-ridden*. People can be too.

And Hamlet was truly haunted by the false memory of his father.

'No!' said King Claudius.

'Outrageous,' said my father.

'Barbaric,' said the queen. 'Sweet, but barbaric.'

'He *deserves* this,' argued Hamlet. We were in the queen's chambers, three days later. Elspeth had brewed us a posset of ale, butter, and spices that warmed our insides, but lizard tongues of cold still flicked about my toes. King Hamlet had lain in state for the requisite nine days, and the funeral rites were to be celebrated on the morrow. Hamlet continued, 'The death of a great man demands great ceremony. As my father blazed through life, so let him blaze his way into death. It would be infamy indeed to toss him into a grave hole like the meanest of peasants.'

'We will not toss him into a hole,' the new king said in a tight voice. 'We will see him to his final resting place with the proper pageantry and obsequies.'

'The king, my father, wasn't the man to creep meekly underground like a tame cat crawling beneath a blanket. No! To take his place among his forebearers, he should sail boldly, a warrior. Send him forth, I beg you, on a blazing ship so that his passing turns the water to fire, the night to day. Thus much has he deserved of you and Denmark, and much more.'

'My son,' the queen said gently, 'it has been hundreds of years since the last king went forth in the manner you describe.'

'It has been hundreds of years since Denmark saw a man as great as my father.'

King Claudius leaned forward. 'Nephew Hamlet, it's commendable that you wish to do such honour to your father, but we're a civilized nation now. These pagan rites would be impious, a crime against God, to desecrate your father's body by setting it aflame. My brother was above all a gentle, Christian king who would want above all a gentle, civilized, Christian burial.'

'My *father* was a gentle, Christian king, but he deserves a passing to rattle the very gates of heaven.'

Did no one but me remember the king as he was? It was bad enough that Hamlet saw him as a loving father when the truth was the old king could scarcely stomach his younger son, but now everyone was nodding at Claudius's description of the cruel, capricious reprobate of a king. He had been neither gentle nor civilized. Perhaps he'd indeed been a good king, but he hadn't been a good man and yet these folk were treating him as if he'd been the spit and image of the beloved St John. I wanted to scream. Were all these folk play-acting, or had they come to believe these comforting falsehoods? I wanted to shake them and shout, 'Tell the truth, tell the truth.'

Then I caught myself up short. I was hardly one to chastise them. I dared complain about their blurred vision when I myself was throwing sand in their eyes. I was a murderer. I'd killed the old king, just as much as Claudius had, and here I sat as meek as milk. How could I be so indignant that the truth about the king was blurred when I was determined that my own truth would never come out?

'We have slaved night and day to build that ship in time,' Hamlet shouted. 'You have seen it. Is it not rare, a thing of surpassing beauty?'

From the corner where he sat in the shadows, Lord Rosencrantz spoke up. 'The ship is indeed a gem, my dear lord, and therefore it would be a travesty to destroy such a lovely bauble.'

Lord Guildenstern, who sat next to him, said, 'Let us preserve it, rather, as a treasure for Denmark so future generations might see how glorious a thing our longboats were.'

Hamlet sprang to his feet, his face flushed with fury. 'I built this ship for my father, not for future generations. What care I for future generations when my father is dead?'

Claudius said smoothly, 'Your father would be mightily pleased by your act, nephew, but—'

'But you will not use it in his funerary rites?'

There was a moment of silence. I could hear the logs crackling in the fireplace and Hamlet's laboured breathing. Then Claudius said, 'No. We will not use it in his funerary rites.'

A cry was torn out of Hamlet like the cry of a bird who discovers her nest violated and all her chicks killed. Then he ran from the room. The queen stretched out her arm toward him, but let it fall. She turned to the new king. 'Claudius?' she said in a voice heavy with worry.

'This is a bad business,' my father muttered. 'A bad, bad business indeed.'

Rosencrantz and Guildenstern exchanged troubled looks, and only old Elspeth, huddled sleepily by the fire, seemed untouched by what had transpired. My heart felt swollen to the bursting point with pity for Hamlet. Nothing he ever did seemed good enough in this unforgiving kingdom. Try as he might, he could never win a tithe of his father's love, and now his uncle dashed on the rocks his efforts to honour his father in death. It was discourteous, but I ran out of the room so I could find Hamlet and console him. Behind me I heard both my father and the queen call out my name, but I ignored them.

I asked the guard outside the room which way Lord Hamlet had gone, and I had to ask the same of two more guards and one log boy before I realized that he'd head down to the sea shore. I didn't stop even to snatch up a cloak, but I ran after him as fast as I could.

He was taller than I, but he was accustomed to the life of a scholar, so he was slow of foot, even when he ran. By the time he reached the ship, I was only a few paces behind him. The completed ship was indeed beautiful, stretched gracefully on the sands just out of the water. She'd been painted scarlet and gold, and now the builders were aboard giving her one last polishing in the lights of the lanterns and torches that made her gleaming surface bright as day. Lord Hamlet ran to her prow and shouted up at the men on the deck, 'Help me push her out into the water.'

The men looked startled, but Hamlet repeated his request.

The men hesitated, but Ragnor, who had been polishing the railings, shouted, 'Do as the prince commands.'

The men scrambled off the ship and leant their shoulders to Hamlet's. The ship slid smoothly into the water like a child tumbling from a tree into his mother's arms. Hamlet struggled aboard.

'My lord,' Ragnor called, 'you cannot sail her alone. Give us a chance to board her, too.'

But it was clear that Hamlet had no desire to sail her. Instead he'd grabbed a wooden cask and was sprinkling its contents all over the deck and railings of the ship.

'My lord, have a care,' Ragnor called. 'You are courting danger with your reckless behaviour. My lord—'

Hamlet paid him no heed. He threw the cask down and tugged a torch out of its holder. Then, to my horror, he pointed it downward to the railings. With a whoosh of wind, the railings caught on fire.

'Hamlet!' I screamed. I ran down to the water and started to the ship. It wasn't yet far out from shore, still in water that I reckoned was no deeper than my chest. But the sea pushed against me and the tide tugged at my sodden skirts so I couldn't move swiftly.

Faster than I could have believed, the fire spread across the ship, turning it into a blazing star on the dead black waters. Lord Hamlet was clearly outlined against the golden flames. 'Jump!' I screamed. 'Hamlet, save yourself! Jump!'

But he seemed incapable of hearing me. Behind me I heard Ragnor mutter a string of curses, and then he pushed past me through the cold water. He was a dark shape shoving his way onto the ship. He lunged against Hamlet and toppled him into the water, then he dived himself. The golden flaming ship continued to drift serenely out to sea.

I pushed on through the water to where Hamlet was struggling to stand. My waterlogged skirts were immensely heavy so it seemed to take forever to reach him. I wrapped my arms around his shivering body. 'Shh,' I said. 'Shh.'

Ragnor surfaced on the far side of the prince. He put a hand under the prince's elbow. 'Get him to shore,' he said curtly.

We led the dazed prince onto the shore, and Ragnor called out for wrappings to be brought. Soon the prince was swaddled in one man's cloak, while Ragnor and I were tucked around with blankets that smelled of sheep and sweat. I still had my arms around Hamlet who shivered with a cold that was deeper than the cold of the body.

When we were warm enough to speak, Ragnor said, 'My lord, that was a foolish thing to do.'

Few nobles would allow a peasant to speak to them in such a fashion, but Hamlet only whispered, 'If my father cannot have the ship, I don't wish it to go to the service of anyone else.'

'You could have killed yourself,' Ragnor said.

Hamlet gave a little laugh. 'Would that have been such a bad thing?'

His answer scared me. I pressed tighter to him, and his arms closed tighter around me.

'The son of a king shouldn't ask such a question,' Ragnor told him, and he directed one of the men to take Hamlet over to the fire and pour him some hot wine. When I made to follow him, though, Ragnor pulled me back.

'How stand things, Cat, between you and the prince?'

I pulled away. 'My friendship with Prince Hamlet is no concern of yours, Ragnor, and I'm not one to flap my tongue about nothing.'

'Keep yourself far from him, girl, for he's not a good one for you to know.'

I looked hard at Ragnor in the flickering firelight, dark and sturdy and solid of body, and then I looked past him to the prince, pale and finely drawn. He looked so fragile in the play of light and shadow, and I could feel my face soften as I looked at him. He was so beautiful, even wet and cold and huddled in a peasant cloak.

Ragnor's rough fingers closed around my chin and forced my face over to look at him instead. His eyes were hard as sea glass. 'Cat, he's a bad bargain. Leave him alone.'

I was outraged. 'He is the best man I know. Kind, noble, caring—'

'He is in love with death, Cat. Perhaps he loves you, too, but I wager he will, in the end, choose death as his mistress.'

'Don't be so daft. How can you, a peasant, ever hope to understand a prince?'

'Then let me say the same thing to you, Cat. How can *you*, a peasant, hope to understand a prince?'

'I'm a peasant no longer! I've changed into a lady, Ragnor, and if you cannot recognize that Hamlet is a prince beyond price, then your eyes are too filled with the mud in which you wallow!'

That surprised a laugh from him. In a gentler tone he said, 'Cat, I grant him noble, kind, and a thousand desirable things, but once a man falls in love with death, he's a danger to all around him. My girl, steer your craft to a different ocean for there's no safe harbour here.'

I jerked my arm free. 'Nothing in this world can make me forsake the prince.'

Only when I was leading Hamlet back to the castle did I notice the beauty of the night. The sky was scattered thick with stars, and the moon was as full-bellied as a woman in her eighth month. Hamlet didn't speak all the way back, but he clung to me, and when we parted at the bottom of the stairway that led to his chambers, he kissed me gently. His lips were rough and tasted of salt, and I didn't know if that was from the sea or from his tears.

'Rest well, my good lord,' I whispered as he climbed the steps, 'for the morrow brings us a long day.'

When I reached my chambers, a fresh surprise awaited me.

26

Sprawled on a chair in the antechamber of our rooms was a young man in a fine silk doublet as green as a peacock's feathers. Underneath he wore scarlet trousers cross-gartered with gold. I was uncomfortably conscious of my wet, salt-stained clothes and my dishevelled hair.

'Where have you been, Ophelia?' my father demanded in a voice so full of irritation that it squeaked.

But the young man leaped over to me and clasped my arms. 'Dear sister!' he cried out. 'For my entire life I've wanted a little sister, and now at one blow do I not only have one, but I have a sister who is doubtless the fairest maid in all Christendom as well!'

'She's passably fair when she's clean and tidy,' my father grumbled, 'but now she plays the hoyden and must give you a disgust of her.'

The young man winked at me. He was taller than I by half a head, and his hair was brown and curly. He wore it clipped closer to his scalp than was the custom in Denmark, and a diamond earring dangled from one ear. His nose was a little flat, as if it had been patted down when he was a baby and had never sprung back into place, but over all he was handsome enough, and while he was more carefully curled and groomed than even the queen herself, there was nothing of the woman about his strong shoulders and muscular arms and legs. His eyes twinkled, but it seemed to me he stood back a few paces behind his eyes as if his merry friendliness were a well-polished role.

'Then you are my brother, Laertes?'

He swept a magnificent bow that included a flourish of hands. 'The very same.'

'In faith,' my father said in his querulous voice, 'I don't know which of my children I should scold the more, for it's impudent of you to show up garbed like a popinjay at this court of mourning. Black, sirrah, is the proper colour to wear when your king dies. Black! Black! If you and I slight our betters, slight indeed will be our portions.'

Laertes flung up his hands. 'I cry craven, sir. I did bring with me fine black velvet clothes, but I had only the one set so I thought it better to travel in colour so that my black garb wouldn't be journey-stained at the funeral.' This gave my father pause, so Laertes thrust home with, 'I promise you, sir, I took pains to keep my present finery well-covered with my drab cloak, so none but you and Ophelia know that I haven't been swathed in black the entire time.'

My father fussed about a little more, but he accepted this. Since my bedraggled gown was my black one, I first had to wash out the salt stains in a basin and then lay it out to dry, but then I listened with fascination to my new brother's tales of his life in Paris. I didn't know whether he spoke true or not, but according to him, Paris was a wondrous place that made Elsinore look rough-hewn and oafish. My father's chief concern was that Laertes was insinuating himself into the graces of folk of high rank, but I loved hearing of the theatres and balls, the entertainments, the grand shops.

The king's funeral was the next day. My gown was still damp and scoured with the faint marks of salt, but I doubted anyone noticed. The service was long, and much of the time as I stood or knelt, I kept thinking, 'I'm the one who did this. I'm the one who killed this king.' How folk would stare to discover that one thin girl had toppled a warrior monarch. Then I began to imagine the fires of hell in which I'd roast for eternity, and next my thoughts slid to imagining the tortures that would await me on earth should my part in his death be found out. I knew there was a dungeon under the castle, and if Claudius were to betray me, I would, at the least, have my belly slit open and my entrails pulled out before I, still living, was hanged and then cut down alive only to have my arms and legs tied to four horses who'd be whipped into setting off in different directions so that I'd be pulled to pieces. That would be the *best* for which I could hope.

Nevertheless, if I were given the gift to play the scene again, I'd still do what I did. I couldn't allow the queen to be tossed from the ramparts like the contents of a chamber pot emptied into the sea, and I still could puzzle no other way to have prevented it. Worse, though, than all my imaginings of the hell that awaited me either in the dungeon or after death was my fear that one day Prince Hamlet might discover what I'd done.

We were a huge company that trailed the king's body to the ruined monastery and the castle graveyard. All manner of visiting folk joined us for this procession. I spotted several men from my village, and I thought I caught a glimpse of Horatio, the prince's friend who'd accompanied him on his visit last summer. It took near an hour for us to reach the graveyard since we walked so solemn and slow. The dead king was carried into a great stone tomb. *He's lucky he's a noble with a stone tomb, for often in winter the ground is frozen too hard to dig a grave.* Laertes whispered to me that soon King Hamlet's likeness would be carved in stone and laid atop his resting place.

The court was in official mourning, so all entertainments were suspended for the thirty days following the king's death, during which we could wear nothing but black. Since most folk, even the nobles, had but one black gown, the smell of the unwashed cloth grew high as the year slid into spring.

Most of the visiting gentlefolk left as soon as the funeral was done because this was the time of ploughing and planting, and they didn't dare be absent in case their peasants failed to sow enough to see their estates through the entire year. Hamlet kept to his chambers almost entirely. One time, when I asked about him, Rosencrantz said that he'd covered all his windows with heavy drapes and sat in the darkness, day and night, weeping and sleeping. He never appeared in the Great Hall, and he could have been back in Wittenberg for all the good his presence did me.

The queen was punctilious in observing all the rites of mourning, but in no way did her grief for her husband match the floods of grief she'd felt for Holger. Although I attended her faithfully each afternoon, she had little need for me because Claudius usually made one of our company and her eyes were only for him. They behaved with propriety. In my presence they talked of no private matters. They exchanged no tokens of affection nor did they touch, but even Blind Jorgen from the village could have seen that they were deep in love.

I disapproved.

Oh, my mind was glad that the queen had found a considerate and courtly lover after the loutish behaviour of the old king, but my imagination was revolted that folk as old as they would fall in love. The skin on their hands and faces was slack and creased with many wrinkles, and I didn't want to think of what their bodies looked like beneath their clothes. Love should be for the young with smooth, firm bodies and wild hearts. I said as much to Yorick one morning when I joined him up on the battlements.

'Doubtless that's why the old king brought so many young wenches to his bed,' he said.

'At his age he should have been beyond all desires of the flesh.'

'Desire of the flesh is the main thing that separates the living from the dead,' he said. 'I cannot fault any man or any woman either for living fully in the body because it's lonely beyond belief to no longer feel with the body and to feel only with the mind.'

I know that should have made me more tolerant of Claudius and the queen, but I still pushed from my mind all thoughts of their physical coupling.

Laertes was wild to return to France. 'It's as dead as a convent in Lent here,' he often said, but my father counselled him to be patient and wait out the month of mourning.

'You must then cultivate our king Claudius as you'd cultivate the rarest rose, Laertes. Rather let me say, cultivate him as you would a field of wheat, for while a rose offers much adornment, it provides no sustenance, and in Claudius you find both adornment and sustenance. His favour will suckle you and help you grow, and grow you must when nursed with the favour of a king, for –'

'I'll wait,' Laertes assured him.

He spent the afternoons in training exercises with the soldiers, confiding in me that he'd learned much of sword-craft in his time in France and was able even to teach some of the officers some new passes and thrusts. There were more soldiers in Elsinore now. Perhaps the biggest change that Claudius made after he took the throne was to increase the size and the activities of our army. He was convinced that we faced some danger from Erik Strong Arm, and he wanted to make certain that Denmark was well protected.

One month to the day after the old king's death, Claudius convened the court and announced the end of the mourning period.

'For our good brother's death, there's no length of mourning long enough to do him courtesy and justice. Should we mourn until we ourselves do come to die, it would still fall short of what is due.'

Hamlet had appeared in court this day. My eyes flew to him to see how he received this, but his arms were folded across his chest. He seemed to mumble something, and his mother who stood next to him gave him an impatient look, and he threw himself down into his chair. There was a gasp that ran through the court. It was discourtesy bordering on treason for anyone – even a prince – to sit unbidden in the presence of a king. We waited nervously for Claudius's response.

He glanced over at his nephew, and his mouth seemed to harden. He chose to ignore, however, Hamlet's boorish behaviour. His voice showed no sign of anger or disapproval. 'Tomorrow we order all of you to lay off your mourning and take up your lives again.'

A murmur of approval ran through the court. The proper dues had been paid, and folk would be glad to garb themselves in fresh clothes.

'No matter how full our hearts may be, life demands a return to life,' Claudius went on. 'Therefore, as a further pledge of this, we do hereby announce that tomorrow morn, we'll take to wife Gertrude, the widow of the late king.'

The murmur grew to a roar. Hamlet sprang out of his chair so abruptly that it toppled to the ground with a great crash. He clenched his hands into fists, and his eyes were as spooked as a horse in a fire.

Claudius held up one hand, and the noise subsided. The queen had cast her eyes down, but she was blushing like a shy girl.

'Under the rule of our brother,' Claudius said, 'Denmark dwelled in golden days. We wish to demonstrate that nothing is different under our rule. Where once you had King Hamlet, you now have his faithful brother. Where once you had his good queen Gertrude, you have her now again. It shall be as if nothing at all has changed.'

Hamlet gave a strangled exclamation and stalked down the length of the hall and out the door. All eyes followed him.

'Nothing has changed,' Claudius repeated.

27

The wedding was a private affair with none of the usual festivities following the ceremony. Afterwards Claudius went to the queen's bed at night, but in the presence of the court, they behaved with the same quiet friendliness that ever they'd shown. They didn't hang on each other or follow the other's movements with their eyes, and so all but one of the folk at court soon grew easy with this new development.

All but Hamlet.

He now came to both meals of the day. He alone had failed to cast off his mourning clothes, and so he stood out among the company, a black bruise on the colourful body of the court. He wouldn't speak to anyone at meals, sprawling on the dais in his chair next to the king, listlessly pushing food around on his plate or crumbling bread onto the table cloths with angry fingers. Claudius treated him with unflagging courtesy, but his mother often looked worried when she looked at him. He never noticed me. As soon as each meal or ceremony was finished, he pushed his way to be first out of the door and once more shut himself away in his chamber. His friends, Rosencrantz and Guildenstern, had returned to school, but everyone at court knew that he still kept his windows shrouded with black curtains he'd ordered specially made, and that he didn't eat enough to keep a spider alive.

'Give him time,' Yorick counselled me again and again when I complained to him of my impatience to be with Hamlet. 'Let a little of his grief and anger drain. At present he's too full of pain to have any place for you.'

Laertes stayed on. My father speculated that Claudius's marriage would make him both jovial and generous, and that Laertes might benefit from this expansive state of affairs. Laertes was much happier now that court had resumed its usual activities. He was a great favourite among the folk there. Men liked him for he listened attentively to anything they had to say, seeming to drink it in with great appreciation and asking their advice on every matter under the sun. The unmarried women were attracted by his good looks, liveliness, and cosmopolitan air, but he preferred to spend time with the matrons. He flattered them and flirted with them as if they were still pretty maidens, and they'd grow all a-flutter under his attention. One time when I ventured to tease him about his triumphs, he said, 'Remember, Ophelia, old folk like two things – to be seen as wise and to be made to feel young. I treat every man as if he were Solomon and every woman as if she were the Queen of Sheba, and thus they adore me.'

My eyes widened to hear this calculating account, but he chucked me under the chin and said, 'Our blood is not great, and therefore we must make our fortunes, you and I. So adventurers let us be. Now tell me, is what I've heard true, and you have indeed captured the notice of the prince?'

'He noticed me once,' I said bitterly, 'but now he notices me no more.'

'Then you must push yourself back within his notice. Study him as you would game you wished to trap. Discover where his fancy takes him.'

'Not to me. That much is certain. He is too full of grief to notice anything else.'

Laertes gave my arm a playful tug. 'Then use his grief, dear sister, to catch the nearest way.'

'What do you mean?'

'Use his grief to thrust yourself back into his attention.'

'How can I do so? He rushes away from the hall at the end of meals as if all the legions of hell were hot on his heels. Other times he stays locked in his chamber. I have no chance to come near him.'

'If you cannot come near in body, then come near in words, dear sister. Write to him. Commiserate with his grief.' He twisted a strand of my hair around his finger. 'Particularly now that his friends have left him for school and his mother has left him for the bed of his uncle, he may be susceptible to your sympathetic overtures.'

In the next two days, I penned more than two dozen notes, discarding one after another, judging this one too brusque and that one too flowery, this one too prim and that one too bold. Because of my part in his father's death, you might well accuse me of playing the hypocrite, but I was careful never to write that I sorrowed over the death of the king, only that it broke my heart to witness Hamlet's pain. It was a small distinction in the face of the enormity of my sin, but at least it gave me a few shreds of self-respect.

I wasn't much pleased with my final product, but by the end of the second day I despaired of ever writing the perfect message. I settled on one which said:

My dear Lord Hamlet,

My own Heart is Heavy with Pain when I see your Very Great Grief for the Loss of your Father. As One Who Lost a Mother at an Early Age, I do know what it is like to be without a Parent although you had your Much Loved Father for Thirty Years and I never had the Luxury of Knowing my Mother or Her Love. Still I long to Give you Comfort and Ease. If there is aught I can do to soothe your Suffering, please hasten to let me know. If I could, I would trade you my Heart for Yours that is laden with Pain. I am always and Forever your Servant and Admirer, Ophelia.

I showed my composition to Laertes. At first he frowned over it, but then said, 'The sincerity shines through, and that's more seductive than style.' He offered to see that it was delivered to the prince.

The next afternoon, there was a tap on the door of our ante-chamber. A page stood there. 'Be you the lady Ophelia?'

'Yes.'

'I am ordered to give this to you direct.'

He handed me a great packet of folded papers. It was a letter from Hamlet. More than seventeen sheets of writing, some of it cross-hatched. It took me almost the entire afternoon to read it all. He wrote of his love for his father, his despair for his own future, his guilt over his brother's death and that a younger brother should surpass an elder one, his anger over his mother's marriage, and his yearning to do something to set things aright but his failure to understand what there was to do. When Laertes returned that evening, I held up my trophy.

'Your advice had a sound bottom! See! He wrote back.'

Laertes grinned. 'I pegged him as a plum ripe for shaking.'

I felt lifted upon clouds of glory. I gave my brother a quick kiss. 'When I'm a princess, there will be no end to your advancement.'

Laertes looked startled. 'What is this?'

I smiled back at him. 'Once I've wed Hamlet, then I'll see that you receive all manner of reward.'

Laertes ran his hand through his brown curls and twisted his head to one side and then the other like a man whose collar has shrunk. 'Ophelia,' he said, taking my hands into his. 'I hadn't thought . . . I'd forgotten that you are new come to court . . . it didn't enter my mind that you'd expect Hamlet to *marry* you.'

I was confused. 'I love him and I think he loves me. Why

else would you help me bring myself back into his favour if you didn't expect him to wed me?'

He gave a groan. 'It's all my fault.' He closed his fingers more tightly onto mine. 'Ophelia, Hamlet cannot wed you. He is now the only heir to the king. He must marry for the good of the state, not from private desires and inclinations.'

Things made no sense. 'Then why did you help me win my way back into his good grace if you didn't expect him to marry me?'

'Ophelia, dear sister, I knew that if people at court saw you'd attracted the love of a prince, your own worth as a bride would increase ten times over. Men much prefer women coveted by other men. You and I, we haven't a great family name or much wealth to use as barter in the marriage trade. If men see that a prince is sick with love for you, then we might aim as high as a younger son of a nobleman when we come to marry you off.'

I was revolted by his mercenary, calculating words. 'I want the prince for himself, not so that he can puff up my value.'

'And I want to live forever, but neither of us can have these things.'

I pulled my hands away and pressed them to my ears. 'I will not listen to this.'

He grabbed my wrists and forced my hands down. He seemed honestly distressed. 'If you'd grown up at court as I did, then you'd know to your bones that Hamlet must marry a foreign princess to buy allies for the country. Don't send your heart to sea in a paper boat.'

'King Hamlet once spoke to me of marrying his son.'

'But that was when Prince Holger was alive. Now there are no more heirs after Claudius, your marriage to Hamlet is a pretty dream that's not to be, no more substantial than a soap bubble.'

I still couldn't make sense of it. 'Did you wish me, then, to be his mistress?'

'No!' His fingers dug into my wrists. 'Without your virtue, then you're without worth to our family. Guard your chastity well, Ophelia. It's perhaps our greatest treasure.'

For a moment I hated him. 'Ophelia,' said Laertes gently, 'it can be amusing to play at love with a prince. Just remember always that it's but a game and hold fast to your virtue and your heart.'

That night I lit a candle in my closet and read back over Hamlet's letter. Its contents didn't smack of playing or pretence. I wrote him back, another short note, expressing my sympathy for his feelings and reaffirming my earnest desire to serve him. I was fearful that my father might intercept our correspondence, so I told him not to send the letters to our rooms, but that every evening after supper I'd walk for an hour up on the battlements unattended and that a messenger could deliver a note to me there.

I didn't tell Laertes of this second note. I'd henceforth keep my own counsel.

The next day, on my way to the queen's chamber, I slipped my letter under the door to Hamlet's room. That night after supper I'd walked along the battlements no more than five minutes before a servant appeared with a folded note.

It was too dark to read it, but I clutched it to my heart and gave Yorick, who was seated on a wall watching me, a smile that nearly cracked my face in two.

And thus for several weeks we wrote back and forth. Occasionally a clever trifle accompanied his letters: a sonnet, a sketch of my face, a riddle, a tiny painting of a sphinx. We exchanged no spoken words. Every day, though, he sent a servant to deliver a new instalment of letters in which he poured out his pain over the emptiness of life, the fickle nature of women, his own desire for death, his disappointment in his mother, his admiration for his father, his hatred of his uncle, his ambition to be himself a great man and a famous king, and countless other things. I did note that he showed little interest in what I did or felt, but I knew he was crippled with grief, too consumed by his own pain to have space left for the pain of others. As the days passed, I was surprised that his own suffering didn't seem to ease a jot, but I comforted myself with the thought that if he could feel so much for a father, how much more he would be able to feel for a wife.

One day as I walked on the battlements waiting for his letter, I received perhaps the worst shock in my life.

Moving slowly toward me, his back to Sweden, was the ghost of King Hamlet himself.

'What do you want?' I said, but my voice quavered.

He stared at me with no expression on his face, and then he disappeared.

I stood trembling, and when the messenger spoke behind me, I screamed and frightened him so much that he screamed as well.

I wanted to talk with Yorick about the king's appearance, but I couldn't bear staying any longer up on the battlements in case the dead king came again, so I clattered back to my own closet and curled up on the bed, my heart thudding like the shuttle of a loom. That night I had trouble falling asleep, and when I did, the king walked in my dreams.

The next evening it took all my courage to climb back up to the battlements, but my longing for Hamlet was greater than my fear of his father's ghost.

Yorick was waiting for me. I told him of seeing the old king the night before.

'I knew he walked,' Yorick said.

'Why didn't you warn me?'

'He doesn't know your part in his death. I reckoned he'd keep his distance.'

'What would he do to me should he find out?'

Yorick sighed. 'Nothing. Ghosts cannot harm living folk direct. At most they can work on the minds of some of the living to manipulate them to effect a revenge.'

I was still nervous, and each night I had to grab my courage with both hands in order to wait for Hamlet's messenger up on the battlements. Twice more the king's ghost walked over to me and disappeared, but now I told him, 'Be off, for you cannot do me harm.'

Hamlet's long letters more than made up for having to face down his father's ghost.

Still it irked me not to be able to speak to Hamlet direct. Once or twice, up on the battlements with no living person to hear, I screamed out my frustration that Hamlet and I met only through letters. The sight of the queen and Claudius so happy and tender together acted on me like fingernails in a wound. I had trouble sleeping. In the past I might have climbed to the battlements and paced until I'd walked off my restlessness, but now Claudius had armed guards aloft from the hour of nine until dawn, so the battlements were no longer my private place. In my brain jangled an unceasing prayer, *Let him come to me, let him come to me, let him come to me.*

At last he did come, but not in the manner I expected.

28

I found myself roughly shaken awake. A hand was pressed over my mouth.

'I've seen him!' Hamlet hissed.

With eager hands, he pulled me to my feet. He wrapped my blankets around me in a clumsy fashion and led me out into the corridor. The wooden floor was cold beneath my bare soles, and, to my surprise, Yorick watched us from the shadows in the hallway.

I began, 'My lord, who have you—'

'Hush! We mustn't be overheard.' He gave a laugh whose unearthly sound lifted the hair on the back of my neck. I'd seen him excited before, but never as giddy as this. He hurried me along the hallway, his head flicking back and forth as he looked for a place for us to be private. Finally he pushed me into a tiny prie-dieu, no bigger than a clothespress, that had been built to accommodate a sickly grandmother who'd been too much an invalid to travel to the main chapel. There was a minute altar, scarcely bigger than a kitchen tray, and a tiny glowing lamp in front of the stained glass window. In the faint light of dawn, the purples, reds, and greens of the window glowed sullenly like a bruise.

He pulled the heavy curtains closed behind us.

'What is it, my lord? Who have you seen?'

He almost danced around the small floor. 'The king.'

I was bewildered. 'You see the king each day, my lord, so why—'

'Not Claudius! The king, my father.'

My legs grew weak underneath me, and if he hadn't grabbed my elbow, I'd have tumbled to the ground. 'The king, your father?'

He nodded and grabbed my hands, twirling me round and round the room. 'He has returned. My father has returned. More than that, he needs my help, Ophelia. Mine! For the first time in my life, my father has turned to me for aid! Not to my brother, not to my mother, not to my villain uncle. The king, my father, has come to me!' I'd been worried since I saw the ghost of King Hamlet, and now the worst had come to pass. 'He spoke to you, then?'

'He spoke to me. He wouldn't speak to Marcellus or Bernardo or Horatio, but he spoke to me!'

My throat tightened. 'What did he say?'

'I am to avenge his murder!'

It was as if all my muscles had turned to claws. It hurt to breathe. It hurt to speak. Still I forced the words out. 'His murder?'

'The ghost brings word that he was most foully murdered, and I am to avenge his death.'

Things were spinning out of control. 'Did the ghost tell you who had done the deed?'

Hamlet threw back his head and laughed. 'It was as I expected. My uncle Claudius. When my father was sleeping in the orchard, my good uncle poured a vial of poison in his ear.'

I began to tremble. 'And did the ghost tell you where he got this poison?'

Hamlet gave an impatient shrug. 'What does that matter? All I care about is that my uncle killed my father, and I am to avenge his death. Now, finally, I have my chance to prove myself worthy to be his son.'

What was to be done? I couldn't bear for Hamlet to learn

that I'd given the poison to Claudius. I could never make him see that his vision of his father wasn't his true father, nor could I ever hope to make him understand the reason for my action. *Do not let him ever learn of my part in this affair.* I was fearful of losing his love, but I was just as fearful of losing my life. Now I wished I'd played the whole business differently. I should have contacted him and informed him of his father's plan to marry me, disinherit him, and murder his mother. I could have been clever and arranged for him to overhear his father talk to me about it. That's what I should have done. But once the wool is spun, it cannot again grow on the sheep's back, and once the fish is eaten, it can no longer swim. There was no way to walk upstream through time, and now I must figure out how to play the cards that were dealt.

'I don't know that I'd trust the word of a ghost,' I said carefully. 'Although he has the form and voice of your father, evil often assumes a familiar shape in order to win our souls to damnation.'

Hamlet paused. The bruised light from the stained glass window gave his face a mottled, beaten look. 'There is some sense to what you say, although I believe the ghost to be an honest ghost and not a spirit of evil.'

'Still,' I said, pressing my slight advantage, 'you don't want to kill an innocent man on the strength of nothing but the words of a ghost.'

'My uncle Claudius is not a good man. He is a lecher, an upstart who snatches away the crown before I can return from school, no more than a pebble next to the watchtower that was my father.'

I didn't mention that the council gave the throne to Claudius because they feared Hamlet's instability or that Claudius's feelings toward the queen smacked more of love than of lust. Instead I croaked out, 'What do you intend to do, my lord?'

Hamlet slid his head one way and then the other as if he

were checking for people spying on our conversation. 'I have a plan,' he whispered. He tugged me over behind the altar, as far as possible from the hallway, and pulled me down so we both knelt together in the tight space. 'From time to time, I've displayed an antic disposition, a giddiness amounting almost to madness. I'll let this fit come upon me again, but from craft, this time, and not from happenstance. In such a manic humour will I creep about the castle, looking for proof of what the ghost speaks. Madness, Ophelia, conveys a marvellous freedom, and I'll avail myself of this freedom to ferret out the truth.'

This plan seemed foolhardy at best, but I dared not protest.

He continued, 'Therefore, dearest Ophelia, don't marvel at me if I should play the zany or the fool, but know that I'm mad in craft and not mad indeed.'

I touched his face. His cheeks were flushed and hot to the touch. 'My lord, I'll do anything you ask of me.'

Hamlet pressed kisses upon my hands, then looked up to say, 'More than this, if you love me, aid me with your actions as well as your silence.'

'My actions?' I could hear my voice falter.

He nodded. His hands burned hot against my cold skin. Even his face seemed to give off warmth as if his crusade had kindled an inner fire. 'In a few days, once I've successfully begun to weave my disguise of mad antics, I need you to go to your father with a story of how you've witnessed directly strange behaviour from me.' His eyes glittered. 'Tell him something like this. Say that I came to you . . . came to you in your chamber . . . and what I did there convinced you that I'd lost my senses.'

'What should I say that you did, my lord?' *By all the saints, this was bacon-brained indeed.*

He gave an impatient shrug. 'You are a girl of a lively

imagination. You will think of the right thing to say. Weave some story or other. Say I appeared with a face painted blue or I leapt to your bed and began to crow like a cock. Say that I pulled on some of your clothing or pulled off all of mine. I don't care what lies you spin, only persuade your father that I'm mad to my fingernails.' He turned my hand over and pressed a kiss into my palm. My whole arm tingled. 'Will you do this much for me, Ophelia?' He pressed his cheek against my hand the way a tired child might lean against his mother. 'There are so few people that a prince can trust, but I've put all my faith in you. I'm lost, Ophelia, and you're my light in the darkness. Will you help me, my dearest love?'

What could I say but, 'I'll do as you ask, my lord. But—'

He crushed his mouth against mine and cut off my words. I clung to him, confused and sick with dread. We heard footsteps passing in the corridor, and he pulled me tight to his chest, hugging me till I couldn't breathe, the sound of his heart pounding in my ear. As soon as the steps died away, he whispered, 'You must go at once back to your chambers for the castle is starting to be up and about, and it will do your reputation no good to be seen with me wearing only your shift.'

'But, my lord—'

He pulled me to my feet. 'My love, you're cold as ice and trembling like a leaf in a gale. I was cruel to snatch you from your warm bed, but I wished to share this news with you.' He stroked my cheek with the back of his hand. 'Know that I wish to share every bit of my life with you, my one and only love.' Before I could speak, he drew the curtain to the hall aside and peeked out, kissed the top of my head, and gave me a little push into the empty passageway.

'Pray you, keep silent, for both our lives and souls hang in the balance,' he whispered. 'Go quickly.'

Without giving me time to say anything, he tugged the

curtain back across the archway. I stumbled back to my chamber and into my bed, but not to sleep. I drew my knees up and rested my chin on them, alarmed by the turn events had taken. The man I loved was trusting me to help him root out the murderer of his father. That murderer was in fact the girl he loved and trusted. Somehow I needed to stop his search. But how?

I toyed with the idea of going to Claudius, but almost at once I saw danger there. Claudius had murdered his brother, so what would stop him murdering his nephew who was, after all, trying to kill him in return? More than that, if Hamlet confronted Claudius with his suspicions, what would keep Claudius from exposing me as the supplier of the poison? How I longed for advice from a wiser, cooler head, but to tell this to anyone would be as much as to sign my own death warrant and perhaps even Hamlet's as well.

My only comfort was that Hamlet was a reasonable man, a good man. He wouldn't accuse Claudius without proof. My best hope was that it wouldn't be easy to obtain that proof. His whole life he might harbour suspicions about his father's death and the words of the meddling ghost, but there was no evidence to be found to substantiate the ghost's message, so nothing would come of it. Claudius would never confess the truth, and I most certainly wouldn't.

Still, I felt the need for advice for I was sailing in a cold, dark sea and needed the voice of someone else to serve as my true North. There was no question of going to anyone at court, and while I trusted Piet as I trusted myself, I didn't think his love of surfaces would let him sound the depths of my confusion. The Herbwife was wise and loving, but since I'd used her poison in the act, I dared not let her know that I'd laid her open to a charge of complicity in the deed. The more I thought about it, the more it seemed that Ragnor was the very person I needed to talk with. He was courageous to the point of recklessness, and it was important to have a confessor, one who, if things grew dangerous, wouldn't toss you to the wolves to lighten his own sleigh.

God seemed to steer me in that direction, for that very afternoon a fearful storm blew in from the sea. Odds were that Ragnor had beached his boat and was sitting out the storm, so I fought my way through the terrible weather down to the village and found Ragnor in the shed in which he keeps his gear, mending some frayed rope.

'I've done a dreadful thing,' I burst out, not waiting for even a word of greeting.

While most folk would protest, 'Oh, it cannot be as dreadful as all that,' Ragnor did me the courtesy of keeping silent. He just looked at me curiously, his hands continuing to twist the strands of the rope.

All at once, I was at a loss as to how to continue. The queen had schooled me in many arts, but she'd never taught me how to confess myself a murderer. I groped about my mind for the proper thing to say until Ragnor finally said, 'Give me the words with no bark in them, Cat.'

I took a deep breath and then blurted out, 'I've killed a king.'

For a moment Ragnor's hands froze, and then he continued to braid his rope. His face never changed. 'Did you, indeed?'

'Oh, Ragnor, I poisoned King Hamlet.'

Suddenly it was as if my bones had turned to water. I sank down onto the folded sailcloth and wanted to keep on going, sinking deeper and deeper into the earth until all was silent and peaceful.

After a while, Ragnor said, 'Doubtless you had a good reason.'

His comment unloosed my tongue and I poured forth my tale. He said nothing, but I could tell he listened hard. When

I'd emptied myself like an upturned pitcher, he didn't speak for a long time until finally he said, 'It's a serious matter to kill a man.'

His voice, though, was dispassionate. Not judging, but simply stating the truth as he might say 'It's foul weather today' or 'The parsnips need salting'.

What struck me most was that he, like me, regarded the murder primarily as the death of one man, not the death of a special man. It was that I'd killed a human being that mattered to him, not that I'd attacked a king. I didn't know why, but I found this reassuring.

'Oh, Ragnor, could I have laid out our lives like a sampler to be stitched, I wouldn't have included Hamlet's father's execution in it at all, but I didn't have a choice, as I saw it, of either killing someone or not. No, Ragnor, I'd been given the devil's hind choice – *someone* was going to be killed, and my only choice was whether it would be the king or the queen.'

'I reckon most folk would disagree with your decision,' he warned me. The rope gave a little scraping hiss as it wove through his rough fingers. 'They would argue numbers.'

'Numbers?'

'Most folk are shopkeepers at heart. They'd point out that King Hamlet was profitable for Denmark, so the sacrifice of one woman – even if she was queen – would be a small cost in order to keep this prosperous king on the throne.'

'But what about all of his bastard babes that he'd had my father put to death?'

'How many babes might we be speaking of?'

I shrugged my shoulders. I didn't know the sum of these small executions.

'Five? Ten? Even a hundred. Even if you drag his murdered bastards into the equation, folk would point out that most children born alive never make it into adulthood and that this swift death was kinder than one through starvation, neglect, or disease.'

No! The king's rank didn't outweigh his wife and his dead offspring. 'So you think I did wrong, Ragnor?'

For the first time he looked surprised. 'It's not my place to judge you, Cat.'

I felt relieved. 'Then you think I did right?'

He repeated, 'It's not my place to judge.'

'Oh, Ragnor,' I said, unlocking the worry deepest in my heart, 'what shall I do about Lord Hamlet?'

Ragnor kept his eyes fastened on his ropemaking. 'Do you plan to murder him, too?'

I grabbed up a wooden peg that lay on the floor and threw it at him. 'My transgressions are not a matter for jest, pirate boy. I've trusted you with information that I've given to no one else, and I'll not let you mock me.'

He still didn't look at me. 'What frets you about Lord Hamlet?'

I didn't want to bring up the matter of the ghosts, so I simply said, 'He suspects that his uncle has killed his father.'

'Can he find proof?'

'No. Claudius is an astute man. A man of much self-control. He would never give himself away.'

'Can Hamlet find proof in any other quarter?'

'There's no other proof that can be found.'

Ragnor laid the mended rope aside and picked up a thicker one. 'Then it seems you have naught to worry you. Leave the matter alone. For your ease of mind, though, leave Hamlet alone as well.'

His advice was good, but he asked of me the one thing I wouldn't do. 'Ragnor,' I said softly, 'I love him.'

His fingers closed tightly around the rope. 'I know.'

'I love him and I killed his father. What am I to do?'

Ragnor didn't answer immediately. The room was filled

with the scrape-hiss of the ropemaking and the terrible pounding of the rain and wind against the sides of the shed. At last Ragnor said, 'He is not a good man for you, Cat.'

I sat up, furious. 'How can you say that? Prince Hamlet is a very good man.'

'A good man, yes, but not a good man for you.'

'He is the best man for me. The only man for me.'

In two heartbeats, Ragnor had flung the rope to the floor and was standing in front of me, pulling me upwards. His strong, rough hands were nothing like the prince's, and he smelled of salty sea air and woodsmoke. 'Cat, you've lost yourself in that castle, and I fear that you're losing your wits as well.'

I struggled to get out of his grip, but he held me fast. 'Listen to me, Cat. What you did in murdering the king – that wasn't wise or politic, but it was courageous and true and noble. You loved the queen and you loved justice, and you acted bravely, in spite of risk to yourself, for a noble cause. But I cannot bear to watch you shrink the way you're shrinking. When you lived in the village, you were daring and clear-sighted. But look at you now. You were made to live a life as grand as the sea, yet you've shrunk your being to fit in a walnut shell—'

His words knocked the breath clean out of me, but as soon as I could, I interrupted him. 'Of all men in the world, Lord Hamlet is the most wonderful, the most magnificent, and I love him with all of my heart. It's you who are but a patch on the sum of his greatness.'

At that Ragnor released me so suddenly that I tumbled back down onto the folded sail. 'You don't love him,' he said, and his voice sounded tired, 'because you don't truly *see* him.'

'I *do* see him. He fills my eyes, my thoughts, my soul.'

'In truth, he fills your eyes so much that you cannot see him for what he is.'

'He is a great man. He is witty and artistic and noble and

high-spirited. He stands above the common herd as a stallion will tower above a flock of geese. He sees the world in a fresh way, and he has the will to carry out his visions. He is beautiful and glorious . . . and he loves me, *me*, an ignorant girl from a forgettable village. He—'

'You love him not for himself, but for those very parts you're trying to cut away from yourself. Down deep it's a grand life you crave, not a grand man.'

How wrong I'd been to come to Ragnor. He was a fool. An absurd fool. I'd come to him for comfort, for counsel, and now he was sounding just as mad as Hamlet.

Oh, God. I immediately thrust away that thought. Hamlet wasn't mad. It was Ragnor who'd poisoned my thoughts. Hamlet was high strung, but he wasn't mad. Ragnor was a peasant, unable to understand a man who was infinitely his superior. And no matter what Ragnor said, I hadn't become weakened or muted. I'd merely grown refined, a concept that Ragnor, in his coarseness, was incapable of appreciating.

I pushed my way out in the storm, feeling a grim satisfaction that the drama of the weather matched the drama in my soul. I hated Ragnor for all those lies he was hurling at me.

No, I'd never meet with Ragnor again.

The storm outside faded during the night, but my inner storm continued to rage. By the morning, the sea was as smooth as glass, and word was sent that Laertes's ship would depart a little after noon.

After middag he took leave of the king and queen who graciously wished him a speedy voyage. Claudius held our father back to ask his advice about some matter of state, but I hurried back to our chambers with Laertes to help him bundle up the last of his things.

Lord Hamlet didn't attend middag that day.

The day was mild, so Laertes and I followed two young

servant boys as they carried his baggage down to the ship. I was sorry to see my brother depart. It was true that he was, like my father, slippery of tongue and always with one eye peeled to catch the nearest way to advancement, but unlike my father he had a merry heart and charming manners and had made a most pleasant companion. He had the beauty and elegance that my father lacked, and while Laertes was perhaps a little too fond of his own opinions and a little too pleased with the man he'd fashioned himself to be, it was still very satisfying to have such a fine brother. My eyes welled up with tears as I saw the servant boys heave Laertes's luggage into the skiff that would ferry him out to the main ship. Just for a moment I didn't feel strong enough to face the loss of one more person I loved. Piet had all but disappeared into his work in the kitchen, Hamlet spent all his time cloaked in his misery, Judith had run away, and Ragnor had turned against me. Even the queen was lost in her excitement of her new marriage. Try as I might, I couldn't bring myself to feel anything but a tepid sense of duty toward my father. I was fond of Yorick who'd served as my chief advisor at court, but loving a ghost is like dining on air. I despised myself for being such a self-pitying maw-worm, but I longed ferociously for someone who would stand still long enough for me to love him.

Laertes handed the servant boys each a coin. They pulled at a forelock and departed. He turned to me, and when he saw my sad expression, he stuck out his lip and pretended to cry in big 'Boo hoo hoo's' until, in spite of myself, I laughed. 'If you're to succeed in this world,' he said, 'you must learn to school your face so you don't let others know what you feel inside.'

'I will,' I said and burst into tears. I threw my arms around him, and he closed his arms around me in return, saying, 'Ophelia, Ophelia, you have so much to learn.'

'I wish you'd stay,' I wailed, all my decorum forgotten.

'Write to me. Write often. Give me all the news at court.'

'Can you doubt that I will?'

Then he held me out at arm's length. For once his face looked troubled. 'Sister, there's one thing that I must say before I go, one warning I must give.' For a moment I thought perhaps he was going to caution me against our father, but his next words set me straight. 'It's true that Lord Hamlet is much attracted to you, Ophelia, but remember that such attractions pass as quickly as a cloud floats across the sun.'

Now I wanted to laugh. For all his wordly wisdom, he was like Piet in only seeing the surface of things. I kept my mouth prim, but I could feel my eyes dancing. 'That quickly, brother?'

He nodded and smoothed a strand of my hair back into its netting. 'You must not give in to your own attraction to him. Remember always that he's a prince, Ophelia, and he cannot choose a wife willy-nilly. Never let yourself forget that he must marry well, marry to please the country and not his own desires.'

Inwardly I smiled like a kitten at a cream pot. I didn't think Claudius would dare toss any obstacles into the way of my marriage to Hamlet. After all, I knew too much about Claudius's role in the death of his brother, and I was certain he'd rather have me under his eye here in the castle safely married to his nephew than have Hamlet make a grand foreign alliance that left me free to flap my lips about Claudius's deed.

Laertes continued, 'More than that, my dear sister, you must not risk the loss of your honour in this business. Your chastity is an even more valuable coin than your beauty. A youthful spendthrift will end up an elderly pauper.' He nattered on in this vein for several minutes until I finally promised to keep in mind what he was telling me. 'But,' I warned him, 'don't you preach to me the narrow strait of virtue if you're going to strut down the primrose path of vice. The sauce for the hen tastes just as sweet on the cockerel.'

He laughed then, and I laughed with him. It was a glorious day indeed, with a sky as blue as the eyes of a newborn baby and a wind gentle as its mother's caress. Before we could talk more, our father bustled up, a windbag of advice, speaking no words of love to my brother, only platitudes about how to advance in the world. The sailors began to gesticulate wildly, trying to loosen Laertes from the grip of my father's lecture so they could set forth in time to catch the winds.

Finally even my father caught onto the grimaces and arm-wavings of the ship's company and let my brother go. Laertes gave me one more hug.

'Remember, Ophelia, my warning and heed it well.'

I stood waving until he disappeared below the deck and his ship drew anchor.

As soon as my father and I began to walk back to the castle, he said, 'What did Laertes warn you about?'

I didn't want to answer, but I could think of no way to sidestep his question. 'He said something about Lord Hamlet.'

My father ruffled up like an angry peahen. 'Lord Hamlet. What is going on between Lord Hamlet and yourself, daughter, that your brother feels the need to warn you about? Are you bothering Lord Hamlet?'

I wanted to slap him. 'On the contrary, my lord.' I drew myself up proudly. 'Lord Hamlet has shown me many indications of his love for me.'

I expected my father to be impressed, but instead he gave a snort like an angry whale. 'Do not talk to me of *love*. I myself know how easy it is to swear love when the blood burns. Never expect a man in the throes of lust to speak the truth.' He studied me as if he was seeing me for the first time. 'Lord Hamlet is a man, and therefore he may carry on as he pleases, but I don't want it said that I have a trollop for a daughter.'

'Father—'

'From this time forth, you're not to waste your time with Lord Hamlet. Do you understand me?'

I stood there, in the middle of the road, hating him. Because he was himself a man who lied and cheated and spoke false and worried only about what he could trick away from others, he believed every man was like that. He couldn't see that Hamlet was as different from himself as a star was different from a stone. My father, who understood self-advancement so thoroughly, was incapable of understanding love. I inwardly fumed at my father, my brother, and Ragnor. Dogs in the manger, all of them. All of them loveless, and so they wanted me to be just as loveless as they.

Then it was all I could do to keep from laughing as I realized that the wording of my father's demand would make it no great hardship to fulfil. He'd ordered me not to *waste* time with Hamlet. He had *not* ordered me not to spend time with Hamlet. Time spent with Hamlet was never wasted.

I put on my sweetest smile. 'I will obey you, my lord.'

29

That night, when I went to bed, I found a folded scrap of paper pushed underneath my pillow.

I have primed the pump, and now it is time to let the waters flow. Within the next day or two, do something to convince your father that I have run mad indeed. My life depends on you. Do not fail me, my dearest love. It is vital to the success of my plan to persuade my villainous uncle and the rest of court that my wits have gone a-begging. Present some tale to your father that he can take to the king.

I slammed the letter down on my bed, and the crude oath that escaped my lips was one that I'd neither heard nor used since my village days. In the bustle of my brother's departure, I'd let myself forget Hamlet's silly scheme to mask himself in madness to investigate his father's death.

'What's amiss?'

Yorick appeared in my chamber.

'Hamlet wants to probe the wound of his father's death. He believes that if he feigns madness, he'll be able to investigate more thoroughly.'

Yorick's lips curled into a smile. 'Clever boy!'

'Clever?' Another long-forgotten oath popped out of my mouth. 'This is the most foolish plan imaginable.'

'Not at all. If folk think him mad, then he'll have the freedom to roam about the castle at will. To ask or say anything. To paw through papers, to listen at doors. If anyone challenges him, he can pass it off as madness rather than stealth.'

Now I liked his plan even less. 'What do I do, Yorick, if the end of his scheme is to bring him to a knowledge of my part in his father's death?'

Yorick leaned toward me. 'You must make sure that such a thing doesn't happen.'

'How?'

'One way might be to get Hamlet so caught up in playing his part that he forgets why he's playing it.' He touched a finger to his nose and nodded.

'Do you truly think such a thing could come to pass?'

Yorick motioned to me to lean closer. 'There's a special quality to pretending to be mad. Once we throw open the portals of reason and venture across their thresholds, it's hard to remember to come back inside and shut those doors again. Your chief safety lies in encouraging Hamlet to be as mad as possible. More than his love of acting, his own unfettered imagination will help betray his quest and render him ineffectual.'

'I don't want to betray him.'

'Then do you want him to learn that you were the one who supplied the poison to kill his father?'

'Of course not.'

'You cannot have the goose both strutting in your barnyard and roasted on your plate, Ophelia. You must choose.'

I hesitated.

'Look at it this way. Will knowing that his father was indeed murdered make him one jot the happier?'

'No.'

'So keeping him from the truth will be good for him as well as for you, for Claudius, and for Denmark.'

This made sense. I myself hadn't thought of it in that light.

'So if you encourage his madness to run riot, he'll at last exhaust himself and come to believe that the ghost wasn't his father's shade but an incarnation of the devil. You can help him come to this understanding. Whenever you can, cast doubt in his mind about the veracity of the ghost. Above all, keep your focus on what you most desire.'

I nodded.

He continued, 'Tell me what that is.'

'I want Hamlet deep in love with me.' I added, 'And sane.'

'Is he sane now?'

'He pretends not to be—'

'But do you see any madness beyond his play-acting?'

'He is a little mad with grief for his father and his part in his brother's death.'

'Hamlet cannot come to his full wits until he has let his mad grief run its course. Therefore, Ophelia, the farther you push him into his madness, the sooner he'll sail through it and dock at his native sanity on the other side.'

I opened my mouth to question him, but before I could speak, he said, 'This is for Hamlet's own good. Remember the best way you can help him, Ophelia, is to feed the flame of his madness so that his guilt over Holger and grief for his father can burn away.'

So the next morning, before middag, I practised in front of the glass in my bedroom. I made my eyes wide and my expression frightened. I pulled several hairs out of their pins and tugged my clothes about until they looked tumbled. With my looking-glass as audience, I played out the scene over and over until I was perfect.

When all was ready, I went running for my father. He was standing in the courtyard with a man I didn't know, a man bundled in cloaks and holding the reins of a sad-dled horse. I hadn't thought to play my scene all out in the open, but a quick reflection told me that I couldn't have asked for a better setting since even should I fail to shiver in my part, the very cold air itself would set me a-shivering.

'Father!' I cried out as I tripped down the steps to the courtyard. 'Oh, Father, I've been so afeared.'

A look of concern flickered across my father's face. 'What's the matter?'

I launched into the tale I'd concocted. 'My lord, as I sat sewing in my closet, Lord Hamlet appeared suddenly before me. I knew at once something was amiss.'

'How?'

'His doublet was all unlaced. His stockings were stained and tumbling down to his ankles. He was as pale as milk, and the expression on his face was as terrified as if he'd just witnessed the worst horrors of hell.'

Before I could tell my father how Hamlet had seen a legion of ghosts, his next question caused me to change direction. 'Was he mad for your love?'

Instantly I saw that my father had associated Hamlet's half-clothed state with lust, not terror, but I quickly realized that for my purposes this wasn't such a bad thing. I hung my head and whispered, 'I fear it's true.'

'What happened then?'

'He grabbed me by the arm and held me hard.' How far should I go in my tale? 'He held me at far arm's length as he studied my face as if he'd paint it. After a long time he shook my arm back and forth, back and forth like this.'

'Did he violate you?'

I shook my head. 'No.' I didn't want to taint him with an accusation of rape, so I quickly said, 'Then he let go of me and backed out of the room, saying nothing and keeping until the last his eyes fixed on me.'

In truth, I'd liked my original story better – one in which Hamlet was screaming about the ghosts who chased him –

but my father seemed convinced by this version. 'Have you two quarrelled recently?' my father asked.

I shook my head. 'I've done only what you commanded – not communicated with him by speech or letter.'

In fact, my only recent contact with the prince had been last night's note slipped under my pillow.

'That has driven him mad,' my father said in a satisfied voice. 'Clear it is that he's mad with love for you, daughter. I'll inform the king of this.'

He looked at me with naked speculation in his eyes. 'Perhaps I was wrong,' he said in a dreamy tone as if he was talking to someone deep within himself. 'When the old king broached the matter of you marrying Hamlet, I'd feared that the two of you'd be shut away like your mother and so the alliance would do me no good in the end.'

'My mother!' I repeated, dumbfounded. 'My mother died of childhood fever.'

My father ignored me. 'Then, when Hamlet became the only son, I doubted that he'd ever look so low for a wife.'

At once I didn't want to talk of Hamlet. Here was matter more urgent. 'What do you mean, Father, about my mother?'

My father's face broke into an approving smile. 'It might do. It might just do very well indeed. In fact, this might be the only chance we'll have to marry you to a prince and make you a queen. If he's to rule, his wits must be restored, and if the only way to restore his wits is to marry my daughter . . . it may answer. It may answer very well indeed. Come with me, Ophelia, and let us tell the king.'

I stamped my foot. 'I'll go with you nowhere until you tell me what you meant about my mother being locked up.'

He looked at me with irritation in his eyes. 'Surely you know her history.'

I wanted to scream. 'Judith said she died of childbed fever. She said nothing about locking her up.'

'Judith spoke true, and yet it was not all the truth she spoke. Sometimes we can lie while speaking the truth if, in truth, the whole of the truth be hidden and only a limb of the truth – if we can speak of truth having limbs and—'

I wanted to grab him by the throat and shake him back and forth. 'Tell me about my mother!'

He stopped his rambling and patted his own belly several times as if he were debating how much to tell me. 'No credit to her memory is it to bring this up, daughter, but if you're to wed a mad prince, perhaps it is best you know the whole. Your mother's childbed fever entered her brain. She'd been a pretty-mannered, biddable girl, but once you were born, her wits turned. Two hours after your birth, she tried to drown you in a basin of water. We took you at once to a wet nurse, and the king gave permission, for her own safety, that she be locked in one of the abandoned watchtowers along the coast. I left her there with a woman to attend her, but no more than five days had passed before the woman appeared back at court to tell us that your mother had flung herself out of the top window and drowned in the sea.'

The news turned my bones to sawdust, and I sagged against the wall for support. My poor mother. Was she in her right mind when she leapt from that window? Was she seeking out death . . . or freedom?

My father took no notice of my bruised feelings. 'Now that he's the last of the bloodline, though, they'll never lock Hamlet away, so perhaps there's much gain to your own bloodline should you be wed to the prince. If I can persuade the present king that you can restore his nephew to his right mind, there's no end to the riches that might flow into our family coffers. Let us go immediately, Ophelia, to see what we can make of this matter.'

My feelings were a gale that swirled about me. I couldn't stand meekly in the presence of the king as my father reported on all of this. More than anything, I wanted to let Hamlet know that his first gambit had succeeded.

'Pray make my excuses to his majesty, but I'm too agitated to go with you. I need some time to compose myself.'

I could tell that my father was chomping at the bit to deliver my tale to the king, so in a perfunctory manner, he wished me a soothing repose even though it wasn't yet midday and galloped off to talk to Claudius. The news about my mother's madness and death had unloosed some restraint in me, so I ran wildly to the prince's chambers, calling out to the guards that I delivered a message, not even caring that girls were never given messages to take to a man's chambers. I was gambling away my maidenly reputation, but I wanted Hamlet or no one as husband, so I didn't care if I was ruining myself beyond social redemption. This whole court seemed a bog of lies and Hamlet the only solid truth.

I pounded on his doorway. 'Let me in, for it's I, Ophelia, come with news.'

His voice sounded surprised as he bade me enter. But it was I who was surprised as soon as I pushed through the heavy doorway.

30

Hamlet's bedchamber was a miracle of light and colour. I'd thought the queen's rooms beautiful, but they were nothing compared to Hamlet's, a snowdrop next to a cathedral. Instead of the heavy woven hangings in the queen's room, Hamlet's walls were painted with scenes so lifelike that I half-expected to be able to walk right into them. One wall featured a marble temple with a group of young men sitting at the feet of an older man who seemed to be teaching them. All the people wore short white tunics and sandals, and the sunlight shimmered around the whole scene in a glorious brightness. The wall by the windows contained a vast meadow with three beautiful women standing before a man who was pointing at the plumpest and pinkest of the three. The man wore a white tunic draped with a goat skin, but the three women wore nothing but a few wisps of filmy white. The wall next to it showed the yawning mouth of a cave. A man carrying a small gold harp stood just outside the cave in the sunshine, his head turned back to look at a beautiful woman just inside the shadows of the cave. She was reaching a small white hand out to the man but behind her a slender youth – naked except for golden sandals with wings at the heel – was pulling her back inside the cave. On the fourth wall there was no colour at all, just the charcoal lines of a drawing that showed a beautiful young man lounging by a well. He held a goblet, and long ribbons of ivy trailed down his long curls. He was surrounded by beautiful girls who wore nothing but the skins of animals, and a beast much like a lion sat at his side.

I was dazzled in part because the folk in the paintings looked so alive, so real. All the pictures I'd previously seen, in books and on the walls of churches, featured flat figures decorated with slabs of a single colour. The folk on Hamlet's walls had a roundness to them, and the countryside behind was just as marvellous as the figures because through some enchantment the landscape looked as if it actually stretched away into the distance. I could have studied them for hours and not seen everything there was to see – the trees, the flowers, the rivers, the distant towns. More than that, I'd never seen such wonderful colours – bright, soft, and glowing – that often flowed from one shade to the next. Imagine the most beautiful music you've ever heard made visible, and that's what these paintings were like. I was so rapt in wonder that I didn't even notice Hamlet until he spoke.

'Do you like my art work?'

All my thoughts were too big for my mouth so I just gaped like a landed cod.

Hamlet laughed. 'My fingers cannot keep pace with the glories in my mind, but they're a start.'

Finally I managed to gasp out, 'Heaven must look like this.'

Hamlet laughed again, but I could tell he was pleased. 'You like them, then, Ophelia?'

'Like them?' I gasped. 'I didn't know such beauty could exist in this world. Did you indeed paint them, my lord?'

Hamlet looked softer and younger than I'd yet seen him. 'I did indeed paint them, my lady.'

I eyed him with new respect. 'You? You created these beautiful paintings?'

He nodded, very proud. 'I've been working on them for nearly ten years. Each time I came home, I've done a little more. I got the idea from a visit I made to Italy many years since. I saw churches in which entire walls were given over to painting scenes from Roman myth. While others here at court are busy drinking or wenching or hunting, I shut myself in my room and try to make my dreams visible.'

'My dearest lord,' I said earnestly, 'give over all thoughts of kingship. You were made to be a painter, a very great painter. Being a king is nothing compared to that.'

He laughed. 'My girl, we are subject to our birth. Had I been born of common stock, I do think I'd have turned my hand to painting for I love it most dearly, but I may not choose for myself as lowborn folk do. I was born to reign, so I must cast aside all thoughts of painting.'

I shook my head so vigorously that my hair ribbons slipped. 'God wouldn't have given you this talent if He didn't expect you to use it.'

Hamlet gently smoothed my ribbons back in place. 'You speak like a green girl, Ophelia. I may not carve out my future to suit myself, so let us have no more talk about it. You shouldn't be here, you know. A girl should play a strict duenna to her reputation. Women are frail creatures at the best of times, and they're lost indeed if they court disaster. Now get you gone before you give rise to idle tongues.'

'I'm here on important business, my lord.'

He looked amused rather than impressed. 'Why have you come?'

'I've set the cart rolling down the hill, my lord.' I quickly told him how the scene had played out with my father.

'He thinks me mad with love for you?' he asked.

I nodded.

Hamlet took a couple of paces about the room, and then he stopped and studied me. I knew I didn't look my best. I hadn't taken time to tidy myself, and a hank of hair still dribbled over my shoulders and my bodice was askew.

'Why not?' Hamlet whispered. 'Why should it not be so?'

I didn't pay him much mind, for I was looking again at the wondrous paintings. Hamlet seized me by the shoulders and twisted me to face him, standing as he was in front of the wall with the three nude women.

'Ophelia,' he said in a merry voice. 'What say you to marrying me as quick as catch can? What say you to marrying me this very day?'

31

What in the world did he mean? 'My lord?'

'Are you willing to have me as your husband, lady? I'm a poor thing, but I'm heir to the throne of Denmark, and I can make you a queen.'

I felt the colour rising in my cheeks. 'Do not mock me thus, Hamlet.'

He gave me a twisted smile. 'In faith, I swear that I don't mock you, lady. On the contrary, I see that a fruitful marriage will much advance my plan. It will show my monstrous uncle that I'm not his plaything, and it will bring me much pleasure. I'm thirty, Ophelia, and my first duty to Denmark is to provide an heir. So what say you? Will you marry me right now?'

His mention of advancing a plan jangled out of tune with my desires, but in the end all that mattered was that he wished to marry me.

He caught up my hands and spun me around. 'Marry me, Ophelia. Marry me, O bright and beauteous lady. I'll keep you twirling till you grant my wish or till you tumble to the ground in a faint, and afore God, I have no desire for you to bruise your fair white skin against the hard and cruel floor. Say yes, Ophelia. It's a little word, yes, but in it crowds all my future and the future of my entire country. Say yes.'

I pushed hard against him and staggered just out of reach. The room spun around me. 'Hamlet, it's not so simple.'

He stretched out his arms and began to twirl himself around in a circle. 'Ophelia, it is the simplest thing in the world. As simple as breathing. As simple as dying. Say yes, my lady of the mysteries. Say yes, fair maid of spring. Say yes, my dear Jeptha's daughter, O queen of the elves, our lady of innocence.'

'My lord, stand still and talk sense!' I shrieked at him.

He staggered and fell to the floor, laughing.

I tried to pull him to his feet. 'You jest, my lord, or else you're disguised with drink or merriment. Our marriage would be no simple matter indeed. I doubt not but that you, as prince, must first win the king's permission to wed me. Then—'

'Radiant Ophelia, wise Ophelia, beauteous and chaste Ophelia, do but assure me that you love me in truth, and all obstacles will fly right out of our path.'

'I love you, sire. I've loved you since first we spoke, but—'

'Then let us be wed at once, for there's no one else in the world I'd sooner take to wife.'

He *was* jesting. I'd suspected as much, but now I felt a sword pang of bitter disappointment. 'At once? My lord, even should you obtain permission, the banns must be read for three weeks before—'

'Pah!' He made a gesture as if he were sweeping cobwebs away. 'We are in a new world, a new age, and we have no patience with the turtle's pace of the past. Three weeks indeed! No, as the writings of Johannes Kepler and many of the other church scholars show us, God doesn't expect us to use a priest as an intermediary. No, Ophelia, God has shown us time and again that He will talk to us directly and He expects us to be direct with Him in turn. I have no patience with the superstitious nonsense of the old Church, and while I keep silent here on these matters so as not to upset my mother, when I'm at Wittenberg, I don't give an ear to the fusty-musty old ways.'

I made a quick gesture with my fingers to ward off evil that might be tempted to slip in, emboldened by his wild talk. 'How can there be a marriage, sire, without a priest?'

'As Kepler makes plain in all his writings, for a man and woman to marry, all they must do is plight their troth before God and swear to cleave together as husband and wife until they're severed by death.'

I was scandalized. 'No more than that?'

He pulled me onto his lap. His body was hot, as if his twirling about had worked up a sweat, and his clothes had the familiar smell of cloves and oranges. 'No more than that,' he said, 'and I'm a scholar so you know I speak true. For a marriage in the sight of God, nothing else is required but our honest pledging, but in the eyes of the law,' he went on, 'there must be at least two witnesses. God doesn't need a witness, but there are scoundrels who would tumble a maid in the name of marriage and then deny to the world that the marriage had ever taken place, so Kepler as well encourages us to have worldly witnesses.'

I'd never heard of a marriage taking place without a priest, and I told him as much.

'What a little prude I'd take to my bed,' he teased. He scooped me onto the floor and knelt in front of me, his nose almost touching mine. 'Ophelia, we're the parents of the new age of Denmark. It has been given to us to give birth to a new way of life, a better way of life. Ophelia, my dearest love, there's no one else in my life that I love as much as you. There's no maid that walks this earth that I'd rather marry. Although Saint Paul said it's better to marry than burn, I do indeed burn for you, Ophelia. What say you, my dear? Will you have such a clumsy fool as I for your husband?'

It's easy to long for something with your whole heart, but it can feel like madness to have your wish suddenly granted.

I whispered, 'Do not trifle with me, my lord, for you'd break my heart past the mending.'

His voice was husky and heartbreakingly tender. 'I know I'm a broken thing, but I do love you more than anyone in this world, Ophelia.'

More than your father? I wanted to ask, but I knew I couldn't face the answer and so I kept silent.

'I ask you to trust me, Ophelia, and to marry me in the sight of God. Why do you hesitate? Do you not love me enough to marry me? Or do you think I set your maidenhead at a pin's fee, that I speak honeyed words and plan to tumble you and betray you?'

I moved to my knees in front of him and wrapped my hands around his. 'My lord, I do love you best in all this world and in all worlds that might come. I ask for no greater joy than to be your wife, and I'll follow you anywhere, even to death and beyond.'

He gave a cry of joy and pressed his lips against mine. I felt as if I was somersaulting head over heels down a flight of stairs and nothing could stop me. He sprang to his feet.

'Let me fetch two witnesses, and we'll pledge our troth at once.'

'Now?'

He covered my face with kisses. 'Forge the blade while the iron is hot, love. We don't know what the morrow may bring, so let us do what we can today.'

To my amazement, he pressed on a carved rose at the edge of the mantelpiece, and a door in the wall sprang open. He gave me a grin and galloped out it. Through the opening, I could catch a glimpse of dimness and a narrow stairway. I saw Yorick in the shadows there.

'Yorick!' I called out. I needed some cool advice. 'Yorick, what should I do?'

He stepped into the light. 'It's what you've dreamed of, and if you don't seize this moment, there's no telling if he'll catch hold of the notion again. Hamlet is changeable. He is a cloud, and once he's drifted out over the sea, it's doubtful he'll again float over the land.'

Oh, my heart loved the adventure, but my head screamed at me to slow down. Still, Yorick was right. If we're not ready to seize fortune when it bows to us, then we may lose it forever. At that moment I realized that for all I'd dreamed about becoming Hamlet's wife, I'd never really expected it to come to pass. It was like my dream of being the Flying Catgirl, an intense longing but not one that I'd located in the realms of the possible.

'Why not seize the opportunity?' Yorick said. 'Think of your life if you lose him. Watching him marry some whey-faced foreign princess who cannot even speak our tongue, married yourself to some blockish landowner who buries you in a backwater. Would you prefer that life, Ophelia?'

Before I could answer, Hamlet clattered back into the room with his friend Horatio and a man in a guardsman's tunic, a burly soldier named Marcellus. Events were moving too fast, as if on greased skates, and yet I didn't choose to slow them down. Once a flower has blossomed, it cannot be sealed again in the bud, and while this wasn't the marriage ceremony I'd dreamed of, it was the marriage ceremony offered to me. Hamlet must have already explained the whole matter to his two companions as he was fetching them, for they didn't offer one word of protest, although Marcellus looked as nervous as a spooked mare.

Hamlet directed me to kneel next to him. I did so, although my actions felt unreal, as if I was dreaming rather than living. Was this what it felt like, being a ghost? Being aware of what was taking place around you, yet feeling as if your real life was being lived miles or years away?

'Listen to what I say, Ophelia, and then you say the same words,' he directed me.

'I, Hamlet, son of King Hamlet of Denmark, do take Ophelia as my true and lawful wife in the sight of God and of these two witnesses.' He nodded to me, and Marcellus cleared his throat nervously.

I said, 'I, Ophelia, daughter of Polonius, Counsellor to the king of Denmark, do take Prince Hamlet as my true and lawful husband in the sight of God and of these two witnesses.'

'I will forsake all others and will cleave faithfully unto you, so long as we both shall live.'

Unbidden, an image of Ragnor flickered into my mind. What would he think, I wondered, when he learned I was the wife of Prince Hamlet? Quickly I repeated, 'I will forsake all others and will cleave faithfully unto you, so long as we both shall live.'

There was a long pause, as if Hamlet was trying to remember what else needed to be said. Marcellus broke the silence. 'My prince, do you think it meet to marry her in such a havey-cavey fashion? Might not King Claudius construe an act such as this as treason? Would it not be better to—'

'Silence!' thundered Hamlet. He stood up and brushed off the knees of his trousers. 'I decree that the marriage is complete.'

'What about the rings?' Marcellus said. 'It surely cannot be a lawful marriage without the rings to seal your troth.'

I too wondered that, but Hamlet gave me a merry wink. 'We have given our words. With such a valuable bond, I need nothing as cheap as gold, for a man's words – if crafted fine enough – can outlast all other baser stuff. Do you not agree with me, Ophelia? Or do you crave a marriage gift.'

'You yourself are the only gift I crave,' I told him.

'Oh, ho!' he laughed. 'Then you're indeed a jewel among women.' He plucked a small pouch from off his belt and undid the drawstrings. 'But now that we speak of jewels, what think you of this jewel, my jewel and wife?'

He turned my hand over and spilled into it a grand necklet on a chain as fine as embroidery silk. Hanging from it was a cone of woven silver that clutched a pearl as big as a knuckle.

'It's beautiful,' I breathed reverently.

He slipped it over my head. 'The chain is too long,' he said smiling, 'but since it's so long, you can wear it tucked beneath your shift. No one but us two – and the two witnesses of our nuptial – need ever know that it rests secretly tucked between your beautiful breasts.' He leaned down and kissed the top of one breast and then the other. I felt myself grow warm and a little breathless.

Horatio spoke up. 'May we have your leave to depart, my lord?'

Hamlet smiled at me for several heartbeats, and then he let me go. He turned to his comrades. 'I need you gentlemen only to sign your names to this statement.'

He scrawled a message on a piece of parchment: *On this day, I, Hamlet, Prince of the Danes, do take Ophelia as my wife in the presence of God and of these witnesses.* Hamlet signed his name. Then he handed the document to Horatio.

'Write "witnessed by" and sign your name, brave Horatio.' As bidden, Horatio signed his name and handed the paper to Marcellus.

The soldier tried one last protest. 'My lord, should the king dislike this union—'

'The king and the queen will be most pleased, I promise you that.'

Marcellus looked as if he'd like to say more, but instead he scribbled his name with such force that the quill ripped the paper. He handed the contract back to Hamlet, saying, 'My mind dislikes this clandestine affair, but I am sworn to you, my lord, and even if it means my livelihood or my life itself, my word is a bond that must not be broken.'

Hamlet thanked him and dismissed him to return to his duties. After he was gone, Horatio spoke for the first time. 'When means your lordship to make this marriage public?'

There was a silence long enough to ring twenty strokes on a bell, and then Hamlet stretched out his hand to me. I could see worry in his heavy-lidded eyes. 'My lady, my wife, should you mind it very much indeed if we keep this union hidden till the time is ripe to bring it to the notice of my uncle and the court?'

I smiled and took his warm hand in mine. I myself needed time to think about what had been done and what needed to be done to pave the way so our union could travel smoothly on greased wheels on a level road. 'My husband, I'm yours to make or mar, to conceal or reveal at your will. Whatsoever you choose to do with me is my greatest pleasure.'

He kissed my hand and held it to his heart, but as I continued to smile at him, I thought, *Now that I'm his wife, I must use our closeness to keep him from the truth about his father's murder*. I could plant the seeds in his mind that the ghost wasn't his father but an evil spirit come to steal his soul. There was no evidence, none, that he could root out about Claudius, and Claudius was a man with a cool head so it was doubtful that he'd give himself away. No, we'd be safe. I'd encourage Hamlet to play the madman and investigate for a few more months, and then I'd lead him to conclude there was no truth to the ghost's report.

Hamlet's eyes twinkled. 'Leave us, Horatio, for there's one more thing that must be done to secure this marriage.'

Without a word, Horatio bowed and departed.

'One more thing?' I echoed. 'Do you need my signature on the marriage contract?'

Hamlet laughed the laugh of a carefree boy. 'No, love. It's

just that a marriage is not valid until it's consummated.'

So on that morning in a grey March, in a room whose walls were painted a permanent May, on a bed piled high with the softest furs and smoothest silk sheets, I became Hamlet's wife in every sense of the word.

ACT THREE

My Second Murder

32

For all his beauty, Hamlet seemed awkward in his embraces, although perhaps it was just his eagerness made him clumsy. Or perhaps all men were awkward in their coupling. I had no way of knowing otherwise. Still, he treated our lovemaking with the reverence and awe that most folk would reserve for a meeting with God.

'Have you been with many women?' I asked him afterwards as we snuggled against each other.

'Not many.' He coloured up as if embarrassed. 'None, in fact.'

I was at first startled, but concluded he'd held himself apart from women because he hadn't wanted to father bastards and condemn them to their harsh and lonely legacy. I kissed him tenderly on his chin and then rubbed my head against his smooth chest. It was strange to think of how all the men in court were like this – so large in their bulky clothes with the padded doublets of stiff leather or brocade that made them look as broad as bears, but how underneath was a small, soft, animal body.

'How old were you when you first went off to school?' I asked.

'Seven.'

I sat up abruptly. 'You left here when you were but seven?'

He sat up too and swung his legs over the side, his naked back to me. The sight of his thin, pale, defenceless back with its rippled spine and a few freckles sprinkled across his shoulders almost undid me with tenderness. 'My father decided that year that it was time for me to leave. He feared . . .' Hamlet's voice trailed away.

'What did he fear?'

Hamlet gave a little shake to his head and sighed. 'I don't remember what I was going to say. It was just that he decided that I was grown enough at seven to be sent away to school.'

'Did you come home often?'

He lowered his head. 'I didn't come home at all the first five years. Since then, I've returned every two or three years, usually staying each time for a month or so.'

I did some rapid calculations in my head. Twenty-three years he'd been gone. His first visit home came when he was twelve, and in the eighteen years since then, he'd visited only every year or two. Say he'd come back every two years for a month at a stretch . . . that still meant he'd seen his father at most for a total of nine months in the past twenty-three years. By our Lord of the loaves and fishes, I'd seen more of my father in my handful of years here at court than Hamlet had seen in the last twenty-three years!

'You didn't know him at all!' I blurted out.

Hamlet stiffened. 'What do you mean?'

'Since you were a small boy, you've been far away from your father. How can you be so loyal to his memory when you've spent less than a year in his company ever since you were seven?'

Hamlet twisted his head to look at me over his shoulder. Icicles dripped from his voice. 'I didn't have to be in his presence to know that he was a great man and a great king. His sending me away, that was for my own good. I'm certain it broke his heart to be parted from me, but he cared more for me to be schooled than to indulge his inclinations to keep his son close.'

He kept Holger close, I wanted to say, but I didn't. I knew I should keep my lips pressed tight, but I heard myself saying, 'If your father loved you so much, then why does his ghost ask you to risk life and soul to kill Claudius? A truly loving father wouldn't so imperil the life and eternal soul of his son.' As soon as the words were out, I wanted to herd them back into my mouth. They would do no good. After all, how can you tell someone that the person they think they love is no more like the real person than a dragonfly is like a dragon?

Hamlet stood up and wrapped a sheet around him. He didn't look at me. 'You are a woman, Ophelia, and so, as my father often said about my mother, your brain is not fashioned in such a way as to permit you to understand things like honour and such.'

Just as you don't understand your father's true nature and how he never loved you the way he loved your brother. But I wouldn't fan the fire of Hamlet's rage. I'd let the inferno burn itself down to embers. His father was dead and, over time, his influence on my new husband would fade till it was as faint as the memory of a childhood love.

The bell rang to summon us to supper.

'Forgive me, Hamlet,' I said, forcing my voice into meek tones. 'You are right. I don't understand these things, so I shouldn't speak of them.'

He inclined his head. 'Forgive me, Ophelia. I know it's a common fault for women to speak without thinking.'

I longed to tear into that remark like a hound attacking a marauding badger, but I kept the peace, saying only, 'Shall we to supper?'

'Dress yourself and go,' he said, still not looking at me. 'I'll send for you when it's safe to come again.'

As I crept away from his chambers, I felt more like one

of his father's tumbled kitchen wenches than a princess of Denmark.

Hamlet himself didn't come to the hall for supper. I didn't see him for two days, and sometimes I fancied I'd dreamed the entire marriage. Then on the third day, after supper, Horatio approached me and said he'd been sent to bring me to the prince. To my surprise, instead of leading me through the corridors to the royal chambers, he escorted me down to the courtyard.

For a wild moment I feared that Hamlet repented of the marriage and had sent Horatio to spirit me away. 'This is not the way,' I said to him, and a ghost in scarlet tunic and with a thick line of blood across his neck overheard me and gave a wild laugh.

'It's best for you to travel through the secret passageway,' Heratio said.

I remembered the hidden door in the wall in Hamlet's room. 'How came he to have a secret passageway?'

'The passageway leads to all the royal chambers.'

He would say no more but showed me the little door in the courtyard, veiled with ivy and nestled into a shadowy niche behind a huge rain barrel. He gave me a heavy golden key and showed me how to unlock the door, then led me up some long stairs that, at the top, branched out like a flattened hand. Hamlet, holding a lamp, stood at the top of the third branch.

'My door doesn't open from your side,' Hamlet said, 'but you can tap against it three times, and I'll hear you and let you in.'

We made love, and afterwards, as we lay there and listened to the crackling and tinkling of the logs in the fireplace, I asked Hamlet about the hidden passageway.

'The king who had built the castle, one of my ancestors, wasn't popular in Denmark and therefore feared the possibility of an uprising. Thus he built this secret passageway.'

He chuckled. 'It's so old that I may be the only member of the royal family who remembers its existence. I learned of it one day when I was thumbing through an old heap of notes about the building of the castle. It took me days of pulling and tapping to find the exact place to press to open the door.'

As soon as I stepped into his chambers, I was astonished to see how much work he'd accomplished in two days on the unfinished wall painting. The young man and several of the women now had ivory-pink flesh, and the young man's draped furs looked real enough to touch.

'Did you have elves to sneak in and help you, Hamlet, that you painted on this in two days only?'

He wrapped his arms around me and rested his chin on the top of my head. 'I cannot sleep, Ophelia. The sad hours of the night ravel slowly, and there's little to do save joining my uncle in his drunken revels that bring no credit to Denmark.'

I didn't remind him that his father had presided over identical drunken revels.

He tightened his arms around me. 'I like to have my rooms ablaze with torches, to throw defiance in the very teeth of night, to say—' and here he let me go and leapt upon a chest as if it were a stage, '"Hamlet the Dane is such a great king that he can turn night to day and make the dead live again" . . . at least here in my chambers.'

'Make the dead live again?' Did he too see ghosts?

He laughed and held out a hand to me. 'In my paintings, Ophelia. In my paintings.' I took his hand and he pulled me up to stand with him upon the chest. 'When I'm painting, I know how God felt when He created the world.' He threw back his head and gave a long howl like a primitive battle cry, and I howled with him until there was a knock at the door to the corridor and a rough voice called out, 'My lord, is all well within?'

I began to giggle, but Hamlet called, 'Yes, thank you,

Bernardo, all is quite well, and all is quite well, and all manner of thing shall be well.' He looked over at his painting with a fond eye and said to me, 'I'd prefer to work with sunlight instead of flame, but even the king of Denmark cannot command the night turn to day.' He leaned back against the wall. 'Did you ever hear the story of my ancestor, Cnut? When his courtiers fawned and lisped and told him he was as great as God Himself, Cnut ordered them to carry his throne down to the seashore and then he ordered the flowing tide to ebb.'

'Did it?'

'Of course not. He staged the whole pageant to show his court that no matter how great a king is, there are things he cannot command.' He climbed down from the chest, his mood now sombre. 'Even my father, great as he was, couldn't command the tides. Or death. Oh, it gnaws at my heart, Ophelia, to think of my great warrior father being slain in his orchard like a helpless peasant babe.'

Like all those babes of his that your father ordered slain. All I said was, 'Even the greatest among us, Hamlet, are powerless over the kiss of a snake.'

He stepped back as if I myself had bitten him. 'Unless that snake wears the crown!'

He reached up and lifted me down from the chest.

'My dearest husband, a snake killed your father. A snake, not your uncle.' Hamlet started to turn away, but I grabbed his sleeve. 'After all, it was a snake that turned mankind out of Eden. Surely that renders him a suitable foe for a king. There's no dishonour for your father to die from a snake's bite.' It made me sick to lie to him, but it made me sicker to think of him discovering the truth. I rubbed my cheek against the soft black velvet on his arm. 'For this night at least, leave it. Can you not step away from this coil and find some joy with me?'

He crushed me into a hug so tight that I couldn't breathe.

His words were muffled by my hair, but I heard them plain enough. 'My dearest wife, in these two days I've found such joy, such profound joy.'

He loves me. He can use this love as a rope to pull himself out of his caverns of melancholy. I tilted my head up to look at him, and he looked down in my eyes. His next words, though, threw cold water on the embers of my heart. 'I know now that I draw close to the truth about my father,' he said. 'I know that soon, like Oedipus, I'll solve the riddle of my father's death, unmask my traitorous uncle, and come into my rightful kingdom to rule in such a way as to make my father smile down from Heaven and say, "This is a proper son." What more could I want to make my joy complete?'

Me, I wanted to cry out. *Want me*. Let me be enough. Let me take the place of father, mother, kingdom, art, and God. Let me blaze so bright in your eyes that you cannot see the shadows of death. Let me be more important than truth. Want me more than anything.

But there would be time enough to ring all the changes. I said nothing more as I drew him to the bed.

33

I crept back to my own chamber before dawn. My father didn't notice my absence since he was much involved with the present negotiations with Norway. Information from spies indicated that Erik Strong Arm was indeed preparing an invasion of Denmark, and my father and Claudius were frantically trying to arrange a peace. In fact, Claudius was so preoccupied with these affairs that my father refrained from relating to him the story I'd manufactured of Hamlet's visit to my chamber. In any case, it wasn't much needed, for the whole court was buzzing about Hamlet's antics.

For the first weeks of his madness, he'd contented himself with wandering about the castle muttering vague phrases such as 'Well, well, we know,' and 'There be, an' if they might,' but I pointed out to him that if he truly wished to clothe himself in the appearance of madness, he needed bolder strokes. So he took out the little tablet that he always carried and set down the ideas we devised. It turned out to be as good as writing a play. We decided that one day he'd claim that he could smell the devil in the castle and he'd wander about, sniffing his way along the floor joints and around the cracks in the doors. Another day he went about with his clothes backwards – all except his shoes because we couldn't figure a way to keep shoes on when they were turned rear to front. When asked he told the folk that, 'If the devil sneaks up behind me to steal my soul, if I wear my clothes backwards he'll sneak up to my front thinking it's my back, and thus I can see him coming and run away.' He spent one day doing nothing but repeating any speech that was said to him, and the day after that we draped linen sheets about him instead of his usual clothes, and he informed everyone that he was Mercury, the messenger of the gods. Hamlet took to these schemes with great zest, and he soon became even better than I was at thinking up new, outrageous notions.

One day he stripped off all his clothes and walked naked as a newborn babe up and down the corridors. Another time he wore a chamber pot upon his head and strutted about the great hall proclaiming he was King Netherworld. Otherwise he continued to wear his mourning clothes all through the spring, and once he appeared at supper with his face and skin painted as black as his dress. It took nearly two weeks for all the traces of the paint to fade.

'You should give up the throne and become a player,' I told him, only half jesting for he was remarkably good at throwing himself into a part. 'Let us leave Denmark and travel about the world, you and I, writing plays together and directing a band of actors.'

To say truth, this notion held great appeal for me.

'The world has need of good players,' I cajoled him.

'It has a greater need for good kings,' he said.

It pleased me that Hamlet concentrated so much on finding a new way to play mad that he forgot that the end of his search was to discover the truth about his father's death. Part of my soul was always like a clenched fist, tensed against his finding out my role in his father's death. As weeks went on, though, he seemed more and more fascinated with acting out his madness and less interested in digging up truth.

It became almost a game at court for folk to share tidbits of his odd behaviour. My father caught him in the counting room, rifling through the recent treaties, and when he questioned him, Hamlet claimed that he was looking for a needle to sew up a rip in my father's clothes, and when my father ventured to say that he could see no rip, Hamlet grabbed my father's sleeve and tore it in two. Elspeth caught him in the still room, opening all the vials and tasting them, and he told her that he hadn't eaten in seven days and was hungry for a good dinner. Often he wandered into Claudius's chambers to root through everything stored there. When challenged he argued that husband and wife were one flesh and that mother and son were of the same body, so this was actually his own chamber and he had the right of ownership. Finally Claudius posted special Swiss guards at the door of his chamber to keep Hamlet out.

His exploits always made me laugh, especially seeing the long faces of all the courtiers. I loved the drama and audacity of Hamlet's imagination. By this time he often came to meals in the hall, and frequently he'd smile or wink at me. I didn't come to his chamber as often as I'd have liked, though. Horatio appeared with a summons for me once a week or so, but by this time we were moving toward the season of white nights, so I had to sneak away earlier and earlier to be back through the courtyard and into my own room before dawn. Hamlet made great progress with his painting. The background was nearly finished, and he had only the faces and figures of the women to go. He told me the young man in the painting was the son of Jove who had been shut out of Mount Olympus and condemned to madness, and that the women who travelled the earth with him were known as the Bacchantes, driven mad and wild by their love for the beautiful, doomed young god.

'If you weren't a prince,' I said several times, 'you should turn painter.'

'But I am a prince,' he always answered.

One night as we lay in his bed, he turned my words back on me. 'If I weren't a prince, I might turn playwright and pen the tragedy of Bacchus so all could know the truth of the struggles of that poor, doomed, misunderstood lad.'

Excited, I scooted up to my knees in front of him. 'Do it, Hamlet. Even though you be a prince, write that play.'

He laughed and ruffled my hair and said that his own doom was to be a ruler and not a writer, and then he called me by many of his pet names: his undiscovered country, his mouse, his wanton girl, his newfound home. He received great pleasure from the secret of our marriage, and I, too, hugged this private knowledge to my chest like a much-loved babe, but I was eager for the winds of his wildness to die down so we could begin to knit the fabric of our lives. He still talked much of his suspicions of his uncle, but he moved no nearer the truth. He spoke often of the emptiness of his life and how the only times he felt truly alive were my visits and during his outrageous pranks. I did notice that his mad adventures grew increasingly dangerous, as if something increased his appetite for wildness and what had once been a feast was no longer even a mouthful. I grew frightened to hear how he'd balanced for several hours up on a turret, a pole in his hands, shouting that his father's death had made him a weathercock and he must do his duty. Then, during one of my visits, he leapt out of the bed and began to scream.

'Hamlet, what is the matter?'

He cowered in a corner, shrinking down until he was crouched on the floor. 'Give it back to me,' he whimpered. 'O false lady, restore what you've taken or my heart will burst with grief.'

I ran over and knelt before him. 'My dearest love, what have I taken?'

'O Delilah,' he wept, 'you've played me false. You have shorn my hair and taken away the better part of my manhood. Until you give it back, I have no hopes of pulling the temple down.'

I kissed his hands and pleaded with him to give over this behaviour, that there was no need to act the madman with me, but he wouldn't leave off crying and moaning so at last I crept back to my room.

He didn't come to middag that day, but at supper he was merry as a gig, and several times he winked at me and pulled comical faces.

I didn't understand why he'd given me such a show, but I accepted that I might not know everything about my husband, and so I didn't let myself think any more about that strange episode. The next time I visited him, he was cheerful and spilling over with conversation. He talked for almost two hours without my fitting a single word into the wall of his chatter. He talked of flying machines, a Persian king, of how pelicans feed their young, the philosopher's stone, mathematics of the Moors, and the emperor Nero. I lapped up his talk as a starving kitten laps up milk.

Yorick had led me to understand that Hamlet's show of madness would tire itself out, but, if anything, he waxed rather than waned. When I shared my impatience with Yorick, he counselled me, 'Give him time.'

The worst part of it was that in order to appear mad, Hamlet stopped bathing and cutting his hair. He didn't often change his small clothes, and where he'd once been a pattern card of beauty, he now was as rumpled as a leper. Where he'd once smelled of oranges and cloves, he now stank of dirty linen, sweat, and worser things. It was indeed comical to watch, for when he approached folk at court, almost like clockwork you could see them lift a perfumed handkerchief to their noses to ward off his smell. When I went on my secret visits, I'd soak my hair ribbons in rosewater to help mask his smell.

Horatio stayed on at court. Hamlet moved him out of his lodgings in town into a chamber in the castle. In the middle of June, Lords Rosencrantz and Guildenstern returned to celebrate the Midsummer revels.

Neither they nor I had the least suspicion that those revels would change all our lives.

34

The queen informed me of their arrival as we sat sewing in her chambers.

'Did Lord Hamlet expect them?' I asked.

Would he tell them of his plan, why he was feigning madness? Or would he shut them out of his heart? I puzzled over this and then realized that the queen had waited a little too long to answer my question. 'Did Lord Hamlet invite them here?' I asked, looking hard at the queen.

She coloured slightly and bent down to her stitching. 'I believe it was an unexpected visit.' I knew her well enough to hear a strain in her tone. She was hiding something.

'Unexpected by everyone?'

She tugged her thread so tightly it snapped, and then she looked down at it in surprise. 'Yes, I believe so.'

The queen wasn't skilled at dissembling. 'That's a thing most strange,' I said, studying her. 'I've never before heard of folk riding up casually to a castle as if it were an inn, to burst in on a visit without sending a word of warning of their arrival.'

The queen twisted the needle round and round in her thin fingers but said nothing.

I asked bluntly, 'Did you send for them, Majesty?'

She turned to me a face full of misery. 'What else should I do, Ophelia? My son is suffering the torments of the damned, and I cannot find out what tortures him. Was it wrong to send to his two closest friends and ask them to help me sort him out?'

Now I was the one who made no answer.

Hamlet didn't make an appearance at supper, but Rosencrantz and Guildenstern sat on the dais, flanking the king and queen. At a table in the back of the hall sat a group of men I didn't recognize, and I asked my father who they were.

'Marry,' he said, 'they are the players come to perform for us.'

Players at last! I clapped my hands with joy.

'These are said to be good,' he told me. 'I gather Lord Hamlet often attended their shows in Wittenberg, and he was most pleased with their antics. I'm told they're the best actors in the world for tragedy, comedy, history, pastoral, pastoral-comedy, historical-pastoral, tragical-historical, comical-tragical-historical-pastoral, and so forth. Seneca is not too heavy for them, nor the airy Plautus too light. They can give you—'

'When will they perform?'

'Tomorrow night. They will perform "The Murder of Gonzago".'

I was agog with eagerness, and as soon as the queen's departure released us from our places, I hurried up to welcome Rosencrantz and Guildenstern. I wondered if they'd yet met Hamlet and if he'd told them of our secret marriage.

Rosencrantz greeted me warmly, a smile both on his lips and his soft, doggy eyes, but Guildenstern, as usual, was stiff in his manner.

I said, 'I didn't expect you to return so soon to Elsinore.'

Rosencrantz glanced at Guildenstern, a guilty expression on his face, but Guildenstern looked as bland as a rain-washed stone. I was sick to death of other people's secrets. First the queen, and now Lord Rosencrantz. Something was clearly afoot.

'This is like a second home to us,' Guildenstern finally said.

'Do you not mean third home?' I countered. 'There is your birth home and then there are your apartments at Wittenberg. Or do you not count one of those abodes?'

Rosencrantz blushed and even Guildenstern looked a little flustered. Before I could press my advantage, Guildenstern bowed and excused himself. 'I wait upon the king. He has promised to show me a new gelding in his stable.'

Rosencrantz made as if to follow, but I tucked my hand into the crook of his arm. 'Walk with me a little,' I said, and he had no graceful choice but to obey.

We strolled through the labyrinth of passages toward my chambers. I decided to give him my words with no bark on them. 'You have come to spy on Hamlet, have you not?'

Again there was that pause that was a little too long.

'We come in friendship, lady. No other reason.' He didn't meet my eye.

I ventured to draw my bow at a possible target. 'I understood it was the queen who sent for you.'

He stopped in his tracks. His scarred eye twitched. 'Lady, she did send for us indeed, but we share her concern for the prince.'

'Concern?'

He looked away.

I pressed on. 'If you're loyal to a friend, then you don't turn him round, looking for minor flaws.'

'Minor flaws! Ophelia, Hamlet is mad.'

And you're a credulous fool! 'Have you even spoken with him since last you were here?'

'We spoke with him this afternoon.'

Scorn dripped from my voice. 'And you judge him mad after one short afternoon's visit?'

'I say this, lady, after a lifetime of knowing him. His madness comes in fits and starts, but he's mad all the same.'

He disgusted me. 'I thought you loved him.'

'No man loves Hamlet more than I do. Nor no woman, either.' He looked down at the floor, and when he lifted his eyes to mine, they were filled with tears. 'I'd give my life for him, Ophelia, if he required it. He has the gift of inspiring unreasoning loyalty.'

'Then it's all the more lamentable of you to slander him this way. Loyalty demands that you see only what is good and beautiful and glamorous in him.'

'Loyalty demands that I see him honestly.'

I gave a disgusted sniff.

'Ophelia, no matter how much we love him, our love cannot heal the disease in Hamlet's soul—'

'Villain! You are wrong!' My voice rose like a wind from a March sea. 'You are wrong in all that you say. Hamlet has no disease in his soul, and even if he did, love can heal all such defects.'

Rosencrantz grabbed both my hands. His own hands were dry and a little leathery, more weather-beaten than I'd have anticipated in a scholar. 'Ophelia, I know that you love him, too. I know how he can feel like the sun that draws the flower of your soul to him. I know how he can fill your eyes and heart so that everything around you seems shadowy and insubstantial. So listen to me and know I speak out of friendship and nothing else. There's much greatness in Hamlet but there's no foundation in his soul. He is like a bird with broken legs. He soars high, but when he tires of soaring, he has no way to come to earth without a crash. At times – and these times are becoming more frequent and long-lasting – Hamlet's moods consume him as fire consumes dry wood so that his mood of the moment runs leagues before his sense.'

'Stop it!' I twisted free and pressed my hands over my ears to shut out the nonsense he was babbling.

I could still hear his voice even with my ears covered. 'Much of the time Hamlet is fine, but when the wildness comes upon him, he's capable of much harm to himself and to others. Other times he disappears under a black cloud of sadness, unable to move or think or speak. When he's seized by the right hand of antic excitement or the left hand of despair, he is out of himself and becomes a dangerous creature, but when he's between his personal Scylla and Charybdis, there's no one more enchanting on the face of the earth.'

'You lie! I grant you he's high-strung, but he's no more mad than you or I, and he's less capable of harm than either of us. You cannot be his friend if you'd speak thus of him, betraying him to the queen through your actions and betraying him to me through your words.' I swept up my skirts. 'You sicken me!' I ran down the corridor to my chambers. Rosencrantz called after me, but I wouldn't turn back.

There was no refuge in my chambers. My father was there. As soon as I saw him, I wheeled about to depart again, but he stopped me before I could take flight.

'Ophelia! Daughter!'

'Father, not now, for I'm in too great a passion to listen.'

'You must listen. The king has a plan that involves you and Lord Hamlet.'

35

His words stopped my flight. 'What plan?'

'I showed the king your letters from young Hamlet—'

Jesus in the temple with the money lenders didn't have one-tenth the fury that leapt into my heart. 'My letters! What do you know of my letters?'

'The letters you keep hidden under your mattress.'

He had snooped through my room! 'Those were private, Father!'

He didn't show the least bit of shame. 'Pooh! A daughter is the property of her father. Ergo all her property is also therefore the property of her father so any letters sent to her are thereby letters to her father—'

'So, Father, you say Hamlet is writing love letters to *you*?'

'Do not try my patience, Ophelia. Do not try it. This is no matter for levity, no matter at all. Let us rather find the lever with which we can levitate the heaviness that sinks the reason of young Hamlet, and the *reason*, I reckon, for his unreason is his unreasoning love for you.'

I was sick of the way folk at Elsinore used words to show off their own cleverness rather than to convey plain truths. 'You had no right to paw through my possessions.'

'Go to! I'm your father, and I have the right to know everything about you. What is more, it's my duty to know everything that can be known about you.'

'Father—'

His face blazed with excitement. 'I've persuaded the king

and queen that Hamlet's madness derives from his love for you. If we can prove this is the case, then they'll give consent for you to marry the prince.'

Too late, I thought, *for we've been wed near three months.* My father clasped his hands together. 'I'd thought myself cursed years ago when I found out my wife had given birth to a daughter rather than a son, but now I see that it was great fortune indeed for the house of Polonius. Father to a king. How well that sounds. Trust me to guide you and shape you, Ophelia, and we shall see great days yet.'

'Do you care at all how I feel about these matters?' I asked, curious.

'Pooh!' he said. 'When it comes to kings and their ways, our feelings don't matter any more than the tooth of a flea. Do you think I myself have had the luxury of indulging in feelings all these many years I've served first King Hamlet and now King Claudius? Had I indulged my feelings, I wouldn't now be chief counsellor to the king and you wouldn't be a fine lady at court and your brother wouldn't be well-schooled in France. Had I given in to each feeling, I'd have felt our way all the way out of court and far into obscurity. Do not wave the banner of feeling at me, girl, and expect me to surrender.'

I still didn't like my father overmuch, but now I saw him highlighted by the glow of a kind of shabby heroism, scrabbling to the top of court and swallowing slights and insults that would choke most of us just to keep his family elevated.

'What is Claudius's plan?' I asked.

'He will tell you himself on the morrow.'

No matter how I questioned, I could tease no more information out of him.

Hamlet needed to be warned that this new plan was afoot. As soon as darkness fell, I let myself into the secret passage and crept up to the door of his chamber, but since he didn't expect me, the door was locked tight. I banged and kicked against the panel, but he didn't open it and the door didn't budge on its own. I returned to my chamber and penned a note and hastened to the front door of his rooms, but four of the king's Swiss guards stood there, and I dared not let them witness me pushing my letter underneath Hamlet's door.

I passed a restless night. I mistrusted Claudius's plan, and I vowed to approach Hamlet after *middag* and tell him about it.

Unfortunately, I was summoned to the king's presence *before middag*.

As my father led me down to the lobby of the Great Hall, I felt like a heifer being led to the axe. The king and queen stood there in fast conversation with Rosencrantz and Guildenstern.

Claudius was asking, 'Can you not learn why he puts on his confusion?'

'He does confess that he feels distracted,' Rosencrantz said, 'but he'll not tell us the cause.' His eyes flickered to mine and I fancied I saw guilt in them.

'He keeps himself apart from us,' Guildenstern said.

The queen interjected, 'Did he receive you well?'

'Like a gentleman,' Rosencrantz said.

'But he had to force himself to be polite to us.'

As well he might, I thought, *since you've come as spies for the queen.*

The queen continued, 'Can you catch his interest in anything?'

Rosencrantz said, 'We informed him that certain players had arrived at court, and he's ordered them to perform a play tonight.'

'That's true, very true,' my father piped up. 'Young Hamlet has begged me to entreat your majesties to attend the performance.'

The king and the queen both looked pleased. Claudius dismissed Guildenstern and Rosencrantz and asked the queen to leave us as well.

'Gertrude,' said the king, 'we've sent for your son so that he, as it were by accident, may bump into Ophelia.' King Hamlet had referred to himself with the plural *we* only when he addressed the court in a formal proclamation or ceremony, but I'd noticed that Claudius liked to use the royal pronouns whenever he spoke. 'Her father and ourselves will hide behind that curtain and spy upon them to discover whether or not it's love that causes Hamlet to run mad.'

I was speechless with horror. In the first place, there was something obscene about having my father and the king eavesdrop on my encounter with the man I loved. Second, I feared that Hamlet would, justifiably, grow enraged and suspicious if he thought I was conspiring with his uncle.

Before I could object, the queen hugged me. 'Ophelia, I pray that it is indeed his love for you that has driven my son to wildness, and I also hope that your love for him will bring him home again.'

'I hope so, too,' I said through gritted teeth.

My father thrust a book of prayers into my hand and ordered me to pretend to stand and read . . . as if anyone indeed had ever strolled the lobby reading any kind of book, prayers or other. Like hares into a hole, he and Claudius popped behind the curtains just as Hamlet appeared in the distance, muttering to himself.

I couldn't make out his words, but I dared not run away for fear of exciting Claudius's suspicions. Too soon Hamlet spotted me and approached.

'Nymph, in your prayers remember all my sins.'

I was terrified he'd say something to give away the truth of our relationship, so I pressed a finger to my lips, willing his discretion. He looked confused.

'My good lord,' I said in a tight, squeaky voice, 'how have you been for this many a day?'

He kept a small tablet looped to his belt with a small pencil attached so that he could set down notes to himself. I moved close enough for his body to shield my movements, and I worked the tablet free.

He stared at me, bemused, saying only, 'I humbly thank you. I've been well, well, well.'

On the first page I scribbled, *We are watched*. 'My lord, I have some love tokens of yours that I need to return to you. Please take this.' I held the tablet out to him.

He read the note and looked up at me, bewildered. 'I never gave you anything.' He took the tablet and wrote down, *Who?*

I kept talking as I wrote my reply. 'Indeed, my lord, you did give me many gifts and accompanied them with words so sweet that they made the things much richer.' *My father and the king*, I wrote. 'That perfume is now gone—' I held out the tablet. 'Take these again.'

Hamlet took the tablet and pencil.

So as not to arouse suspicion in the king and my father, I kept babbling on with a village proverb. 'To the noble mind, rich gifts wax poor when givers prove unkind.'

He wrote, *Where?* and held out the tablet to me.

I tilted my head toward the curtain that hid the onlookers. 'There, my lord.'

Hamlet let forth a great laugh that shook the hall. I couldn't read him. 'Are you honest?' he asked me in a loud voice.

'My lord?'

'Are you fair?'

What game was he now playing? I was scared of making a false move. Cautiously I asked, 'What do you mean?'

'A maid who is honest and fair will grant no one access to her beauty.'

His words made no sense to me. Was he saying that since
I married him in secret, he couldn't trust my honesty in this?
Surely not, but what message was he trying to give me?

Playing for time, I asked, 'Could beauty have a better
companion than honesty?'

'Yes,' he said, his eyes glittering, 'for beauty can turn
honesty into a bawd sooner than honesty can turn beauty
chaste.'

What was he saying? Was he calling me a whore for
sharing his bed in lawful marriage? I wanted to end this
strange encounter. My head began to ache with confusion.

'I loved you *once*,' he said in a cold voice, looking at me the
way you might look at a wheedling beggar.

'Indeed, you made me believe it.' I knew he was just
play-acting, but his acting had a chilling reality to it.

'You shouldn't have believed me.' Was it indeed mere
play-acting? Or was he out of his head with anger at being
spied on? Was it anger toward his uncle, toward me, toward
both of us? Surely he couldn't believe that I had volunteered
to conspire with Claudius in this present course. 'Your virtue
can't inoculate our bloodline, Ophelia.'

'My lord—'

'I never loved you!'

The words thudded like a stone on the floor of a pit I'd
thought bottomless. *He is acting. He is just playing a part. After
you're away from here, the Hamlet you love will be restored to you.*
The words in my brain were more prayer than thought.

'Then I was deceived,' I said softly.

'Get to a convent,' he snarled. 'Above all, don't become
pregnant and breed more sinners. I myself am fairly virtu-
ous, but I could accuse myself of such sins that it would
have been better if I'd never been born.' He continued to
rant, a catalogue of his sins tumbling from his lips faster
and faster. His words were a blur; I couldn't focus. Then

a question slapped me out of my reverie. 'Where's your father?'

I'd indicated where father was hiding. 'At home, my lord,' I said. I rolled my eyes over to the curtain where my father stood listening. *Had Hamlet forgotten?*

He raised his voice. 'Let the doors be locked at him there so he'll play the fool nowhere but in his own house.' He turned and walked away, calling over his shoulder, 'Farewell.'

Relief at having this uncomfortable scene finished swept over me. I decided I could contribute my mite since I'd added very little to feed the eavesdroppers' appetites. In my best theatrical fashion, with a grandeur of style suitable to the Flying Catgirl, I fell to my knees and screamed, 'O help him, you sweet heavens.'

I was startled to see Hamlet turn abruptly and stride back into the lobby. His eyes were wild as if he was persuaded that I'd indeed contrived with the king to arrange this encounter. 'If you ever marry, take this curse as your dowry,' he screamed like an eagle swooping onto its prey. 'Be as chaste as ice, as pure as snow, and even then you won't escape slander. Get you to a convent. Farewell.'

I was too stunned to speak. My mind understood he was playing a role but the Hamlet I knew seemed to have departed from his body, leaving a stranger in his place. In the eyes of the man in front of me I saw no trace of the man I loved.

'If you have to marry,' he screamed, 'marry a fool, for wise men know what monsters women make of them. So get to a convent. Go quickly. Farewell.'

He started away again. I made the sign to ward off evil and whispered, 'O heavenly powers, restore him.'

As if I'd summoned him, he wheeled around and charged back to me. 'Women!' he screamed. 'I've heard how you paint your faces. God has given you one face and yet you make yourselves another one. You jig, you wiggle, you lisp, you nickname things, and you pretend to be all innocent when you're goading a man to blaze with lust. Damn you all! I'll take it no more. It has driven me mad!' It took all my will to keep me there, listening to his fury. *Play-acting*, I told myself, but I no longer believed it. Some dark tide had drowned the husband I loved. He raged on. 'I say that we shall have no more marriage!'

I looked up at him, stricken, and for a moment he softened. 'Those that are married already—'

'Yes?' I whispered, but it was as if my words had called down the storm again.

He shrieked, 'All but one shall live. The rest shall keep as they are.' He dug his fingers into my shoulder. 'To a convent, go!'

He gave me a great push that sent me tumbling backwards. My head banged against the stone floor, and for a moment the room reeled about me. I heard the rustle of the curtain and turned my head to see the king and my father stepping back into the room, looking almost as shaken as I feel. For several heartbeats, we three held ourselves in stunned silence.

Choose to believe he was acting, I told myself. *Now play your own part to back up his performance. Show yourself a faithful wife.* I wanted nothing more than to lie quietly on the floor, but I dragged myself back to my knees. I struck a prayerful pose. *Think performance. Think Flying Catgirl.* 'Oh, what a fine mind has been destroyed.' I gave a bloodcurdling moan. 'The courtier's, the soldier's, the scholar's. He was the eye, the tongue, the sword, the hope, and the flower of Denmark. The looking-glass of beauty and the pattern of gentility, the sharpest mind in all Denmark – gone, all gone.'

The words sounded forced and hollow to my ear, but I'd always used an elevated diction in my play-acting, and I didn't know how to make my speech more natural. 'And I, of all ladies in the world, am the most miserable and broken, I who once sucked the honey of his poetic vows of love. Now I see indeed that his noble and powerful reason – like sweet bells jangled – all out of tune and harsh. Alas, alas, his mind has been blasted with his madness. O, woe is me!'

Through my sobs, I could hear Claudius talking to my father, but I couldn't make out his words. Even though my own words seemed artificial, I was still shaken by Hamlet's performance. Doubtless it was just a nod to his great talent, but it had felt to me more like madness than craft. I badly needed to talk with him.

My father patted me on the shoulder, and I involuntarily winced as his hands tapped the sore place. 'How do you fare, Ophelia? You need not tell us what Lord Hamlet said. We heard it all.'

He helped me to my feet, and I limped out of the lobby, stiff and shaken by what I'd seen in Hamlet. The push had hurt my shoulder, and when I put my fingers up to probe the bruises, I discovered that it had ripped my gown as well. I needed to change clothes, but more than that, I needed to talk with Hamlet, to find out what had just taken place.

I slipped down to the courtyard, torn gown and all, and as soon as I made sure there were no eyes in my direction, I crept into the secret passage and made my way up to his door. I tapped and scraped and finally banged against the panel, so desperate was I to talk with him, but he never opened the door. At first I thought he wasn't in his chambers, but after a while I laid my ear next to the crack, and I could hear someone stirring within. My first thought was that it must be a servant, but then I realized a servant would either have fled at the sound of my banging or he'd have come over to the panel to investigate. No servant then. To my horror, I realized that Hamlet was in his chambers, but he didn't want to admit me. I banged more wildly, and then I pressed my ear back to the crack. Now I could hear him talking within, a wild tumble of words like water over a cliff, but there was no other voice answering back. From time to time he even gave a little laugh. I banged harder until my hands were bruised, and I called out, 'My husband, let me in,' but the door never opened.

After perhaps half an hour, I gave up and returned to my room.

What was happening? I felt dizzy and sick. Had Hamlet turned against me? Did he think I was now the ally of his uncle and had betrayed him? Life felt as if it had gone mad indeed, and sense had been usurped. Rosencrantz's words about Hamlet haunted me: *His madness comes in fits and starts, but he's mad all the same.* No! These words were lies, slanders, calumny. There was so much greatness in Hamlet that there was no room left for madness.

Nevertheless, doubt now had become the serpent in my paradise.

It can't be that he suspects my part in his father's death. I closed my eyes and whispered a quick prayer for protection to Saint Ursula, patron of virgins. Then I remembered that I was no longer a virgin. I didn't know to whom married ladies prayed. I was floundering in waters too dark and too deep. The memory of Hamlet shouting at me down in the lobby, his angry face so like that of his angry murdered father . . . All at once my stomach twisted, and I vomited up all the contents of my stomach into my chamber pot. The foul smell made me vomit up again. Then, to my disgust, I began to cry. With tears streaming down my face, I shoved the pot out into the corridor and lay upon my bed till this unaccustomed weeping spell would run its course and I could return to myself again.

I woke to my father's shaking my arm. 'For shame, Ophelia. For shame. The bell has rung to summon us to the play, and you lie here a slug-abed. Rise up, my girl. We must hurry for no one will be admitted after the king has entered the chamber.'

Oh, Lord. I'd fallen asleep. Time had turned the corner into evening. Drugged by misery, I'd slept the entire day away, slept past both middag and supper. I was still in my torn gown, and I knew my hair must be as frowsy as a haystack. 'Father, I'm not dressed—'

'You look charmingly, charmingly,' he said, pulling me to a sitting position. 'We dare no longer tarry, daughter.' He jabbed a few loose strands of my hair back into their restraining net. 'The queen would be most displeased if you missed the play, so no more of this, but come along.'

'I look like a wanton—'

'No such thing.' He pulled me to my feet. 'And even if you do, I dare not let you be absent from the show, for the queen most pointedly said to me after supper that she was glad you were to have this treat after your ordeal of this morning.'

The pain of the morning came flooding back. 'Father, it wasn't well done of you nor of the king to spy on me in such a fashion.'

'Pooh! You have no more sense than a gosling. Unless we unpuzzle the cause of Hamlet's madness, Denmark totters, for there's no one else in the royal bloodline to take the throne once Claudius – God grant him long life – passes from this earth.'

'Do you truly have no notion of the pain you caused me?'

'Go to! What is your pain in the face of our country's welfare? For the good of Denmark, I'd spy in the same fashion upon the queen herself.'

'Then next time hide yourself behind a curtain and spy upon the queen, for I'll no longer be your hare's foot.' I loathed him. I was a tool for advancement to him, nothing more. I was no more a person in his eyes than the shawl that he'd snatched off a hook and wound around my shoulders.

To my surprise, he smiled and rubbed his hands together.

'That's a very good notion, very good indeed. A capital notion, in fact.'

'What?'

He put a firm hand in the middle of my back and pushed me out into the corridor. 'I'll try the same thing with the queen that I did with you. Under some pretence or other, I'll entice Hamlet along to her chamber. I can hide me behind an arras and overhear their conversation. Ophelia, that's a good notion indeed.'

I was horrified that he'd taken my impulsive words as advice instead of censure. I started to tell him that there was no need to spy on the queen, that she'd certainly confess to Claudius all her private conversations with her son, but by this time other courtiers were jostling past us in the corridors, and I decided to save my protests until later.

As we neared the hall, my father hissed in my ear, 'Sit toward the back and do nothing to draw attention to yourself.'

'Father, my gown is torn, and—'

'A trifle, a trifle.' He gave an impatient cluck. 'Hide the tear under your shawl, and if anyone comments on your being bundled up in June, say you're cold. What people don't see, doesn't matter.'

All at once I had an idea. 'Father, let me creep up to the minstrel gallery. From there I can watch the play unseen—'

'Unseen even by the queen! This I cannot permit. I own I would that you were tidier, but in the eyes of her majesty, a tumbled daughter is better than no daughter at all.'

Outside the doors to the hall he stopped. 'Find you a place where you're unlikely to be noticed. I must go check that all is in readiness for the play to begin.'

He left me. All the supper tables had been removed from the hall. The chairs from the dais were clustered close to a space at the far end that I guessed would serve as the stage, and the rest of the hall was filled with benches. Already the rear of the room was crowded with servants, pressed so tightly together that I couldn't make out Piet.

The dais end of the hall had been rigged up with straw-coloured curtains. I looked around for a seat, but most of the benches for the courtiers were full, and no one scooted to the side to make room for me. I noticed that most folk wore their finest clothes, and I felt shabbier than ever. Part of me wanted to run back to the safety of my chamber, but another part of me very much wanted to stay and listen to the play. Even more than that, I wanted to stay and see Hamlet. Which Hamlet would I find – my brilliant, huge-hearted husband or the cruel, snake-tongued man of this morning?

A horn rang out, slapping me back to the present moment. I stepped to the side of the doorway so the royal party could pass in. Claudius looked particularly regal in a new satin doublet the colour of wine, and the queen wore a new gown of silver. Hamlet wasn't with them. As soon as she stepped over the threshold, the queen caught sight of me and held out her hand.

'Ophelia! Join us. This is your first play at court, and you must have a good seat.'

There was no way to refuse. I moved forward to join her party. Behind me I could hear people whispering. I knew they were tut-tutting over my slovenly appearance, but I just lifted my chin and pretended there was nothing amiss. I saw Osric's eyes widen at the sight of my wrinkled gown, and Elspeth stared at my untamed hair in frank disapproval. This steeled my resolve to brazen it out, so I lifted my chin and pulled the shawl tight around my shoulders.

Foppish Osric was next to me as we strolled to our seats. He lifted a finger and tapped it against my hair. 'A new fashion?' he mocked.

'My brother writes me that the fine French ladies often

wear their hair thus,' I shot back, even though in his letters
Laertes had said nothing of the kind.

Then Osric was gone from my mind for I caught sight of
Hamlet stepping out from behind the curtain and advancing
toward us, his arms outstretched like a host who welcomes
folk to his inn. He looked so beautiful that he took my breath
away. He still wore his customary black, but now he sported a
new suit, a watered-silk doublet in which sprinkled diamonds
glittered like stars against the night sky. I loved the way the
darkness set off his fair beauty. In his face there was no trace of
the enraged monster I'd seen that morning in the lobby. *Look
at me*, I willed him. *Look at me*. I was scared, but, more than
that, I wanted to see how he'd respond when he saw me.

As if on cue, his eyes drifted over to mine. For two
heartbeats we locked eyes, and then he smiled a welcome
with no trace of his previous rage.

My father bustled over.

'Lord Polonius,' Hamlet said, 'did I hear that you performed once in a play at the university?'

My father had once been an actor! I felt my heart warm
toward him. It was as if he kept his worst qualities on display
– his long-windedness, his obsequiousness, his bowing and
scraping to those in power – and he hid the things that were
most endearing: his struggles to raise himself up from poverty,
his acting in a play back when he was little more than a boy.

'That I did, my lord,' my father replied, 'and I was
accounted a good player.'

How odd! I'd never before suspected that it was from
my father that I'd inherited my own love of theatre and
play-acting. I'd never before thought there was anything
of my father in me, but in this, at least, I was his true
daughter.

'What did you enact?' Hamlet asked.

'Julius Caesar. I was killed in the Capitol. Brutus killed me.'

'It was a brute part of him to kill so capital a calf there.' Everyone laughed at Hamlet's pun. I felt a rush of affection toward both my father and Hamlet, grateful that my husband had made only a mild jest and refrained from making my father look the fool.

Rosencrantz appeared and informed us that the players were ready to begin. As we moved toward our places, the queen called out, 'Hamlet, sit by me.'

To my surprise, he moved toward me instead.

36

'No, Mother,' he sang out, ignoring the queen who patted the seat next to her. 'Here's metal more attractive.'

I flushed as I felt the eyes of the whole court turn to me. I saw my father lean over and whisper something to the king.

Hamlet took my hands. The candles in the hall were so numerous that I could see myself reflected in his eyes. He eased me into a seat next to the queen, winked and asked loudly, 'Lady, shall I lie in your lap?'

A gasp ran through the crowd near enough to hear his coarse words. His eyes were twinkling. I hadn't seen him in such a good humour since our wedding night. It was clear that he loved playing the double agent, treasuring his secret knowledge of our many nights together and walking on the razor's edge to see how far he could go in public without giving the game away. For all my love of play-acting on the stage, I was discovering in myself a dislike of playing parts in real life. I frowned a warning to him. 'No, my lord.'

His grin grew. He said in mock innocence, 'I meant my head upon your lap.'

At that moment I felt I could die of love for him. He was as beautiful as Lucifer, and he belonged to me. All in all, it would be no bad thing to let the court witness his fondness for me. I felt like I was starving and he was all the food in the world. 'Yes, my lord.'

His eyes twinkled brighter than the diamonds on his clothes. 'Did you think I meant crude matters?'

I twinkled back at him. 'I think nothing, my lord.'

He sank down on the floor in front of me, his back pressed against my legs. He'd cleaned himself up, bathed and washed his hair, and once again he smelled of oranges and cloves. It looked as if this morning's rage had perhaps burned out the last bits of his debilitating grief. He leaned his head back to rest on my knees. 'That's a fair thought, to lie between maids' legs.'

The devil! If he wasn't more circumspect, he'd betray our private relationship to the entire court. I tried to sound as repressive as possible. '*What* is a pleasant thought?'

He caught my warning and backed away from the subject. 'Nothing.'

In spite of myself, my hands began to stroke his hair. 'You are merry, my lord.'

'Who, I?'

In that moment, I felt I would indeed die from love. 'Yes, my lord.'

'Indeed, I am God's jester. Why not be merry? Look how merry my mother looks, and my father died just two hours ago.'

Something in me stiffened. I tried to reassure myself. *He is pretending to be mad. He hasn't really forgotten how long ago his father died. He is playing his game.* Still, I'd become skittish in the matter of his moods. Carefully I said, 'Your father has been dead four months.'

'That long? Then there's hope a great man's reputation might last as long as six months after his death!' I glanced over at Claudius to see how he took all this talk about his brother's death, but he sat impassively talking with my father, apparently paying Hamlet no mind.

Just then the oboes sounded. Most of the light about the hall was doused, and the play began. The first part was a dumb show. Actors dressed like a king and queen appeared, and they mimed great affection toward each other. Hamlet kept looking over at his uncle, but Claudius and my father continued to talk in low tones and showed no inclination to watch the performance.

Hamlet motioned me to lean down, and he whispered in my ear, 'This night will make or mar the fortunes of my father-ghost. Keep a close watch on Claudius, for I use this play as my final weapon. This next hour shall end it all. If, as the play unfolds, Claudius betrays himself, then I'll know my course. But if he fails to respond, then will I understand the ghost to be an evil spirit indeed come to tempt my very soul to perdition, and I'll give over this whole foul business and live the obedient nephew-son and play the loving husband to the most beauteous maid in Denmark. So fasten your eyes to Claudius's face to see if he betrays his guilt.'

Then he turned his head to study his uncle. All I could think was, *once this play is done, then Hamlet will give over his suspicions and we can settle into marriage and a regular life.* I didn't understand how this play was supposed to trigger a guilty reaction in Claudius, but I'd never seen a man with more self-control than the king, so I had no fear that Claudius would betray anything at all.

On the makeshift stage, the actor playing the queen left and the player king lay down upon a bed of flowers to sleep. Then a scurvy looking fellow crept in, and the audience booed and shouted out insults. He unstopped a vial and, to my horror, poured poison into the ear of the sleeping king. The crowd booed even louder. My eyes flew over to Claudius, but he was lost in his private conversation with my father. Hamlet sat upright, his eyes darting back and forth between Claudius and the performers. I could sense Hamlet's tension growing. I didn't know if Claudius was indeed paying the play no mind or if his conversation with my father was a pretence so he could ignore the play, but it was clear that he wasn't going to betray himself. *How had Hamlet found a play so close to the circumstances of his own father's death?* At least the play in front of us didn't feature a girl who handed the poison to the murderer.

On stage, the queen discovered the dead body and made a great show of wailing and weeping. Then the poisoner reappeared and wooed the queen. The crowd booed louder than ever. The players all bowed and exited. I was confused. Was the play over?

I could see Hamlet was plunged in despair that his uncle was taking no notice of the action. I whispered to my husband, 'What does all this mean, my lord?'

Hamlet answered me although he kept his eyes fixed on Claudius. 'Mischief. Dire mischief.'

Then a flourish was blown on a horn and an actor entered. I realized at once that the play wasn't over. 'Perhaps this first part did but serve as a prologue.'

Hamlet gave me a quizzical look, and I blushed at the knowledge that he'd understood all along that the dumb show wasn't the play entire. 'We'll find out from this actor. Players can't keep secrets. They tell you everything.'

'Will he tell us what that first part meant?'

'Yes, or he'll talk about anything you want to show him.' He began to slide my skirt up my leg in a teasing fashion, but I slapped his hand before he could expose all my nether parts to the court. 'Hush, my lord. I want to watch the play.'

The player's speech was only three lines long. After the actor had bowed and left, Hamlet announced loudly to the entire court, 'Was that the prologue or the inscription in a ring?'

A ripple of laughter ran through the crowd.

'It was brief,' I admitted.

'As woman's love.'

He stared pointedly at his mother as he said this. Above

his smile, his eyes were cold as flint. The court obediently laughed again, but I fancied there was some unease in their response. Much as I loved Hamlet, I did hate it that he said degrading things about women. At those times he sounded more like his father than himself.

As the body of the play proceeded, I began to hear lines that I suspected had been inserted by Hamlet himself. The actor playing the queen, for example, proclaimed that she'd be accursed in her second husband because the only people who took second husbands were women who killed their first. Even though Hamlet had ordered me to watch Claudius, I sneaked a glance at the queen to see how she took this, but her face was as smooth as a pond on a windless day. A few lines later, the player-queen argued that every time she kissed a second husband she'd kill her first again. Queen Gertrude still showed no reaction, although Hamlet gave a crow of laughter. Then the actor playing the king told his wife that if she married a second husband, she'd be killing him a second time. These lines were so blatant as to make me most uncomfortable, but the queen still gave no sign that she applied them to her circumstance. I looked at Claudius. He listened with the weary courtesy of one who doesn't much care for the theatre.

After a few minutes, Hamlet looked up at his mother, 'How do you like this play?'

On stage, the player-queen prayed that she'd be damned if she was widowed and then married again.

'I think the lady protests too much,' she said.

Claudius bent down to Hamlet. 'Have you heard the plot? Is there anything offensive in it?'

A nervous excitement rose in Hamlet like a tempest wind. He laughed, although Claudius had said nothing comical. 'It's all a jest. Anything poisonous is just a jest. There's no offence, not the least little bit.' He laughed again and began plucking at my skirt.

'What's the play called?' asked the king.

'The Murder of Gonzago.' Hamlet's speech was growing more and more rapid, and now I saw the faint sheen of sweat upon his brow. 'It's the true story of a murder done in Vienna. Gonzago was a duke; his wife's named Baptista.' He laughed again. 'It's a wicked piece of work, but what do we care about that? We're innocent, you and I. Let the guilty flinch, but you and I are untouched.'

He was talking too much. I saw the king look at him suspiciously.

'Here comes Lucianus,' Hamlet babbled on, seemingly unable to stop his words. 'The nephew to the king.'

In hopes of calming Hamlet down, I quickly said, 'You are a good chorus, my lord.' I gave him a little pinch.

He raised his voice. 'I could even interpret what goes on between you and your love if I could witness your private matters.'

Oh, Lord. He was going to give away the whole show, both the one acted out on stage and our private one as well. He was too excited. 'You are keen, my lord. You are keen,' I said, shooting him a warning look. *Calm down. Don't do anything you will regret.*

His hand slipped underneath my skirt. 'It would cost you a groaning to take off my edge.' He began to stroke my leg, his hand moving faster and faster.

'Still better, my lord, and worse.' I reached down and firmly pushed his hand away. I cut my eyes from side to side to remind him that we were in public and must not indulge in our private play here.

He showed no sign of understanding my gesture. 'So you women *mis-take* your husbands.'

I was terrified that his rising frenzy would prompt him to blurt out things that should be told gently. I was confident that we could win the favour of the king and queen for our marriage, but not if Hamlet shouted it out baldly in front of the entire court. I was even more afraid that Hamlet might, excited by the play, leap to his feet and accuse the king of murder right here in the Great Hall. There would be no backing down from such a charge, and if the king didn't have him executed on the strength of it, he'd at least have to lock Hamlet away. I tried to think of a way to bring Hamlet back to his senses, but just then the action of the play itself caught his notice.

On the stage, the villain, nephew to the duke, was showing off a vial of poison. The crowd erupted with hisses and shouted warnings. With a great flourish, he poured its contents into the duke's ear.

Hamlet sprang to his feet and began to shout. 'He's poisoning him in the garden for his estate. His name's Gonzago.' He darted to Claudius and grabbed hold of his doublet. 'It's a true story and written in very choice Italian. Watch and see how the murderer gets the love of Gonzago's wife!'

Then my life tumbled head over heels.

Claudius leaped to his feet and pushed Hamlet backwards. 'No!' I screamed, but there was so much noise in the hall that no one heard me. Now it was Claudius I wanted to stop. He had only to sit calmly through the play, betray no feeling, and Hamlet would have been convinced of his innocence.

Above the babbling of the court came the king's shouts for lights. Then he blundered out of the hall like a wounded bear. I looked back at Hamlet, and there was a look of unholy glee in his face. He was staring after the king avidly like an imprisoned lecher who has just seen his first maiden in twenty years.

My father seized my arm. I tried to hang back. I wanted to talk with Hamlet, but my father dragged me along with the crowd that pushed its way out of the hall. I felt sick with despair. So close. We'd been so close to shutting the door on this Pandora's box of troubles, and then Claudius

– of all folk – betrayed himself. What would happen now? Would Hamlet challenge Claudius to single armed combat? Claudius was at least twenty years older than Hamlet, but he'd been a soldier while Hamlet had never seen a day of combat. Such a challenge would bode no good for my husband. Would Hamlet now make his accusation public? What would happen then? Hamlet would have no hope of taking a king to court. More than that, with no hard proof to substantiate his accusation, Hamlet himself could be accused of treason and made outlaw in his own country. Or would Hamlet now gather an opposition army and lead them against Claudius's troops. Had I just witnessed the start of civil war?

Would my own part in this whole affair be revealed?

'Get you to our chambers,' my father commanded.

'Are you not coming?'

'I have business for the king. I'll be along shortly.'

I took a few stumbling steps toward our chambers when my father's voice stopped me.

'Ophelia! Tonight you behaved with sweetness and dignity in the face of Hamlet's lewd remarks. If it were actions and not birth that ennobled a person, then tonight you proved yourself the most royal of all of us. I was proud indeed to be your father.'

He looked small and stooped in the long corridor.

I hadn't expected such sensitivity from him and I was both surprised and touched. 'Thank you, Father.'

'Now get you to your chambers, for daughters, like jewels, can come to grief if they spend too much time out of their caskets.'

In truth I felt battered by the events of the day, and I was glad of a few moments to puzzle out my way. I crept back to my chambers and wrapped myself in a thick wool blanket, so even though it was a fair June night, I was shivery with

cold. But as soon as I'd curled up on my bed, I was hit with
a dreadful thought.

What if Claudius tries to kill Hamlet?

A familiar voice spoke from the shadows.

'Now the fox is truly among the hens!'

37

Yorick stepped forward to sit down beside me on the bed. Even in my flurry of concern for Hamlet, I was startled to see him take such a liberty. 'Young Hamlet has the entire castle in a flutter,' he said.

'Yorick, Hamlet has shown his hand to Claudius. I'm afraid that Claudius will now do away with his nephew to protect himself.'

'Not an unreasonable assumption.'

'Hamlet is not –' I fumbled for a word, '– worldly. He is brilliant in the world of ideas, but in the world of people, he's not as wise as most of his servants. He is no match for Claudius, especially now that Hamlet's presence means a danger to Claudius's state.'

'You wish to rescue Hamlet?'

'I want to preserve his life, and so I must be one step ahead of Claudius. I need to protect my husband. Help me. Tell me, if he tries to murder Hamlet, what means will he use?'

Yorick thought for a moment, and then he said, 'It seems to me that once a murderer has found a method that works, he'll employ that method again and again. Claudius used poison the first time . . .'

I shook my head. 'He doesn't have access to my store of poison.' I ran my fingers through my tangled hair. 'What else might he try?'

'The easiest thing will be to send one of his own guards or servants to kill young Hamlet.'

I considered this for a moment, but then rejected the thought. 'He is too wary, I suspect, to take some other man into his confidence. Even a servant.'

'Perhaps he will order the prince arrested and executed on the grounds that Hamlet's accusations show treason to the crown.'

'No. He loves the queen too well to place her in that coil.' I began jiggling my leg with impatience. I had to hurry. Hamlet was like a half-cocked pistol that could discharge itself at the slightest touch. Claudius was canny enough to know that if he wanted to ensure his safety, he needed to silence Hamlet immediately If I didn't move quickly, by morning Hamlet could be as dead as his father.

'What if Claudius—' began Yorick, but suddenly there was a rap on the door to the antechamber.

'Lady Ophelia!' called out a voice I recognized as that of Lord Rosencrantz.

I scooted out of bed and ran to the door. Rosencrantz stood in the hallway, breathing hard, his face drawn.

'What is it, my lord?'

Without waiting for invitation or permission, he brushed past me into the sitting room. 'Lady, have you no attendants or servants about?'

I shook my head. 'We summon those of the castle as we have need.'

He bit his lip and glanced at the door. 'Perhaps I should fetch a lady to attend you.'

Something was wrong. 'Lord Hamlet?' I cried out.

He jerked. 'Let me find a woman—'

'No. Give me your tidings at once. Do not delay.'

He looked at me gravely. 'The news I have is very bad, lady. My heart misgives me to—'

'Quickly let me have it!' I closed my hands around the back of a chair for support, and I caught my breath.

'It's the worst—'

'Hamlet!' I cried out again, and tightened my fingers until the wood pressed painfully against them. I'd been too late. Claudius had moved more swiftly than—

'Worse than that.'

This caught me up short. Out of the corner of my eye, I saw Yorick hovering in the doorway to my room, but I forced my attention back to Rosencrantz. 'My lord, I don't understand.'

He began to rub his hands against each other as if he was washing them with air. 'Lady, it's your father.'

I felt a flush of relief. Hamlet still lived. I didn't know what foolish business my father had been involved with, but if Hamlet was safe—

'Lady, your father is dead.'

I looked at him blankly. The words rang hollow coin against my ear, not carrying the gold of sense. 'No,' I said calmly. He was mistaken. 'I left my father not half an hour ago. He is well.'

More than well, for he'd praised me for the first time since I'd come back in his life.

'He is dead, Ophelia. Stabbed to death.'

This was ridiculous. My father wasn't the sort of person to be caught up in a brawl. 'You are mistaken,' I said gently, a little amused that Rosencrantz had obviously fallen the victim of some hoax.

'I wish I were mistaken, lady, but there's no doubt to the matter. The queen herself was witness to the deed.'

'But who would stab my father?'

Rosencrantz hesitated.

'Tell me,' I insisted.

'It was Hamlet,' he said finally.

'No.' This made less sense than all the rest. The country indeed had run mad. 'Why would Lord Hamlet stab my father?'

I'd killed his father, and now he'd killed mine. Did this show that he knew about my part in his father's death? Was this his revenge?

Rosencrantz said, 'Your father called out for help to protect the queen—'

'Protect the queen from whom?'

'From her son.'

'What nonsense is this? Hamlet loves his mother. He wouldn't harm her.'

'Polonius thought that Hamlet was about to murder the queen, so he cried out for help in her defence.'

'You lie!'

His face whitened. 'I heard the story from the queen herself.'

'It cannot be true.'

His hands tightened into fists, not as if he wished to hit me but as if it was hard to drag the words from his mouth. 'After Hamlet's outburst upset the play, the queen commanded Hamlet to speak with her privately in her bedchamber. Your father was hidden behind a tapestry to overhear their conversation—'

Suddenly my knees gave way, and it was only my hold on the back of the chair that kept me from tumbling to the ground. Virgin of virgins, my father had taken my flippant words to heart and acted on them. Because I'd put a silly notion into his mind, he was now dead. Foolish, foolish old man.

'According to the queen, Hamlet heard a noise and ran his sword through the hanging before looking to see who was there. At first he thought he'd killed the king.'

My poor, poor father. He'd lived for the king and now he'd died for him as well. A comic figure in his life, condemned to a farcical death. Worse than that, there would be no one to truly mourn for him. I myself hadn't loved him, but he had died unshriven, so the least I could do now was say a prayer over the remains. 'Will you take me to my father's body?'

To my surprise, Rosencrantz didn't answer at once. I was confused. Mine was a simple request. 'Tell me,' I said. 'I must go to him and offer up a prayer.'

'There's a problem, Lady Ophelia.'

'I'll not faint at the sight of my father's mangled corpse,' I assured him.

'It's only that . . . well . . . we cannot find the body.'

It took a few seconds for the meaning of his words to sink into my brain. 'Cannot find the body?' I echoed. 'A body cannot evaporate into thin air.'

'No. That much is true. It's only that . . . Lady Ophelia, Hamlet has hidden the body.'

'Hidden the body? Does he hope to hide the murder? But you said the queen was witness—'

Rosencrantz sighed. 'We don't know *why* he's hidden the body, but he dragged it out of the queen's chamber and up and down stairs, and in and out of rooms until no one knows where he's put it, and Hamlet will not say—'

This was one matter I could set to rights. I took off running.

I would find Lord Hamlet.

ACT FOUR

More Murders

38

I found my husband up on the ramparts. There was a thick fog, blank as a winding sheet, and he was capering about wildly, laughing and dancing and singing bits of song. The damp had plastered his hair to his face, and his face was flushed a deep red. Like some demented troll in one of the old tales, he warbled:

> *Clever Hamlet; clever me!*
> *Solve the riddle, neat as can be.*
> *Kill a king and wed my mother—*
> *Caught you out, my father's brother!*

There was no sign of my father's body.

'My lord,' I called out. 'Lord Hamlet!'

He sprang to me and caught up both my hands in his, kissing them passionately.

'Oh, Ophelia, my love, my life, my dove, my wife – we've triumphed more greatly than ever we dreamed.'

'Hamlet, where is my father?'

He giggled. 'At supper, my love. Polonius was ever the good trencherman, especially at someone else's board.'

Keep calm. 'My lord, supper has been finished these many hours past.'

'Not for your father.'

He bounded over to the section of the wall from which his brother leaped to his death. He jumped onto it, windmilling his arms frantically at first to keep his balance, shouting out to the sea, 'Oh, ho, brother of mine, magnificent Holger! Golden son, apple of my father's eye – where is your glory now? It is I, Hamlet, lowly second son, the send-him-off-quick son, the mad son, the bad son, who has solved the riddle and avenged our father's murder. Where were you, superior brother, when it was I who carried out my father's wishes and you lay like a slug-abed in a snug grave?'

'My husband,' I said urgently, 'my father is not at supper.'

Hamlet giggled again and turned carefully to face me. A couple of times his foot slipped against the wet stone and he had to lurch about to keep from falling in a twin path to his brother's fate. 'At this supper, Ophelia, your father is not eating, but eaten! Polonius, who ever licked the feet of kings, now is himself being gummed by worms!' He broke into song:

> *Know that I am chief of Danes*
> *And Hamlet Hamlet's son is my name!*

It wasn't the cold damp of the night that made me shiver. It was clear that Hamlet was now dwelling far from his wits, exiled from his right mind. Moments of understanding don't arrive gradually like a plodding traveller come from a great distance. They come instead with breath-stopping rapidity, as if the world has suddenly been ripped apart like a worn sheet flung over the truth to disguise it. I'd been so sure that I was the right one and all the folk in the castle were wrong, that Hamlet hadn't been subject to these manic fits of unreason but only misunderstood. All at once I understood that I'd indeed been wrong. So many people had warned me that Hamlet wasn't the master of his wits, but I'd ignored them, and now it had cost my father's life.

'Bring me to my father,' I said.

His face blinked into surprise. 'What's that?'

'Bring me—'

He motioned me to be quiet. 'No,' he said. 'I don't intend to harm her. It was only that old fool got in my way.'

I whirled around and cast my eyes all over the battlements, but there was no one else there, not watchmen or even ghosts. 'Hamlet,' I fought to keep my tone level, 'to whom do you speak?'

'Do you not see him?' I glanced around but the place was still as bare of company. It was clear he wasn't speaking to me. 'Look!' he shrieked, waving his arms so violently that he wobbled and might have fallen to his death below had I not grabbed hold of his shirt. He closed cold, trembling fingers over mine. 'Tell me that you see him.'

I looked for a third time. Now I made out Yorick standing at the top of the stairs. Doubtless he'd followed me up here, but there was no one else in sight. To calm Hamlet down, I said, 'I cannot quite make out who it is that talks to you.'

'It's the king!'

'Claudius?'

'No, the real king, the true king, the king my father. Do not pretend that you cannot hear him and see him as clear as can be.'

There was no one at all there, not even the shadow of a ghost. I played for time. 'What does he tell you, my lord? The wind is in my ears and I cannot quite make out his words.'

'He says I've buried myself too long in the world of women, but I must now be about my father's business. He says that I must kill Claudius and take my rightful place as king of the Danes.'

My immediate task was to get him down off the wall and to safety. 'My husband,' I said, making my voice as gentle as I could, 'please bring me to my father.'

'Not I!' he crowed. 'When a woman marries she must leave her father and cleave to her husband. So, Hamlet, put from you all thoughts of that rash fool, Polonius.'

'Fool though he was, he was my father, my lord.'

'Nay, Hamlet. Your father was the dead king.'

'You are Hamlet, my lord, and I'm Ophelia, your wife.'

He gave a hoot of laughter. 'Nay, you are Hamlet, for husband and wife are one flesh, so you are Hamlet as well as I.'

Nettled, I snapped, 'Then you are Ophelia as well as I, and you've killed your father Polonius!'

At that he leaped from his perch and ran across the roof, giving a full-throated battle cry. As he clattered down the steps, I heard him shouting, 'Come Trey, come Stony, come little Dobbin, for we must ourselves outrun the hounds of heaven!'

My heart full to the breaking point, I leaned against a cold stone pillar to catch my breath. All was a dark muddle with no firm hope of dawn. What was to be done?

'Are you all right, Ophelia?' Yorick called out.

'I didn't see his father's ghost here, Yorick. I thought I could see every ghost in the castle.'

'You can.'

'I cannot!' I snapped. 'His father's ghost was invisible to me.'

Yorick moved closer. 'That's because his father's ghost wasn't here with us.'

'But Hamlet saw it.'

'Yes,' he said in a voice as thin as the wind. 'Old King Hamlet no longer haunts the castle. Now the only place he walks is in the corridors of Hamlet's mind. Hamlet believes that he sees a ghost who has long since faded from the castle. People, as well as castles, can be haunted, you know.'

'Is it a real ghost, the ghost in his mind?'

'Are any ghosts real?'

I was sick of these riddles, sick of this castle with its secrets and its hundreds of halls that snaked about like a labyrinth. I wanted to get back to a place like the sea that was flat and open and clean. If I could get my husband away from this troubled castle, then he'd surely return to himself again.

First, though, I needed to make sure he was safe from an attack from Claudius.

Now I had what seemed to be a foolproof plan to do just that. I'd go to Claudius and beg his aid. He was in my debt, for, after all, I'd furnished him with the very poison he'd used to gain the throne. More than that, I'd kept my silence. Claudius owed me a favour, and now it was time for him to grant it.

Claudius was the answer.

39

I found Claudius closeted with the queen.

'Oh, Ophelia!' the queen moaned as soon as she saw me. She enfolded me in her arms and pressed me close to her. I hadn't noticed how thin she'd become. Now her body felt like that of a brittle old lady. 'My poor child. My poor fatherless child.'

'It's our fault,' the king said, the anger in his voice as jagged as the teeth of a saw. 'We knew Hamlet's affliction. We should have kept him on a short leash as did our brother. We have known since his childhood that he's most unfit for the large world, but my pity for his loss of both a brother and father in the space of a few months led me unwisely to grant him too vast a scope.'

The queen's arms tightened around me. 'He is mad as a tempest,' she sobbed. 'I've lost one son to death, and now I've lost another to the dark places of his own mind, and neither shall return to me in this world.'

I eased myself out of the queen's embrace. 'What's to be done?'

Claudius said quietly, 'We've sent Guildenstern and Rosencrantz to find the prince and persuade him to deliver up your father's body.' The queen gave a moan. Claudius continued, 'You have heard about that sad game that he plays?'

I nodded.

'Then,' Claudius said, 'we shall ship him away to England

at first light, for this will keep him from the anger of the populace and the demands of justice.'

'He is a prince,' I said. 'What justice dares touch him?'

'A king might carry off such an accusation as the one he makes about his father's death,' Claudius said, 'but a prince is not so fortified against censure.' His face softened as he looked at his wife. 'Go, Gertrude. You are pulled to splinters over this business. Seek you out some rest tonight for you've been much troubled.'

The queen laid her soft hand on my arm. 'Come with me, Ophelia, and we can comfort each other in this time of sorrow.'

'I thank you, Madam, but I must first speak some private business with the king.'

The queen looked uncertain, but Claudius lifted her hand from mine and kissed her fingertips. 'Go, love, and Ophelia will join you as soon as she's able.'

The queen gave him a faint, shy smile and slipped from the room. As soon as she'd departed, Claudius stiffened and said in a hard voice, 'What would you have from us, Ophelia?'

I felt through my words as carefully as a blindfolded prisoner might feel his way through a forest. 'My gracious lord, I'd know your complete plan for taking care of young Hamlet.'

A faint smile played around his lips. 'Do you seek revenge, girl, for your father?'

'No, my lord. I have a fondness for Hamlet—'

'Even though he killed your father as one might kill a mouse?'

Forgive me, Father. 'Even so, my lord.'

'Then you're not a very dutiful daughter.'

But I'm a dutiful wife, I wanted to shout. 'I would know everything you've planned for Lord Hamlet,' I repeated.

'We told you our plan. We're sending him off to England with his school friends.'

'And how will that help him?'

'It will get him away from the law,' he said. 'God knows it will take all our skill and presence to face down this deed. We don't yet know how best to paper over it.'

'My lord,' I pressed on, 'I don't understand why you send him to England and not back to school in Wittenberg.'

Claudius turned his head to the right and left, making certain that we were alone. Then he said, 'The king of England owes us a favour in return for a kindness we once did for him. We send Rosencrantz and Guildenstern with a sealed letter to the king. In that letter we ask the king to kill Lord Hamlet.'

My stomach clutched like a fist.

He continued, 'Now shall we both be profited. You will be avenged for your father's death, and your king will be safe from his murderous nephew.'

No, no, no! I stammered, 'His friends would never carry such an order.'

Claudius smiled smoothly. 'They don't know what the letter contains. They assume it is a formality, one king saluting another. That's why they're so good for our purpose, why Hamlet will suspect nothing. He will go with them as meek as an Easter lamb to the butcher's knife.'

I felt dizzy. Life was careering out of control like a runaway wagon over a cliff to the sea. My immediate task was to prevent Hamlet's execution.

'You cannot have him slaughtered like that,' I protested.

'He killed your father in cold blood. Had you been there . . . or our own self . . . and we could have just as easily been the dead one. You heard, did you not, that he stabbed your father through the curtain, not knowing or caring who he killed. He is a danger to all around him.'

'But he's well loved of the people of Denmark. They adore their golden-haired prince. His death—'

'Why else do you think I send him to England? Should he die there, the people might be sad for a few days, but people are fickle, Ophelia. Once he's safely gone away, they'll start to forget him.' He stepped closer and lowered his voice. 'He is a danger to us both, Ophelia. He has tumbled to knowledge that we were the one who poured the fatal draught into his father's ear, but do you think *you* will escape the edge of his knife once he learns that you supplied the poison?'

My stomach lurched, but I held fast to my course. 'We've had too many deaths here at Elsinore, Majesty. I cannot permit you to add Hamlet to the roll of the dead.'

Claudius frowned. 'Do you not hear us aright, girl? As long as he lives, Hamlet is a danger to us both. What we do is the salvation of Denmark, preserving her from a nasty civil war between the lawful king and our hasty nephew. It's the preservation of *your* life as well. Don't play the idiot with me, Ophelia. Should our nephew learn you supplied the poison to slaughter his father, then he would kill you as surely as we stand here.'

'You must not do this.'

As if my remark had snapped his patience, he shouted, 'Then, tell me, what should we do, Ophelia? Wait tamely until he murders us? The death of his father wasn't a step we undertook lightly. It haunts us, Ophelia, it haunts us. We cannot sleep, we cannot pray. If we could, we'd go to the priest, confess our crime, accept our penance, even if it meant we had to give up the woman we've loved for so many years. But we cannot do that, Ophelia. We cannot leave Denmark with no one to steer her course.'

'Hamlet,' I said. 'It's his right.'

'Our nephew is mad. History itself is a cautionary tale of the havoc that comes to a country with a mad ruler at its helm.'

'His madness—'

'His madness comes in fits and starts, true enough, but

when it seizes him, there's no telling what violence he might wreak.'

'The death of my father – it was an accident. An impulse. Hamlet will not repeat that offence. His life as king will not be filled with folk skulking behind curtains.'

He thundered back, 'This wasn't his first murder, girl.'

How dare he bring up Holger's death. 'You cannot lay the death of his brother at his door. That was Holger's arrogance and foolishness, not Hamlet's fault.'

His face changed as if a shutter had been pulled across a casement. 'Tell me in plain words, Ophelia, how stand things between you and our nephew?'

Caution urged me to equivocate. 'What means your majesty?'

'When you offered us the poison for his father, was it indeed out of concern for the life of the queen? Or have you and Hamlet conspired in some plot too deep for us to see until now? Did you manipulate us into murdering his father on *Hamlet's* behest so that he advance one step closer to the throne?'

His words stunned me, but I saw him growing calmer and more expansive as this false understanding spread through his brain.

'No,' I said urgently. 'Hamlet was no part of it.'

'And if he'd indeed charmed you into tricking me to kill his father, would you answer any different?'

What he imagined was outrageous! 'Hamlet played no part in the murder of his father.'

His eyes narrowed, and he smiled. 'How blind we've been. All this time we've thought Hamlet a fool, but he's played us like a mouth organ. We've been his puppet. You have, too. Ophelia and Claudius have twitched and jigged while he pulled our strings. Clever boy! He knew that if he confronted his father direct, he'd lose, so he charmed *you* into seducing *us* into murder. Can you not see the truth? This madness is a ruse to let him now remove his uncle so he himself can inch his backside onto our throne.'

'It wasn't that way at all,' I said desperately, but Claudius paid me no heed.

'So now he tricks us into betraying ourself in front of our entire court. Very clever indeed.'

'You said he was mad and out of all self-control. How then can he be this cool and careful usurper you describe?'

'We said he has fits of madness. And never did we deny that he has the best brain in all Denmark. A prince who is mad and stupid would present little problem to a country, for wise counsellors could always manipulate him, but one who is brilliant and mad is more dangerous than Satan himself.'

'He played no part in his father's death.' Claudius flung up an impatient hand, clearly not believing me. I drew myself up tall and said, in my most queenly voice, 'I'll not permit you to kill him, even if I have to tell both him and the queen of your violent plan.'

His hand shot out and grabbed my arm. 'You cannot stop us.'

'I can warn Hamlet. I can tell Lords Guildenstern and Rosencrantz what their sealed envelope contains.'

'You are a silly, ignorant girl who is dabbling in matters far beyond her understanding,' Claudius said coldly. 'This cannon has been fired, and now we must wait for the ball to fall to earth. He called out, 'Guards!'

Five or six of his Swiss guards pushed into the room.

'The lady Ophelia is overcome with grief about her father's death. Her sorrow pushes her to the very edge of reason, so much so that we fear for her safety. Escort her back to her chambers, and let a guard be set to keep her within. Keep from her all means of self-harm, and don't let anyone come to her until she's released. More than that, don't give an ear to her mad ravings, for it's fantastical speculations that fall from her lips tonight rather than the truth.'

'No!' I couldn't let him lock me away. I needed to warn Hamlet about the sealed note that contained the orders for his death. 'I'm not mad and pose no danger to myself.' Nevertheless, two of the Swiss guards took me into their grip. 'Let me go!' I twisted about in an effort to free myself. 'I don't need to be guarded. I don't need to be taken to my room. Let me go.'

'Stay with her until further instruction,' the king said in silky tones. 'Let us keep her safe through this sad night.' He looked pointedly at me. 'Perhaps in a few days she'll be restored to the clear-thinking girl I believe her to be.'

As they dragged me, screaming and kicking, from the room, Claudius called out, 'I pray God you will soon be restored to your right mind. But know this, Ophelia. We will not leave you to be tortured by your wild, mad fantasies. If you're not soon restored, we have a medicine that will give you peaceful rest.'

40

How stupid I'd been to show my hand to Claudius. Since I couldn't now pour the milk back into the cow, I turned my energies to finding a way to elude the guards and warn my husband about Claudius's secret orders to the king of England. Failing that, I needed to contact Rosencrantz. He was devoted to Hamlet and would never willingly escort him to his execution. Try as I might, though, I couldn't escape from my chambers. Each time I tried to sneak out, one of the guards stopped me and firmly shoved me back within again.

I begged them to take a note to Hamlet for me if they wouldn't let me go to him, but they were the king's men, and nothing could budge them. For a few moments I thought about telling them all, telling them about the fatal sealed orders, but common sense pointed out that they wouldn't believe me, and that they might even carry that story direct to the king. That was another danger. Claudius now distrusted me, and, as his final words made clear, he wouldn't hesitate to kill me if he thought me a real danger.

I screamed with frustration and banged my fists against the doors until my skin was red and sore.

Then I flopped down on my bed to think.

Two unpalatable truths confronted me. First, unless I was a bird, once Hamlet's ship had sailed I had no way to communicate a warning to him. Second, it would be to Claudius's advantage to have me dead. I was the only person with knowledge of his role in his brother's murder.

Until tonight he'd trusted me to keep my silence, but now that he thought I was a confederate of Hamlet, he trusted me no longer. I had to provide him with a reason to keep me alive.

In June, it's dark for only a few hours. Dawn comes early. Just before daybreak, Yorick appeared in my room.

'Oh, Yorick,' I said, 'we're in the awfullest mess.' I told him what had happened with the king. 'My only hope lies in you. You must go to Hamlet and warn him.'

I hadn't lighted any candles, and in the darkness I couldn't read the expression on Yorick's face. 'This is something I cannot do.' There was a looseness in his voice, almost as if he were drunk but trying not to show it, but I didn't see how ghosts could become drunk.

'You must attempt it,' I said, 'or the prince that we both love will be dead shortly after he steps onto English soil.'

'I cannot talk to him. I can talk only with you.'

'Try,' I begged. 'Go to him and try to speak. At least you can try.'

He shook his head, the silhouetted points of his cap bobbing.

'At least go to him.' Surely, once he saw Hamlet, he'd be overcome with pity and find something to do to preserve his life.

'Ghosts cannot cross water, Ophelia. We are all held prisoners here by the moat that surrounds the castle.'

I buried my face in my hands. 'Oh, Yorick, what am I to do?'

He vouchsafed no answer, and when I looked up, he'd vanished.

As dawn filled the window, I grew more frantic. I tried screaming, shrieking, thrashing about the floor while squealing and moaning. When at last two of the guards came into the room, I threw myself to my knees in front of them and begged while tears coursed down my cheeks. I shouted at them that

Prince Hamlet's life depended on my reaching him before his ship sailed. To each of these entreaties, they turned a deaf ear and a blind eye. I was so frantic I made myself sick, puking my stomach out into my chamber pot.

Nothing moved the guards.

A little after midday, they brought me a plate of food, but I lay on my bed and turned my face to the wall and refused to touch it. By now, Hamlet had sailed.

Late in the afternoon, Claudius appeared. He motioned the guards away, and he stepped into my closet. His nose wrinkled at the smell of the stale vomit in my chamber pot, and he frowned at my dishevelled appearance.

'You look like a mad thing indeed, Ophelia. But calm yourself and lay salve over your distempered conscious. Hamlet has sailed these eight hours since on a wool merchant's ship. There's nothing you can do now to stop our plan, so wash your face and change into these fresh black garments sent to you by the queen for we've found your father's body and all is prepared for his burial on the morrow.'

Even though he was king, I refused to stand up. It was as if despair had turned my bones to sawdust. Hamlet was gone.

'Dress yourself and come to the queen,' he said coldly. He started to leave, but then he wheeled back. 'Ophelia, there was nothing else to be done. We'll weep for him most sincerely, especially for the tragedy of his madness. We know well it wasn't a portion he chose for himself, but madness in great ones cannot be allowed to flourish unchecked. We've sacrificed one life to save the many that would certainly die should he rule Denmark.' I turned my face to the wall, but the words went on. 'It's much the same choice you made when you gave me the poison to use on his father.'

I lay rigid, saying nothing. I refused to let him know that his words struck home. After a moment of staring at me, he strode out of the room.

I levered myself up to sit on the edge of the bed, the black gown from the queen clutched in my fingers. Tears ran down my cheeks and splashed onto the dark silk cloth. I wept for Hamlet, for my father, for myself, for all who are made the pawns of life. I wept for all those deaths in the past – Yorick, the little dog Blanche, my mother. When I was emptied of weeping, I tried to calculate how long it would take Hamlet's ship to reach England. Wool ships were large vessels that had no need of great speed. Depending on winds, Hamlet had at most a handful of days remaining upon the earth.

All I wanted to do was lie in my bed and cry, but my weary brain pointed out it would do me no good to stay locked and guarded in my chambers. I made myself get up and take out pen and paper. I composed a note to the king.

> *My Grief over my Father's Untimely Death did turn my Wits for a spell, but now I am come Home to myself. I much Repent me of anything Foolish I said in my Madness of Grief, and I Humbly ask Your Highness to Forgive me for I am your Most Loyal Subject.*

I signed my name and tapped on the door. When a guard cautiously opened it a crack, I asked him to deliver this note to the king.

After a long while, I went back to the door to see if the king had sent any answer.

The doors were unlocked, and the guards were gone. I was again free.

What should I do? Go to the Herbwife for a potion and kill Claudius? That at least might satisfy my deep-rooted anger and appease my husband's ghost.

No. I'd forgotten. I'd be deprived of even his ghost since the spirits couldn't travel across water. If my husband walked after death, he'd walk in a far-off land. It was true, something in me would be eased if I killed Claudius . . . but what then?

Such an act would leave Denmark without a king, deal the queen another blow – the death of the last of her family. What woman could survive such tragedy? I might just as well push her off the parapets myself. In addition, as much as I hated it, part of me understood that like a snarling dog who saw no way out but attack, Claudius himself had been backed into a corner. Hamlet had shown Claudius that he was being hunted for the murder of the king. What other action could Claudius have taken to ward off Hamlet's attack? Confess all? Yes, and thereby expose me as his fellow conspirator. I'd be justly tried and executed for my part in the old king's death. Then too, why was I demanding that Claudius behave according to higher standards than my own. After all, I wasn't leaping to confess to my misdeed, so how could I fault Claudius for not doing what I myself refused to do?

He could have shut Hamlet away in a place where he could do no harm. But Claudius would answer that by saying exiles can escape, and that was true as well. Besides, what good did it do me to puzzle out what other ways Claudius had to respond to his nephew's attack when all the while his nephew was sailing slowly on his way to death.

Then, all at once, I saw how Hamlet's death could be prevented.

41

The fog was as thick as uncarded fleece. As I pushed my way through it, I thought of the tales of some of the old folk in the village. The Christian fathers taught us that hell was a place of unquenchable fire, but the old folk talked of the underworld realms of Hel, the old goddess, and her caverns of ice through which lost souls could wander alone for all eternity, where there was neither day nor night nor time nor companionship. The sailors had told tales, too, of ships lost on cold Northern seas, becalmed and shrouded in fog without any way to take bearings, drifting too long and too far ever to return home again even after the fog lifted. Some folk whispered that a few of these ships discovered, once the fog had lifted, that they'd crossed over to a new world or came to rest against the shores of undiscovered lands. No one could ever prove those tales true or not although I preferred to picture the sailors exploring an uncharted island rather than lying cold and still on a cold, wet deck. As I struggled through the clinging fog, I felt as if I were clawing my way into an unknown land. Just before I reached my village, the fog began to break up, great clots of mist drifting off like the sodden souls of the damned slowly moving up from the surface of the earth.

I burst into the Herbwife's hut. I must have looked quite a sight. My clothes were themselves sodden from the fog, muddied and torn. My hair bushed around my head, as tangled as a thicket. The Herbwife had gone to bed, but she sat up alarmed.

'Who is it?' she cried out.

'Ophelia.'

'Who?'

'Myg's girl.'

'Child,' she said, rising up from the bed, 'whatever be the—'

'Ragnor,' I gasped out. 'I must see Ragnor.'

Do not let him be adrift on the sea, waiting for this weather to lift. Lord in Heaven, I'll ask nothing else of you if you just made sure that he read the weather beforehand and moored his ship securely to wait out the fog.

'Dear one,' she said, 'you look as if the hounds of hell have chased you all the way here. Come sit you by the fire while I brew a warm posset—'

'I must see Ragnor now!'

Her brows drew together in worry, but she said only, 'He is down tending his ship.'

Without a word, I fled out of her cottage and down to Ragnor's ship. He'd built a small driftwood fire on the white sand next to it. By its light, through the fog-dappled air, I made out Ragnor, tying some bundles onto the deck.

'Ragnor!' I called out as I ran. 'Ragnor!'

He straightened up immediately and moved toward me, catching my arms before I stepped onto the deck. 'Cat, what is the matter?'

He felt wondrously solid, the first safe thing I'd touched in days. 'Oh, Ragnor, all is at sixes and sevens up in the castle, and I need your help to set it to rights.'

I felt him stiffen. 'It's not my duty to set castle folk aright.'

'My husband's life hangs in the balance.'

'Husband!' He let go of me and took a step backwards as if I'd suddenly burst into flame. 'What mean you by husband, Cat?'

I hadn't meant to blurt it out that way, but there was no way to take back the words. I lifted my chin and said, 'I'm married to Prince Hamlet, Ragnor.'

He stood perfectly still, but I saw something flicker in his eye. For a moment he said nothing, but I could hear the heavy rasp of both our breathing. Then he said, 'I don't reckon that to be the way of it, Cat, for even here in the village we'd have heard such great news.'

'Ragnor—'

He held his hand up to silence me. 'More'n that, with his father so freshly dead and all, I don't reckon that even the royal folk would have ushered in two hasty marriages, both the queen's and yours.'

'I've married him in secret, Ragnor. Not even the queen knows about it.'

'And your father gave nod to this havey-cavey affair? Pull my tail, Cat, for believing such tiddle-tidings.'

'My father does not – *did not* – know of it.' He shook back his thick dark curls in clear disbelief. 'Our marriage was secret even from him.'

He made a sound of disgust. 'I'd thought you slap up to the mark, Cat. Back here in the village, you were ever the knowing one, tumbling to the truth faster than all the rest of us combined. I cannot fathom how you'd fall for such an alepot scheme. Married in secret indeed. What priest braved the anger of the king to perform the rite? You tell me that.'

I could feel my cheeks redden. 'There was no priest, Ragnor.' He gave a disbelieving laugh, and I added defiantly, 'Hamlet explained that it's enough for a man and a woman to make their vows directly to God.'

'And you fell for that fol-de-rol? Cat, Cat, when did you lock your mind into hiding? Or has it been turned into porridge in your stay up in the castle?'

'It's not like that, Ragnor.'

'No? Since the beginning of time, I reckon, noble folk have been giving peasant maids a slip on the shoulder. Even you've heard tell of great lords who pretend to wed a lass and then turn her out when they tire of her.'

'It's not that way!' In my anger, my voice began to slide back to the accents of the village. 'Lord Hamlet married me in honourable fashion. He even brought in Horatio and Marcellus to bear witness.'

Ragnor laughed again. 'Aye. His cronies. Fine witnesses they be! And when Lord Hamlet says that he never took you to wife, they'll swear that all this is a mad tale from a love-besotten peasant girl. What they'll end up witnessing is you being thrown right out of the castle.'

'I'm not a peasant girl! I'm now a fine lady—'

'And that's the greatest loss of all!' Ragnor turned away from me and bent to tighten a rope.

I clutched his arm desperately. 'Ragnor, I didn't come to you for a sermon. I came to you for help.'

'You're the wife of a prince now, Cat. Let him help you. He is much more powerful than a sailor lad.'

He pulled away, but I lunged forward and seized hold of his coat with such force that my wedding necklet swung out from its hiding place beneath my shift. He grabbed it, and his eyes were so dark and wild that for a moment I feared he was going to strangle me with it, but he just held it on his palm and asked in a tight voice, 'Do these trinkets mean so much to you that you're willing to barter yourself away for a handful of glittery stones? Do you now understand, Cat, that you yourself are a jewel of more value than any of these trifles?'

I yanked the necklet out of his hand and stuffed it back inside my shift. 'Damn you, Ragnor! Leave off this nonsense and listen to me!'

He jerked away as if my hand had burned him.

I wouldn't be stopped by his churlishness. 'King Claudius

has sent Hamlet off to England with an order that he be put to death. He is being transported by a wool trader.' I stopped, considering how to proceed.

After several moments, Ragnor said, 'I don't understand why you rushed down to tell me this, Cat.'

It was as if his words pulled away the boards of a dam. My own words tumbled out. 'Oh, Ragnor. I need you to pursue him, to rescue the prince. Your ship is built for speed. Can not you and your brothers do this one great deed? You can outsail the wool ship. Reach it before it reaches England. Rescue the prince. You will be the hero of Denmark.'

'And the enemy of King Claudius.'

'Dress as pirates, and the king will never know who attacked his boat. Think of this – when he's at last king, Hamlet will owe you much.' I laid my hand on his arm. 'Please, Ragnor. Please. You are the one hope left for Lord Hamlet.'

A bitter smile played about the corners of his mouth. 'Do you know what you ask, Cat?'

'I ask you to save an innocent man's life.'

'And, in return, you put me and my brothers under a sentence of death. Even should we succeed, Cat, piracy is punishable by death. You would brand us all pirates—'

'I don't ask you to kill anyone. Just stop the ship, board her, rescue Lord Hamlet, and then be off. It's not piracy, Ragnor. It's Christian charity.'

'Under the law, it's piracy indeed.'

'Then disguise your faces. Paint your ship a different colour once you've returned. Cling hard to the knowledge that you've saved a life and earned the undying gratitude of your next king. Can you even imagine the riches Hamlet will shower upon you once he takes the throne?'

'You forget that I and my brothers worked with Hamlet, losing a week's business to build that damned funeral ship that he so easily destroyed. He is fickle, Cat, with a mind as changeable as a leaf in a stream.' He shook his head. 'This is a May-mad scheme, Cat. You would do better to go to your father. He knows his way around court and noble folk. Ask him for advice.'

There was no way I could tell him that Hamlet had killed my father. Instead I said, 'There's no time, Ragnor! Did I not tell you that even as we speak, Hamlet is sailing his way to death in England. I *know* you, Ragnor. I know you for a decent man and one who loves a challenge. You and your brothers are the only men in Denmark who can save this doomed prince. Please, Ragnor. Please.'

He stared at me for a long time before saying, 'I'm sorry, Cat, but I don't have such a high regard for Lord Hamlet that I'd risk my life and that of my brothers—'

'Then do it for me, Ragnor.' He started to pull his arm away so I tightened my grip. 'We were ever good friends, Ragnor. You and Piet were the best friends I ever had. I love you well, Ragnor, and I think I don't flatter myself in believing that you love me well in return. Please, Ragnor.'

He turned his head away as if I'd struck him. Then he turned back to me, lifted my hand to his lips, and kissed my fingers. 'I loved the girl you were, Cat. I don't know if I love the woman you've become.'

His words sucked the air right out of me. How could he say such a thing? I'd worked so hard to fashion and shape and squeeze myself into a fine woman, doing all in my power to kill that unruly, harum-scarum girl. How could he prefer that shaggy beast to this fine lady? But this wasn't the time to argue the matter. I curled my fingers around his. 'Then for the love you once bore that girl, Ragnor. Save Hamlet.'

Slowly he said, 'If I do this for you, Cat, then understand this pays out my account. Your friendship has become too costly. I cannot afford to keep you in my life.'

Suddenly the world felt very bleak indeed if I could see him no more. 'Surely we can still stay friends, Ragnor.'

'No!' I was taken aback by the savagery in his voice. 'Cat, you're another man's wife. I'll bring him back to you, but then you must hold fast to him, come better or worse. I'm not of a humour to die for love, but each time I see you it carves away a little of my heart, and I will no longer pay that price. Let this rescue be both my wedding and parting gift to the one girl I ever loved.'

I felt as if the world I knew had turned to quicksand beneath my feet. Ragnor loved me. He'd loved me these many years. It was as if I'd bolted stones to my eyes so I'd never seen the truth, and now, all at once, my blindness had toppled away.

Then a harsher truth slashed its way into my understanding.

I loved him.

I loved his wild tangle of hair, his flashing black eyes, his shame-the-devil courage, his passion for life just as he found it without needing to make it prettier or more philosophical. He'd known me when I was uneducated, wild, strong-willed, silly, and he loved me for all those things I'd tried to scrape out of myself. With Ragnor I wouldn't be large in worldly status, but I'd be large in character. Loving Ragnor was like finding my way to the kingdom of myself.

But—

I was already married. I'd married Lord Hamlet.

Damn Ragnor to the coldest cavern of Hel! he'd been right all along. It wasn't Lord Hamlet that I'd loved. I'd been dazzled by him. I'd fallen under the spell of his beauty, of his creative spirit. I'd fallen in love with the magic, not the man himself.

Now suddenly I had a chance to transform my life into what I truly wanted. All I had to do was to tell Ragnor not to pursue the wool merchant's ship. Lord Hamlet would die, but Denmark would be made safe under the reign of the careful Claudius. Ragnor wouldn't be branded a pirate, and I could have my true heart's desire. I could leave the twisted, dangerous castle and become Ragnor's wife. Let Hamlet's ship sail. After all, he was himself in love with death. His execution might even come to him as a relief, delivering him into the yearned-for embrace of oblivion. A gift, in fact. He'd talked incessantly of how he was weary of life. No doubt but he'd welcome death, welcome the chance to escape from his madness, from the conspiracies and betrayals of royal life. In addition, I was the king's subject, and to let the ship sail on would be nothing more than an act of obedience to the king. The queen would weep but, better the swift mourning than years of slow grief that Hamlet's madness would cause.

All I had to do was do nothing, and everyone would find a happy ending and win their deepest heart's desires.

Unfortunately, nothing was the one thing I couldn't do.

Yes, I'd been a glamour-dazzled little fool when I'd taken Hamlet as my husband. But even if I hadn't married him, I couldn't let an innocent man sail off unawares to his death. Not when I had the means to stop it. If Hamlet preferred to die, then his must be the hand to end his life, not mine. No, my foolish ambitions had cost me Ragnor, but I wouldn't sacrifice the poor broken prince to buy my own contentment.

So I pushed words heavy as boulders out from my mouth. 'I accept, Ragnor. After you rescue the prince, all will be at an end between us.'

42

As I started to leave, Ragnor called out, 'Don't return to the castle.'

I looked at him, bewildered. Was he saying he'd changed his mind about helping me?

'I don't reckon you'll be safe there,' he said. 'If Claudius wants to kill the prince to buy his silence, you must be in danger as well.'

He was right, of course. Especially when Hamlet returned. Since Claudius's safety lay in my silence, my death would make my own silence absolutely secure. But where should I go? It wouldn't be safe to remain here in the village. Claudius could easily find me here. My knees suddenly wobbled, and I leaned against the sides of the ship for support. Anywhere I tried to hide, the king could find me out. If he was brazen enough to murder his royal nephew, the son of his beloved wife, then nothing would stay his hand from killing his accomplice.

'I'll think of something,' I said to Ragnor. 'You make ready as quickly as possible. I'll find a safe way out of this coil.'

He hesitated, and then he nodded. I felt a flea's breath better that Ragnor had enough faith in me to trust I'd think of a plan.

'Thank you,' I said, and I tried to memorize Ragnor's appearance as he stood there framed by the light of the fire. *This may be my last time ever to see him.* With all my inner energy, I branded his image on my heart. Then I quickly stumbled back to the Herbwife's cottage. She was stirring a small pot over the fire, and the air was thick with the smell of bittersweet herbs and something else that smelled like the damp soil after a spring rain.

'Sit you down by the fire, lass, to warm your outsides. I'll pour you a drink to warm your insides as well.'

One of the things I liked best about the Herbwife was that she asked few questions. Unlike most folk, she didn't poke her nose into everything or shower you with advice. Her son had learned from her this trait of trusting that folk could rule their own lives.

I was cold, but it wasn't the mild night that had chilled me. It was the December in my heart that was making me feel frozen. The Herbwife handed me a warm cup wrapped in cloth so it wouldn't burn my fingers. The first sip of her posset made my insides want to purr like a stroked cat. 'Thank you,' I said, and took another drink of the soothing potion.

'You look pale,' she said. 'Have you been well?'

'Things have been all a-jumble up in the castle,' I told her. 'And the past two mornings, I've been sick to my stomach with worry.'

She looked at me closely, then laid a warm hand against my forehead. 'Would you like me to look at your water, child, to see if you've taken an illness?'

I shook my head. 'I'm fine. It's just that things are out of joint. I feel the strain.'

I knew I should tell her about my father's death, but I took the coward's way and kept mum. I'd let her hear the news from other sources. Could I ask her, I wondered, for advice about how to handle Claudius? But then it hit me that if I told her my whole story, I'd be putting her in the way of danger, and so I said nothing about it.

She moved to a crock in the corner and extracted a small, tied packet. 'These herbs might help,' she said. 'In the morning, brew them in boiling water – just a pinch in a cup. Sip them as soon as you feel a little sick.'

'I don't think to get sick again.'

She smiled. 'We will hope not, but if you should, try my herbs.'

She handed the packet of herbs to me. Beneath the thin cloth the herbs were dry and prickly, but they smelled of mint and something astringent. I looked over at the locked cupboard from which she'd given me the vial of poison that had killed Blanche and the king. In her faint English accent, the Herbwife kept talking, but I paid her little mind for now I'd thought of how to control Claudius and turn all events to my own advantage.

43

All the way back to the castle, I polished my scheme the way a warrior would shine his battle sword.

The previous night I'd slept on a pallet on the Herbwife's floor, and now I moved through the dew-dappled grass and the soft grey light of early dawn. There was a calm deep down inside me that could be either exhaustion or resolution or a mixture of them both. My plan was the simplest thing in the world. First, I'd take a leaf from Hamlet's book. I'd pretend to be mad. Saint Berengaria knew I currently looked the part, my clothes muddied and torn, my hair wild, even my skin spattered with flecks of mud and tiny tears from twigs and thorns that had slashed against me when I'd wandered through the fog.

By now Ragnor and his brothers had surely set sail to rescue Hamlet. I'd left a note with the Herbwife to give to Ragnor on his return, telling him where to bring Hamlet. More than anything I hated biding my time, but bide my time I must until Hamlet was safely returned to me. Only then would I go to Claudius with my plan that would solve all our problems.

Of course, my plan meant that I'd never see Ragnor again, but it would be foolish beyond belief to let myself see him again, now that I knew that he was the man I loved. I didn't believe myself to be a person who could be married to one man and lie with another, but then for most of my life I wouldn't have believed myself to be someone who would murder a king. By all the saints and the old gods, too, we may know who we are, but we don't know who we might become.

No, it was best that I'd made my final parting from Ragnor.

Someday the pain would go away.

When the castle came into sight, I stepped behind a tangle of bushes. With my teeth I tore at the hem of my gown, and then I ripped my skirt into tattered strips. I did the same to my sleeves, and tore my bodice until slashes of my shift showed through. There were a few berries on the bush, halfway between green and ripe, and I squeezed them up and down my arm and streaked my face with their juice. Small wildflowers puddled about my feet, and I plucked a handful and wove them into my matted hair and tucked them between my laces. I hid my slippers beneath a bush. All through my childhood, except on the coldest of days, I'd run about barefooted, but now my feet had grown shoe-pampered and tender, and I didn't walk very many steps before they began to ache. I had no relish of walking across the stones of the courtyard.

My life depends on my acting out my plan. My life, and doubtless the life of Hamlet as well. In truth, the whole history of Denmark would be changed by what I did this day. I had to marshal every one of my faculties to do it successfully. I could afford no traitors from within, no turncoat gestures or emotions.

As I drew within earshot of the castle, I began to sing a ditty that I'd heard the village boys sing, a rude drinking song. I sang it in a sweet, shy little voice, stopping from time to time to speak to folk who weren't there in the same way, two nights earlier, Hamlet had addressed his father's ghost up on the ramparts. 'Yes,' I said, 'Good Mother, I will indeed dance at my wedding.' I wobbled a few steps forward, then turned to the right. 'Indeed, my father, you don't need to tell me, for there are hawks and geese enough at court to furnish a dozen feather beds.'

Then I switched to a love song that the older girls in the village often sang, and when I couldn't remember the words, I just made them up. Out of the corner of my eye, I saw the porter and a few of the Swiss guards staring at me open-mouthed, and I sternly suppressed a smile.

To my mind, Hamlet's moments of madness – feigned or otherwise – had sometimes lacked drama. If one is to be mad, there's no fun unless one goes at it ferociously. I'd go at it full-flower, holding nothing in reserve. I'd give the court a performance that would put to shame my childhood play-acting. I swept regally across the moat, bowing and nodding to imaginary subjects as if I were the empress of air and emptiness.

'How now, Lady Ophelia?' asked the porter in a tone that sounded almost frightened.

'Lady Ophelia?' I said, pitching my voice a little higher than usual. 'Fie, there's no Lady Ophelia here.'

'Then who do you be, pretty lady?' he asked nervously.

I twirled around, pleased with the way my tattered skirt floated out about my waist like the ribbons on a Maypole. 'I be the daughter of one who was and who is no more. If the candle is snuffed, then the sparks must go in the dark. I am darkness. I am the winter wind come on a day in June. I am the bird who flies alone over the dark seas, calling *too-loo, too-lee*. My father is dust and ashes, and my mother is the same, so what can the child of dust and ashes be but the mud that lurks beneath the stepping stones?'

I began to dance on my bruised feet, humming a tuneless song.

'Go fetch the king,' I heard the porter mutter to one of the soldiers who stood there. 'This affair is much beyond my experience.'

My plan was working. By pretending to be mad, I'd remove from Claudius all worry that I might betray his part in his brother's death. What threat could a madwoman pose him? Any accusations I might hurl at him would be excused since I was clearly far from my wits. This would ensure my safety until Hamlet had a chance to arrive back upon these shores. Then I'd go to Claudius in private and put the second part of my plan into motion. In truth, I was much pleased with myself for coming up with such a cunning scheme. I was young and untrained, but I'd devised a plan that would control a king, save a prince, and set things to rights in all of Denmark. This business of ruling wasn't so hard after all.

In addition, I was quite enjoying my performance as the mad maid of Elsinore. It was great fun to say whatever came out of my mouth, to do anything I had a mind to do. There was a freedom in madness that wasn't to be had in the life of a proper young lady. It was a marvel to me that more women didn't turn mad in their time. I bowed to an imaginary partner and began a jig, calling out instructions to invisible musicians. It was difficult not to laugh at the dropped jaws of the porter and the soldier. For once there were no ghosts about, and I regretted they too couldn't witness my fine performance.

In a much shorter time than I'd have thought possible, Claudius appeared. The porter slumped in relief. 'See, my lord. It's just as I've said. Lady Ophelia is mad, mad as poor Lord Hamlet.'

I plucked a flower from my hair and held it out. 'Good sir, good dove, O duckling of state and prince of the primroses, you must weave this posy into your crown and come a-dancing in the moonlight. They say you have a good voice, and so you must provide bass to my soprano.'

I looked for the confusion in his face, but instead it was pulled tight as a starched collar, and his eyes were hard.

'You spoke aright,' Claudius said, and his voice was as cold as winter. 'The Lady Ophelia is indeed far from her wits.' He turned to the soldiers. 'Take her into custody and, for her own safety, lock her in the dungeon and post double watch outside her door.' His eyes slid over to mine. 'We much fear what harm she may do to herself and others should we let her roam free.'

Now it was my mouth that dropped open. I hadn't expected this turn of events. I'd been sure that Claudius would regard me as harmless in my madness, not as someone who might offer danger to the throne. Claudius turned on his heel and marched back into the courtyard.

For several heartbeats, the soldiers and I stood frozen as a picture. Then the porter said, 'You heard the king. Take the poor lady into your care and shut her up so she comes to no harm.'

The poor man had no idea that the harm that awaited me was in Claudius's grip, not from roaming free. It was as if the porter's words had released the soldiers from a spell, for they moved toward me, one on each side. I gave a yelp, and then I began to run.

44

For a moment the soldiers hesitated, confused, and then they gave chase.

I thudded down the stretch of road leading from the castle, my mind whirling. How had my beautiful plan gone so horrifyingly wrong? I dared not let myself fall into Claudius's hands, for once I was locked away, I doubted whether I'd ever again see the light of day. Already my feet began to throb, and for a moment I regretted casting my slippers aside, but then the slippers of a lady weren't made for running and they'd have given me no purchase across the ground.

I could hear my pursuers behind me. I had the benefit of being lighter, but in my years in the castle I'd taken little exercise, so I knew that I'd tire rapidly. My chief advantage lay in knowing the countryside. For the first time I was glad that Claudius's guards were Swiss. They didn't know the area outside the castle. As I ran, I cast about in my mind for the best way to go. I knew I could never make it all the way back to the village without slowing down. Even if I could, it would be be churlish to place a friend in danger of the king's enmity by hiding in his hut. I gave a jump over a nest of meadowlark eggs half-hidden in the grass. Turning to the shore would be a bad idea as well. It's weary work to run across the sand, and there would be no hiding places along the seaside. So at the bottom of the rise to the castle, I turned and headed across the country to a small nearby wood. To my horror, my side ached from trying to catch my breath. The one good thing was that

I'd torn my skirt to shreds. A proper skirt would have hobbled me, but now I could stretch my legs and fly.

I tried to imagine the Flying Catgirl at my side. 'You can do this,' she said proudly. 'You are a hound made for hunting, not a tame lapdog who dreams his life away, curled up on a silken cushion.'

I leapt over a tiny stream that the town women used to wash clothes and headed toward the churchyard. In the ruins of the old monastery, behind tumbled-down stones, lay a wealth of nooks and hidey-holes. Unfortunately, already I was losing labour. I couldn't keep running much longer. A stitch in my side began to ache like one of Jesus' wounds, and my throat was raw from my great gulps of air.

'This is something you can do,' the Flying Catgirl told me calmly. 'Think of this as the kind of high adventure you always craved.'

Now we were dodging through the trees in the patch of woodland. The chase had made me sweaty, and I was grateful for the cool shade. I ran like a rabbit, leaping over fallen logs and darting this way and then that among the trunks of trees. I could hear my pursuers crashing behind me, and I risked turning my head to see how near they were. They were closer than I liked, so I put on a burst of speed. Up ahead I could make out the wall around the monastery and swerved toward the gate.

And ran headlong into a man who was standing there.

45

'What have we here?'

He seized me and held me in a firm grip. His accent was the thick, strangled speech of Norway. I had to strain to make out his words.

'Let me go,' I gasped, struggling and kicking to free myself. He was dressed like a soldier, but his outfit wasn't that of any Danish troop. The Norwegian soldier just laughed and held me tighter.

Now my two pursuers had drawn level.

'Give her to us!' one of them called out in his gluey Swiss accent.

I heard the clink of a drawn sword as the other one said, 'Who are you and why are you here?'

My captor jerked me so hard that the breath was knocked out of me. 'I serve in the army of Prince Erik Strong Arm of Norway.'

I heard a second sword drawn. 'Then what business have you here?'

My captor twisted me around and pulled me so that my back was pressed against his chest. 'I come under the protection of a safe conduct from your own king.'

'You had safe conduct to pass through many days since,' said one of the soldiers. 'Not to skulk about like a spy.'

The second Swiss soldier said, 'The last battalion passed through this area three days ago. Why do you tarry behind?'

My captor said, 'I'm not a spy!'

'Then why are you still here? You should have been long gone.'

'I rest. I gather strength before I go as a replacement for the first wave.'

'It wouldn't have sapped your strength to travel this little distance from Norway. I think there is other business afoot. Give us that girl, and then come along with us to the king.'

My captor gave me a push that sent me sprawling onto the ground. 'I think not,' he said, and I heard him pull his sword.

'Put your weapon away,' said the second soldier, 'for you're outnumbered.'

'I think not!' said the Norwegian soldier. He called out something that I didn't understand, and suddenly three other Norwegian soldiers appeared. The first lunged at one of my pursuers, but I didn't stay to see any more. I scrambled to my feet and took off running. Behind me I heard the shouts and swords clanking against each other, but I ran off into the nearby wood. Then I circled around and crept back into the ruins of the monastery. The safest place to go would be the old cellar where Piet and I had played so often when we were children. As I moved cautiously through the remains of the old refectory, I kept one ear peeled for sounds. I was fairly certain the soldiers wouldn't fight unto the death. To do so could catapult the two countries into war, and it was unlikely any of the soldiers on either side would have taken that risk. The most likely result was that after a sufficient show of bravado, the soldiers had broken apart and raced back to inform their commanders of the encounter. The threat of war outranked the dangers of a mad young girl any day. With luck – and I was certainly due some luck – Claudius would be so preoccupied with the discovery of enemy soldiers hiding out in his land that he'd concentrate on clearing that up before he worried about recapturing me.

The cellar might be the safest, but it would afford me no

way to watch for an attack. Better to climb up in the tower. At its very top was the belfry, and, if need be, I could hide up in the shadows of its rafters. The old tower looked more cracked than ever, but I found the huge stone torso of Saint Peter blocking the passageway to the stairs in the same place that it had been when we were children. I shouldered it aside enough to wriggle through, and then I grabbed hold of the outstretched stub of a stone hand and tugged the stone shut behind me. If soldiers tracked me here, they might not suspect a stairway lay behind the fallen statue.

I picked my way carefully up the winding stairs, amazed to see how much more it had crumbled in just a few years. Several times sharp shards of stone cut my feet, and once I slipped and banged my knee hard enough to make tears swim into my eyes. But soon I was safe in the old belfry looking out over the old chapel beneath. The bells themselves were long gone, and by now almost all the tower's roof had fallen through, although the little bit that remained provided me with a bit of ragged shelter. I was both thirsty and hungry, but I'd wait until darkness to try to remedy that. After dark I could creep down to the old well, and poke among the old garden to see what might be growing there. All along the walls of the graveyard grew apple trees, and I could fill my belly with green apples if it came to that. For the present, I curled up in a niche of the stone wall next to the stairway and set myself to puzzling out my best course of action.

I could hardly credit that not three days since I'd been a fine lady at court, daughter of the chief advisor to the king, the loving secret wife of a beloved prince. How swiftly turns the wheel of Fate. Now I was outlaw in my own life, wed to a man condemned to death, in love with another man entirely. *Do not waste time thinking of such things*, I sternly told myself. What mattered now was finding a way out of this tangle. I could waste years indulging in philosophy once I'd taken myself and Hamlet to safety.

If only I could find a way to talk to Claudius in private, I could set everything to rights. Especially with enemy troops lurking about, it would be difficult to make my way to him. Perhaps I could make my way to the queen and beg her help to intercede with her husband. Yes, that might be the best . . .

I sat up with a start. My body was cramped and aching, and I realized, to my shame, I'd fallen asleep. At first I couldn't believe I could sleep at such a time, but my body felt as weary as if it had been plunged into the stream with laundry and beaten over and over. Then, too, much had happened to tire my spirit as well during the past few days. I gave a few cautious stretches to ease my cramped muscles. Overhead the sky was spangled with stars, each as bright as a jewel on an emperor's robe. Suddenly, I realized that one of the stars was shining below me, not above.

There was a small light moving around the chapel. A lantern.

Then I heard someone call out my name.

46

On my hands and knees, I crept down the stairs, careful to stay in the shadows. I couldn't make out the figure holding the light at the mouth of the stairway.

'Ophelia!' the voice called again. 'Be you here?'

With a flash of joy, I recognized the voice. Piet. I started to call back to him, but caution reined me back. What if he'd been sent by the king? After all, he was in Claudius's service. Perhaps the wily king had laid a trap.

I pulled farther into the shadows and waited.

'Ophelia? If you're here, it's now safe to show yourself.'

I didn't move.

Only when the candle began to leave the chapel did I call out, 'Piet?'

The joy in his voice tugged at my heart. 'Ophelia! Then you're alive! I hoped to find you here.'

'Are you alone, Piet?'

'Mus has come with me, but there be but us two. Shall we come up, or will you come down?'

'I'll come down!' I was overjoyed to see Piet. As usual, he didn't hug me or fuss, but he did thrust out a small parcel wrapped in a cloth.

'Here,' he said. 'I knew you'd be hungry, so I brought food.'

I brushed the dirt and splinters off a toppled block of stone and sat down to unwrap his parcel. Piet set his lantern on a ledge and squatted in front of me. I saw that Mus, his sweetheart from the kitchen, stood next to him, muffled in shawls and scarves so that she looked as wrapped as the package he carried. He'd brought me a wedge of cheese, two small loaves of bread, and several long strips of dried cod. As soon as I smelled the food, I realized I was starving, so I broke off a huge wedge of bread and crammed it all into my mouth. 'How did you know where to find me?' I asked, my words muffled by the food.

'I heard tell in the kitchens that you be mad and gave the slip to soldiers sent to protect you. Our king has set forth that he fears you'll do violence to yourself.'

'And do you believe it, Piet?' I broke off another wedge of bread and stuffed it into my mouth.

Calmly he said, 'I know you, Girl. I know you be no more mad than me nor Mus here. I reckon you couldn't turn mad, even if'n you wanted to. You've always been a deep'un, Girl, and I doubt not but that you have some deep scheme to play out.'

I leaned down and hugged him. As always, he wriggled away. 'Leave off that silliness, do.'

Mus said nothing, but through the thin candlelight she watched me with scared eyes.

'Do you want to know my scheme?' I asked.

Piet thought about this for a moment before saying, 'No. It'll do neither of us much good to know it, and it might do Mus and me harm. Best you keep it close-buttoned to your own chest.'

I was disappointed. It would have given me comfort to confide in him, and, to speak true, I was proud of my plan and I wanted someone else to admire it. On reflection, though, I saw that his way was the wiser. As they say in the village, the fewer people sharing the mug, the less chance beer will be spilled. 'Tell me this, though, Piet. Has the king sent his guards back out to find me?'

'Tonight?' Piet asked amazed. 'Find you tonight?'

'Yes, find me tonight.'

He clucked in disapproval. 'The king would hardly seek you out tonight.' Both he and Mus regarded me as if I'd just said the silliest thing in all Denmark.

I snapped back, 'I didn't know his soldiers to be so afraid of the dark.'

It was Mus who answered. 'Not the dark, lady, but bethink you what night this one be.'

I'd lost track of time entirely. Only when Piet added, 'It be Midsummer's Eve,' did I understand what she'd meant.

Yes, of course. The Midsummer celebration was even bigger than that at Midwinter. Midsummer was the other turning point of the year. Spring, for all its beauty, was a lean time. You were most likely to starve in the spring as food supplies ran low while the new world of nature hadn't yet begun to produce. Once you reached Midsummer, though, a new abundance began. Crops had begun to swell, and baby animals had been born and were growing and fattening in preparation for the winter's slaughter. Cows, sheep, and goats were all in milk. On the trees were green apples and nubs that would be pears and apricots. Seeing so much bounty made you sure you'd live forever. On Midsummer Night, people took themselves to the meadows rather than the shores. Again bonfires were built, but these were smaller than the ones in winter, made for the beauty and fellowship and not for warmth or calling the sun. First there'd be contests in the long afternoon, foot races, competitions to see which woman could spin the longest length of thread the fastest, and barrel rolling. Finally all would end with dancing. Folks at Midsummer were light of heart and friendly, and lots of folk liked to travel to nearby villages to visit with distant neighbours as the slow evening wore away. Girls would gather flowers and weave wreaths for their hair, and folk would eat bread baked with dried fruits and the last of the winter nutmeats, honey cakes, and sallets of new-laid eggs and the first greens of the season.

'Even the foreign soldiers wouldn't willingly miss the Midsummer festivities,' Piet said. 'Not for anything short of an attack. Certainly not for one scrawny little girl.'

Mus said, 'Being it was Midsummer made it easy as cream for us to slip away. Most of the kitchen folk be gone back to their own villages to celebrate, so they just reckoned we were headed to our village as well.'

I felt myself flooded with affection. I didn't deserve such a generous gesture. I'd wrapped myself up in concern for the noble-born folk, and yet it was my foster brother from the village who'd risked his safety to come help me.

Laertes! This put me in mind of my own true brother. Doubtless a messenger had hurried to him once our father was killed. With good roads and good weather, Laertes could be here soon. What would he do when he arrived? I didn't think he could tamely swallow our father's death. His murder was an insult to our family. Honour demanded vengeance. But how? Since Hamlet had been sent away, Laertes couldn't challenge him. By our Lady and her murdered son, would Laertes be rash enough to challenge Claudius instead? After all, Claudius had failed to restrain his mad stepson.

Laertes might even now be racing straight into danger. Honour led men to do reckless deeds, to throw over every shred of common sense and self-preservation. Most importantly, though, Laertes was an innocent pawn in the dangerous game that Claudius and I now played for the life of Hamlet. It was all my fault that he'd been drawn into the deadly game at all. I needed to do what I could to gird him in safety.

My one advantage was that Claudius liked to work in secret. His murder of his brother, his secret orders for Hamlet's death – these acts took place behind the scenes, not on the stage where everyone could see them. Thus I needed to keep my brother Laertes in the glare of the public sun to protect him from Claudius's backstage violence.

'Piet,' I said, 'I have one more favour to request of you.'

He looked at me steadily, but Mus nervously slid her hand into his.

I continued, 'I need you and Mus to go to our village and talk with the folk there. Tell them about my father's murder. Tell them Prince Hamlet is mad and no fit ruler of Denmark. Tell them that Denmark must have an heir to the throne, and that from all your observation in the castle, Laertes is the very man to rule us. Stir them up. Convince them that Laertes is a good man, a fine young man, the very cream of Denmark. Make them understand that he had nothing to do with the strange and dark affairs up at the castle. Tell them that if they surround Laertes with their support, when he comes to his fortune, he'll be a generous and grateful overlord. Cram their ears with dreams until they agree to accompany Laertes when he returns and goes up to the castle to meet with the king. Will you do that much for me?'

'Why?'

'To save Laertes's life! Unless my brother is surrounded by people, Claudius may try to kill him.'

'Why?'

'To prevent Laertes from demanding retribution.'

Piet thought about it for a moment. I knew better than to rush him, although my temperament chafed at his deliberate pace. Finally he said, 'I can do that.'

'I must do one thing more to make Laertes safe,' I told Piet and Mus. Laertes was skilled with his sword, but he needed a weapon of stealth in case he demanded a private audience with the king. 'Come with me.'

We crept out from under the toppled stones of the monastery and wove our way through the churchyard. Mus clung tightly to Piet, but she offered no sound of protest, only jumping and squealing each time a branch snapped. I myself was almost as nervous.

I led them back to our village. A few times we spotted bonfires in the distance, but we didn't see another living soul. I hurried us along. I needed to be back out of the village before the morning light, and the short night was already far advanced. Once in the village, it was a little unsettling to see the houses deserted and no folk around. Did death feel like this? A familiar landscape but finding yourself the only living creature about? I refused to show fear, but I pressed a little closer to Piet.

I pushed the Herbwife's heavy trestle door open and crept inside, motioning Piet and Mus to follow. I could tell from their expressions that they didn't want to be there, but they didn't resist. I took up a candle and lit it from the banked embers on the hearth. I remembered she'd hidden the key to her potion cupboard in the blue crock on the mantelpiece, so it was but the work of a moment to shake it out. I unlocked the cupboard door.

Mus watched me with huge, terrified eyes. I held the candle up, surveying the three shelves of dangerous potions, casting my mind back to that day long ago when she'd shown me which was which. Pray God that I remembered aright. I wished the candle threw a better light, but I closed my shaking fingers around a tiny red bag with a golden drawstring. I then set my candle on the table and opened the bag. Inside was a tiny vial, no bigger than my thumb. *Let this be the liquor I sought.* I held it out to Piet.

'You must give this to Laertes,' I whispered, although as far as I could tell, we were the only folk in the entire village. 'Tell him that on no account must he tell anyone about it. Tell him to pour the contents in a small bowl and dip his knifeblade in it. Tell him this is a poison so powerful that he need but scratch his opponent, and then no power on earth can save his attacker from death. Tell him that, pray God, he'll not need it, but he must be on his guard when he tries to sort out all the circumstances of his father's death, and he should carry his drugged knife at the ready at all times, just in case he find himself surprised and must defend himself.'

Mus gasped, and Piet backed away. 'I'll have no commerce with murder,' he said.

'It's not murder!' I snapped, my voice sliding back toward the accent of the village folk. 'This be but protection for Lord Laertes. I doubt he'll have need for it, but I don't wish to send him all unguarded into the dragon's mouth.'

'Do not take it, Piet,' Mus whispered in her squeaky little voice. 'If you are caught it will be your death and mine, too.'

'If you don't,' I said, 'it could be the death of Laertes. Do you wish that death on your head?'

It seemed to take an eternity, but finally Piet plucked the vial from my fingers and slipped it back into its drawstring pouch. Carefully he tied the strings of the pouch to his belt. He didn't say anything, but it felt like something had died between us, some bond or some faith.

'My only wish is to save the life of an innocent man,' I said.

Piet said nothing. Mus began to weep.

'In truth, I'm trying to save two innocent men,' I said. 'My brother Laertes and Lord Hamlet . . .'

'Do not tell us anymore,' Mus said between teary sniffles. 'All this dark knowledge be dangerous.'

Piet said, 'I think it best we go now.'

'Leave the poison here,' Mus pleaded, but Piet shook his head.

'I offered my help, and I'll see it through,' he said.

'And you will rile up the village folk to throw their support to Laertes?' I begged. Piet was no orator, but village folk trusted him and would listen to his words.

He nodded.

'I owe you more than I can say, Piet. More than that, you do heroic work, for you will save the life of two innocent men.'

He gave no reply, and in a twinkling he and Mus were gone, leaving me alone in the Herbwife's cottage. I quickly locked the cupboard and restored the key to its hiding place. I wet my fingers with my tongue and pinched the wick to snuff the flame before restoring the candle to its place. I cast a look of longing at the ladder leading up to the place between the ceiling and the roof. I knew that Ragnor slept up there, and for a moment I wanted nothing more than to stretch out atop his bedcovers, to smell his scent, to think of him so bold and sensible. It would be so comforting to lie under the thatch in this snug cottage, fragrant from all the drying herbs.

But I'd chosen a different course. It was my lot to sail into uncharted seas, and it would never do to steer back to harbour now. So I wended my way back to the ruined church and climbed back into the tumbledown tower. Hunched chin to knees, I let the night spin away as I puzzled out plans to keep Hamlet safe.

By morning I was stiff, cold, and hungry. No one was about, so I made my way down to what remained of the monk's garden. As a child, I'd sometimes come here with the Herbwife, gathering plants from the deserted herb garden. Even though all the monks were long gone, the descendants of many of the herbs they'd planted hadn't only survived, but also spread in merry abandonment.

I pinched off a few sprigs of fennel, woodruff, rue and rosemary to chew on, hoping that the bitter flavours would

quiet my grumbling stomach. There was still the remains
of the bread and cheese and fish that Piet had brought, but
I didn't know how many days it must last me, and I didn't
want to gobble it down too soon.

The herbs didn't agree with me, and I leaned over the wall
and retched them back up. I felt shaky, but I no longer felt
hungry, so I stepped across a crumbling stone fence into my
favourite part of the garden, where the flowers grew. It was
over-run now with vines that snaked about the plants, but
I loved how the flowers hadn't given up the fight but still
clung on fiercely for a toehold. In the shadows of the wall I
could find only one remaining violet, but there was a crowd
of pansies huddled together and in the centre of the patch,
several May daisies defiantly poked their blossoms high above
the vegetation. Tall, slender stalks of columbine stretched
sunward through the remains of the brick walkways. It was
as good as a sermon, seeing how such a delicate flower could
nudge a path through the stone and brick in its quest for light
and sun. I didn't know how many days I'd need to play outlaw
in this place, and to pass the time, I plucked a lapful of flowers
and began to weave them into a garland as the village girls did
in preparation for Midsummer festivities. As the sun rose, a
few fat bees began to buzz lazily and several butterflies flitted
about to keep me company. In spite of myself, I grew drowsy
and finally drifted off to sleep, dreaming that the humming in
my ear wasn't the bees but the chanting of small brown monks
carrying armloads of fragrant blossoms.

Quicker than I'd ever believed possible, I lost count of
how many days I spent hiding in the ruined church. I'd
seemingly contracted some mild illness. I spent much of the
time sleeping and was often a little sick, but I usually found
myself in better health in the afternoons. After I finished
the last of the food Piet had brought, I managed to find
wild strawberries and was able to fish in a little stream. In

the nearby fields I discovered some nests of wild birds and took a few eggs from each, and in the late afternoon I'd risk a small fire to cook my meal so I did well enough. I passed hours upon hours polishing my plan to save Hamlet, once Ragnor brought him back to me. I was pleased with the result. My head reminded me that no plan could be foolproof, but I secretly thought mine was.

Three times soldiers passed by. I was certain that Claudius was looking for me still. Fortunately they didn't take pains to muffle their approach, as if they'd thought me struck deaf as well as mad, so I always heard them in time to hide.

One particularly beautiful afternoon, I risked a nap down in the walled churchyard. One of the kings was buried under a monument with a wide ledge all around his effigy. The ledge was broad enough for me to lie on, and the stone was pleasantly warmed by the sun. The statue of the dead king was big enough to hide me from the eyes of anyone entering the churchyard, so I felt fairly safe there. The heat from the stone beneath and the sun overhead was glorious, and the air was scented with the roses and shadow lilies that grew wild about the gravestones. The buzz of the bees was a lullaby lulling me to a dreamless sleep.

A touch on my shoulder snapped me awake. I leapt to my feet, poised to flee.

There stood Hamlet. He looked more beautiful than ever in this sun-dappled garden. His time at sea had scoured his cheeks to a ruddy hue that much became him.

'Have I stumbled upon the lair of the fairy queen,' he said, smiling, 'or is this some woodland sprite who appears once a year only to celebrate summer?'

'Hamlet!' I threw myself into his arms. His body was warm from the sun and beneath their usual fragrance of dried orange peel and spices, his clothes carried a faint hint of the sea wind.

His arms tightened around me, but as soon as I started to loosen my grip, he let me go.

'Did Ragnor come with you?' I asked, looking around.

'Ahh, a good fellow for all that he's a peasant and a pirate. I must reward him well when I come into my estate, for he's done me a good service. He saved my life.'

I started to tell Hamlet that Ragnor wasn't truly a pirate, attacking that one ship only to rescue the prince, but I held my tongue. There would be time enough to explain the whole to him. Instead I asked again, 'Is Ragnor here?'

Hamlet shook his head. 'Ophelia, since we parted, I've had such adventures!' He grabbed my hands and whirled me around, but my feet caught in a snare of vines and I tumbled against him, sending us both crashing to the ground, me on top of him. I laughed ruefully and sat up and pulled him up to a sitting position. I was suddenly conscious of the very odd figure I must cut. My clothes were tattered and dirty from my days of hiding out, and no comb had touched my hair for a long time, so it bushed out madly across my shoulders.

'Hamlet, you must wonder to see me looking so wild . . .'

It was as if he didn't hear my words at all. 'You'll want to hear all that has come to pass to cast me up so untimely back on these shores.'

I began, 'Much has come to pass at the castle, too, and—'

He cut me off. 'Ophelia, ere I was two days at sea, this pirate ship gave us chase, but we were too slow of sail to escape. We were forced to fight—'

'Ragnor!' *Damn him. I'd told him there was no need to fight.* 'Was the pirate captain hurt?'

'None of the pirate folk were hurt,' he said in an impatient tone. 'But you will wish to hear of *my* adventures, not theirs. In the general grapple, that long-haired pirate captain seized me and hauled me onto their ship—'

'Were any of the pirate folk killed?'

'You miss the point of my tale,' he said, frowning. 'This is *my* story that I tell. I don't believe that any of them suffered more than the merest scratch, but they were pirates after all. I want to tell you of my grand adventure. Truly, it was as if Providence herself took a hand in writing my tale and helping me to right the wrongs done to me. Don't worry. I'll reward those pirate rogues well once I come into my kingly fortune, and that's, after all, what those knaves care about.'

I felt a moment's impatience with him. These remarks smacked of the high-handed ways of his father, not of the man I loved. *Of course he doesn't realize what he's saying. He's too caught up in the plot of his own drama to notice the others about him. Once he's restored to himself, he'll show himself again to be the kind and considerate prince with whom I fell in love.* So I contented myself with saying merely, 'What an act of grace those pirates saved you.'

His eyes twinkled. 'It was tidy-handed, true, but I didn't need their interference for all that it was timely. I'd already saved myself.'

I stared at him. 'What do you mean?'

He gave me a smile so much that of a carefree boy that it near broke my heart. 'Since my uncle knew that I'd tumbled onto the truth of his part in my father's death, I was certain he meant me harm. So the first night on the ship, when we were at table, I excused myself to empty my bladder but whisked instead into the cabin of my two school friends. It was but the work of a moment to find the letter they carried to the king of England. Those fools had left it lying in full view atop Guildenstern's sea chest.' He winked. 'You wouldn't credit what Claudius had written, Ophelia. His letter begged the king of England upon receipt of this to tarry not, but at once to strike my head from my body.'

That letter was our salvation. 'Hamlet, have you kept the letter as proof against Claudius?' Even though a king had almost an unlimited licence to do as he would, this letter was proof positive that Claudius had exceeded his authority. It would destroy his reputation among the people of Denmark once they saw he'd ordered their beloved prince killed. No court of law, perhaps, could convict him, but the letter would turn his people against him, the one obstacle that even the power of his crown couldn't overcome. 'Oh, Hamlet, that letter can save everything for us!'

He leaned closer.

'You suck the milk from my tale, Ophelia, and don't wait for the cream! Attend while I tell you what I had the wisdom to do next.'

'Tell me you had the wisdom to bring this signed order with you. What more wisdom do you need?'

'O foolish virgin, hoard your oil a few moments more until I pour forth the flame of my tale!'

'Tell me this only – did you keep the letter?'

Impatiently he shook back his hair that shone like gold in the late afternoon sun. 'Claudius's letter is naught. Leave it awhile.'

'But do you have it on your person, Hamlet?'

'It's not of Claudius's letter that I wish to speak, woman!' he shouted at me. 'You are acting more the shrew than the loving wife!'

I held my tongue. It wouldn't hurt me to let him finish his tale. Claudius's letter would keep. In truth, I'd been shrewish. A few nights in the wild had scraped away all my castle gilding and left me rough and wilful. I needed to prune away these tendrils of wildness and fashion myself into a lady again. So I smoothed my face to show naught but tender concern and wrestled my voice into meekness. 'I do heartily beg your pardon, Hamlet. Pray tell me your tale at your own pace. It was wrong of me to interrupt you.'

He looked a little mollified. 'I doubt not but that you will much rejoice when you hear of my cleverness and readiness. Mark you, Ophelia, no sooner did I find this letter commanding my own execution than I whisked it away with me. That night, in my own cabin, I sat me down and wrote out a new commission in my fairest hand. I had that of the king next to me, and I made the pen strokes on my new one so like the hand of the king that I'd defy even your father to tell them apart.'

His mention of my father shook me. 'My father?'

He nodded eagerly. 'When this whole business is ended, I must write out a new letter in Claudius's hand and see if your father can spot the counterfeit.'

Horror rose in me like a floodtide, but I kept my voice steady. 'My father is dead, Hamlet.'

'Dead?' He sounded genuinely amazed.

'Have you forgotten,' I said, spacing my words carefully like beads on a rosary, 'that my father is dead?' I didn't add, *and you were the one who killed him*.

He knitted his brow. 'Indeed,' he said in a worried voice. Then he shrugged. 'Well, then, no matter. We must then find someone else at court to examine my hand and see if it's not the very likeness of Claudius's. My mother, perhaps. Or one of his other ministers.'

I leaned against a gravestone for support. *Angels of grace, he has no remembrance of my father's death or his own part in it. He butchered my father, a man he'd known all his life, and it had flitted from his memory as easily as if he'd slapped at a mosquito that nipped his skin.*

'No great matter,' he continued, 'but I was very proud that I'd made my letter look so like the original.' He paused, expectantly, and then said, 'Do you not wish to know what I wrote in the new missive?'

Not trusting the steadiness of my voice, I nodded.

He grinned. 'You will like this, Ophelia. I wrote all manner of flowery phrases about how peace and friendship should flower like a rose betwixt our two countries, warmed by the sun of Denmark and the fertile soil of England, and nonsensical fol-de-rol such as that. But then, mark you, I came to the very meat of the feast.' He leaned forward. 'I wrote then that the king of England should immediately put to death the two bearers of this letter.' He gave a bark of laughter and threw up his arms in sudden joy. 'Clever of me, wasn't it? I wrote that their death should be so sudden that they shouldn't even be given time to confess their sins!'

I shut my eyes. *Let this new nightmare go away. Let it be that I misheard Hamlet's words.* But when I opened my eyes again, I was still sitting in the ruined graveyard with my gravely ruined husband. My throat felt as tight as if a giant's hand was squeezing it shut, but I choked out, 'You condemned your two friends to death?'

He looked annoyed. 'They were carrying orders for my own death, Ophelia.'

'Hamlet, they didn't know what orders they carried.'

He shrugged one shoulder impatiently.

'Hamlet, the orders were sealed. Claudius would never have taken them into his confidence. They loved you well, Hamlet, and they were escorting you to England for what they thought was your own good. You'd killed an innocent man, Hamlet—'

'They betrayed me, Ophelia. I'll not weep for them.'

'Hamlet, they were acting out of love for you. They were the dupes of your uncle—'

'Then they should have been wiser, Ophelia. I hold no wake for them. Why do you take the part of the men who would have killed your husband? They were inferiors, Ophelia, who presumed to meddle in matters of those far above them. Let their fate serve as a warning to all who reach above their station.'

Into my mind flickered pictures of gentle Rosencrantz with

his twisted eye and his hopeless devotion to my husband, of Guildenstern the cocky bantam rooster who had strutted his way through life. By now they'd perhaps reached England. By now they might be no more alive than the gravestone pressing against my back.

'I had my father's signet ring,' Hamlet continued in a breezy voice. 'So I sealed up the new orders, and, at the first opportunity, sneaked them back into the sea chest in place of the others. Wasn't that clever of me? Then the next day the pirates attacked and snatched me away. It was indeed the luckiest chance, but I still do regret that I wasn't there to behold the faces of my two Judases when the king of England whisked them off to their death.'

Hamlet beamed at me, as beautiful as ever, with the ruined church behind him. I felt sick and empty inside. It struck me that he, too, in his own way was a ruined monument.

He lounged there, beautiful and damned, wholly unconscious of either trait. At that moment I learned that hearts don't actually break, but they can dissolve into a bruise in your chest. I realized I was witnessing the death of his future, the death of his ever being able to live a life grand enough for his gifts. Had he been born a normal man, perhaps he could have channelled his wild, mad energy into being a painter, a sculptor, an actor or even a playwright. If he'd been free to live one of those lives, his madness might have never led to murder. He was cursed by having been born a prince and thereby not being able to live a life to suit his talents. Tragically, this creative madness would make him disastrous as a king. I thought of Piet, Ragnor, the Herbwife, my childhood friends in the village. I couldn't unloose this mad king upon them. If his madness continued unchecked, there was no way to reckon how many other innocent folk might be slaughtered on impulse. If he ever became king, he could easily be seized with a wild notion and bring the whole country to ruin. I wanted to weep . . . for the tragedy of his inner madness that betrayed his gifts, for Rosencrantz and Guildenstern who were faithfully on their way to their undeserved deaths, for my father, and, if truth be told, for my own future, married to this superb and superbly mad man. I was filled with shame and self-loathing, for I now bitterly regretted our over-hasty marriage. Fool that I was, I'd been too dazzled by his glory to see the man beneath the glamour.

Nevertheless, he was my husband, and thus his welfare was my responsibility. I held my arms out and he flew to my embrace like a bird winging its way home. As I held him, I thought how fragile a thing a body is, how quickly it can be turned to cold clay. For all his flaws, I couldn't let the light that was Hamlet be snuffed out.

I laid my cheek against his sun-warmed hair. 'I'll take care of you, my lord,' I murmured and tightened my arms around him. 'Don't worry. I have a plan that will make everything right.'

47

'I wish to see the beauteous queen of Denmark,' I told the porter.

My heart fluttered in my chest like a snared sparrow, but this was the time for boldness. 'I come bearing tributary from the kingdom of posies.'

The porter looked at me askance. I'd thought it out thoroughly in my days in the wild, and my best chance lay in seeing the queen before I saw Claudius. In her presence, Claudius wouldn't dare to lay violent hands upon me. If he tried, I'd shout out unpleasant truths about his failed attempt to kill Hamlet. I'd threaten that if Claudius tried to lock me up, folk would take that as proof positive that what I said about his attempt to murder Hamlet was true.

'I don't think the queen . . .' began the porter.

At that I let loose a screech that must have scraped the very underside of heaven. 'I will see her!' I screamed. I hopped up and down, pounding the ground with my feet. 'Do not hinder me. I will see her at once! I will! I will!' I fell to the ground and rolled about, beating my chest with a fist.

'Calm yourself, lady,' the porter said nervously, clearly uncertain how to deal with madness in one whose station was so much above his own.

'My father will hear of this,' I screamed, 'and he'll have you whipped for such insolence.' I scrambled to my feet. 'Oh, there's mischief afoot here at Elsinore, and trickery that stains the hems of those on high. The tale I might spin you if I had

the time would curdle your blood and wring from your eyes
the very liquor of your heart. Elsinore is awash in shadows,
and you'd be much moved should you hear what rustles about
in the dark.'

Fearing I'd been too plain in my drift, I then burst into
song, croaking out a ditty from my days in the village about
a maid who wishes to marry one lad after another only to
find out that they're her brothers, sired by her philandering
father. The porter, alarmed, frantically gesticulated a page
to run to the queen. He was back so fast I didn't make it
to the final verse, my favourite, in which her mother reveals
that she, too, was unfaithful so that the girl herself was sired
by someone else.

As I was escorted to the Great Hall, many of the castle folk
made a point of gathering where they could gawk at me as
I passed. Clearly they'd heard Claudius's account and now
wanted to see the mad girl with their own eyes. The ghosts,
too, were out in full force, clogging the stairways so that I
had to shove my way past them.

I was shocked by how pale the queen looked. Horatio stood
next to her holding her elbow in his hand in support. The
queen stammered out a greeting, but it was clear that it hurt
her to see me like this. I felt awful deceiving this woman
who'd been so kind to me, more of a mother than any I'd
had. Doubtless the sight of my madness reminded her of her
own beloved son's condition. Nevertheless I shored up my
resolve by reminding myself that the life of her son depended
on the success of my masquerade.

To buy time, I warbled another song, this one about a
knight who's ambushed when he visits his own true love in
her bedchamber.

Partway through, Claudius strode into the room. My heart
gave a flop of fear. This was a duel, as deadly as any ever
fought by knights, although our weapons were our wits instead

of rapiers. I kept singing although I realized I was warbling the verses in a scattershot fashion. At least this made me seem even more mad.

'How do you do, pretty lady?' Claudius asked, his eyes boring into mine, probing whether I was mad in deed or in craft.

My own eyes met his and held them. 'May God reward you in kind for all that you deserve,' I said, and his eyes flickered. Then I made my voice dreamy. 'They say the owl is a baker's daughter.' I knew that legend was one of the queen's favourites, the story of how, when Christ asked a baker for a piece of bread and her daughter complained about a beggar getting so large a piece, Jesus turned the girl into an owl. The queen looked at me blankly, but I could see understanding rising in Claudius's eyes. 'We know what we are, but we don't know what we may become,' I warned him. I could tell by his expression that he caught my warning. Then, to soften the effect, I burst into a rude song about a man who seduces a young girl and casts her out.

A couple of times the king tried to interrupt me, but I kept singing and dancing around the room. I was glad that Horatio and Elspeth were also witnessing my performance. The more people who could testify to my madness, the more successfully I could bring Hamlet and me to safety.

All at once I saw Yorick also watching me. 'What is this show of madness?' he demanded in an irritated voice.

It was clear that no one else could see or hear him. 'I hope all will be well,' I told him. 'We must be patient.'

I turned back to the king. 'I cannot choose but weep to think they'd lay him in the cold ground.'

But Yorick wasn't done with me. 'I can tell you have some scheme in your head, but do you dare imagine you can bring everything to pass all alone?'

'My brother shall know of it,' I told him.

'Let me help,' he begged. 'I can advise you well.'

The weight on my shoulders lightened. It would ease my burden to let Yorick aid me, advise me. 'I thank you for your good counsel,' I told him.

The queen and Horatio looked at me aghast. I had to laugh. Since they couldn't see Yorick, my sensible utterances to him seemed as daft to them as the rest of my nonsense. 'Come, my coach,' I called out, giddy with delight at how well my plan had begun. I backed out of the doors, wishing the queen and Elspeth good night, over and over.

It was a relief to be out in the passageway. My nerves still jangled, but ease began to seep into me for pulling off my performance. Before I had time to suck in five or six deep breaths, however, Horatio appeared.

'Lady,' he said, 'may I keep company with you awhile?'

For a wild moment I thought of confessing everything to him and confiding in him about my plan. After all, I knew him to be a faithful friend to Hamlet, and that, too, he'd witnessed our marriage and had kept that secret from the king. But I let the impulse pass. I didn't know how accurately he saw my husband, or if he, still dazzled by Hamlet's glory, didn't yet see the madman underneath.

'Do you dance, my lord?' I asked him.

'Dance, lady?'

'This is the feast of Saint Valentine, my lord, and I would foot it awhile.'

'Nay, lady.' His voice was tender and grave. 'We are at the end of June, not Saint Valentine's.'

'Then it's even more a day for dancing. Will you partner me, lord?'

'But there's no music.'

'There is always music. It's just that some of us are deaf to the tones.'

His brows knit together. 'What music do you now hear, Ophelia?'

'I'd rather know what music *you* hear, Lord Horatio. Do you jig to the pipings of the king? Or do you tune your ear to the strains of my lord Hamlet?'

Before he could answer me, I did hear something . . . but it wasn't music. It was shouting below in the courtyard. Horatio heard it, too. Then I heard a great crashing. He ran to the window and looked out.

'They have broke open the doors!' he cried.

Several guards ran past us to join the others at the doors to the queen's chamber. Horatio shoved me into an ante-chamber. His hand groped at his belt, but he had left off his sword in order to wait upon the king. He looked quickly about the room, and his eyes fastened on an iron rod from which some curtains hung.

'Keep back by the window, lady,' he called out as he wrestled the rod from off the wall. 'This doorway is narrow, so I should be able to keep the attackers back until help can reach us.' With his knife he ripped the fabric off the rod and kicked it toward a corner so that it would not tangle about his feet. 'The mob looked to be full of peasants and such, so I do not expect them to be of sufficient skill to get to you past my singlestick.'

Almost at once footsteps clomped up the stairs and we heard a multitude chant, 'Laertes shall be king! Laertes shall be king.'

My brother! My brother had returned to Denmark, and he was armoured in the crowd of villagers incited by Piet. O wonderful, faithful, efficient Piet!

I opened my mouth to inform Horatio that we were in no danger, but he stood looking out the door in a tense, warrior stance, and I knew he wouldn't heed my words. Just past him I saw the passageway filling with youths, many from my village and many others that I didn't recognize. At the head of the rabble was my brother Laertes, pale and exhausted, but brandishing a staff. They swept past Horatio, paying him no mind, intent on reaching Claudius.

'Laertes shall be king!' the mob cried out. 'Laertes as king!' I rejoiced at Piet's industry and my cleverness. Claudius would never dare to stage a shadowy assassination of Laertes while he was in the full sun of the crowd's affection.

Several men carried logs, and as the crowd chanted Laertes's name, they battered the logs against the locked doors of the Great Hall until they smashed open. Even as I rejoiced at the vigour of Laertes and his followers, a small part of me mourned the destruction of the doors, for they'd been a thing of beauty, finely carved with scenes from the Saga of Sven Sigurssen, a Dane who had, in the olden days, sailed his ship deep into Russia and fought a dragon for his hoard and captured a fiery Russian princess.

I darted under Horatio's arm before he could stop me, and plunged into the roiling mass of the rabble, squirming among the bodies until I could see my brother.

The mouth of the Great Hall was lined with the Swiss guards, looking huge and fierce, their weapons drawn.

'I will see the king!' Laertes commanded in a bold voice that I would never have suspected him of possessing. He appeared flushed and confident. 'I demand a parlay.'

The commander of the guards hesitated, but he seemed to hear a voice from behind him giving orders, so he took a slight step to the side. 'You alone may pass,' he said in his mushy Swiss accent that was like stockings sopped in milk. 'But you must not carry with you any weapons.'

'No!' cried the crowd. 'It's a trap. Don't go!' They began to make threatening sounds as if they would charge the guards, and I saw several of the older soldiers looking decidedly nervous. But Laertes turned back to his followers and raised his hands until they quieted down.

'I need no weapons,' he shouted, 'for I have you.'

The crowd gave a cheer.

'The king knows well that should he hurt me, he would never get past you to safety.'

The crowd cheered again.

'I need no swords, for you good men will give me a greater protection than a thousand swords and ten thousand silly foreign soldiers.'

The crowd gave their loudest cheer of all.

Laertes made a great show of unstrapping his scabbard and handing his sword to the man next to him. I myself was a little worried. He did indeed inspire a fanatical loyalty in this mob, but there were no more than thirty or forty youths, armed principally with logs and hoes and homemade weapons. Certainly they had surprised their way through the castle gate, but I was sure that even now there was a troop assembling below, and Laertes's followers would be caught between a handful of Swiss guards in front of them and a large army behind. In this narrow space they would be chaff to the thresher's flail if the army chose to attack.

'Wait for me here!' Laertes ordered the crowd, and he boldly strode forth into the Great Hall to confront Claudius. Never had he looked to better advantage than now. There was a fire in him, a purpose. I'd liked him well on his earlier visit, but I'd found him, like my father, a little too oily, too unctuous, too willing to lick the soles of those in power. I much preferred this defiant flame, even though it was sparked by the desire to avenge a father who'd held him in no special affection. For the first time I thought how alike my husband and brother were, both of them risking their lives for fathers who hadn't really loved them, both of them staking their lives to avenge the father of their imagination, not the cold father of their actual history. Had Laertes, like Hamlet, forgotten the real father and replaced him with a legend? Do all men transform their fathers into myths?

In any case, I dared not leave Laertes too long alone with Claudius. In addition to the loyalty of the mob, Laertes had his dagger which he had surely anointed with the poison I'd sent him. Besides, I knew Claudius. It was unlikely that he'd make so bold a move as to kill Laertes with witnesses waiting just outside the hall. No, my present fear was that Laertes would kill Claudius, and without Claudius's aid, I had no chance of my own scheme's going forth.

So I shoved my way through the raggle-taggle crowd. The first to recognize me was Behag who'd been one of my childhood players' band, the merry-hearted son of the harbour master's assistant, who'd willingly undertaken any role given him.

'It's Lady Ophelia,' he shouted. 'Laertes's own sister, Lady Ophelia herself.'

A murmur rippled through the crowd. I didn't know whether they marvelled more at my appearing there or at the strangeness of my tattered gown draped with garlands of dead flowers and herbs.

'I must go to my brother,' I said, and the crowd made way for me, shouting out, 'Let her pass.'

I pushed my way past the Swiss guards into the hall.

As soon as he saw me, Laertes turned white and made a sign to avert evil. 'By heaven,' he cried out to me, 'your madness shall be avenged as well as the death of our father.'

The queen looked whiter than the palest ghost in the castle. One of her hands gripped a wad of her skirt so tightly that the knuckles looked like bony skulls, but she stood tall and dignified. Claudius too stood there with bluff magnificence, but I suspected his calm was less the result of inner strength than his knowledge that Laertes's supporters were sandwiched between the Swiss guards and the army. I could tell that before I joined them, the three of them had been discussing my father's death and had reached some sort of precarious balance, but I couldn't read that outcome in the wary expressions of the king and queen. Laertes merely looked stunned by my apparent loss of wits. I felt ashamed to deceive him, but there was no way to tell Laertes why I was putting on my show of madness. Hamlet's life hung on the slender thread of my plan. I burst into another village ballad about a deceitful servant who seduces his master's daughter who then kills herself. *Console yourself with this . . . if Laertes is convinced that you've overturned your wits, it will move you further along toward winning what you seek.* So I danced and capered wildly around Laertes, rejoicing in the shock in his eyes and pity in the eyes of the queen. Claudius, however, watched me the way a skilled hunter might watch a wounded bear, trying to gauge whether it would charge or not.

My hand brushed across the withered garland draped about my waist, and I broke off one of the herbs I'd woven into it and held it out to my brother and swept him an elaborate curtsey.

'Rosemary,' I said, 'for remembrance.' His fingers closed around mine. I would indeed be sorry to see him no more, for he'd been kind to me, but if my plan worked, I wouldn't return again to the court. 'Pray you, love, remember,' I whispered. I must have been very tired, for I felt tears prickle against my eyes. I broke away and danced over to Claudius. I plucked a flower out of the garland and held it up. 'Here's a pansy, for thoughts.'

I heard Laertes whisper something to the queen, but I couldn't make out the words. I handed the king some more herbs and flowers, and then I handed a sprig of rue to the queen and to my brother. There was still more rue, so I gave it to the stone-faced Claudius. 'You must wear your rue with a difference,' I told him.

Our eyes locked for a few moments. *He knows that this is but play-acting. We are both playing deep games.* I forced myself to slide back into my daft expression, dancing and handing out a few more flowers, babbling out whatever popped into my mind. There was no reason to linger. I'd established my madness in the minds of my brother and his followers. I needed to do no more at present. In fact, I needed to give Laertes some time for the impact of my change to sink in. So I warbled a little more of a song and swept out of the room.

The crowd fell silent when I reappeared. I decided to give them as good a show as I gave to the royals, so I sang another mournful love ballad and twirled around, handing out flowers and ribbons to those that I recognized in the crowd. To my shame I rather enjoyed being the centre of their attention again. Before I could finish my new ballad, the crowd tensed and several of them clutched at the hilt of their daggers or tightened their hands on the long sticks they carried. I turned. Claudius and Laertes stood in the doorway between the smashed doors. The crowd surged forward, but Laertes held up his hands and they pulled back, although I sensed they were like a hound straining against the leash of their self-control.

Time for the next step in my plan.

'I would speak alone with the king!' I cried out and spun around and around so wildly that my petticoats spread wide like the petals of a flower.

'Do you witness this, O heaven?' called out my brother in an agonized voice.

'Laertes,' said the king, 'take your followers to the kitchens and tell any of my staff that's still on duty to prepare them drink and bread and such foodstuffs as have been left for tonight's feast.'

A suspicious rumbling rippled through the crown.

'You have done well,' Claudius said in a loud voice so the entire mob would hear him. 'It is honourable and loving for a son to seek revenge for his father. We would never impede you in that quest.' He let his eyes sweep across the gathered folk, and he raised his voice. 'My subjects, you too have done well to champion this unjustly bereft young man. We grant you safe conduct out of our castle.'

You want to disperse them without harm to yourself, I thought.

'We will confer with Laertes apart, and if we cannot satisfy him that there is no need for this revolt, then you have our leave to come again.'

I knew they would never be admitted through the castle's gate a second time.

Claudius turned to Laertes. 'Once you have your loyal followers safely bestowed, join us in our chamber where we'll commune with you straight.'

Laertes glanced back and forth between me and his followers. 'What about my sister?' he asked.

'The queen and ourself will summon attendants to give her care. Fear not. She will be gently treated.' His eyes flickered across me. 'We have much hope of her soon being restored to her right wits.'

Laertes considered for a moment, then nodded and raised his voice to the mob. 'Let us to the kitchens straightway, for I have no doubt but that you're in need of sustenance to fuel your bodies and hearts.'

'Come to us as soon as you've seen your people well bestowed,' Claudius said.

The cheering crowd followed Laertes out of the hall.

'Pretty Ophelia,' the king said in a low voice, 'we must talk.'

'Fetch the queen,' I said, 'for I would speak of matters that concern her nearly.'

Without taking his eyes off me, Claudius called out, 'Gertrude!' In a moment the pale queen appeared. She clung to Claudius's arm for support. 'We will withdraw to our chambers and speak with Ophelia.'

'No more,' she murmured. 'I can take no more of this. The sight of poor Ophelia breaks my heart.'

'We feel sure that her wits will soon be righted. Come, love.' Claudius threw an arm around the queen's shoulder and led her toward their chamber. I trailed after them.

'Well?' Yorick appeared at my side, his eyes glittering.

'The plan goes forward apace,' I whispered.

Ahead of me, the king and queen paid no heed to my whispering if indeed they heard it at all.

'Tell me your plan,' Yorick begged.

I quickly explained to him what I had in mind.

He nodded in approval, his small eyes dancing with delight. 'Very clever. Very clever indeed, Ophelia,' and his praise warmed me. 'I have but two small suggestions.'

As we tripped along the corridors behind the king and the tottering queen, he whispered his suggestions to me. They made sense. It was odd indeed to have the king and queen take no notice of me as I carried on a whispered conversation with Yorick, but I knew they couldn't see the ghost. To them I must have looked as if I was chatting with the empty air.

I stepped into the king's chamber. I'd never been here before. I was surprised that it wasn't as luxurious as the queen's chamber or as elegant as Hamlet's. There was a warrior austerity about it, the chests and tables and even the bed of simple polished wood. The style suited the old king more than Claudius. In his four months as king, I supposed he'd not had time to make it over to fit his own taste.

'How now, Ophelia?' he asked in a cynical voice. 'Have your wits still gone a-begging?'

'Hush,' the queen said. She looked distressed. 'Do not

torment the poor child further. She can no more help her madness—'

'An interesting madness, is it not, my love? We've seen many mad folk in my time . . . including my own nephew . . . and never have we seen madness so pretty or so musical. It's as good as a play.'

'My love,' the queen began, but just then Horatio stepped into the room.

'Your majesties,' he said with a bow, 'I would like to be of help with the Lady Ophelia.' He looked genuinely worried. 'Let me take her from court,' he said. 'I'll find her a quiet place in the country. I'll find a good woman to care for her. Perhaps with rest and fresh air and kindness, she'll come again unto herself.'

I hated to deceive him, yet I didn't want to speak my truth in front of him. His first loyalty was to Hamlet, and I couldn't afford to let Hamlet know of my plan. First, I couldn't trust Hamlet to keep silent counsel. In a fit of madness he might blurt out the whole intelligence to any who would listen. Second, and more importantly, I knew he wouldn't approve of it. No matter that it was for his own good. His mental infirmity was something he denied. Once the plan had been carried through, he'd adapt, but it would be fatal for him to learn beforehand what I intended. So much as I wished to confide in Horatio, I had to deny myself that luxury.

In fact, I needed to get rid of him before I spoke my heart to the king. I knew I had little time to do both things. Laertes might even now be on his way to the king's chamber after settling down his followers at their repast. I thought quickly about ways to send Horatio out of the room. For once, luck sat at my table, for before I put this stratagem into action, a page appeared in the doorway.

'Forgive me, sire,' he said, 'but there be sailors below with a letter.'

Claudius flinched. 'Sailors?' he said, and his tone sounded fearful. 'Letters from whom?'

'I know not, sir. I know only that they come bearing letters.'

'Bring them up.'

Claudius turned away to signal he was done with the page, but the page didn't depart. Instead he said, 'Your majesty misunderstands me. The letters be not for your majesties. They be for Lord Horatio.'

Horatio looked surprised. 'I don't know from what part of the world I should be greeted if not from Lord Hamlet, and he's had scant time to reach the English shores.'

'Bring the sailors here,' Claudius commanded.

'Begging your pardon, your majesty, but they said they were to meet with Lord Horatio in private, sire.'

The queen broke in. 'Perhaps you had best go down, Horatio. I doubt not that the letters bring tidings from my much-missed son.'

Claudius looked like a clenched fist, but Horatio gave a quick bow and then turned to the page. 'Bring me to these sailors.' The two of them hurried out the door. Claudius frowned to see him go, but almost at once he turned back to me.

'Now, Ophelia,' he said in a voice as taut as a rigging rope, 'what means this masquerade?'

48

'For pity,' the queen said, 'leave the poor mad child alone.'

Yorick slipped into the room. He withdrew into the shadows next to the fireplace, although if he stood in full light, no one but me could see him. He leaned forward, his face eager, looking ravenous to hear all that transpired.

'Be of good cheer, Gertrude,' Claudius said. 'This madness is too pat, too pretty. Too like a play to be madness indeed. This is a madness of stage, not the ugly, slovenly madness of the soul.' He cocked his head and regarded me through narrowed eyes. 'Speak, Ophelia. What is it you want of Denmark?'

I hadn't fooled him, but fooling him wasn't necessary to my plan. Indeed, I would have been on a more precarious ledge if he had been fooled. I'd misled the common throng and the folk at court, and that was what I needed to do. 'Safe conduct,' I said. 'That's the first thing I need.'

The queen gaped to hear me speak so reasonably, but Claudius's mouth tightened in grim satisfaction. I kept talking to the king. 'Denmark rules many little islands. I need an island far from this castle, one that can sustain life. I ask that you send me there . . . along with Lord Hamlet. House us and keep us as befits his station. It will be good for his troubled mind to be lodged in a peaceful place far from the strains of royal life. Tucked away thus, he'll not have to answer for the killing of my father and he'll trouble your realm no further. All of us then can rest in peace.'

'But my son is on a ship to England,' the queen cried out. 'I don't know how we can recall him from his present voyage.'

Claudius's eyes bore into mine. 'We don't expect him to return any time soon. Or is it that you know something that we don't?'

I didn't let my gaze waver. 'Should he come back, Majesty, will you give me your word that you will not harm him but only spirit him off with me to the island of your choosing? Think, sire. It will be a good thing for you, for exiled on the island he'll speak no slander against you. Or should he speak them, there will be none on the island in whose hearts his wild words can root and grow.'

'Yours are the wild and empty words, Ophelia, for we don't look to see Hamlet returning to Elsinore.'

The queen added, 'At least not for a long, long time.'

'We don't expect our nephew to cause any more trouble,' said the king.

'Heed me well, sire, for what I propose makes good sense,' I said.

I could hear all three of us breathing hard as if we'd been racing. The queen was the first to speak. 'Ophelia, then are you truly not mad? Was it indeed all a show?'

I ignored her. The sands of my time were running out. Laertes might appear at any moment, and I needed to lay out my entire plan before he interrupted us. 'Claudius, if what you state is true, then the promise I seek will cost you little,' I said. 'If Hamlet doesn't return, it will cost you nothing at all.'

The king's heavy lids closed briefly over his dark eyes, and then he nodded. 'Very well, Ophelia. If Hamlet returns to our shores, we'll spirit him away and set him up to dwell in exile on a distant island.'

The queen gave a little moan.

'Gertrude,' said the king, 'it's for the best. It's dangerous for you, for ourselves, for all of Denmark, even for Hamlet himself, for your son to roam unfettered.'

The tension drained from my body so suddenly that I felt limp as a wet sheet. 'Thank you, your majesty.'

Before I could say more, he held up a finger in warning. 'I give you this promise only on the condition that you tell me how we can spirit this proud young man away. I doubt he'll go willingly, and should we drag him through the streets in chains, then surely his many supporters will rise up against us.'

'I've thought this all out,' I said eagerly, 'and I know just what is to be done. I'll fetch you a potion, that, once in the blood, gives its drinker the identical semblance of death. No breath can be felt, no heartbeat detected. For three days the drinker will sleep, the very picture of death itself, but on the third day the drinker will regain full consciousness and full use of all his faculties. Therefore, when Hamlet returns to Denmark, you must dip a knife, a needle, even a hook in the mixture. Then scratch him until he bleeds, and the potion can enter his blood. In a very few minutes he'll fall fast asleep. I also know a sea captain who can smuggle Hamlet away. Only give me directions to the island of your choosing, and I'll take care of all the other arrangements.'

I could see that Claudius was thinking furiously. The queen still looked dazed. 'I don't understand the least part of all this,' she said.

'Every one of us is the victor in my plan,' I said. 'Even Denmark. We all agree that Hamlet cannot come to rule. The country would indeed founder should he assume the helm of state.' I turned to the queen. 'By the laws of justice, he should himself be put to death for the rash murder of my father—'

'No!' The queen recoiled, her face frightened. 'I've lost one son. I cannot bear to have another slip out of life.'

'Even so! This way Hamlet need not face censure for the murder which, in his madness, he couldn't prevent. Under the aegis of my plan, your majesties will be safe on the throne, safe both from the threat of usurpation by Hamlet or his followers and safe as well from any further calamities his madness might bring about.'

'I don't like to think of him exiled all alone,' the queen objected.

I tried to sound as reassuring as possible. 'He will not be all alone. I'll keep him company.'

It wouldn't be the life I'd dreamed of, but how many of us actually live the life of our dreams?

'You love him well,' the queen said, reaching out to stroke my hand.

I felt a pang. I *had* loved him, but neither wisely nor well. I couldn't confess that I'd loved him in mistake for what I wanted him to be rather than for who he was. I'd loved him because it gave me someone to rescue. I'd loved him because I wanted to attach myself to someone grand and glorious rather than go to the trouble of becoming grand and glorious myself. I'd loved him because it was easier to love someone who appeared to live the life of my dreams than to hammer that life out for myself. Nevertheless, I *had* loved him once, so now I'd care for him as ferociously as if I loved him still. 'He will be well-tended,' I countered.

'The rabble cries out for your brother to be crowned king,' Claudius said. 'We doubt therefore that they'll let us whisk you yourself away and bury your beauty on a distant island. We doubt your brother will permit it, even though it's the very course you yourself have chosen.'

'They will not know,' I said.

'You cannot disappear without a trace. Suspicion will breed that we killed you to make safe our own way.'

'Listen to me. I've thought all this through.' Out of the

corner of my eye, I saw Yorick gesturing me to speak faster. 'I've made certain that dozens of folk have seen me act the madwoman. Now I must disappear, and you will set forth that I've killed myself. Thus they'll besmirch you with no stain from the deed.'

'Kill yourself!' echoed the queen. 'Indeed you must not, dear Ophelia. Self-slaughter is a sin against God—'

'I shall not kill myself in fact,' I told her quickly. 'But that will be the tale you tell, I've worked out all the details.' I was proud of the story I'd created describing my suicide. 'Tell folk that I went wandering for flowers and fell into a brook.' I remembered how my father's second wife was said to drown. 'That my madness prevented me from understanding my own danger. Tell them that I lay in the water, singing snatches of old ballads, until my skirts, weighted with the water, dragged me to my death. Tell this even to my brother. None will doubt the tale if you can make Laertes believe it, and he looks so shaken by my madness that I don't think he'll question this account of my mad death. Once I'm announced as dead, I'll hide me until it's time to board ship with Hamlet and supervise his journey to the island of our exile.'

Claudius tapped his chin with a forefinger, running over my plan in his mind. Then he said at last, 'Your plan has merit. We do think it can dispose of all our difficulties.'

'What of the burial?' the queen asked. 'Dead bodies, even suicides, have to be buried.'

'Tell the people that my death was doubtful. Say that for fear that I might have killed myself, you buried me secretly in an unmarked grave.'

The queen looked nervously at Claudius. 'I don't think our credit with the people sufficient to bring off another hasty burial.'

'Another?'

'Your father,' said Claudius.

I was bewildered. 'My father is not yet buried. Why, he hasn't even lain in state.'

Claudius and the queen exchanged worried looks. Then Claudius said, 'We buried him the very night of his death.'

This thudded into my consciousness. 'Do you say that my father has been three days buried without the rites and honours deserved by one who spent his life giving faithful service to the king?'

The queen looked away, shamefaced, but Claudius met my angry gaze. 'We thought it best to bury him hugger-mugger. We didn't want to fan rumours to full blaze about the manner of his death.'

Poor father. Killed in such an ignoble fashion and then denied the state funeral his fidelity to the crown had earned him.

'Then bury me in public view,' I said, 'but bury me quick. Use as your excuse the suspicious manner of my death.'

'But there will be no body to bury,' said the queen.

This gave me pause, but Claudius had an answer. 'Leave that part to me. I can have something or other wrapped tightly. We will seal it in a coffin and nail the lid shut. None will suspect that there's not Ophelia's body locked within.'

Yorick gave a deliberate cough, and I remembered one of his suggestions. 'There is one danger that remains,' I said. *Laertes.* 'Once my brother understands that it was Hamlet who killed our father, he may wish to kill Hamlet in revenge.' Yorick was correct about this. If Laertes had any inkling that Hamlet wasn't dead, he might hunt him even to the ends of the earth. The success of my plan rested on this need to appease Laertes.

'All these plans are but an empty exercise,' Claudius said, 'because Hamlet will not be returning.' The queen gave a little gasp, and Claudius added, 'At least, not for a while.'

I caught the sound of steps coming down the corridor. It

could be Laertes. I needed to be brief. 'If Hamlet does return, we must not let Laertes kill him.'

'No,' moaned the queen.

I ignored her and continued. 'Majesty, you must channel Laertes's anger instead into something harmless, like a contest of capped swords. That can draw the head off the brew of Laertes's anger. If Hamlet is in his right mind, he'll feel guilty enough about our father's death to oblige Laertes's challenge. I leave it to you to find a way to convince Laertes that a contest of capped swords will pay off his honour and his passion for revenge.' The footsteps were getting louder. 'Tell him it will not be to his credit to kill a madman. Tell him such an act will tarnish his good name.' I couldn't tell if the footfalls were Laertes's or not. I spoke more rapidly. 'All who know you, Majesty, know that you're every inch the diplomat, that you have a silver tongue. Use that to persuade my brother. Convince him that there's greater glory in showing that he can bring Hamlet to the point of death but then stay his hand than to kill the feeble prince outright.' I could see Claudius weighing and measuring my words. 'You may have to offer Laertes something in return, an advancement or a reward of money or some such stuff. But you're the master of persuasion, Majesty. You will know just how to manipulate my brother to your will.' The footsteps turned into this corridor. I spoke more rapidly. 'What might work best is to blend the two acts, the contest of swords and administering the sleeping potion. Anoint Laertes's sword with the sleeping mixture. He is the better swordsman. Let him scratch Hamlet enough to draw blood and thus the potion will enter Hamlet's body and we can carry off our plan.'

'Get out of the room before you're seen conferring with the king!' Yorick urged.

'Someone approaches!' Claudius said. In three strides he reached the wall and lifted one of the hangings to reveal a door underneath. 'Gertrude, take her quickly into your chambers.'

The queen put a hand on my arm and began to pull me toward that door which must join her room to her husband's. As she dragged me away, Claudius called, 'How shall I get the sleeping potion?'

Yorick's instructions about this flew into my mouth. 'Send a messenger to the Herbwife in the village of my childhood. Summon her to the castle this very afternoon. Tell her the queen has a disordered belly. and she must mix a potion to give the queen ease. Within her cottage she has herbs I can use secretly to mix our sleeping potion.'

Yorick spoke up. 'Tell him to send a trusted servant with you who can carry your potion to the king, for afterwards you must straightway go into hiding.'

He was right. It would be foolish of me to risk returning to the castle to seek another audience with the king.

'Send a servant with me,' I said, 'and then he can carry back the sleeping draught to your lordship while I disappear.'

The door to the king's chamber began to edge open.

'Come,' gasped the queen, and she pulled me from the room just as Laertes burst in.

We ducked into the queen's chambers just in time. Laertes didn't spot us. The queen was trembling, and, while we stood there waiting for her to regain her composure, she threw her arms around my shoulders and burst into tears. 'Things are so toppled and scattered that I have no inkling what I should believe.'

I patted her on the back. 'Hush, your majesty. Hush.'

'Everything is out of joint,' she sobbed, 'and I don't see how it can ever be put right.'

'It's as simple as breathing,' I said. 'We give your son the sleeping potion. You tell the world that I've died and you bury a coffin quickly. Then your son and I are off to one of the islands where we shall live forever in peace.' For a moment I debated telling her that I was already her son's wife, but I didn't see how the knowledge would help her at all. Once we'd gone to our exile, let her send a priest to the island to marry us in the ways of the church.

But the queen was as good as a fountain for she couldn't turn off her weeping. For a long while, I just let her weep. Finally I whispered, 'Your majesty, it has been given to you to save all of Denmark. You must go now to the king and my brother and weave them a tale of my death by water.'

'I cannot do it,' said the queen. 'I'm but a poor dissembler.'

'You can,' I countered. In fact, the moment was becoming overripe. She looked half-mad herself with her tear-blotched face and her veil slid halfway down her head. 'Your son is a fine actor, and talent like his isn't a wild weed. He must have inherited his abilities from you. It's only that you have never had the chance to use your own acting skill. At least not until now.'

'No,' she said, but she looked a little pleased. Then, 'Tell me what to say. Give me the very words I must speak.'

From the adjoining room we could hear my brother's voice raised in anger, but I couldn't make out the words.

I wove together a very pretty speech about my death. In my tale, I climbed out on a willow branch to pick flowers. As I spoke, I could see the pictures in my mind. I climbed out farther on the branch when, crack! My armful of flowers and I went tumbling into the water. Even there I didn't give over my crooning, but I continued to sing as the envious water bore me downwards. I even grew misty about the eyes as I worked out this tale of the death of a poor mad girl.

I ordered the queen to repeat the tale. I made one or two corrections, and then I had her tell the tale two more times. At last I sent her forth.

'You will be marvellously persuasive,' I said, 'for all folk know that you've never told a lie in your entire life.'

She still looked troubled.

'We have practised the story, and you have it by heart,' I assured her. 'You tell it well.'

This was a lie. I didn't find her performance convincing, but there was no purchase in telling her so. I'd composed a beautiful speech describing a beautiful death, but I felt a moment's pang that I'd made it perhaps too poetic. Would Claudius object to it, as he did my madness, claiming it was more like a play than like real life? I shoved these doubts out of my mind. I had no time to waste on such bubbles. Besides, real life would improve by being more like plays.

'Go to it,' I said. Perhaps I should have taught her a few gestures to give while she recited my speech, but I didn't think the queen had it in her to be an actor. Only later would I discover how very wrong I was. 'I must to the village, Majesty, to fetch the sleeping potion.'

'Wait until I return,' she said, but I shook my head.

'I must go now while it's still daylight.'

'Remember that the king's messenger must spirit the Herbwife away before you riffle though her potions,' Yorick reminded me.

'Without fail, send a horseman to bring the Herbwife to the castle,' I told the queen. Straightway I pushed her back into the king's room.

From its peg on the wall, I took the queen's blue cloak and pulled it down low over my head. It was a simple matter to slip out of the castle, for the guards watched folk coming in, not those going out. As I crossed the courtyard, I could hear the sound of revelry back by the kitchens, and I knew that Laertes's band was still at table.

About a mile from the castle, a horse and rider galloped past. I was sure the steed carried the Herbwife's summons.

About half a mile further, I heard a voice puffing behind me.

'Lady Ophelia! Good lady . . . stay your steps till I've caught up with you.'

49

Osric, the king's attendant, tottered up to me. His face was bright red with his effort to catch me, and he snatched his blue silken cap off his head and fanned himself with it. 'I was sent by the king . . . to bear you company . . . and to bring something . . . you would send . . . back to his majesty,' he panted.

I disliked Osric heartily. He was a painted popinjay of a fellow, puffed up with his own importance, caring for nothing but currying favour from Claudius, just as he'd fawned on the old king. Osric had sanded himself until he'd smoothed away any knobby bits and splinters of character, and he'd fashioned himself carefully, improving on God's handiwork until he was little more than a magical looking-glass that came to life only when it was reflecting back a glorified image of the ruler of the land. Most ghosts are made ghosts through death, but Osric was a kind of living ghost, killing off his own life in order to haunt the life of the king. My first thought was that I couldn't fathom why Claudius would choose such a hollow, slavish fool to play a role in our private drama, but almost at once I realized that Claudius couldn't have found a creature less likely to betray him. Osric lived only to give pleasure to the king. If Claudius had told him that day was night, I doubted not but what Osric would fall a-yawning and say he must make at once for bed.

I didn't like him, but I could see that Osric was well suited for Claudius's purpose, and after all, it didn't matter a groaning to me which courtier Claudius sent as my escort. All that mattered was my task.

'We must keep still,' I told him. 'If there be any village folk about, it will not serve Claudius's plan should they see us.'

He nodded so vigorously that a length of his long yellow hair fell across his eyes.

We reached the village in good time. I'd put the hood back during our walk, but now I pulled it low again, so that no one would recognize me. I led Osric through the handful of streets to the Herbwife's cottage and motioned him to follow me as I slipped inside.

Her house was cool, dark, and scented by the herbs hanging from the rafters. Once I'd shut and latched the door behind us, Osric fanned himself again with his cap. 'The day is hot,' he said. 'I'm not used to trot around the countryside like a sweating gelding.'

'Hush!' I told him. His face grew even redder, but whether it was from embarrassment or anger at a chit of a girl who dared chastise him, I didn't know. I slipped the key out of its hiding place on the mantle and opened the cabinet that contained the dangerous potions. I wondered if the Herbwife had yet discovered the theft of the potion for my brother's safety. Thank God he was so armed against attack. I ran my eyes quickly across the three shelves of vials and bags as I tried to remember the day that the Herbwife had shown me each one. I couldn't afford to make a mistake now.

'Ooh, what is this?' Osric had crept over beside me and had lifted a vial of green liquid.

'I don't know.' I snatched it from his plump fingers and set it back in its place. 'Don't mess with things that you don't understand.'

'Is she a witch?' Osric asked, his voice excited.

'She is just a woman who studies the properties of herbs. Now hush your tongue so I can concentrate on my task.'

Which was the sleeping draught? I narrowed it to two choices, both in the same squat little jar, both corked with the same little cork. I pictured the Herbwife explaining the different poisons to me. She'd picked up the little jar . . . but which one?

Osric squealed again, and I jumped. 'Pearls!' he said, plucking a glass jar from the shelf. 'Is she so rich, then, as to fill her cabinets with precious jewels?'

'Put that down at once!' I thundered. I remembered the Herbwife explaining to me the properties of those beads. 'Those aren't pearls, fool, but a potent poison. Drop one in a cup of wine, and a single sip will kill you dead.'

His eyes grew wide, and he quickly set the jar back on the shelf.

Then I realized I'd been so busy looking for splinters that I'd missed the log that lay across my path. Of course the Herbwife would take precautions with her potions! All the poisonous ones were marked with red, either in a red bag or with a little red thread tied about their cork or else she'd used berry juice to stain a cross on their stopper. The ones that weren't poisoned were marked with other colours: mustard, green, or brown. I didn't know what each of the other colours signified, but one of the jars I was considering had a red thread wrapped tightly around its stopper. At that moment, I saw clearly in my mind that she'd reached for the other one, the one with the yellow thread, when she'd told me of the sleeping draught.

I snatched that one up and held it out to Osric. 'Take this to the king,' I said. 'Remember, too, he wishes this task carried out in secrecy and in haste.'

Osric nodded and tucked the little jar into a pouch at his waist. 'His majesty bade me tell you, lady, that after you fetched what he needed, it would be best for us to depart single spy and not in tandem. He said it would be easier to slip away unseen if we didn't travel together.'

I was glad of the excuse to be rid of this fool. 'You go,' I said. 'I'll count to a hundred and follow you.'

Osric shook his head. 'Lady, the king said I was to let you be the first to get away. That way if you encounter danger, I can bring up the rear and come to your aid.'

I couldn't imagine what aid this plump, silken-suited partridge could give me, but it made no matter which of us was first to depart. I've never liked waiting, so I saw no reason to cavil at this offer. I locked the cabinet back up and returned the key to its hiding place. Then from a shelf I got down a scrap of paper and the little bottle of ink that I'd brought years ago when I first taught Ragnor his letters.

'Why do you delay?' Osric asked, alarm in his voice. 'We must be swift.'

'Then you be the one to go first. It makes no matter to me, but I must pen a note before I go.'

His alarm seemed to grow. 'What madness is this? Do you leave a record of our theft? Such folly will bring all to ruin.'

He was truly the most despicable man! 'I write a letter on a different subject entirely,' I said. He continued to splutter, but I paid him no more mind. Instead I wrote:

Ragnor, I have Need of one more Favour at your hands. I need you to put your Ship at my Disposal with yourself as Captain. I cannot yet tell you when or what our Destination will be, but if ever you held me in the Smallest Part of Esteem or Affection, I beg you to do as I ask. As soon as I need you, I will send you word. This should all come to pass in a day or two. Please do not fail me.

At the bottom of the page, I drew a sphinx.

'Where are you going?' Osric screeched.

I ignored him and climbed up the ladder to Ragnor's loft. It must have been a merry place back in the days that all the brothers shared it, but now tucked among the piled sacks of herbs, there was but a single pallet and a single chest. I laid my letter atop the pallet, and then I pressed my cheek against the pillow, trying to sniff his scent, but the odour of the drying herbs was too strong, masking all other smells.

I know he told me that he'd do no other task for me, but let him do this one last thing. He knows me well. I wouldn't ask if for myself, but I need him to save Hamlet one last time. Surely he knows I'd never ask this unless it was of the utmost importance.

From below Osric called up, 'Lady Ophelia, we must no longer stay. The day wanes, and we dare not be caught here by any villager who might come a-calling.'

Ragnor had to help me or else I was lost. I didn't trust Claudius. If I left the choice of ship and captain to him, I doubted that Hamlet and I would reach our exiled island alive. My only security was that he wouldn't dare to try to kill Hamlet in such a way that the queen could lay the death at his door. At sea, though, it'd be easy to dispose of us both and then spin a tale about a tempest or pirates with none the wiser. My nervous fingers reached under my collar to twist my necklet back and forth as I tried to think of a way to let Ragnor know there was deadly peril for me indeed if he didn't come to my aid this one last time. Then I got an idea. I lifted the necklet off over my head and laid it on top of the letter. He'd accused me of selling myself for a handful of jewels. Surely if I left my jewels here, he'd see how urgent this matter was.

'Lady Ophelia!' wailed Osric from below. 'You will be our ruination if you don't hasten away.'

'I'm coming,' I snapped. I climbed back down the ladder. Osric looked like a plump babe about to cry. 'Count to a hundred before following me!' I snapped.

I replaced the hood down over my head and slipped out of the house and moved quickly through the village. I had no doubt that folks would tell the Herbwife of a figure in a Virgin blue cloak who'd come to call and left when it was discovered she was out, but, after all, plenty of cloaked figures slipped through the streets to visit her. Chiefly maids who begged for love potions or tired women wanting something that would lengthen the time between babes, so no one in the village would waste time puzzling out the identity of one more disguised visitor. I doubted that Osric would tarry for the entire hundred count, but it made no matter. My plan had been set in motion. Perhaps some of my fellow players – most notably the queen and Osric – didn't have as much skill at this drama as I'd have liked, but my childhood plays about the Flying Catgirl had taught me that it's possible to bring a drama off even if some of the actors have less ability than others. Now all that remained to do was to bring Hamlet to the castle. Once Claudius had fed Hamlet the sleeping potion and let me know the island to which we were to go, I'd send word to Ragnor. Then Hamlet and I would sail away into exile and live out our lives. The cricket in the porridge was, of course, Hamlet's madness, but it might be that on a peaceful island far from the buzz of other people, his madness would fade. After all, Rosencrantz had said that in Wittenberg the spells of madness had been infrequent.

Rosencrantz! A pang went through me. Had he and his companion reached England? In spite of myself, I pictured their startled, terrified looks as they heard they were being put to death. Would they realize it was their friend who had so betrayed them? Or would they think it part of Claudius's scheme?

I didn't want to think of such things. In truth, it wasn't Hamlet's madness that had snuffed out my love. Rather his madness had created two Hamlets – one who was kind, creative, loving, and loyal. One that had seemed to step out of legend. One I'd dreamed myself into loving. But there was also the other Hamlet, the one who hadn't only killed my father or his friends, but who felt not the smallest drop of remorse for his deeds. Both men dwelt in the same body, but Hamlet couldn't control which man would pop out at any moment. If there were a way to slice out the killer and leave the artist, I'd willingly do so. I wondered, though, if his darkness was gone, would his golden light be able to shine as bright? Without the madness, would there still be the magic in him?

Stop it! I lacked Hamlet's appetite for idle speculations. These thoughts were too deep for me to sound, and I suspected in any case they had no bottom. Instead I must trust that in our exile I'd survive his dark times and revel in the bright ones. I wouldn't wallow in thoughts about how bleak it would be to spin out a lifetime on an island with a madman, or that my future with Hamlet was a high price to pay for the indiscretions of a childish heart that had craved a hero. No, from this time forth I'd be a pattern card of virtue, a good and faithful wife. Life on our island wouldn't be bleak beyond endurance. The queen would surround him with comforts. Perhaps there might even be visitors from time to time. Surely the queen herself would come to check on her son, or Horatio—

As if by magic, just as I thought his name, Horatio popped into view, walking purposefully toward the churchyard.

With him was Ragnor.

50

'Gentlemen!' I cried out without thinking. Then it hit me that it would have been wiser to have stayed silent, but it was now too late to call back my greeting.

They wheeled about. Horatio looked wary, and I recalled that when we'd met that morning, I'd been busily playing the madwoman.

'Lady Ophelia?' he asked in a tentative way as if he feared I'd start frothing at the mouth and biting the heads off goslings. 'How fares your ladyship?'

Ragnor merely scowled at me.

I made a quick decision. I'd confide my plan to Horatio. After all, he'd kept counsel about my secret marriage. Surely I could trust him.

'The winds of my madness have blown themselves out, leaving me as sane as an August sky.' I turned to Ragnor. Next to the tidily-groomed Horatio, Ragnor looked wild and strong. 'Ragnor, how do you fare this morning?'

He didn't answer me. Instead he bowed to Horatio. 'You have no further need for me, my lord. This lady can be your guide.' Then he bowed in my direction without looking at me. 'Your servant, lady.'

He began to stride away, but I ran to him. I grabbed hold of his arm, but he jerked away as if I'd become a pillar of flame.

'Ragnor—' I began, but he cut me off.

'Go with this lord, for he's your world, Cat. You and I sail different seas.'

'Ragnor—'

He bowed again. 'I pray you, excuse me, lady.' This time I didn't run after him. I contented myself by calling out, 'Ragnor, don't believe anything you hear of me. You are tired. Lay your head upon your pillow, and all will come right.'

Understand my message, Ragnor. Find my letter upon your pillow. Pray God that you do what my letter asks. He looked savage as he strode through the meadow without a backward glance.

I returned to Horatio who stood there bewildered. 'Lady Ophelia, what means all this?'

'Why are you here, Horatio?'

He hesitated, and then he said, 'I received a letter from Lord Hamlet directing me to this place. He has been brought back to Denmark—'

'I know.'

He blinked, surprised. 'He sent this sailor who rescued him to bring me to where he was.'

All at once I remembered the page who had summoned Horatio to leave Claudius's presence. This must have been what all that was about.

Had Hamlet sent messages to anyone else?

I knew that Horatio was loyal to his friend, so I said, 'Hamlet has a plan to make everything right. My show of madness, that was but part of Hamlet's plan.'

I was certain that Horatio would offer allegiance to the plan more readily if he thought it of Hamlet's devise than if he believed me to be the author of it. I needed to make sure that events didn't speed too rapidly into motion. I didn't want Hamlet to return to the castle just yet so I couldn't risk Horatio's escorting him back there right away. Osric needed time to transport the sleeping potion to Claudius. Of a certainty, I needed more time for Ragnor to read my letter and prepare his ship.

'Lord Hamlet is within the ruined church yonder,' I said, 'but he's sleeping now.' *Do not let him take this moment to show himself*, I prayed. 'He has asked me, his wife, to beg you to return to him on the morrow. He bade me tell you that this afternoon he's too tired to speak with you, but on the morrow he'll reveal all.'

Horatio hesitated, clearly uncertain whether he should go or stay.

'Come in the middle of the morning,' I said, 'for he has much news he longs to tell you.'

By then all the pieces of my plan should be firmly in place.

Horatio looked troubled. 'His letter asked me to come at once.'

I forced myself to give a light laugh. 'You know how changeable my lord is. But I do know, Horatio, that there's no one in all Denmark he longs to see more than you. But Hamlet is weary to the bone. And you understand well that he has much still to confront back at the castle. Grant him this one day's rest to grow stronger before you plunge him back into the maelstrom that is his life.' Horatio still didn't look convinced, so I added, 'I myself will guard him well all through the night and see that no harm comes to him.'

'Let me guard him, too,' Horatio offered.

This was something I most definitely didn't need, Horatio mucking up my plan. 'Your absence at the castle will be noted,' I said quickly. 'All could be lost should the king send out a party to search for you. We cannot allow him to discover Hamlet hiding here. As you love Hamlet, I – his wife – beg you, don't fret him now, but return on the morrow.'

Doubt was still scratched across his face, but he bowed to me. 'It gladdens my heart to see you restored to your right mind, lady. Let us pray that your wits never take their holiday again. Moreover, since you are indeed his wife, I will do as you ask. Let him sleep this night, but I shall be with him early in the morning.'

As he began to leave, I quickly said, 'Horatio, don't let anyone know that my madness wasn't true madness indeed.'

He bowed. 'Lady, I shall tell no one—'

'And if you hear tell of my death,' I added, 'offer no contradiction. Let your mouth be as silent as the grave.'

This made him stop short and stare at me. I stared back, raising my chin. After a moment, he said, 'This seems a havey-cavey business, Ophelia.'

'Hamlet would have it this way,' I said desperately, and once again, the mention of Hamlet's name acted like a charm to soothe him. 'It is Hamlet's wish.'

'I'll remember,' he said. He caught up my fingers and kissed them. 'Guard him well, lady, for he's both my dearest friend on earth and my liege lord.'

'Would you die for him, Horatio?' I don't know what made that question pop into my brain and out of my mouth, but it was in the air before I even knew I was thinking it.

He lowered his head in assent.

'Why?'

He looked surprised at this question. 'Life without loyalty, lady, is no life indeed.'

Then he was off across the fields, and I picked my way through the churchyard to the decaying monastery.

Hamlet wasn't asleep. He was lying on his side on one of the tombs that lined what had once been the nave of the monk's church, reading a book, his back resting against the carved stone effigy of an armoured knight. The entire roof had collapsed, so he lay in dapples of sunlight. When he heard me, he swung himself into a sitting position. 'Ophelia, I have just now learned the most remarkable thing from this volume. Did you know that swans live silent their whole life long, but just before they come to die, they burst into glorious song?'

He looked so vulnerable, unmindful of all the danger and intrigue that swirled around him, that it tugged my heart. At the same time, I was annoyed. *Your life hangs in the balance, and you read a book of natural lore!* Still, I tamped down my irritation. I sank down next to him, snuggling behind his back, and wrapped my arms around his chest. 'It will all be well,' I whispered in his ear.

I spoke as much to myself as to him.

He patted my hand, but rather absently. 'Did you further know that Egyptian geese mate for life, and that if one of the pair comes to die, the other one flies high up in the air and crashes to earth, killing itself in its sorrow? This book claims that parts of the desert in Egypt are cross-laced with the white bones of those geese who died for love.'

I'd been around geese and swans my entire life. I'd never heard a swan sing or seen a goose kill itself from a broken heart. More than that, it seemed to me absurd that a waterfowl like the goose would ever fly through the deserts of any country at all. I didn't know whether to laugh or cry. 'Hamlet, how can you gibber about the deaths of geese and swans when even now our own deaths could be stalking us?'

'Death,' he sighed and tightened his grip on my hand. 'Death stalks us all, but whether to run *from* it as from a dread monster, or whether to run *to* it as to a mother's arms, that's the question that haunts us all.'

It wasn't a question that haunted me. I couldn't imagine running toward death, at least not while I had the strength to run.

He craned his head to look up at the heavens. 'I hate our sky in Denmark. It's so vast that it mocks us, reduces us all to specks beneath its vast, mindless space.'

That surprised me. I didn't see how anyone could help but love the grand expanse of sky over our land – as opulent as a nobleman's cloak.

'Denmark is, in its own way, Ophelia, a desert. A flat land, a land that lays us open to view. Man wasn't meant to live in these bleak, flat spaces.'

I couldn't believe that we were sitting here, talking of philosophy, while our lives were in danger. 'Do you then prefer mountains, my lord?'

He sighed. 'They dwarf me with their height and breadth.'

'Then in what landscape do you feel at home?' Perhaps a small island would indeed be his salvation. He could himself be large in such a small space with no towering crags or windswept breadths of flat land to mock him.

Abruptly he changed the subject. 'What do you think, Ophelia? Is death a long sleep from which we wake not, a communion with darkness and forgetfulness? Or do our very nightmares pursue us even past the grave to a land where we haven't the luxury of waking to escape them? Do you not think, Ophelia, that it's only the fear of those haunted eternal dreams that keep us reluctantly clinging like a frightened babe to our tortured lives rather than racing toward death as toward a lover's embrace?'

I chose my words carefully. 'I think death would be a cold lover, Hamlet. If I could, I would live a dozen lives at once and still not live my fill.' He looked down at a leaf that had drifted onto the tomb from a branch above. Gently I asked, 'Do you not like being alive, Hamlet?'

He gave me a rueful, shamed, secretive little smile. 'I think I'll like it better being dead.' His grin widened. 'Unfortunately you cannot try both states before you make your choice.'

My flash of irritation was drowned in a flood of remorse. It was easy for me to relish life. I didn't have that monster within that overwhelmed my reason and turned me into its puppet. I didn't have spells of blankness, only to be confronted with the horror of the deeds I purportedly committed while I was lost in my dark places. Not knowing what to say, I opened my arms wide, and he snuggled into my embrace the way a tired babe might cuddle against his mother's breast. We sat like that for a long time, and after a while, the light bled from the sky, leaving us in darkness. How I longed to cure this poor, cursed prince. In truth, things might have been easier for him had he been mad all the time, not drifting in and out of madness as a traveller might pass through a floating mist. Perhaps the worst thing of all was that in his lucid times, he learned of the mad things that he did when his wits went wandering. No wonder he feared nightmares. His life as the golden prince had turned into a living nightmare, but here there was no enchanted thread to follow, no key, no path that could lead him out of the labyrinth of his tormented mind.

'I'll keep you safe,' I crooned, even though I doubted he could hear me since he'd fallen asleep. 'Soon, soon, I'll spirit you away to a place where you'll have your paints and books, and there'll be no one you can harm when the madness comes upon you.'

I wriggled to a more comfortable position and wrapped the queen's Mary blue cloak around us both. Then I began softly to sing songs from my childhood. Spinning songs, and the slow, soft songs that women sing to calm fractious babes. Songs of longing from generations of seafarers and songs of loss from centuries of heart-shattered lovers. As I sang, a meadow of stars blossomed over our heads, and for this one night at least, no ghosts disturbed our rest.

51

'Where is it?'

Rough hands shook me awake. Ragnor's face was tight with fury.

There was no sign of Hamlet.

'I don't know what mad game you're playing, Cat, but I'll not let you skip about the countryside, murdering at will. Have you grown as lunatic as that mooncalf you shelter?'

I tried to blink the sleep out of my eyes and brain.

'I rescued your mad prince for you, and even though I told you I'd aid you no more, I was prepared to have my ship ready to whisk you away. But poisoning is the act of a coward, and in the days I knew you, girl, you were no coward.' His grip tightened, his fingers digging painfully into my arm. 'More than that, I cannot believe you'd mix my mother into this murderous plot of yours. How dare you condemn her to death! Mighty cool of you, Cat, to repay her many kindnesses to you with theft and execution.'

I pulled away from him, but he didn't let me go. Clearly he'd discovered last week's theft of the tincture to put on Laertes's sword. I snapped at him, 'I took that tincture only to safeguard my brother—'

'Don't lie to me, girl! We both know that it wasn't a tincture you stole.'

Saint Olaf preserve us! What, then, was he talking about? He glared at me, angrier than ever I'd seen him. I tried frantically to puzzle out his meaning. What I took yesterday was a sleeping potion, not a poison. The only other poison I'd used was the stuff the Herbwife had given me long ago for poor little Blanche . . . and that I'd then given Claudius to use on the king. But Ragnor had known about that. I'd confessed all to him months ago. How dare he wait till now to tax me with that? Indignation gave me strength, and I yanked my arms out of his grasp.

I told you, I told you a long time ago about my role in the death of the old king. How churlish of you to let this lie in you like a sleeping serpent, waiting till now to strike? More than that, Ragnor, what right have you to accuse me of theft? It was your mother who gave me that potion—'

He leaped on my words like a snarling cur. 'Don't come over the innocent with me, Madam. You know very well it's not of that poison I speak.'

He was insufferable! Of course it was that poison, that or the poison that I'd taken for Laertes for I'd had dealings with no other poison. 'If your mother is so afraid of arrest and execution, then why has she such a collection of poisons at all? Tell me that, Ragnor. It seems to me that she collects poisons as a queen might collect jewels—'

'Don't play the fool, Cat. It ill becomes you. We both know very well that she does no harm with her poisons. At most she uses them to ease the passing of a creature past cure.'

'I did filch a poisonous tincture a week since, but I needed it to protect my brother and the future of Denmark itself,' I said.

In spite of himself, his lips twitched. 'Just my ill luck in life to have a mother who jousts with Death Himself and to be bewitched by a girl who wants to save a kingdom single-handed.' Then immediately his face hardened. 'Still and all, you betray my mother with your base actions, Cat. You betray me. Haven't I kept your secrets and done your bidding? I've kept my faith with you, time and time again. Even yesternight when word came to the village that you'd gone out of yourself and drowned yourself in a stream, even then I said naught about the matter.'

So Claudius had spread the story of my death about. I was now officially a ghost. Even though I knew the announcement was forthcoming, it was unsettling to learn of my own death, to be erased from the land of my birth, no longer one of the living.

Had Yorick felt this way when he discovered he was dead?

Had the old king?

Ragnor continued to scold. 'No, I held my tongue until last night when my mother discovered that yesterday when she was gone to court, someone broke into my mother's cupboard, some mysterious woman all muffled up in a blue cloak, and she realized it must be you. Do you deny it?'

'It was true that I went to her cupboard yesterday—'

'I knew it!' he said triumphantly.

'But it was no poison that I took, Ragnor. It was naught but a sleeping potion.'

He gave a mirthless laugh. 'Have you lived so far from truth in these years with the castle folk that you no longer recognize its face? Yesterday you took her deadliest poison of them all.'

The ground fell away. I felt as if I was plummeting from a tower with no way to stop my fall. How could I've been mistaken? My legs and arms turned to ice. 'I thought it a sleeping potion,' I whispered. 'The little jar . . . it wasn't marked with red. I'd thought all the poisons were marked with red.'

Ragnor snorted with disgust. 'Lies, Cat. Lies even now. I see you haven't lost your acting skills, for you could almost convince me of your innocence with those wide eyes, the

way you made your skin go pale. You should open a school
for players, Cat, for you could teach them much about
counterfeiting emotions on the stage.'

I grabbed hold of his shirt. 'Tell me, Ragnor. Was that
little jar I took yesterday filled with poison instead of a
sleeping draught? Tell me quick, for lives depend on your
answer.'

His strong hands closed tight around my wrists. 'Do not
play the fool with me, Cat, for I've tumbled to your tricks.
Yes, you took a sleeping potion, but my mother cares nothing
for that other than to wonder why you didn't ask her for it free
and open. It's the other that worries her sick. That poisoned
pearl you stole. The deadliest poison in her whole collection.
You must give it back, Cat, for it's a jewel too deadly to be
out in the world.'

'I didn't take—' I began, but then I snapped my mouth
shut. Osric! Osric who'd been so curious about the contents of the cupboard. To puff up my knowledge of the
poisons, I'd boasted to Osric about the properties of that
pearl. Osric who'd seen me take the cupboard keys from
their hiding place. Osric who'd told me to go ahead, that
he'd stay behind in the cottage for a count of a hundred
before he followed me. At this my stomach gave a sudden heave, and I turned my head and vomited up a thin,
sour liquid.

When I shakily sat back up, Ragnor had pulled the kerchief
off from around his neck. He blotted my mouth with it. 'Have
you aught to drink?' he asked in a subdued voice.

'No.' It was as if, with that retching, I'd coughed out
all my life force. I felt exhausted, dead. 'I didn't take the
pearl of poison. But I think I know who did. I fear it was
stolen by the man who accompanied me and stayed behind
so that we shouldn't be spotted together as we left the
village.'

For a moment we stared helplessly at one another. Overhead I heard the rasping cry of storks winging their way from far south to their summer home.

'Can you get the poison back?' he asked quietly.

I had to. I had no other choice. Somehow I had to get to Claudius and wrest the poison from him. Failing that, I had to find Hamlet and warn him not to take any drink that Claudius offered. My mind whirled faster than a spinster's wheel. Which to do first?

I'd prefer first to find Hamlet, to alert him to the danger, to beg him to stay in hiding until I'd sorted out this matter. The rub was that I had no notion of where he'd wandered. He could have headed to court to challenge Claudius to a duel, but it was just as likely that a spasm of madness had seized him and he'd meandered off to the Witch Wood – a stand of windblown trees twisted into grotesque shapes – to raise the power of the old, dead gods. Equally he could now be sprawled out in a meadow, rapt in a book about the mating habits of eels. There was no way to know where he'd gone.

Therefore the more efficient course would be to confront Claudius. I just had to think of a ploy to sneak the poison away from him. Could I threaten to expose him to the populace about the old king's death? No. That was my very last coin. If that didn't work, then the pockets of my imagination would be to let. No, I needed to hoard that secret in reserve. It would be foolhardy to take on Claudius with an empty coffer. Better instead to threaten to tell folk about the poisoned pearl so that if Claudius tried to use it, Hamlet's death would be laid to his hands.

Most of all, I'd threaten to tell the queen.

Perhaps that was my best weapon. Claudius, above all things, loved Gertrude. I could go to her, expose his plan.

'Cat?' Ragnor's voice broke into my reverie. 'Are you ill?'

'I must go to the castle to set things right. Please believe me, Ragnor, that it was a servant of the king who took the poisoned pearl. I didn't know that till now. So I must force the king to give it back to me before he does any harm.'

I started away, but Ragnor's hand stayed me. 'Cat, you've forgotten one thing.'

I was sure that I'd forgotten a great many things, but, unlike Hamlet, I didn't choose to moon and dream about the deaths of swans when events needed to be brought to a close.

'Folk think you dead, Cat.'

He was right. I'd forgotten. Do the actual dead similarly sometimes forget that they're dead? Well, there was no help for that. 'Then folk must think me alive again. When they see me in the flesh, they'll know that it was all a hum about my death.'

'They do bury you this very morning.'

I shrugged an impatient shoulder. 'That they don't, for they'll see clearly that I am not in my grave. Now let me go so I can reach the castle in a timely fashion.'

Ragnor didn't let go. 'Cat, even should they believe you to be you and not a ghost, folk now think you mad. Should you start bleating about the king and a poisoned pearl, they'll think it naught but the ravings of a poor witless maid.'

By all the warrior saints, he was right! I could easily show I wasn't dead, but it would be hard to prove that I wasn't mad. Oh, I'd thought myself so clever to peacock about in front of so many folk, showing off my madness, thinking it would protect me. Now it'd proved my own snare. My very weapons had shot me down.

'Come away with me now, Cat,' Ragnor urged. 'Let me sail you to England. You will like it there. My mother's people will help us, and Judith will give you safe harbour. You can start a new life, free from this castle of madmen and murderers. My ship lies ready. Come with me now, Cat, and all will be well.'

For one craven moment I was tempted. The thought of exploring new lands, of finally sailing far out to sea, to see Judith again, to start over clean and new . . .

To cast Hamlet adrift. To leave him to his death.

He seeks death. He loves death more than he loves you.

In my mind's eye I saw the Flying Catgirl watching me closely. 'I cannot,' I told Ragnor sadly.

'Why not?'

'If you were shipwrecked and had a wounded passenger clinging to the board on which you lay, you'd never kick that passenger off into the sea so that you could make faster headway, would you?'

Ragnor frowned. 'Our cases are different. I'm captain of my ship so my duty is to care for even the lowliest member of my crew.'

'We are all of us, in our own ways, captains. So I must tow Lord Hamlet to safe waters.'

For a moment we stared at one another across a chasm as wide as the sea itself. Then he said harshly, 'He wouldn't do the same for you.'

Into my mind flickered so many memories: Hamlet atop the castle at the Midwinter festivities, the torches blazing behind him; Hamlet reading sonnets to me in the candlelit palace of ice; Hamlet nestled in my arms last night beneath the panoply of stars.

'Unless I save him, he'll be lost forever,' I said slowly.

Ragnor's face tightened. 'And you've always longed to be a queen.' He swept me a bow. 'Forgive me, your majesty, for trespassing on your royal business.'

He turned and strode out of the ruined church. I wanted to call him back, but I doubted he'd believe me if I tried to tell him that I wasn't battling for Hamlet because he was a prince, but because he was a broken man who lacked the skills to save himself. My chest hurt as if my heart had been carved out leaving only a bleeding wound in its place. I still felt queasy and a little dizzy, but I wouldn't sit about, paddling in a pool of speculation. If I was to set everything right, I must be up and doing. I'd go to the castle and talk with the queen. Ragnor was right. My show of madness had closed off my chance to enlist the populace to my ranks, but the queen had the power to turn all to rights.

In her lay all my hope.

52

I kept off the roads. Once in the distance I spotted a large procession heading toward the churchyard. *That crowd must be my funeral procession.* If so, it was all to the good, for with the king occupied and the castle emptied of folk, I could more easily creep into the queen's chambers. Fortune finally smiled on me.

My chief concern was how to slip past the porter and so gain admittance to the castle, but there Fortune also seemed to offer me a helping hand. When I reached the gate, I saw the porter engaged in laughing conversation with the driver of a wagon full of straw. I was able to burrow down in the back of the wagon, and so ride all the way to the stable. When the driver left to fetch some lads to help with his unloading, I tumbled out and ran back to the keep. The courtyard was otherwise empty, and while I could hear a few faint grumbling voices from the stable behind me and some laundry maids singing as they pounded their washing tubs, the only other living creature in the courtyard was a limping hound sniffing out the foundations of the guardhouse.

As I drew near the door to the secret passage to the royal chambers, Yorick rushed out to greet me.

'Our plan proceeds apace,' he said, his little eyes twinkling. We ducked into the shadows. 'The king is prepared to set Laertes and Hamlet at swordplay. It lacks only Hamlet's presence in the court.'

'Did the king anoint Laertes's sword with the sleeping potion I sent him?'

Yorick closed one eye in a wink. 'The sword has been anointed. All is ready.'

I felt my muscles relaxing. If the king had used the sleeping potion on Laertes's sword, then he must not be planning to use the poisoned pearl. Apparently he'd secured it to use only if the initial plan failed. I was determined to make certain that my plan didn't fail. 'Was that my funeral procession that I passed?'

'The king thought it best to bury you quick, the better to spread the news of your untimely death.'

I gave an involuntary start.

He chuckled. 'Even so. Believe me, I know well what a peculiar sensation it is to watch your own funeral.'

This remark of Yorick's plunged straight into the wound that masqueraded as my heart. 'Have you been dead for a long time?' I hoped this wasn't a rude question.

He gave his twisted smile. 'More than twenty years.'

Longer than I'd been on earth! 'Did you mind so awfully coming to die?'

The smile faded from his lips, and he looked away from me, seeming to peer a great distance into the past. 'Yes,' he said slowly. 'Yes. I'd been at court for less than a year, but that handful of days was more marvellous than my entire past. In my own village I'd been a figure of fun, the mocking post of all who were bigger and stronger than I, but at court I was regarded as a great wit, a popular fellow who had the favour of the king and both his young sons. The queen treated me with a gentleness that I'd never known, and I was the special playfellow of the younger prince. I'd never dreamed that life could be so sweet, and I foresaw a wealth of years stretching out in front of me.'

I started to ask what went wrong and how he'd come to

die, but I instantly decided it would be rag-mannered of me to probe further, so I shut my mouth, my questions stillborn. Yorick seemed heavy-laden with painful memories, and I didn't choose to emburden him the more.

What now should I do? It seemed clear that Claudius had fallen in with my plan. Perhaps the wisest course would be to put the theft of the poisoned pearl out of my mind and concentrate instead on checking that all was indeed in place to whisk Hamlet's drugged body down to Ragnor's boat and away to the chosen island.

As if he could read my thoughts, Yorick said, 'What you should do is hide yourself away. Claudius has things well in hand. Let him take the reins. Above all, don't distress yourself about that poisoned pearl.'

I looked at him, stunned. 'Poisoned pearl? I said nothing about a poisoned pearl. Why do you mention it?'

For a moment he looked discomposed as if he hadn't meant to say what he did, and then he gave a laugh. 'Oh, I know that Osric filched it from wherever you went to get the sleeping draught. But it's nothing, nothing at all. Less than nothing. Put it from your mind.'

Something in his speech didn't ring true. I stared at him, trying to snatch at what was askew, but the answer hovered just out of my reach.

'Your funeral procession will be returning any moment, Ophelia,' he said in an urgent tone. 'You must hide and wait for Hamlet to arrive. If you're found now, then all our plans will come to naught.'

His mention of the poisoned pearl unsettled me. No, I couldn't leave this matter to chance, even though I presently seemed to be Fortune's favoured child. I would still go to the queen and tell her of it. I wouldn't be so churlish as to plant suspicions of her husband in her head. I'd merely warn her that the pearl was in the castle and that it was dangerous.

But why was Yorick so agitated by his mention of the pearl?

'I'll take me off and hide away,' I told him. 'Let us pray that my plan for Hamlet meets with success.'

He bowed. 'I too pray that within the space of a few hours Hamlet will indeed find the peace that he so richly deserves.'

I slipped past the rain barrel to the hidden passageway, and in a few flaps of a swan's wing, I was up the stairs and scratching at the door that led to the queen's chambers.

I'd hoped that Elspeth, on account of her advanced age, had remained behind, but no one responded to my scratching. I knocked boldly, but there was still no response. It would certainly never do for me to wander about the castle, particularly since I was thought dead, so I curled up on the step and leaned my ear against the doorway in hopes of hearing the queen's return.

I wouldn't have believed it possible, but in the quiet darkness, I fell asleep.

It was the sound of muffled voices on the other side of the door that woke me. I was shocked that I'd slept, but the events of the past few days had tired me greatly, and I couldn't seem to muster the abundant energy that I was wont to have. I strained my ears to distinguish the voices on the other side of the door. If it was the queen and Elspeth, all to the good, and if it was the queen and Hamlet, all the better. The only danger was that the king might have accompanied the queen back to her chamber. I strained my ears to listen harder. The voices both seemed female, but I couldn't make them out clearly enough to be sure. This was no time to delay, though. If I didn't act now, I could have no expectation of another audience with the queen. Even if it the king had accompanied her, surely I could be quick-witted enough somehow to turn that to my own advantage.

There's a circle in hell just for cowards. Time to be bold. Seize the devil by the forelock and damn the consequences.

I scratched on the door.

53

Nothing happened.

I scratched again.

Nothing.

A dreadful thought hit me. What if the queen didn't know there was a secret entrance to her chamber? What if she thought the noise nothing more than the scratching of a mouse?

I pounded against the door with my palms, and I cried out an entreaty. 'Let me in, please, please, let me in.' I pounded harder and harder, ignoring the pain in my hands. What if Claudius was pouring Hamlet some poisoned wine, even as I tried to catch the queen's attention? I began to scream like a trapped ferret.

Just then the door swung open. If it had been well-oiled, I'd have tumbled forward on my face, but years of disuse had made it stiff, so I was able to step out of its way just in time.

Elspeth stood holding the door.

'Ophelia!' she exclaimed in her age-cracked voice. Her odd eye whirled in its socket.

I rushed past her to the queen, the only other occupant of the chamber.

In truth, I'd never seen the queen look so ill. Instead of a woman, she seemed a mason's study for an effigy whittled from sickly yellow-white tallow.

I threw myself across the room to kneel at her feet, catching the hem of her gown in my hands. 'Your majesty, all will be lost if you don't bestir yourself to save things.'

'Why, Ophelia,' she said, stooping down to put her hands under my arms. 'What need is there for this passion? Stand up! All goes smoothly according to your plan.'

I let her raise me to my feet, but as I did, I saw with a shock that on the hem of her gown, my hands had left red streaks like smudged roses or pawprints of blood. I must have banged them raw beating on the door. She too noticed the stains. Elspeth,' she called to the old woman who was shouldering the door closed again, 'fetch a basin to wash off Ophelia's hands and some cloth to bind them.'

I blurted out, 'There's no time for that, your majesty.'

She shook her head. 'Everything goes like clockwork, child. Fortune favours us. My son himself appeared at your grave. He was heartbroken to think that you'd died, and he shouted out he loved you.'

By Saint Helga of the snow, I'd forgotten to tell Hamlet that I was faking my own death. Stupid, stupid Ophelia! For a moment my confidence wobbled, but it steadied back in place as soon as I realized that in three days he'd learn the truth, and our reunion would be all the sweeter for it.

The queen went on, 'He grappled with your brother.'

'Right in the hole that was dug for your grave,' Elspeth chimed in.

'But the king seized on your idea and turned their enmity to a formal challenge. It's to take place immediately down in the Great Hall, and the whole court is to witness the swordplay. What could be better?'

'Hamlet's life may be in danger!' I said quickly.

She gave me a tired smile. 'Laertes is the better swordsman, true enough, but the king has spoken with him privately, and his majesty assures me that your brother will not kill my son but will scratch him only enough to let the sleeping drug do its worst.'

'Laertes is not the danger, Majesty. It's Claudius who wishes to kill the prince.'

The queen reared back, and then shocked me to my core by slapping me hard across my cheek. 'Do not speak such nonsense, Ophelia. Claudius loves my son. He would never harm him.'

'But, your majesty—'

'If you keep on with such lies, I shall think you every bit as mad as my poor Hamlet.'

'Claudius knows that Hamlet wishes to kill him because Hamlet is convinced that Claudius killed the old king.'

'Yes, we all know that my son suffers from mad fancies. But don't tell me, Ophelia, that you too have fallen prey to his sick fantasies.'

Should I tell her the entire truth, confess my part in the affair? No, let her live in blissful ignorance. Of late she'd drunk too deep of sorrow. By the end of the day, I'd have the sleeping Hamlet carried aboard Ragnor's ship and we'd be on our way to our new home. Claudius and the queen could then live together in untroubled happiness and peace. What good would it do to rob the queen of all comfort? I said merely, 'Claudius has obtained a deadly poison, Madam.' Words ran out of me like grain through a rip in a sack. 'It's in the form of a pearl. If he dissolve it in a cup of ale or wine and offer it to an unsuspecting Hamlet, then nothing on this earth can save his life.'

The queen's eyes grew enormous in her face, like holes burnt in a shift.

Elspeth glared at me. 'Why do you torment the queen so?'

'In case Claudius tries to kill Hamlet.'

'My husband wouldn't do that,' the queen whispered. 'All

is in place to spirit my son away to an island where he can live out his days in peace and safety. Claudius has no need to kill my only remaining son.'

Just then the air was shaken with the blare of trumpets.

'It's the contest between Lord Hamlet and young Laertes,' Elspeth said. 'It's about to begin.'

'I know Claudius. I love Claudius. He would never hurt the least hair on my son's head,' the queen said.

'Madam, come,' Elspeth plucked at the queen's sleeve. 'There will be no poisoned cup. All shall go off just as planned. You will see.'

The queen stood torn by uncertainty, chewing on her lower lip. Her little dog, Trey, awakened by the blare of trumpets, was frisking about her feet.

'Go, your majesty,' I said. 'Pray God that all will be well, but should you catch sight of the poisoned pearl, promise me you will find a way to stop Hamlet from drinking.'

'My husband would never kill my son,' she said in a voice like a shiver turned into sound.

The trumpets again blared forth.

Elspeth gave her a push. 'Madam, come along. The king and the court are waiting.'

The queen opened her mouth and said, 'Ophelia—'

Before she could say anymore, Elspeth was tugging her toward the corridor. 'Madam, come. If your plan goes off, this may be the last time to see your son.'

The queen gave me a helpless look, but she gathered up her skirts with their blood-daubed hem and hurried after Elspeth. I sank onto the bed, breathless. Trey scampered up into my arms. I patted him absently a few times. *Let the queen take my warning seriously*, I prayed, although it didn't appear that she heeded my words.

Claudius is a cautious man, a private man. He would never

harm Hamlet in view of the entire court. Nevertheless, I couldn't bear to sit here waiting. I hurried after the queen.

Fortunately, by then the corridors were deserted. Since I mustn't let myself be seen, the ideal place from which to watch the contest between my brother and husband was the minstrel's gallery. I slipped through its door and gingerly picked my way up the crumbling stairs, thinking for the hundredth time that it was a shame that such a beautiful castle would be crumbling from within. It would be prudent to watch the proceedings from one of the spy holes, but I couldn't bear to restrict my vision in that way. *If I stay in the shadows in the back of the gallery, I'll be fine. Folk in the hall will be transfixed by the swordplay. There's no reason for anyone to look up at this deserted gallery.*

By the time I reached a place from which I could see clearly, the contest had already begun. My first glance assured me that the men weren't equally matched. For all Hamlet's beauty, he wasn't agile, and Laertes's movements were much more graceful and subtle. Hamlet's face was already pink with exertion, and he was breathing heavily. Under most circumstances, by now Laertes would have made short shrift of this contest, but it was also clear that Laertes was in the throes of passion, and his fury made him over-reach. There was an ugly set to my brother's jaw and he made impulsive lunges. I wanted to call out, *Patience, you fool. If you're but patient, you will wear him down, for even a half-wit could see that Hamlet hadn't the stamina nor stomach for long play.* I hadn't been watching more than two minutes when Hamlet managed to score a touch against Laertes.

Then I spotted something that turned my blood to ice.

54

A servant knelt before the king, a silver chalice of wine in his hand. The king stood tall, holding a pearl high in the air.

The Herbwife's poisoned pearl.

'Hamlet, this pearl is your reward,' he announced, his voice ringing through all the hall. He dropped it into the cup. 'Here's to your health.' Then he motioned the page to take the cup to Hamlet.

Don't drink! Before I could scream out a warning, I saw the queen rise and reach out a hand.

Hamlet shook his head at the page. 'I'll play this bout first. Set it aside.'

The fight began again, but I couldn't tear my eyes away from the poisoned cup. From the corner of my eye I saw that the queen was watching it too.

She will stop Hamlet from drinking, I assured myself. *She saw the pearl and now knows I spoke the truth. She will send the cup away. Since there was but the single pearl, there will be no other poison and all will be well.*

A great shout went up. To everyone's surprise, Hamlet had scored another hit. He moved to where the royal pair sat and mopped his brow. Then, to my horror, I saw him reaching for the poisoned cup.

The queen snatched it from his fingers. He looked surprised, but Claudius turned white. Then, quicker than thought, the queen gave Claudius a hard look and spoke something to him.

As he shrank back, she raised the cup, and drank its poisoned contents.

'No!' I screamed, but the crowd, thinking she toasted her son, sent up a cheer that drowned my words.

Now there was nothing I could do to save her.

She held herself upright through sheer will alone. She reached out a tender hand to Hamlet's face and stroked it, but he broke away impatiently and returned to the contest of swords.

I paid no attention to the swordplay, but kept my eyes fastened to the queen. There had been so many deaths of late, but this was the first heroic one. She'd sacrificed her own life to save her son, and only Claudius and I might ever know. I saw that the king was watching her anxiously, but she kept her face turned away from him. Soon she sank down into her chair, her hand clutching the neck of her gown as if it were choking her. Unbidden, tears began to run down my cheeks.

There was a cry from the centre of the hall, and I saw Hamlet holding his shoulder and glaring at Laertes. Then Hamlet took his hand away, and even up in the gallery I could see the trickle of blood on the cloth of his doublet. He let out a cry and lunged toward my brother, grabbing hold of Laertes's doublet with his hands, dropping his sword. He shook Laertes who pushed him back, and the contest of swords degenerated into a match of fists until the king ordered them parted. Osric and several other retainers pulled them apart and handed them the swords again.

Only then did I notice that the red-hilted sword that Laertes had been wielding was now in Hamlet's hands. Laertes stared down in horror at Hamlet's gold-hilted one clutched in his own hand.

How silly of Laertes to be upset over such a little matter. Since his own sword had been tinted with the sleeping mixture, a scratch now from Hamlet might send him snoring for three days, but that would be nothing. Less than nothing. I was annoyed with my brother for being such a baby, especially in the presence of the dying queen.

Hamlet noticed no difference, but set to work with a fury, carving strokes ferociously through the air. Startled, Laertes fell backwards, defending himself but looking a little bemused like someone awakened untimely from a deep sleep. Then all at once he tripped, and as he fell to the ground, Hamlet slashed him across the upper arm with the sword he now held, drawing blood. I gave a bitter laugh. Now we'd have two sleeping princes in Denmark. It was almost like the start of a legend. Then Hamlet threw the blade aside and leapt again on Laertes, and the two grappled and rolled about on the ground as if this were now a wrestling match.

Folk were shouting in anger, and the king's retainers sprang again to part the two men. They clambered to their feet, still clutching the wrong swords, and glared at each other like two bulls penned in the same pasture. Before they could again go to it, the queen fell to the ground.

Several women screamed. Elspeth knelt on one side and quickly loosened her collar, and the king knelt on the other side and fanned her face. Hamlet pushed his way through the crowd clustered around her. I saw the queen's lips moving but I couldn't make out her words. Hamlet bent his head over her, his eyes widening as he listened, but almost immediately I saw her body give way into the slump of death.

Hamlet sprang to his feet. 'Lock the doors and let no one escape!' he shouted, his voice ringing clear above all the lesser sounds.

Then things began to happen very quickly. My brother fell to the ground, and Hamlet rushed over to him. I couldn't hear what Laertes was saying, but quick as a flash of lightning, Hamlet sprang for the king. One hand grabbed his shoulder, but with the other he plunged the red-hilted sword toward the king's heart. Claudius twisted about, and the sword plunged into his shoulder instead.

Had the queen been alive, all of this would have been as good as a comedy. None of the blows were fatal, and now all three men scratched by Laertes's sword would have three days' nap before being given a second chance at life.

Would God the queen had been so fortunate.

But then Hamlet grabbed up the poisoned cup from off the floor. He held it to Claudius's lips. The crowd was stunned to silence.

'Drink off this potion! Follow my mother!' Hamlet commanded.

Claudius struggled, but Hamlet shoved the cup hard against his mouth, and when he at last let the cup fall, it was clear from the wine stain about Claudius's mouth that the dregs of the poisoned wine had been poured down his throat.

Claudius stared balefully at Hamlet for a moment, and then his knees buckled under him and he fell to the floor, his head banging hard against the polished wood. Hamlet rushed back to my brother whose mouth was moving, but suddenly there was so much screaming and crying in the hall that it would have been impossible to make out the words of a vigorous man and certainly not one as weak as my brother.

A terrible realization hit me.

With the queen and Claudius both dead, I was the only one who knew that Hamlet and Laertes weren't killed indeed, but were in the throes of that powerful sleeping potion that counterfeited death. Unless I did something, they'd both be mistakenly buried. I had to make my way down to the hall and save them, even though I was supposed to be dead myself.

Just then I caught sight of something that nearly undid me entirely.

Yorick had leaped onto the king's throne chair. He was

hopping up and down in a savage dance, a death grin tight across his mouth. He was laughing wildly as he capered around in a circle, whirling like a miniature berserker of yore or a drunken dwarf.

I had no time to sort out this new riddle of his behaviour. I needed to get to the floor of the Great Hall and make everything right. At least as right as it still could be made.

As I pushed my way down the stairs from the minstrel's gallery, the air was shaken by the sound of a cannon's salute. Where had that sound come from? It couldn't already be the guns going off to signal the death of the king. There hadn't been time to send a message to the troops.

Once I reached the floor of the hall, the press of folk was so thick and tangled that I wasn't able to make my way through the crowd, not even a few paces. They all pushed forward to gawk at these unexpected doings, and no one paid the least mind to my cries for passage. I tried this way and that, but there was always a solid wall of folk ahead of me blocking my way.

Then I became aware of the sound of drums. Suddenly the doors to the hall, the doors that Hamlet had ordered closed, were smashed open with a loud crash.

55

The noise in the hall stopped immediately. At first I couldn't see over the heads of people pressed around me, but then the crowd began to pull back, leaving passageway to the dais, and as it pulled, it thinned out till I could see an honour guard of soldiers dressed in the scarlet uniforms of the Norwegians who'd accosted me in the wood several days earlier. In their midst stood an elderly man in elaborate full court dress. Next to him stood a high-ranking soldier who looked to be about Hamlet's age. Prince Erik Strong Arm. He was clearly their leader. His air of command bordered on arrogance. He raised a hand and the crowd fell silent. Then he said, 'Where is this sight?'

Horatio, kneeling on the ground and cradling the body of Hamlet in his arms, was the only one who dared answer. 'If you seek something amazing, then you may cease your search.'

The cool eyes of Erik Strong Arm flickered over all four of the bodies lying there. 'This looks like havoc. What feast, proud death, is this that you've struck so many princes at one shot?'

The older man next to him said, 'This sight is dismal, and my news from England comes too late to tell the king that his commandment is fulfilled. Rosencrantz and Guildenstern are dead.' I felt a pang as I remembered Rosencrantz with his sad, scarred eye and Guildenstern with his thatch of unruly hair and his pugnacious manner that defied his small stature. 'Who now will thank us?' the English ambassador asked.

'Not this prince,' Horatio said, lowering Hamlet's body gently then rising to his feet. 'He wasn't the one who commanded their death.' He walked over to Erik Strong Arm. 'You come timely back from your Polish conquests. Give orders that these bodies be placed high on a stage for the people to view. Let me speak to you and the world how these things came to pass. I can tell you everything.'

'Let us haste to hear it.' Erik's cold eyes seemed to smile, but his mouth remained untouched by expression. 'With sorrow I now embrace my fortune, for I have some rights in this kingdom and now I must claim the throne.'

Whispers rippled through the crowd. Many of the listeners remembered that the old King Hamlet had risked his very life to prevent just such a thing from happening.

Horatio's voice rang out steadily, matching Erik's in volume. I admired Horatio's composure, his courage in giving orders to a prince surrounded by armed guards. 'I'll speak also of that, and of the support the dead prince gave you for this action. As he died, he named you his successor.'

Erik's jaw tightened as if he was suppressing the smile which had crept down to his lips.

Horatio continued, 'But first let the bodies be placed in state so that no more mischance can take place while men's minds are wild with grief.'

Erik gave a single nod. 'Let four captains bear Hamlet, like a soldier, to that stage, for if he'd come to the throne, he would have proved most royal.' It was clear that for Erik there was a practical advantage in presenting Hamlet as both sane and wise since Hamlet had chosen to name Erik as his successor. Doubtless he would have the history of Denmark rewritten to portray Hamlet as the John the Baptist to Erik's Jesus Christ. Erik's voice pulled me back to the moment. 'As

Hamlet passes out of this hall, let the soldier's music and the guns speak loudly for him. Take up all the bodies. This is a sight more fitting for the battlefield than for a royal court. Go, bid the soldiers shoot.'

Four of the honour guard stepped forward to lift up Hamlet's body.

Now was the time. I had to make this new king understand that Hamlet and my brother weren't truly dead.

Desperation gave me strength, and I shoved my way through the stunned crowd.

'Stop!' I called out.

ACT FIVE

My Final Treason

56

Murmurs rippled through the crowd as I passed.

'It's that mad girl returned from the grave.'

'The ghost of Lady Ophelia walks among us.'

'It's judgement day, sure, for the dead have come back.'

Several of them made the sign of the cross.

I ignored them. I threw myself at the feet of the new king. 'You must listen to me for I have something of great importance to tell you.'

The whispers in the crowd grew louder. Even Horatio looked shaken to see me.

Erik Strong Arm's eyes were as cold as a January pond. 'What is this creature?'

Horatio stepped forward and raised me to my feet. 'This is the Lady Ophelia,' he said. 'Wife to Hamlet.'

There was a collective gasp, and then the crowd's sounds grew to a roar.

Someone called out, 'She is dead.'

Someone else called, 'We buried her this very morning.'

The Norwegian prince's icy eyes swept me up and down. 'You don't look like a ghost,' Erik said in his flat voice.

'I am not dead,' I said defiantly, and immediately thought what a stupid thing that was to say.

'Indeed?' Erik murmured. His face was impossible to read.

'I must speak with you,' I said. 'For Hamlet, neither is he dead. Nor my brother. They do but sleep, my lord, and you must not bury them or they'll die for always. Their lives now rest in your hands.'

The crowd began to shout out questions. An expression of fury tightened Erik Strong Arm's face. He made a motion and two of his soldiers grabbed my arms. I struggled to free myself, screeching, 'There was a sleeping potion on the blade of my brother's sword. He didn't poison Hamlet. He merely put him to sleep. Now we must save them both.'

Erik's eyes flickered about the room like the tongue of a serpent. Then he lifted his hand again, but this time the room didn't fall silent. He nodded to his guards, and all but the ones carrying Hamlet's body and the two holding me moved toward the crowd, weapons drawn. They shouted at the crowd to quiet down, and after a few moments, the crowd did indeed grow still.

'What is this creature saying?' Erik asked Horatio in a low voice.

Horatio sighed. 'After her father died, the poor thing went wandering in her wits. For a brief space she became sensible again, but I fear the deaths of her brother and husband have once more sent her mind begging.'

'I'm not mad!' I screamed. 'I speak the truth! If you bury Hamlet and my brother, you will kill them.'

I could see in Erik's eyes that he itched to slap me into silence, but his inner discipline kept him rigid. He told Horatio, 'Come with me at once to sort this coil out out of the hearing of the common herd.' He gave one nod to the soldiers who held my arms. 'Bring her along. I dare not let her roam free, spreading these groundless rumours and inciting folk to foolish ideas and even more foolish acts.' He raised his voice to fill the hall. 'Let the soldiers bear the bodies to the chapel, and let all who were loyal subjects of the royal family follow them and pay tribute even now while grief is green.'

Then he spun about and strode out of the Great Hall. The

two guards hustled me along in a rough fashion. Horatio trotted beside me, urging me to calm myself and that all would be made well.

'I'm not mad. They do but sleep,' I screamed over and over. 'We must not bury them!'

The soldiers dragged me into a nearby antechamber, a room that the old king and Claudius had used to receive members of the lesser nobility and ambassadors from minor principalities. Erik jerked his chin toward the door, and his soldiers released me and went to guard the entrance. Horatio began to speak, but Erik said, 'I would first hear what this creature wishes to say about Hamlet's not being truly dead.'

I poured forth my tale about how the king was going to send Hamlet away into exile and had therefore arranged this whole affair, but how he'd apparently poisoned a cup to make doubly sure that Hamlet wouldn't be free to kill him, and how the queen had drunk the cup to save her son, and now how I was the only one who knew the truth.

When I'd finished, Erik said, 'What say you, Lord Horatio? Is there any splinter of truth in the plank of her tale?'

'It is true that Claudius poisoned the cup and that the queen drank first, but I saw nothing to suggest that it was anything more than an accident, sire,' Horatio said.

'The queen knew about it. She drank to save her son,' I protested.

'More than that,' Horatio said, 'I cannot think that if he'd intended to drug Hamlet merely, the king would also try to poison him. This makes no sense.'

'He'd meant merely to drug him, but he lost his nerve,' I cried out. 'He tried to make assurance doubly sure.'

Horatio ignored my outburst, 'Laertes himself said that Claudius had poisoned the sword that killed Hamlet. He didn't speak of a sleeping drug. He spoke of poison.'

'No,' I cried. 'Perhaps he believed it was poison. The king

was a ready liar, and doubtless he told my brother that the sword was poisoned when in fact it was dipped in a sleeping potion.'

'Laertes spoke of poison,' Horatio said. 'I know only what he said.'

Frantically I said, 'All I ask is that we wait three days. Surely we can hold them in state for three short days. Let time prove me a liar. Just don't bury my brother and my husband before the three days of waiting be up. Then will everything be made clear.'

Erik spoke up. 'Lady, your tale flies in the teeth of sense. I cannot stomach that the king would employ both poison and a sleeping draught.'

'I don't perfectly understand why he did so, but know you this – the queen died to save her son. Do not let her sacrifice be in vain. Keep watch on Hamlet for three days and learn that my wild tale is true.'

'Is it possible, my lord?' Erik asked Horatio.

Horatio hesitated. Then he said, 'I cannot reckon when Ophelia would have been able to tell the queen this, for by her own account, she didn't learn that the poisoned pearl was missing until early this morning. She didn't speak to the queen at her own funeral—'

'I spoke to her back here at the castle, after she returned from the funeral but before she joined the king just now in the hall.'

Erik raised an eyebrow at Horatio, but Horatio shook his head. 'Ophelia, this cannot be. I know the king mounted guards outside his chambers and the queen's. The guards would never have let you in to speak with that poor lady. They would have known you to be dead, so if they'd spotted you, they'd have dragged you before the king, not stepped aside meekly and given you access to the queen.'

'I didn't use the regular door! I used the secret passage.'

Both men looked sceptical, but I explained as clearly as I could about the private passageway.

'Go investigate this tale,' Erik ordered one of the guards.

'Let hours, not my words, prove the truth of what I speak,' I pleaded. 'Delay the burial for three days. Then you will see that I speak true.'

Horatio came to my aid. 'I do believe that Ophelia is out of her head with grief, but it cannot hurt to wait three days on the chance there's a shred of truth in her motley tale.'

O, blessed, logical Horatio. I gave silent thanks that he was Hamlet's friend.

Erik's eyes measured me dispassionately as a housewife might measure out a wheat meal for a saint's day feast. 'My lord,' he said, 'I would have further speech with you for I still cannot make out reasons for anything that has happened, but will you now leave me alone with this girl? Perhaps she'll speak more freely out of your company.'

Once again Horatio hesitated. 'She'll come to no harm in your care?'

Erik's eyes glittered with private amusement. 'I will wrap her in silk as if she is the most precious pearl in all Denmark.'

'And you will delay the burial for three days?' Horatio asked.

Erik gave what seemed an exaggerated sigh. 'There is nothing I would like more to do,' he said, 'but we must think of the good of the state. If she speak true, it would be a sin indeed to consign Hamlet and her brother to a muddy tomb before their time. But if she is indeed mad, to tarry their funerals might be to fuel groundless rumour that would swell and grow, bursting out in rebellion and mutiny. Folk might start to whisper that now it must be three weeks and not three days that must be waited and then that we must wait three years. Three years could become three score of years, and all this time would Denmark be left helpless, without a man to rule her. I myself would like to wait these three days, but I must weigh the good that might arise from such a course against the possible harm. Even Jesus himself didn't ask his apostle to wait three days before laying him in the earth. Let me speak with her alone. Very like she'll confide in me more freely without her husband's friend standing warden over her.'

Horatio considered this and finally nodded assent. 'Ophelia,' he said before he left, 'know that as I was your husband's true friend, I'm yours. It's my fondest hope that we can find a way to bring you back home to your rightful mind.'

'I'm not mad,' I shrieked as he passed out of the room.

Erik ordered the remaining guard to stand watch in the hall. 'See that we aren't disturbed.' As soon as the door shut behind him, Erik moved over to me and took my chin in his hand to look deep into my eyes. I stood there boldly, my chin lifted, for I sensed he was a man who would take advantage of weakness and fear.

'It's not unfathomable,' he said, 'that grief for her husband and brother, dying within a few moments of each other, should turn the wits of a gently nurtured lady.'

I didn't let myself move. 'I'm not mad.'

'Especially since, from what I gathered from that lord, your father is but freshly dead.'

'I'm not mad.'

'We find ourselves impaled on the horns of a dilemma.' He let his hand fall away from my chin. I resisted the urge to rub my chin to wipe off the memory of his touch. 'Let us say you're mad—'

'I'm not mad.'

'—or mistaken and that Hamlet is indeed dead. Waiting three days for the burial would, as we told that Danish lord who seems to know so much of this affair, give rise to wild speculation and weaken our hold on the Danish throne. This would be good for neither Denmark nor ourselves.'

'Hamlet is not dead and I'm not mad.' Oh, how I longed to wipe the sneer from that smug, distant face.

'Hear me out, lady. Humour me. Let us say, then, that you're not mad or mistaken and that you speak the truth. Hamlet was scratched by some magical potion to make him sleep. In three days he awakes to be crowned king of Denmark. Now that's most certainly not good for me, and, from what I've heard about his infirmities – even just now from your own mouth – not good for Denmark. To keep Hamlet alive would perhaps benefit him, but it would be to the detriment of the country and most certainly to the detriment of our own hopes. Therefore, waiting three days to test out your theory would be harmful to Denmark's future.'

'And your own!'

He smiled a thin, frosty smile. 'Certainly, to ourselves as well. I will not disguise myself to you. My father had rights of rule in this kingdom, and he was killed by Hamlet's father. Now Fortune has seen fit to restore those rights to me. Ever since I was a child, it was my fondest dream to avenge my father's untimely death by killing old King Hamlet. Fortune robbed me of that chance. But do I harbour any sorrow for the death of his foolish, useless, mad son?' He paused to drive his point home. 'No, I don't.'

I wanted to smash his chilly composure, to rake my nails down his supercilious face. 'How dare you speak of Hamlet in such a fashion, when even now, to the folk in the hall, you bragged of what a fine king he'd have made.'

'If it would help me obtain the throne,' he said, 'I would have sworn to the folk that the sun rose in the west and Hamlet was the resurrected Jesus who walked on the water across the strait to Sweden and back for his daily constitutional. No, lady, and again no. There is no question what I'm going to do with Hamlet's body. The only question, Ophelia, is how long you are going to continue in this hither-and-yon madness of yours.'

I began to feel afraid. 'What do you mean?'

'Only this. Hamlet is doomed. I do believe he's dead, but if he's not, he soon will be.'

In spite of myself, I flinched. Even the old king had more humanity in him than this monument of ice who stood before me.

Erik looked bored. 'Lady Ophelia, know that I have spies a-plenty in the Danish court. Almost daily I received report about this prince. Every account talked of his attraction to death, how he babbled often – both freely and widely – of his wish to die. From all I could gather, he had but two ambitions in his pretty head. He wanted to kill the man who killed his father, and he wanted to die himself. So let him go, lady. By Hamlet's own reckoning, he's lived a successful life.'

'Except for his bouts of madness, he is an amazing man. Painter, sculptor, poet, architect, scientist, playwright—'

'Who was in love with death! Let him go and seek out death, his own sweetheart.' He tapped his palm against his thigh a couple of times. 'As I said, the question is not whether he'll lie in state three days . . . for that question has been answered . . . but, Ophelia, which direction will your life take?'

That was most decidedly *not* the question. The question was how could I keep Hamlet and my brother above the ground for three days more. Even blind Finn from the village could see I wasn't going to persuade Erik Strong Arm to help me. He was right; saving Hamlet ran counter to his own grain. I needed to get out of his company and seek aid elsewhere.

I made my best curtsey. 'My lord, I'm heartily sorry to have taken up your time with my fancies,' I said. 'I'll leave you now to your own business.' I started to the door. My best hope might be to spread the word among the people, to raise a mob to—

'Stay, Ophelia. We haven't yet finished.' His voice was still low-pitched but hard as obsidian.

I turned back in surprise. Surprise both at his voice and his familiarity at using my name with no title attached. 'My lord, you've made it clear that you will not allow me three days for Hamlet—'

'Leave Hamlet! That ship has sailed. We talk now of *your* future.'

What in the world prompted this concern for me? Nothing about him suggested there was the least shred of kindness or sensitivity in his character. I dared not say *I intend to save Hamlet, and then we'll sail far from here*. But where? I suddenly realized that we had no place to go. I'd have to find another country to take us in. Or would Hamlet wish to stir up the people and try to take the throne back from the son of his father's fiercest enemy? That future could keep. My first task would be to stay Hamlet's burial. There would then be time to sort out the rest. 'Sir, don't concern yourself with my well-being. Doubtless my father has left some properties and monies, and I can—'

'Your father? Who cares a twig about your father? It's of you, Ophelia, that I speak. You are the widow to the prince.' His lips tightened. 'By my reckoning, Hamlet died after Claudius, so it could be argued that you are now queen of Denmark. Thus you cannot just fade away to some tiny country estate.'

I wanted to laugh. How the folk in the village would stare to see me as queen. Instead I gave an impatient shrug. 'I can do just that, my lord. No one need know about the marriage—'

'You are mistaken. That Danish lord who was here just now bellowed it to the full court. It can no longer be hushed up.'

It took several moments for the impact of what he said to

sink into my brain. I then felt a flash of fear. What kind of threat did I represent to his acquisition of the throne? He had no compunction about killing Hamlet. Was I now staring into the face of my own executioner? 'Do you intend to kill me too?' I asked, marvelling that I could keep my voice so steady. My brain whirled. *After all, the second death of a mad girl will not be difficult to arrange.* How would he do it? *Let it be painless at least.* As a new thought struck me, my lips twisted in a smile. *Will I now finally join the ranks of castle ghosts?*

'Kill you? Are your wits still a-wandering, girl? How would your death benefit me?' He took a step closer. 'No, I have a very different fate in mind for you.'

57

Perhaps I was in shock after all that had transpired this day, but all at once I felt at a great distance from what was taking place as if I was watching my own life from one of the castle spy holes. 'What fate is that?' I asked in my new-found calm.

'I propose to propose.'

I looked at him blankly, and he gave a little laugh.

'How else, Ophelia, could I strengthen my grip upon the throne? It's becoming quite the Danish tradition, is it not, having the new king marry the widow of the old king. Claudius did it, and now so shall I.' He again made the sound that in him passed for a laugh. 'How pleased the people will be. They will rejoice to see their foreign king take to wife a girl of good Danish stock. How they'll exult that the pretty wife of that poor, mad prince Hamlet has at last found a sane and lusty husband.'

'This marriage cannot happen!'

'It can and it shall. You know the French proverb that all cats are grey at night? Well, lady, one woman in my bed or at my side is much like another. She is there for show, like the crown on my head or the sceptre in my fist. What matters is that she brings me riches and power, and that she produces sons. So you will suit me very well indeed, lady. You will be the cement joining me to the Danish crown. You are young and healthy. I should be able to sow many litters of sons in that fertile body of yours.' There was no more expression on his face than if he'd been mending a wall or cleaning a pair of boots. 'More than that, it's clear that once you are bathed and groomed, you will be handsome indeed. I certainly do not object to beauty in my wife. In fact I welcome it. A beautiful queen will make me even more popular here in this land, and it will win me admiration abroad.' He yawned. 'Pardon me. It has been a devilishly long day, and there's still much to do before I can seek out my couch and get some sleep.'

I didn't know his adage about the cats, but my life was proving one of our favourite village proverbs, *When the gods want to punish you, they answer your prayers*. As a child, how I'd longed to be one of the grand castle folk. Now a second king had expressed a desire to take me for his wife, and once again I was revolted by the prospect. I lifted my chin. 'I'll not marry you.'

His smile spread across his face. 'Not at once, of course. That wouldn't be seemly. People would disapprove if you didn't take time to mourn your present husband. Doubtless the last royal marriage was overhasty, and I do not choose to repeat other men's mistakes.'

'I'll not marry you.'

It was as if my words were ghost words that he couldn't hear, for he paid them no mind. 'Besides, we must wait long enough to be sure that you do not carry the child of your late husband. I will not play the silent father to another man's offspring.'

'Did you not hear me, sir? I will not marry you.'

'Three months,' he said, ignoring me. 'Three months should be plenty of time to make sure you aren't with child. We will give out word that you mourn in private seclusion.'

'Nothing in the world would induce me to marry you.'

My words glanced off his arrogance like arrows off a stone wall. 'Lady, drop this pretence of fastidiousness just as you dropped your pretence of madness. This coyness ill becomes you and it insults my intelligence. The whole world knows your first husband was a lunatic. The only reason you could have married such a travesty was to secure yourself a throne. You cannot make me believe that you loved that defective prince, so do not even attempt to try. Now I bring you the promise of a healthy king and a secure reign as queen. We both know that never again in your life can you hope for a better offer than mine, so put off this unconvincing show of maidenly simpering and assume the mantle of your new future.'

I wouldn't demean myself by trying to convince him that I'd believed myself in love with Hamlet. 'Send me away, sir, to the island prepared for Hamlet's exile, and then I'll trouble you no further.'

'I am a careful man, as you will find, and I do not throw away valuable tools that are still of use.'

There was a knock on the door, and the soldier who had been sent to look for the secret passage entered. 'Sire,' he said, 'it's just as this woman said. I found the hidden door in the courtyard, and it leads to all the royal chambers.'

'Assemble some workmen,' Erik Strong Arm ordered, 'and see all those portals nailed shut. Nail them on both sides of the door, then brick up the entrance from the courtyard. We will not have such rat holes to let potential assassins come and go in our royal chambers.'

The soldier saluted and departed.

'Sergeant!' Erik called. The other soldier, the one guarding the door, stepped back into the room. 'Escort the grieving Lady Ophelia to her chambers. Post a full contingent of guards at her door. Let no one enter. Most of all, keep the poor widowed lady within, for her heart is breaking over her husband's death, and I fear that if we do not set some watch, she'll do herself harm.'

I stared at him in disbelief.

He took up my hand and kissed it. His hand was cold, his lips hard as if he were snarling rather than kissing. 'Lady, I will visit daily to see how you go on and to make sure you are well treated.'

'I don't need to be locked up, sir. I'll give you my word that I'll not harm myself.'

'Your grief has clouded over your judgement. From this time forth, I will do your thinking for you.' Before I could utter a word of protest, he smiled. 'Take her away.'

The soldier seized me but didn't leave at once. 'I beg your pardon, sire,' he said to Erik Strong Arm, 'but how will I find this lady's rightful chamber?'

'She is Hamlet's wife, sergeant. Take her to his chamber and guard her well.'

As the sergeant marched me away, I saw that many more of Erik's soldiers now filled the hall. The sergeant motioned to some other soldiers to join us, and we were a body of ten when we reached the corridor outside the royal chambers.

'Which one be yours?' the sergeant asked in his thick Norwegian accent.

I gestured toward Lord Hamlet's rooms. 'Those are mine.' I couldn't stay locked up. I had to stop the burials of Hamlet and my brother.

Once inside, I could see from his face that he found the room queer indeed and especially strange for a lady's dwelling, but he said nothing. He ordered four of the soldiers, 'Stay with her until we have blocked up the passageway that leads to the hidden corridor.'

Within half an hour, workmen had nailed the secret doorway shut. I flinched to see the elegantly carved wood of the fireplace split as the nails were thrust carelessly into the wood.

As they worked, I begged the soldiers to let me out, to say I'd run away, to claim that the castle was haunted and that I'd been wafted away by spirits. I recklessly promised them fortunes if only they'd give me a few hours to run free and take care of my affairs, that I'd be back so quickly and faithfully that Erik Strong Arm need never know that I was gone, that riches beyond their most lavish dreams would be theirs if only I could have two hours of freedom . . .

They ignored me. For the most part they pretended they couldn't understand my Danish accent, but from time to time they sneered at me as if they despised my womanly weakness and would never themselves behave in such a desperate way if they were themselves imprisoned. But they didn't have the lives of two men depending on them.

As soon as they were gone, I sent an embroidered cushion sailing across the room. I wouldn't let my husband and brother die like this! To awake in a coffin, alone, struggling for air, fingernails scraping desperately at the lid, scrabbling to get free . . . The image was too horrible. Perhaps Hamlet had longed for death, but my brother hadn't, and even Hamlet would never have chosen this slow, lonely death. I pounded my fists against the door to the corridor, screaming till my throat was raw. My hands were still bruised from beating on the queen's door only a few hours earlier, but I hammered away, ignoring the pain. No one came to let me out or even opened the door to investigate what was happening within. I prowled the room, looking for tools to help. Hamlet's paintbrushes lay in a heap by the fourth wall. *Now he'll never finish that painting.* I snatched up several of the paintbrushes and with their handles tried to gouge the wood around the nails fastening the secret door. If I could loosen them, I could escape down the secret passage. There hadn't yet been time to brick up the door to the courtyard, but if I waited too long, then I'd forfeit all chance at this route. When the paintbrush handles didn't work, I used my own fingernails to scrape, scrape, scrape at the wood. Soon my fingertips were ringed in blood, but I kept scratching until every fingernail had broken off. To my dismay, I failed to work a single nail free. For a wild moment I wondered if I could use my teeth as a tool, but then I remembered the secret door had been nailed shut from the other side as well, so even if I worked all these nails free, I'd still be confined.

If I can just get out of this room, I can go to Horatio. He's a man of sense. He will find a way for me to keep Hamlet and Laertes above ground until three days have passed.

I tried to loosen the tiny diamond-shaped panes in the window, but they were thick and their frame of metal held them fast. Besides, even if I could knock the entire window free from its frame, there would be no way to climb down the wall. The stones were smooth, and there were no handholds.

Just before evening turned the corner to night, the door opened and a soldier thrust in a tray containing a corked jug, a bowl of soup and a loaf of bread. He set it on the floor barely inside the door as if he was feeding a vicious dog.

'Please,' I called out. 'You must—'

He slammed the door shut.

I had no hunger in me, but I was thirsty and drank the soup. *There must be a way out of my imprisonment.* I just had to figure out what it was.

Soon the room was washed with darkness which gave me a new idea. *If they bring in a candle, I can set the heavy drapes aflame.* Then, when they came to douse the fire, I could slip out under the cloak of all the confusion and smoke. Oh, what a pity it was summer and there was no fire in the grate to give me a spark.

The danger was, of course, that they might not discover the fire in time for me to slip out.

Still, I had to take that chance. I'd been the agent of too many deaths already. I wouldn't add two more to my list. Old King Hamlet, yes, I'd deliberately sought his death. If I hadn't killed him, though, then Prince Hamlet wouldn't have run wild with trying to piece out that murder, he wouldn't have confronted his mother after the play, and my poor father would still be alive. If I hadn't shown Osric that poison held within the pearl, then the queen and perhaps even Claudius would also still be wandering this earth. I hadn't intended any of those three deaths, but without my meddling, they wouldn't have happened.

No, that wasn't quite true. Without me, the queen would have died. Her first husband would have killed her.

But now she was just as dead as if I'd stood back and let King Hamlet push her off the castle ramparts. I'd saved nothing, and I'd done much harm.

In some ways, the hardest deaths for me to face were those of Rosencrantz and Guildenstern. In no way was I the direct agent of their deaths, but Hamlet would never have been sent sailing off to England if I hadn't supplied his uncle with the poison to kill his father.

Oh, I could play the philosopher and argue that if I hadn't given Claudius the poison, he'd have doubtless found other sources. But the hard truth was that I *had* given him the poison to kill his brother. I'd chosen to commit that one murder, never dreaming it would lead to another which would lead to another which would lead . . . Five deaths. Five people were dead because of me. And unless I did something soon, Hamlet and Laertes would die for good.

No. I wouldn't kill two more.

I returned to beating against the door and screaming until I had no voice left with which to scream and blood dripped from my hands. The door was never opened. No candles were brought to me, preventing me setting my curtains alight. Finally I curled up on the bed, sobbing with anger and frustration, until I cried myself to sleep.

I woke up screaming, and I kept screaming until I made

myself sick and coughed up a thin, sour-smelling liquid into my chamber pot. *Two days only remaining.* I decided to escape by climbing up the chimney. I crouched in the fireplace and tried to figure out how to do it, but I couldn't get myself higher than a few feet above the floor and ended up covered with soot and ashes. There wasn't enough water in the wash basin to get me clean again, and my bedraggled gown would have disgraced even a ragheap. At midday, when a guard entered to bring me another tray of bread, cheese, and ale, he looked startled by my appearance. Perhaps an hour later a second guard brought in a bucket of water, but I no longer cared enough to wash.

I prowled the confines of the room, looking for anything I could use as a tool or weapon, but I had little success. I did find several lengths of flat metal behind the paint jars. At first I took them for knives, but they weren't sharp. I could probably use them to work the nails free, but now that I'd remembered about the nails on the other side, that scheme was as empty as air. I thought to paint, 'Help,' on the windows, but Erik Strong Arm had probably spread the tale that I was mad again, and no one would take that inscription seriously . . . even if it could be seen. Among the painting jars was a small pot containing a clear liquid that, if sniffed too long, made me dizzy. I wondered if I could soak a cloth in it and, when a guard came in, clap it over his nose long enough for him to faint from the fumes. I doubted, though, whether I was strong enough to hold it to his face. The Norwegian guards were large men, and I was sure any guard I'd attack would throw me off quick as a bull could toss a puppy.

Finally I found something that could work.

Hamlet had paper a-plenty and pens with which to write. I composed a long letter telling of my situation and begging for help. I'd thought to smuggle it out, hidden beneath the jug, when a guard replaced my morning tray with the evening one, but the guard surprised me with my evening meal before I'd finished my letter, so I had to wait until the next morning to try this new scheme.

Only one day remained.

58

This had to work. I had no other plan.

I was awake at first light. I folded my letter and kept placing it in different spots on the tray, seeking a place the guard would be least likely to see it. I tried it under the bowl, under the jug, inside the bowl, under the up-ended bowl, and finally decided that it would work best if I tucked it down into the emptied ale jug. The danger was that no one in the kitchen would notice it there, but that was a risk I needed to take. Of course, the other danger was that if it were found, the finder – in hopes of a reward – would take it directly to Erik Strong Arm. I couldn't, however, see how such a course of action would make my plight any the worse. If I didn't get out this day, then all would be lost indeed and my brother and Hamlet would both be for the dark.

Two lives depended on the success of my stratagem. Once I'd worked my letter down into the jug, I was too nervous to settle in any place for long. I tried to will the guard to come in immediately to exchange the trays and carry my message to the kitchens. I paced the room until I was weary. My stomach was knotted with excitement, and I kept wringing my sore hands. From time to time I threw myself into the bed, but after a few moments I'd hop up to pace some more. I tried to remember how deep into the morning the guards had waited the day before to exchange trays.

Oh, the morning crept by on snail's feet.

Several hours later I heard the tolling of castle bells. I

screamed in frustration. I was certain these were funeral bells. Erik Strong Arm was burying all the dead folk, including Hamlet and my brother. *Let there be enough air in their coffins to last until I can come to them and release them.* Probably Hamlet's coffin would be above ground, in a vault, so he should be fine for at least a day, but my brother would be put down in the ground, and at best there would be air for only an hour or so. *I need to get out of here right away!* Then I realized I'd have to find someone to help me dig Laertes up and break open the door to Hamlet's vault. Perhaps Piet would accompany me. Even little Mus could be of aid. The more hands the better. *If only someone would come to carry my tray away, I could still be in time.*

It was at least an hour after the last bell tolled before the guards took away the tray with the note and left a new one. I couldn't give over pacing the room, pausing every few minutes to listen for sounds in the corridor. I kept recalculating the amount of air that would be in my brother's coffin. Kept telling myself that they'd hold him till the last to be put in his grave, so that perhaps there was still time.

But when the guards brought the tray for my evening meal, I had to accept that it was too late to save Laertes. Even by the most optimistic reckoning, he'd been underground too long to still have air to breathe. My only consolation – and it was cold comfort indeed – was that he'd probably smothered before the potion wore off so that he'd never waked to the horror of finding himself buried alive.

I had only a few hours to save Hamlet.

All through the night I paced, fretted, and prayed. *Let me save him, let me save him, let me save someone from this bloodbath ... God, if you'll let me save him, I'll never ask anything ever again. Mother Mary, Holy Virgin, you watched your own son suffer an untimely death. Don't let Erik add one*

*more slaughter to the world's dark record. Sainted Mary, Mother
of God, let something good come out of all this tragedy.*

By the morning I felt mad indeed. My only thought was to
batter the door down. I tried to lift one of the chairs to use as
my weapon, but it was too heavy for me to budge, so I took
up a long gold candlestick and began to smash it against the
door of the chamber. Soon I'd pounded great dents into the
beautifully carved doors, but to no avail. When a guard came
in with my morning meal, I flew at him, pummelling him with
my bare hands, and he had to call his fellow to pluck me off
and hold me away, and then they threw me onto the bed so
they could slip back out the door.

All through the afternoon I screamed over and over, and
then I howled like some sort of beast, until I had no voice at
all. I used the candlestick to beat again on the door, but I'd
exhausted all my strength. I hadn't touched my food, and I
was getting light-headed, and finally I fell asleep right on the
floor, curled next to the battered door.

The fourth day dawned. I told myself there was still a
slender chance that if I could get out this very day, Hamlet
was still alive in his vault. But for the first time in my life,
I was bereft of ideas. The faces of the people in Hamlet's
paintings stared at me with reproach and disgust in their eyes,
but I couldn't conjure up a meaningful plan.

The fifth day.

Now it was too late for both of them.

Seven deaths.

I lay on the bed, exhausted. I no longer ate the food that
was brought to me. I felt emptied of all desires, all futures.
I saw how madness could be a very attractive thing, and
I wished with all my heart that I could indeed run mad
and forget the seven deaths. Forget my bleak future with
Erik Strong Arm. I'd marry him, of course. I didn't have
the temperament of a martyr or saint. I'd rather be the

queen of a man I hated than to spent my life locked in solitary prison.

On the sixth day, a voice shook me from my lethargy.

'I've come to bid you farewell.'

I looked up to see Yorick standing in Hamlet's room.

'Farewell?' I asked. Did he know something I didn't? Was I being taken away from this castle?

He said, 'Within the space of an hour, I expect to be gone.'

He looked quite pleased, as if he'd been given a secret to relish.

Languidly, I said, 'I wish you'd come to me several days ago. I could have then used your aid. I would have sent you to tell Piet that he had to help me.'

He chuckled as if I'd made a joke. 'I've told you, Ophelia, that we ghosts can speak only to the person we choose to be the tool of our revenge.'

His words made no sense. 'You could have spoken with Piet. After all, you speak to me—'

His smile was so broad that it cracked his wizened face into two parts. 'Just so.'

Had I gone mad indeed? I heard words, but I couldn't string them together into a necklace of meaning. 'I cannot take your meaning, Yorick.'

His eyes twinkled. 'I must thank you, Ophelia, for helping me accomplish the revenge I sought.'

Was he the one who was mad? 'Revenge?'

'Yes. Thanks to you, I'm now avenged on Prince Hamlet.'

59

Was this what madness felt like?

I pulled myself up to a sitting position. 'You mean King Hamlet.'

He shook his head so hard the points of his cap shook. '*Prince* Hamlet. Oh, I'd tried for many years to get my revenge, but no one seemed a suitable weapon until you came to the castle.'

'You are mad!' Horror flooded through me 'Why should you want revenge on Prince Hamlet when it was his father who killed you?'

He roared with laughter. 'It was the son, not the father, who killed me.'

'You lie! Last year, when I was trying to find a way to stop King Hamlet from killing the queen, I asked you if King Hamlet was the one who killed you, and you told me—'

'I told you that *Hamlet* killed me. I didn't say it was *King* Hamlet. If you chose to hear it that way, who was I to disabuse you?'

Inside I began to tremble. 'This still makes no sense. You died when he was but a child . . .'

'Yes,' he said. 'Which makes it all the worse.'

'How can you hope to make me believe that it was a child who killed you?'

His voice turned savage. 'Because it's the truth.'

Then I remembered the awful sight of him dancing atop the throne when Hamlet had seemed to die in the Great Hall.

'Tell me,' I whispered.

He grinned at me. 'I owe you that much, Ophelia. As my partner in revenge, you have a right to understand why I did what I did.' He hopped onto the bed and settled into a cross-legged position opposite me. 'When I came to court, I was so full of pride that I was the favourite playfellow of the comely little prince. He was a regular beauty, that one. His older brother was strong, but Holger had a fearsome temper, so most folk preferred the darling little brother. Oh, little Hamlet was the prettiest child. And so quick with his wit and tongue. He kept the whole court chuckling. I was puffed up with self-importance that this perfect little prince chose me, *me*, to join him in his games. For hours at a time we played at hobble-de-horse, and he'd ride on my back, beating me with the little whip I'd fashioned for him till I bled, as I scampered up and down the length of the hall. One of his other favourite sports was to go exploring in all the forgotten parts of the castle, to roam the roof and the long-abandoned cellars and dungeons. His father forbade him to go down there. He said that some of the foundations were rotten and the young prince could come to grief. But little Hamlet would not be thwarted. He believed the legends about the long-dead King Holger being buried somewhere in the castle's foundations, and little Hamlet was determined to be the hero who found King Holger's grave. He begged me to continue to explore with him, and while I dreaded to disobey his father, I couldn't bear to lose the prince's favour.'

It was easy for me to picture Hamlet as a wilful, charming child with strong ideas for some new plan.

Yorick gave his head a shake. 'I must have been out of my right mind indeed to risk everything on the whim of a child, but I'd never previously been in the forefront of favour. Growing up, I'd been the oaf, the outcast, the butt of all jokes. It went to my head like wine to be the bosom comrade of a prince. I could refuse him nothing. Nothing at all.'

He looked away. 'His father was right. The foundations of the castle *were* rotten. One day as we explored an old wine cellar, a beam snapped and plunged down, slicing through my side and pinning me to the floor. I couldn't move. For a long while, the little prince tried to lift the beam away as I lay there bleeding and moaning, but he was too small. "Go for help," I begged him. "Get some stronger hands to free me."' Yorick's face darkened. '"I cannot," the little prince said. "If my father finds out I was here against his orders, he'll wallop me and I'll be out of his favour forevermore." I pleaded, I begged, I told him I would die without aid. "I dare not incur my father's disapproval," was all he said for answer.'

As the horror of this scene broke over me, I wrapped my arms around my shoulders tightly.

'I lay there for almost three days,' Yorick said slowly. 'On the first two days, Hamlet came to visit me. "I don't like you to have to be here all alone," he said each time. He would sing me songs and tell me stories, but he wouldn't be persuaded to fetch me help. At the end of his second visit, he told me, "I dare come no more, Yorick. My father grows watchful, so I can no longer risk it." He said it earnestly as if I was cajoling him into wrongdoing and he hated to say me nay.' Yorick leaned his head back and shut his eyes. 'I died the next afternoon.'

A silence fell between us. Truly, there was nothing that could be said to sop any pain from that horrible tale, but I finally ventured, 'He was only a child. Children cannot always understand the consequences of their actions.'

His words burst forth like a blood-dried bandage ripped from a wound. 'He left me there to die!'

'And now you leave him there to die,' I said softly, sick at heart.

Yorick stared at me for a moment, and then he sighed. 'No. Oh, I would have if I could have. That would have been a fitting death indeed. But that particular revenge wasn't granted to me. Hamlet never knew what it felt like to see his life seep slowly away while he lay helpless and forgotten. No, Hamlet was dead from the moment your brother's sword drew blood.'

'No!' I couldn't believe that Yorick didn't know the entire story. 'Hamlet was felled by a sleeping potion that counterfeited the appearance of death—'

'Ophelia, Claudius and Laertes didn't dip the swords in your sleeping potion. They used instead the poison that you'd sent to your brother by that kitchen lad, the poison you'd sent him to protect himself. Once Hamlet and Laertes were scratched, nothing on earth could save them, not even you.'

My breath escaped in a little *whump* as if he'd butted me in the stomach.

'You are a good child and a loving heart,' Yorick said. 'Now that Hamlet is safely in the earth, I'm fading from this earth as well.'

'I loved you well,' I said. 'Part of the reason I killed King Hamlet was because I thought he'd killed you. You were my best friend in the castle. My advisor. I trusted you, Yorick. Did you never care for me at all?'

His face looked old and sad in the waning afternoon light. 'I cared for you as a valuable tool, Ophelia. As the instrument of my revenge. Anything else I felt was the servant to my vengeance.'

I couldn't be hearing this. I must be dreaming, lost in a nightmare that exactly counterfeited life. 'But, Yorick, everything I did, I did it all on my own.'

He slowly shook his head. 'If you think back over your history, Ophelia, you'll recall that it was I who put the idea of the poisons in your head. It was I who suggested the contest between Laertes and Hamlet, I who first said that Claudius should send one of his men with you when you collected the sleeping draught. It was I who convinced you Hamlet was mad when I told you that the ghost of his father was only in his mind. You of all people know that it's possible for ghosts to appear to one person and not others.'

'But I see all the ghosts. And there was no ghost talking to Hamlet when I met him on the ramparts, so he—'

Yorick shook his head. 'You see many of the ghosts, Ophelia, but not all of them. Most of the time the ghost of King Hamlet was invisible to your sight.'

'But you told me that I was the one person to see all—' I let my voice trail away. Yorick had lied to me about that as well, making me believe that no ghost could elude my sight. Slowly I said, 'So Hamlet wasn't mad after all.'

Yorick gave me a wolfish grin. 'No, he was mad, all right. Mad as a midsummer lemming. I confess, Ophelia, I played you like the little flute that once hung on my belt. But I was desperate. I had to goad Hamlet into action, and you were my perfect tool.'

He leaned forward. 'For years I'd been terrified that Hamlet would live to old age, tamely in Wittenberg, but it wasn't until an innocent young girl came to court that I saw a way to lead Hamlet to his own destruction. I knew he was hungry for love, you see. For a long time I didn't quite understand how to turn your actions to my own benefit, but in the end you proved to be most useful.'

A pang ran through me. It hurt beyond imagining to learn that all this time that I thought I was acting on my own, I'd actually been Yorick's pawn, that he'd never really been my friend.

I think he saw in my face something of what I was thinking, for he said, 'Console yourself with this. You have won yourself a queenship, and if you're to sit on the throne, you must learn never to expect people to care for you because of who you are. You will always matter more to them as the Danish queen than as Ophelia. In this at least, I've taught you well.'

How stupid I'd been. All the while I thought I was controlling everything, and I myself had been but the weapon of a ghost. I'd chid Hamlet for being manipulated by his father's ghost, when all the time I myself had been Yorick's puppet. My words lurched along like prisoners on their way to an execution. 'And thus you feel compensated for your betrayal of my friendship.'

'No.' He sighed. 'I freely admit that I wronged you, Ophelia. I'd do it again, but I'm not proud of it. I can feel myself fading even as we speak, but before I depart, I want to put one small thing right. I won't depart leaving you to think that Hamlet died because you couldn't figure a way to escape from this chamber. No, Hamlet and Laertes have been dead these six days past, and there was nothing you could have done to save them.'

I felt empty, as if winter had taken up permanent residence in my soul and spring had been banished forever from my own earth.

'My time is almost gone,' Yorick said urgently. Indeed, I could see him begin to fade right before my eyes. He was now as dim as a coloured shadow. 'Listen to me,' he said. 'I used you, Ophelia, but it's time to let that go. Erik Strong Arm wishes to marry you. He will make a fine king, a better king than either Prince Hamlet or his brother. Under Erik, Denmark will see fresh days of glory. The greatest in many centuries. Marry him. Be his queen. You have in you, Ophelia, the stuff of which the best queens are made. You can become a queen of legend, a queen that future generations will look to in wonder and admiration. Marry Erik, and cut loose all the past.'

He grew so dim that he was a ripple of air rather than an

image of a man, and his voice was now only a shiver of wind.

'One last thing.' Yorick's voice grew even fainter. 'Do not fear for the child you carry. The seeds of his father's madness aren't planted in him. He has your loving heart and he has his father's—'

His words faded.

Yorick was gone.

I hardly noticed, for his final words had pulled the rug out from under my feet.

I was carrying Hamlet's child.

All my tiredness, my sickness every morning . . . I was with child. A child that Yorick had declared free of his father's madness. Oh, what a magical child such a one would truly be . . . all Hamlet's brilliance without the madness that attended his father.

Then I shivered.

What would Erik Strong Arm do when he discovered I carried within me a rival claimant to the throne?

60

Erik Strong Arm himself paid me a visit the next afternoon.

His upper lip curled slightly when he saw my slovenly appearance, my tangled hair, my soot-smudged gown, my ripped and bloody hands. 'We have buried your husband and brother,' he said by way of greeting. 'All the dead ones are safely in the ground, and we trust they'll bother us no more.'

I must win his favour. I made myself kneel before him. 'I beg you to pardon me, my lord. I've done you great wrong.'

He stretched forth a hand as if to raise me to my feet, but almost at once he drew it back again as if he couldn't stomach touching my soiled sleeve. Instead he merely inclined his head to signal me to rise. When I did, he gestured to a chair that one of his guards was holding, and I sank down into it. He sat in a chair directly across from me and then waved his hand for his soldiers to withdraw. Once the guards were out of earshot, he asked, 'What wrong was that, lady?'

I kept my voice low. 'I was out of my head with grief for my brother and husband. I convinced myself that they weren't dead in truth but were only shamming, and that I had the power to save them. I understand now that I was mad with sorrow and spoke wild and whirling words with no roots in truth, and so I beseech your highness to forgive me.'

He looked at me suspiciously for a few moments, but then relaxed a little as if convinced that I spoke true. 'Women are weak creatures,' he said, 'and well we know that sorrow can unhinge them in a way that men fail to understand. Indeed, we like that you have such a faithful heart, lady, for we hope in time that you can show such faithfulness to us.'

Already he was using that particular trick of the language reserved for kings, that referring to themselves as 'we' rather than 'I'.

'I hope it too,' I murmured although it made my stomach heave to speak so tamely.

He studied me again before saying, 'Then have you thought of what we proposed to you?'

I looked him straight in the face. 'I've always wanted to be queen.'

He gave a little nod as if confirming what he'd suspected. 'So will you be *our* queen?'

I reminded myself of Yorick's words: *He will be one of the great kings*. He was an able man, a strong leader, not unpleasant to look at. More than that, married to him I'd have the chance to become one of the greatest queens the world had ever known. All I had to do was make myself meek, mild, and demure, for I knew he wouldn't countenance wilfulness from his wife. I made my voice soft and low. 'As your majesty remarked at our last meeting, we must not hurry into this marriage. Can we not take some time to get to know one another first?'

'We must wait three months before we wed, Ophelia. Do you think that time enough for us to learn each other's habits and ways?'

I smiled at him. In the recent events, I'd forgotten to play the well-behaved lady, but three months would give me plenty of time to master that role again.

He rose to take his leave. 'It does our heart much good to have you restored to yourself again, princess.'

That title resounded loudly in my ears. *Princess*. I'd not thought of myself as princess before.

I rose, too. 'Then may I also assume that I'm free to go about the castle?'

He froze. 'That cannot be the case.'

I rushed to set his mind at ease. 'I have no intention of digging up my husband or my brother—'

'Well have you convinced us of that.'

'Then why keep me imprisoned?'

'Before we marry, we must make certain that you are not with child, princess. We told you that we will not father another man's offspring.' He *had* said that. 'Three months of seclusion will, shall we say, restore your virginity. It will let you come to our wedding bed pure, not pregnant with Lord Hamlet's child or with anyone else's. Bloodlines must be preserved.'

I forced myself to ask lightly, 'What would you do if I should prove to be carrying Hamlet's child?'

He strolled over to the middag tray left by the guards. He plucked a grape from a bunch that lay there and held it to the light, examining it. 'Such a cruel truth of life, is it not, that babies are so fragile. They die so readily.' He popped the grape into his mouth and crushed it, swallowing even the seeds. 'Your husband, Lord Hamlet, was of a feeble constitution. I feel certain that any offspring of his would share his sickly nature and couldn't survive long in this world.' He briefly blotted his mouth with the back of his hand. 'Should you have the misfortune to be with child, princess, we would have to wait until after the birth of the child to be wed, but your pregnancy wouldn't be an insurmountable obstacle. It would just slow our course a bit. And what a boon it would be for you to have a new husband to help you through the grief you felt for your poor, dead babe.'

He bowed, but before he could depart, I said, 'My lord, it's not seemly for the woman you'd take as queen to be left with no one to attend her. Think what people would say if it were known that you'd refused to give her waiting women. At the least, you'd be called a nip-cheese, and some might call you a selfish tyrant. I don't ask you to let me roam free, but can you not at least give me some women to attend me?'

He regarded me with narrowed eyes as if he expected a trick. I smoothed my face into innocence and met his gaze. Finally he said, 'I will send for some ladies of the Norwegian court to travel here to attend you.'

He started out again, but I stopped him with my voice. 'My lord, you see my appearance. Until they get here, surely you can find some ladies of the castle to wait on me.'

I could see him calculating the risk, but my dragtail appearance reproached him. He finally said, 'We will send two wenches with water for bathing, and until our Norwegian ladies get here, we will send serving women twice a day to assist you with various women's matters. But—' he held up an admonishing finger '—we will send different ladies each day, just as we assign different guards each time to stand at your door. We will not risk your winning their allegiance. You must now look to form your bonds with the good Norwegian ladies we will import as your attendants.'

'There's no need, sire, to—'

He waggled his finger. 'Let us say only that there have been two many royal deaths in this palace, and that we would be remiss should we leave our most precious pearl of Denmark unguarded.' He gave me a thin-lipped smile. 'Understand us well, Ophelia. Our jewel must learn that we will never allow her to fall out of our grip.'

61

In less than an hour, two laundry wenches a little older than me appeared, lugging a tub between them. Two Norwegian guards accompanied them, carrying huge jugs of hot water. The girls flirted readily with the guards, but they watched their tongues with me.

'Is something amiss?' I asked the girls after they'd failed to respond to several of my pleasantries.

'We'll catch the new king's disfavour if we chatter too freely with you, lady,' one of them said.

Their silence was oppressive, but it was a treat to be clean and clad in a fresh gown. I recognized it as one that had belonged to the dead queen

That night I cried myself to sleep. I wondered what had happened to Elspeth and to the queen's little dog, Trey. I hoped someone had given them both a home.

The next morning, two different maids came to me, one from the milkhouse and one that I didn't recognize. Again, they spoke little to me.

The easiest thing would be to lie back, to let Erik Strong Arm assume control of my life, to drift into the queenship that lay at the end of the present stream. The child inside me would have to die, of course, but most children never lived past their first years. Erik had been right. Children died all the time, and what was the life of this one child against my whole future and the future of the kingdom?

Everything.

I'd been the agent of many deaths, but this was one death that wasn't going to happen, not if I could do anything to change it, and change it I would. I couldn't bring Hamlet or the queen or my father back to life, but I could safeguard the life of their child and grandchild. Not for all the kingdoms in the world would I let Erik kill this child. As I saw it, the child's only chance lay in my ability to whisk it away before Erik became aware of its existence.

So I spent the afternoon composing another letter. I folded it small and wrote *Piet* across it in big letters. Then I drew a picture of a mouse underneath that in case Mus came across it instead of Piet. My first letter, the one I'd hidden in the ale jug, hadn't produced any results, but I would try again and try again after that and I would keep trying. I hid this one under a cloth on my tray.

I kept the language of my note cryptic. I wrote that, upon the death of my father, I had a package I wished to send to my stepmother in England and asked that arrangements be made to transport it right away. The couriers should hold themselves in readiness day and night. I'd send the package to them as soon as possible.

Even should the message be found, I thought I could bluff my way through, pretending that I was sending only a ring or some such to Judith. I'd make up some tale about a christening gift. I doubted my tale would fly if I was caught, but if I wasted time by not acting until all was safe and sure, then I'd die of old age in captivity. Sometimes caution is too expensive a luxury.

If my message just reached Piet, all should be fine. I gave a swift, silent prayer of thanks that I'd taught Piet and Ragnor to read. Piet would be able to read both my words and between my words. He'd understand to go to Ragnor to arrange my passage out of Denmark. Surely Ragnor would come through. No matter how much he despised me, he couldn't fail me now that I needed him so.

If the message reaches Piet's hands.

There was no reply. The next day I wrote another message and tucked it in a nest I hollowed in a hunk of bread. When there was still no answer from Piet, on the following day I tucked my letter in among some fresh green sallat leaves.

The next morning's tray contained a loaf of brown bread and a slab of cheese carved to look like a little book. Assuredly Piet's handiwork. The book was cunningly wrought, its edge even scored to look like pages. As I peered closely, I noticed a few words scratched out like a title along the spine.

ALL IS READY.

Piet had received at least one of my notes! He'd done his part. O blessed foster brother. Now it was up to me to get myself and my child out of the castle and down to Ragnor's ship.

It took three long days to find an opportunity.

Late one afternoon, two scullery girls came up to help me with my bath. I sent the larger one packing. 'Your hands reek of fish. I cannot bear for you to touch me!' I cried out.

She was hurt and embarrassed, but I pressed my hand against my belly to remind myself of why I treated her so unkind. The other girl looked nervous. When she thought I wasn't looking, she lifted her own hand up to her nose to sniff at it, but I crossly ordered her to fill the tub and sprinkle the waters with sweet marjoram and lavender. As she did so, I crept over to where Hamlet's paints were stacked. I retrieved the strip I'd torn off my shift, and I soaked it in the clear liquid whose scent made me dizzy. Then I crept up behind the maid who was carefully strewing a handful of herbs across the surface of the tub. I clamped the sopping cloth over her nose. She began to struggle, and we tumbled to the ground, but determination made me fierce, and I kept the cloth clamped to her face until she fell unconscious.

'You have poured the water too hot,' I said loudly. I

didn't want the guards to catch on to what was happening. I wanted them to think that there were still the two of us talking within.

To that end, I made my voice higher and spoke in the easily retrieved accents of the village. 'Beg pardon, my lady.'

Then in my Ophelia voice I said, 'Now I must needs wait for it to cool before I take my bath.'

Hidden by the tub, I stripped off her clothes. I pulled off the bedclothes and twisted them into ropes with which I tied up her limbs. I stuffed a pillowcase in her mouth and tied it shut with a second strip from my shift. There wasn't much time left. Already her eyelids were fluttering, and I was sure she'd soon wake.

I dragged her over to a clothespress. It took much heaving to lift her in, but I managed to do so and shut the lid. Then I quickly dressed myself in her clothes and wrapped her headdress low over my face. I let my body slump into the posture of a servant. I laid my hand across my belly and whispered, 'Courage, little one. If we hold fast our course, we shall soon wing our way to freedom.'

I gulped a few breaths of air, and then I piled my arms high with small clothes and linens. People seldom paid much attention to servants, and if I kept my head lowered over this pile of laundry, the guards would be hard-pressed to see my face. No doubt the girl would soon regain her senses and set to kicking and bumping the clothespress, but in my mad days the guards had heard me smashing things within the room and had never opened the door, so, God willing, these soldiers would pay her banging no mind.

I looked around the room once last time. I wished there was a way I could carry Hamlet's painted walls with me. Out of spite, Erik Strong Arm would probably paint over them as soon as he discovered I was gone.

I thought I would feel some sorrow at leaving the castle, but all I felt was relief.

I willed myself to move slowly and heavily, like a peasant and not with the light tread of a lady. I was surprised how quickly my village mannerisms came back to me. A few steps, and I was out the door.

A few more steps and I was past the guards.

Then one of them called out, 'Stop!'

62

Stay calm. Play your part.

I lowered my head as if I was bashful to the point of backwardness, and in my thickest village accent, without looking into his face, I said, 'Yes, sir?'

I felt his thick calloused fingers take hold of my chin. He titled my head upwards so I had no choice but to see him. 'Now what have we here?' he asked. His eyes danced.

Courage.

'Yes, sir?'

'Now you and I know this isn't right.'

Courage.

'What's nor right, sir?'

He smiled at me lazily. The other guard watched, equally amused. I calculated if I could give the guard a push and make my getaway, but I didn't think I could elude them both.

My captor spoke. 'You must know, lady, how lamentably ill-paid we soldiers are. When there is a chance of reward, we have no choice but to take it.'

Could I put my hands on enough money to pay more than the king. 'What is the amount of reward you have in mind, sir?'

He winked at his companion. 'So you think you can pay my price?'

I should never have left that necklet with Ragnor. I could have used it to bribe my way to freedom. 'I would need to know that price, sir, to see if I have the funds to cover it.'

He grinned broadly. 'Oh, I have no doubt that you have ample funds.'

I heard footsteps approaching.

His companion muttered, 'Be quick, Carl, or else we shall both be in disgrace.'

The first soldier leaned down and whispered, 'Then pay the toll of one kiss, miss, and I'll let you get back to your work in the kitchens.'

He thinks I'm the serving girl!

My relief must have prompted me to give him a kiss that was overly exuberant, for he looked stunned, but his comrade said, 'Be off quickly,' and they both straightened as Erik Strong Arm stepped into view.

Saint Lucia preserve me! All was indeed lost if he was coming on his daily visit to see how I got on.

I lowered my head to the bundle of clothes in my hands, but I watched him out of the corner of my eye.

'My lord!' the guards said in stiff, formal voices.

'What is this? Erik snapped.

'Sir?' said the first guard.

Without looking at me, Erik said, 'Be off, girl. There's no reason for you to tarry here.' I scrambled down the hall. Behind me I heard Erik berating the guards. 'You had orders not to flirt with the girls sent up to attend the princess. We have a good mind to flog you both.'

But his voice faded as I hurried down the stairs and out into the courtyard. How I wished I could have bid Piet farewell, but I needed to be out of the castle as quickly as possible. I pressed one hand against my belly again to remind myself why I dared not tarry, even to thank Piet.

I set the laundry down on a crate in the courtyard. I'd ignite suspicion if I carried linens out of the castle. I might even be taken up as a thief. As I hurried toward the gate, ghosts began to line my path, but I brushed right past them. The closer I got to the gate, the thicker the horde of ghosts grew. They all watched me with frightened, imploring eyes.

Now the bridge over the moat was in sight. I picked up my pace.

The porter stepped out and blocked the way. 'Where are you going, girl?'

Never before had he prevented folk from leaving the castle, not unless he suspected them of wrongdoing. Was there something amiss about my manner or appearance? Or was this some new policy of Erik Strong Arm's?

I kept my head lowered, trusting the shadows of my headdress to blur my face. 'I received word that my old mother has fallen sick and she needs me.'

I felt the ghosts press around me. It was like being squeezed to death with sacks of down.

'Do not desert me, Ophelia.'

It was the queen's voice. I looked up and saw her standing between me and the porter, her pale face a mask of horror. The edge of her mouth was stained with bloody froth as if she'd vomited up her insides and not yet wiped off the bits of blood and skin.

'You owe us your aid.' Claudius moved next to her, his eyes staring deep into mine. His mouth bore the same nasty stains as the queen's.

Now my father stepped to stand on the queen's other side. He stretched his hands out to me imploringly. 'You have killed my son, and now you snatch my grandson from me. If you depart, I'll never get to see him, so I beg you, don't leave, daughter.' A wound in his chest began to gush out blood, more blood that any mortal man could carry in his body. It poured across the cobblestones and began to stain the hem of my skirt.

'Wait at least until my son's son is born,' the queen begged.

'I've lost both my sons, so let me at least behold my grandson. You owe me that much at least.'.

'Sister, help me.' Laertes now had moved up behind them. He was pale as frost, but he bore no wounds. 'If you leave, our family will be forgotten. Our name will be as dust. Stay and be queen. Because of you, I can never bring glory to our family name. Turn back and be Erik's queen. Leave a legacy that will let our family be remembered forever in the annals of Denmark. You owe us that much.'

'Stay and be queen.' Hamlet had joined the rest. He too was pale, although not as pale as my brother. As always, his hair gleamed like white gold in the moonlight. 'Let my son then take his rightful place upon the throne. If you steal him away, then all I've done and suffered will be for nothing. Don't wipe out the line of Hamlet that stretches unbroken all the way back to Holger the Dane.'

'If I stay,' I whispered, 'Erik will kill your son.'

Hamlet shook his head. 'You will find a way to prevent it. Stay, Ophelia.'

'Turn back and take up your destiny,' Laertes said, 'for you were born to be Denmark's greatest queen.'

'Rule and let my grandson rule,' Gertrude cried out. 'You are the cause of the untimely deaths of me, both my husbands, and my son Hamlet. I loved you well, Ophelia. I never asked you for anything, but now I beg you to stay here in Elsinore.'

'Let me be the father of a queen and the grandfather to kings,' begged my father. 'Turn back. Don't condemn me to oblivion.'

Hamlet stretched out his hand to me. 'My one and only love, you will kill us a second time if you steal our future from us.'

They all began to talk at once, imploring me and stretching their arms out to me.

I closed my arms around my belly to keep the baby safe. I didn't know whether they were indeed the ghosts of those I'd loved and served or if they were evil spirits in their likenesses. In any case, it didn't matter. All that mattered was getting my child to safety.

I shouldered my way through the throng of ghosts, mumbling over and over as if it was a magic charm, 'I must go. I must go.' I even pushed past the bemused porter, and at last was over the bridge, across the moat, and out of Elsinore.

The ghosts didn't follow.

I remembered Yorick's words, *Ghosts cannot cross water.*

Never had air tasted so sweet. The sky overhead was as immense as eternity, and I remembered how Judith had described England as a land of hills and cliffs. I'd miss Denmark. Never again did I want to go back to that haunted, twisting, twisted castle, but I'd miss these flat lands of my childhood.

As I hurried toward the place where Ragnor moored his ship, the sky faded to that shade of twilight purple that makes it look almost bruised. I was lucky that Ragnor was bold enough to sail through the dark. With every step I feared to hear the hooves of horses pounding behind me. Surely by now Erik had discovered my escape. Doubtless soldiers had already been ordered after me. Once or twice I mistook the pounding of my own heart for distant hoof beats.

The light was gone by the time I spotted Ragnor's fire. He and his crew were waiting by his big ship. As soon as he saw me, he barked orders and his sailors sprang into action.

'I knew you'd make it,' he said, helping me aboard. In the darkness I couldn't read his expression. 'We'd best be off at once.' As he released my hand, something metallic and jagged pressed against my palm. The necklet Hamlet had given to me on our wedding, the one that I'd left on Ragnor's pallet when I'd left the note asking for him to sail Hamlet and me into exile.

'I thought you'd want this back,' he said.

'Thank you.' If I sold it in England, it would provide a nest egg for my son and me. If I could, I'd save all the money for my son to use when it came time for him to make his living. At first I could surely lodge with Judith and her family. I hoped to get work in her husband's merchant business. In truth, I'd be glad to be shot of those long, idle days of tamely sewing and letting life drift away like a piece of bark floating on the surface of a lazy brook. It would be much more interesting to work in a shop. Perhaps I'd never sail to the distant ports where Ragnor and his brothers traded, but I'd get to hear their stories, touch all the glorious silks and other cloths that they brought back, smell the strange spices, polish the imported trinkets of silver and gold. To charm their customers, I could weave stories about all the items that we sold . . . Life in a merchant house might suit me very well indeed, and if it didn't, I could always fall back on starching collars. Come what may, I could have a fine life. With the freedom to be a woman and not a princess, I could have a very good life indeed.

I stole a look at Ragnor. I wondered just what role he would play in my new life.

We set sail. More quickly than I thought possible, Denmark began to vanish in the distance.

Yorick had been wrong. Ghosts *can* travel across water. I knew that I carried within me the ghosts of Laertes, my father, Rosencrantz, Guildenstern, the queen, Claudius, and both Hamlets. They would haunt me for a long time. Perhaps for my whole life long. Once I reached my new home, I'd need to spend time mourning all those many deaths. My guilt and sorrow lay in my chest like a heavy stone.

But inside me I carried something else . . . my child. The child for whom I'd thrown away a kingdom and crown. I'd also taken the crown from his hands in much the same way a careful mother might remove a knife or shard of glass, but I'd handed him instead the chance to choose his own life's path. He wouldn't have the chance to be a good king, but he'd have the chance to be a good man, and that was a better bargain. More than that, he'd be far from Erik Strong Arm's assassins and all others who might want to butcher him and seize the throne. For a while Erik Strong Arm might send out spies looking for us, but he'd look in royal courts, not in a merchant business in a small English village, so my son should be safe. I wished I could also save him forever, but unfortunately that was a power given to none of us. The most we can sometimes do is save someone for *now* . . . but *now* can be enough in the face of all the tragedies and disasters that – like evil giants – stomp through the stories of our lives.

I'd saved my son for *now*, and sometimes *now* had to be enough.

'If you stay there in the front,' Ragnor called to me, 'you'll get badly splashed once we hit the high seas. Move to the middle if you want to be safe.'

He was right, of course, but I stayed where I was, facing the future. What did it matter if I got cold or wet, now that I finally had my chance to fly?